THE COUNTERFEIT
CONNECTION

ALSO BY JOHNNY WORTHEN

THE COUNTERFEIT CONNECTION

A TONY FLANER MYSTERY
BOOK 4

JOHNNY WORTHEN

ROUGH
EDGES
PRESS

The Counterfeit Connection
Paperback Edition
Copyright © 2023 (As Revised) Johnny Worthen

Rough Edges Press
An Imprint of Wolfpack Publishing
9850 S. Maryland Parkway, Suite A-5 #323
Las Vegas, Nevada 89183

roughedgespress.com

Paperback ISBN 978-1-68549-325-7
eBook ISBN 978-1-68549-324-0

For the impostors and fakers
who will themselves makers.

THE COUNTERFEIT
CONNECTION

PROLOGUE

"IT WAS A FAKE," said Sergeant San. "The curator said so."

"And how did he know?" asked the colonel, not lifting his eyes from the report.

"He said he did an analysis of it last year. He suspected—"

"Who told him to do that?"

The warning tone in his commanding officer's voice told the sergeant to tread warily. "He didn't say" was the best reply.

"I'll tell you who told him. No one. He had no business doing that. Is this the man's name here in the report?"

"Yes, it is, sir."

"He'll need a talking to," said the colonel.

The sergeant swallowed hard and snuck a glance out the window behind the big dark wooden empty desk, wishing he were outside in the Myanmar sunlight, out of uniform, no longer a policeman. Out of this office. Maybe eating a mango.

"What happened to the first informant?" asked the colonel. "The one who confessed to the conspiracy?"

The sergeant cleared his throat. "He had a talking to."

"Fatally?"

"I'm afraid so, sir."

"This report is good work, Sergeant," said the colonel, now looking up. "Are you nervous?"

San blinked the sweat out of his eye too late to keep the salt from stinging. "Yes, sir."

"Why?"

"The forgery, sir."

"Oh. At ease, Sergeant."

San changed his posture to the prescribed formal military relaxed pose which he'd never found relaxing at all.

"Wipe your face," said the colonel.

He did so with a white handkerchief and nodded gratitude before putting it away.

"Do you think you've stumbled into some kind of state secret with the missing museum piece?" asked the colonel.

"Have I?"

"Yes."

"Will I need a talking to, sir?"

"Do you need one?"

"No, sir."

"Good."

"So my report is meaningless; nothing important was stolen?"

"I didn't say that, sergeant. We know that it was fake. We might even suspect that one of our currently ruling generals took the original and sold it to pay off a horse racing debt and a month-long cocaine binge. We might even know which one of his friends commissioned the replacement copy to keep him from a firing squad."

"General Y—"

"Don't speculate, Sergeant."

"No, sir."

"You are bright. What do you know about the vase?"

"This one?"

"There is only one."

"Of course," he said. "Eighteenth-century jewel-encrusted twenty-carat gold offering container. Sixty-two point five centimeters tall with lacquer and bamboo highlights. One of the most recognizable pieces of art of the royal treasury."

"Straight from the brochure." The colonel waved the very museum pamphlet with the piece on the cover. San would have liked to have seen the real—or—copied piece. He found it beautiful and striking, a symbol of modest power for his country. Uniquely Burmese. It was a covered vase with a tapered hourglass shape rising from a sturdy base through a generous center, topped with a tall tiered lid like a temple tower. He had no idea what thing could be so valuable as to need so precious a container.

"You've uncovered a plot, Sergeant," said the colonel, fixing him with a stare. "It's serious. There's a covert faction working to restore the monarchy. They've been smuggling money and art out of the country for years to finance a plot. We need to find out who's on the other end, which one of a hundred exiles could they be backing."

"How will we do that, sir? Our only lead here has been ..."

"Talked to?"

San didn't respond.

"We know we're looking for someone in America, someone still alive and receiving generous national treasures in order to fund the overthrow of our government."

"That doesn't narrow it down much."

The colonel squinted at him.

"Sorry, sir."

"You're not wrong. But we have another clue, one that I want you to follow up on."

"What's that, sir?"

"You're a good policeman," said the colonel. "I want you to go to America and find the traitor, bring them home for…"

"A talking to?"

The colonel nodded.

San began to speak but hesitated.

"Go on, Sergeant. Ask your question."

"Is this really so big of a threat? We get rumors of coups and overthrows all the time."

"Yes, we do, but this one is different."

"Because of all the money already sent out?"

"Not just that," said the colonel with a deep sigh.

"Then what, sir?"

"That stolen offering vessel was a personal possession of Supayalat, the last queen of Burma."

"But it's a fake."

The colonel shook his head. "Not for what it holds."

San had to ask. "What did—*does* it hold, sir?"

"Legitimacy."

1

WHAT I'D MEANT to say when I met Allison in the parking lot of the Comedy Cellar that Friday night in January was, "How was your drive? Gosh, it's good to see you. You look great." But in the way of nervous and twisted tongues, as she climbed out of her car after not seeing her for weeks and weeks, I blurted out, "I'm a fraud! I'm going to be unmasked as the pretender I am at any minute. You shouldn't have come. Save yourself. I am pond scum!"

Yeah, I was in that mood; had been for a while.

"Oh, for pity's sake, Tony," she said. "Impostor syndrome again?"

"Sorry sorry sorry," I said too late. "My greeting came out wrong."

"Freudian slip?"

"Is that when you say one thing and sleep with your mother?"

"Yes, Tony. That's exactly it."

"Sorry sorry sorry."

"Stop apologizing."

"Sorry."

"Do you want to try again?" she said.

I looked at her face backlit from streetlight glow shining through the dark smog of Utah air. I traced her long straight hair past her cheeks, touching upon her luscious neck, which plunged beneath her collar. Looking up, I found her warm smile reflected in her eyes, and I sighed.

"So far so good," she said.

"God, it is so good to see you," said I. "You look good enough to—"

"Kiss?"

"So far so good."

We swapped spit in the parking lot and held each other. Not for too long because it was cold. She'd been in a car for hours; I'd been in the warm bar. The night sucked our heat away but not our enthusiasm. It would be a good weekend.

We went inside where the impersonator was still on stage.

"Here's Johnny!"

"Seriously, he's doing Jack Nicholson? Fucking hell," said Dara.

We slid into the booth with my friends.

The Comedy Cellar was a basement club in Salt Lake City where my friends and I hang out. We thought of ourselves as comedians, though only Perry Whitehouse could honestly be said to be "making it." We others—me, Dara Sutter, Standard Flox, Garrett and Critter (they're a team)—just did the occasional sets and coat-tailed Perry's fame. Allie wasn't a comedian, but she'd hung out with us enough to join the banter and get in a few good zingers.

"Has he done anyone from this century yet?" I said.

"Fuck no."

"He looks like he's fifteen," said Allie.

"This is the start of a beautiful relationship," said the comic from the stage.

"Bogey?" said Standard. "He's doing Humphrey Bogart."

"Barry must owe someone a favor," said Garrett, and Critter nodded in agreement, his googly eyes rattling on the felt face, his fangs twitching like our broken funny bones at the dying act. Did I mention Critter was a puppet? Well, he is.

Barry is the club owner. Part comedy fan, part entrepreneur, part dickhead.

"If he wanted to save money, he'd have put us up on stage," said Standard.

It was never easy to agree with Standard on anything, but this comic, this kid impersonator, had united the clan.

"You're stale," said Perry.

"Whose side are you on?" said Standard.

"There are sides?" Perry's eyes went wide. He was not the sanest person. Nope, not sane at all. Not even close to sane unless he was firmly on his medications. His paranoid expression suggested he was not. "What are the sides?" he said. "I need to know. Forewarned is forearmed."

"Fight the power!" said Allie.

Perry spun on her like she might raise a Kalashnikov over her head and start the Utah People's Revolution Movement then and there.

"Chill," said Dara.

Perry examined her through squinty eyes. What machinations churned and stumbled behind them, I couldn't imagine. Well, I could but chose not to.

"Perry is never stale," I said. "He's like visiting your demented grandfather, a new person every day."

Perry's suspicious gaze turned to me.

"What's up, doc?" from the stage. He mimed—poorly—eating a carrot or maybe he was reenacting a Dremel tool disaster from his youth.

We shook our heads.

Allie lives in Moab on a ranch. She trains animals, often for movies. Really.

She looked at her phone disappointedly. "I'm expecting a call from Terrance."

"Terrance?"

"My agent. He's in town. We're supposed to meet up. I told you that."

She had told me that, but I'd missed it. Plain words don't always work on me, apparently, and I'm a detective. I'd missed the clue—you know, the unobscured plain-spoken information. Detectives who miss things like that aren't called detectives. They aren't even called alert. They're called dense. They're called slow. And if they continue to call themselves detectives while doing this, they might well be called frauds. This idea, like an allergic rash from lavender essential oil, plagued my brain of late. I was a fake at my career, with my family. My life. I couldn't do anything right—just look at my waistline. And now me the loser had just been outed, at least to me, as a delusional self-aggrandizing putz. I'd somehow convinced myself that Allie had come up to Salt Lake for me because she liked me, because I was worthy to be liked. Fuck that. It was, and I knew it was—had been told as much— that she was here for her agent, Terrance. Unbelievable. This, in my fevered self-hate. also reiterated and reinforced, reinvigorated, regurgitated, remonstrated, and remoulaged my fear that I was a crap detective. All my life I'd sought the right occupation and I thought I'd finally found it as a PI, but lately I didn't think I was any good at it, being more lucky than talented. Thus the shit attitude.

Allie said it was just the shit weather. Salt Lake has this nasty pollution/smog/"no-big-deal-we-don't-need-no-damn-environmental-safe-guards-against-it-you-pinko-communist-treehugging-wimps"   inversions that fill the valley every winter with a greasy rust-colored layer of unspeakable shit. It coats cars and the back of your throat, changes the light to piss, and inspires some writers to envision it killing half the country in horror short stories available now.

But I was used to it. I'm from Utah. I'm acclimated to the crappy atmosphere here. And the pollution.

Not that Allie was wrong. Bad air didn't help, but I realized I was in another one of my midlife crises. Once you're out of high school, most people can expect like one or two of these in their lifetimes, but since my maturity never graduated, they show up in my life like bank holidays when

I'm overdrawn. This current one probably had to do with an upcoming high school reunion as much as anything. And the air was bad.

Garrett shook his head at the comic. "No one here is old enough to know any of the people he's doing."

"I know them," I said.

"Of course *you* know them," said Critter. "You're old."

"And culturally literate," I said. "I know, for example, that Fozzy Bear and Miss Piggy were the same person."

"No, they weren't," said Critter.

"Afraid so," said Garrett.

Critter shook his head in disbelief and turned away. Garrett and I shared a look.

I know I said Perry is the crazy one, but sharing a heart-felt sympathetic look with a ventriloquist while his hand puppet sulks should probably not go unnoticed. In our group of course it was.

"I'll be back," the comic said as Arnold Schwarzenegger for an exit line and raised his hand in triumph.

A table near the front erupted in applause and stood up cheering. It was an older couple, probably orbiting the high seventies—silver hair, Brylcreem, and floral dress. Wingtips and fat heels.

"His parents?" asked Allie.

"Or his grandparents," I said.

The rest of the club returned to their conversations, relieved it was over.

"So are you going to take the case?" asked Standard.

"Do you care?"

"No, but I don't want to get into the whole Frank Oz argument again. Critter takes it personally."

Critter glared at him with his patented plastic stink eye. Standard looked away after a moment, unable to compete in that staring contest.

"I don't like domestic cases," I said. "They're so sleazy."

"Isn't that what you signed up for, though?" said Perry. "There's a reason that one of the nicknames for your profession is 'sleaze.'"

"You have a case?" said Allie.

"A guy wants me to check out his fiancée. I don't like domestic cases."

"It's not that kind of case," said Standard. "Sounds preventative, not punitive."

"You got anything else to do?" asked Dara. "Any other cases?"

"No."

"Taxes all settled?"

"No."

"Any new bills coming due?"

"No comment."

I looked at Allie, actually hoping that she'd say she needed me at her animal ranch, but she shook her head.

"No," I said.

"So fucking do it," said Dara.

"The voice of reason," said Standard.

"It's so boring," I said.

"So you have to enjoy every second of your job?" asked Allie. "I didn't know that was possible."

I stuck my tongue out at her.

"Who is it?" asked Critter. "I wasn't paying attention."

Perry answered. "Tony's been asked to look into the background of this guy's girlfriend."

"Fiancée," corrected Standard. Why had I confided in him? He was my least favorite of all my sketchy friends.

"Right, fiancée. He's late to marriage and a careful man."

"Rich?" asked Critter.

"Well connected," I said. "White middle-aged Mormon man in Utah."

"Is this about your class reunion?" Allie said.

"What class reunion?" said Dara.

"Tony's high school is doing a twenty-year thing a week from Saturday."

"Do not fucking go," said Dara. "Why would you even consider it?"

"I went," said Perry.

"Me too," said Standard. "To my ten-year."

"How was it?"

"Horrible."

"Horrible."

"Don't fucking do it," said Dara. "Dumbest idea you had all night."

"And take the case," said Allie. "You need to keep busy. And the money wouldn't hurt."

"But…"

She gave me a look. If she knew what I was thinking, the look would have been much harder. She saw me as I usually appeared, lazy—I mean, busy. A busy guy. Those cartoons weren't going to watch themselves. What I was feeling, though, was fear that I'll screw it up. Some guy was willing to pay me to help him with a huge life decision, putting his trust in me, and since I sucked and my luck was running out, I'd mess up his life and then have guilt. Well, more guilt. All this because, you guessed it, I was a fraud.

Allie saw only the cartoons, my innate slacker soul. Who was the blind detective now? I wanted to yell. Oh, right. Still me. She'd seen through me, and I knew it.

She wanted me to take the case, challenging me to do something—anything—to get out of the polluted mindset where I found myself. She was right, of course. Allie was usually right. I am hard put to find anything she's been wrong about. Me, maybe. She likes me, so she could be wrong, I decided. Probably was. I don't deserve her. She's too good for me.

See how fucked my thinking was? Still, keeping busy was better than cartoons. Have you seen what passes for primetime animation these days?

I pulled out my phone and texted Moland, Bryan Moland, the client.

> I'll take the case.

> Thank you! :-)

He texted back instantly.

Allie gave me a kiss.

I like Allie. I like her a lot.

"How's the family?" said Perry. He'd calmed down from the sides issue. A good sign.

"Nancy is at a seminar, and Randy is going through phases." I left out the part about Nancy not speaking to me just then. Allie pretended not to notice.

"What kind?"

"Real estate."

"Randy's going through a real estate phase?" said Critter.

I glared at the puppet. He giggled.

"Randy's at that age," I said. "Peer pressure and identity. Breaking free. Hanging on."

Allie said, "Didn't you say that what you call a mid-life crisis, young adults call Tuesday?"

I talk about mid-life crises a lot. "Yep. Randy's got a case of the Tuesdays."

"Shit," said Perry. "Tough time. How are you helping him?"

All eyes pointed to me. I pointed mine at the table.

"I sent him a text yesterday," I said. "He didn't respond."

Eye rolls and head shakes. Swaying felt fangs.

"I'll see him tonight. Probably late. He has a thing. With his friends."

"You're there if he needs you," said Allie, coming to my defense. "That's all you can do. Anything more would be unwelcome pressure."

"I don't know," said Standard.

"Do you have any kids?"

"No…" None of them did but me.

"Then hush your face," I said.

Standard swallowed hard and looked away.

"Okay, Flaner, you get a pass here," Dara said. "Good luck."

"You should go up there, Perry," I said to change the fucking subject. "This place is dying."

"Think I should?"

"Don't do it," said Garrett. "If you're good at something, never do it for free."

"That's not who I am," he said.

I said, "Exposure is good."

"People die from exposure," said Allie.

Now it was her turn to get the looks. Truth hurts.

Perry leaned around the edge of the booth and looked for Barry for the go-ahead. Barry often asked Perry to jump up and save a dead night. Sometimes he even asked us. He paid us in drinks and a fancy-dancey paper "Reserved" tent at our usual table.

I sighed, falling into a pit of doubt.

Allie whispered in my ear. "You are good at what you do. You've just been bored lately. You're in your head looking for something to challenge you. Sherlock Holmes had the same problem."

"He was fictional, you know."

"No way!" Her look of disbelief was worthy of her own act. I cracked up.

"What'd we miss?" said Perry.

Maybe boredom had something to do with it. Most private investigators get domestic cases, which suck ass. It's about peeking in windows and following wives to secret houses and hotels, husbands on out-of-town trysts with dental hygienists named Brooke. They pay, but they haven't invented a soap strong enough yet to remove the stink that lingers afterward.

Barry appeared at our table with a pitcher of cheap (don't call it beer). "Anyone?" he asked, twitching his head at the stage.

"I'll do it," said Dara.

Barry squinted. Dara was the bluest one among us. Her small size and elvish face made the cuss-word-laden jokes she spouted out so much more penetrating. She was an acquired taste. Waders recommended.

"You do need a palate cleanser after that guy," said Perry.

"Okay," said Barry. He set the pitcher on the table and adjusted the little table tent. Payment received.

"Improv?" I said to Dara as she scooted out of the booth.

"I've been working on a new routine," she said, "about sex and food."

"New frontiers in discomfort," said Garrett.

"Uh, Barry," I said, "you might want to clear out that old couple near the front."

He followed my eyes and his went large. "Right." He moved out to save the comic's relatives from Dara's coming onslaught.

"I'm glad you took the case, Tony," said Allie. "How much trouble could looking for a girl be?"

My phone rang.

"Hello?"

"Tony? Tony Flaner. My dear friend. How are you?"

"Ah... Who's this?"

"This is Fah, your friend from Thailand. Are you still in Utah?"

"Oh, Fah. Right. Hi. Um, yeah, I'm still in Utah. Afraid so. What's up?"

"I need your help. There's this girl..."

I MET Fah in Thailand during my first case, the one with the finger trap. He spoke excellent English and better Thai. He told me he also spoke French, German, Chinese, Vietnamese and Swahili. I told him I was American. We only hung out for a few days, but we hit it off really well. I made him a few bucks and he saved me a few bruises.

"You still working at that hotel?"

"What?" he said. "I can barely hear you."

The cacophony of small talk, bottle taps, date fights, and blatant lies bubbled up around me—'Really, sweetheart, I swear I don't know how Sylvia's number got on my phone.'

"Hold on. Let me get someplace quiet," I said.

I moved to the far end of the bar, in a somewhat quiet corner I've taken calls in before. It had a garbage can and a pay phone. Yes, an actual pay phone.

"Welcome Dara Sutter!" Barry on stage.

Applause.

"Fah?"

"I'm here. Are you still a detective? I need your help."

"Who here has ever rage-fucked a pineapple?" It was Dara at the mic.

"What?" said Fah.

"Sorry, that was my friend." The crowd chuckled uneasily from its first shock, automatic psychic defenses still intact, language registering, jaws still movable. Dara would soon put an end to all that.

"You have such friends?" said Fah.

"She's on stage."

"Saying… Did I hear right?"

"I hope not. Hold on."

I covered the mouthpiece and headed outside. Luke, the bouncer at the door, grabbed me.

"Hey, Tony, look at this." He handed me a driver's license. "Does this look real to you?"

I looked at the kid in front of Luke and back at the picture on the card. It was the same face. The birthdate on the ID said he was old enough to drink by a month, but the kid standing there didn't look old enough to drive. It didn't help that he shifted uneasily, sweated in the cold, cleared his throat like he had crickets for tonsils, and wouldn't make eye contact with anyone.

I held the license under the light, tilted it to check the hologram, then turned it over and sniffed.

"Smells kosher," I said. "But I see your point."

"Getting a lot of these," he said.

"Hello, Tony? You still there?" From my phone.

I left Luke to suss out his problems and got out of the bar as Dara moved to the next level. "Here's one for the gents," she said. "I'm told watermelons, when properly ripe…"

"Okay? Better?" I said when I was clear of the door.

"Is it?"

"No, actually," I said. "It's freezing out here."

"That's right. You get snow."

"Snow would be good," I said, smacking the taste of metallic air against the roof of my mouth. "Snow would give the valley a much-needed cleansing, a white enema, so to speak." January in Salt Lake could be damn cold, but snow was never a guarantee anytime. The inversion smog, however— that was like clockwork. Cold and sticky-icky. My breath came out in puffs that joined the lingering miasma like chemtrails into a thundercloud. I'd had garlic with dinner.

"Can you help me?" Fah said.

"What's it all about?"

"I have a friend in Utah United States now. I haven't heard from her."

"She's lost?"

"I don't know."

"Who is she?" I seemed to remember that Fah was married. The thought of another domestic case crimped my belly and threatened to bring up weak beer and over-spiced Alfredo.

"I met her at the hotel. She was going to Utah to visit family and see Sonny dance."

"Is that all she is to you? A friend?" Why let a little thing like propriety stop me from being me?

The long pause was not good. I spent the time spitting a glob of Utah Air™ into a snowbank. It sizzled.

"I'm worrying about her," Fah said.

"Uhm…"

"I have money to pay you."

One of my strengths is that I'm really laid back, which people often mistake for laziness, but I've never had the energy or motivation to correct them. Domestic cases sucked, but so too does all work, by definition. Aristotle said, "All paid employments absorb and degrade the mind." See? I'm in good company. Fight the man! Fight the power! Fight productivity and usefulness! Fight groceries and car payments!

Then there's the commitment issue. When I take a case and people pay me money, they usually expect me to actually do something for them. It's a bummer.

"I have a lot of other cases," I said. Okay, I had one other case and I'd just —like a minute before—agreed to it. Seemed like a lot to me.

"And I'm expensive," I added. In honesty, I've been told I'm actually pretty cheap, but if you converted my fees to pesos and then to Chinese yen, then Euro, Australian dollars and then to Congolese francs using a back-street moneychanger with a lisp and dreams of seeing the arctic, to swap out for Thai Baht for Fah, it could add up, I'm sure, to something significant. Maybe. Think of all those exchange fees and hassle charges. Okay, it was a lie, but lies are just exaggerations blown out of proportion. Amirite? And like I said, I'm a lazy man and I resist work, even when I shouldn't. It's one of the reasons I think I'm a fraud.

"I'll give you a new Rockford price," he said. "A thousand dollars a day plus expenses."

"Fah, I can't be bo—What?"

"A thousand dollars a day plus expenses. I trust you."

"American money?"

"Of course."

"Where'd you get that kind of cash? Aren't you an itinerant butler?"

"I got a nice tip last month."

"From whom? The Saudi Royal Family?"

The long pause this time made my head spin and see bone saws. I was out of spit so I said, "What did you have to bury to—"

"Tony, I need your help. Is that not enough money?"

"Shhhhlllmmmll…sahum…Alabazza…uhm."

"What are you trying to say?"

"I'm not sure," I said in answer to the question about my gibberish; Fah took it otherwise.

"Please, Tony. For old time's sake. I know no one else in Utah, United States."

My money situation was not dire, but it howled. My wife set me up for life on an allowance that would keep any normal human being alive and thriving for the rest of their lives. I'm in debt. I have two houses, one in Salt Lake where the wife stuck me and one in Moab that I picked up after an adventure, the one where I met Allie again. I owe taxes and stuff, and there's this cruise line that's upset about a little trouble they had and are threatening lawsuits for damage. I maxed my credit cards at Thanksgiving to take Allie to Hawaii, and last month at Christmas I might have gone a tad overboard buying my sixteen-year-old son a new Tesla. Since he lives with his mother, there's this air of competition around the holidays. I think it's safe to say I won this year. Nancy still isn't speaking to me because of it. In any event, I'm sure I'll get through my money woes in the end. Or I'll go to prison. In the meantime, a little nudge from funneled Saudi hush money couldn't hurt. I'd love to get that car paid off.

"Tell me about it," I said, wondering if PayPal, Venmo, or Apple Pay would be better for international money laundering—I mean, transfers.

"Of course. But what's that noise, though?"

"What noise?"

"Sounds like crickets."

"Oh. That's my teeth chattering. Not sexy?"

"No."

"Hold on again," I said.

There was an art gallery across the street from the Comedy Cellar, *Spidelits*. I was dressed in jeans and a Dead & Company T-shirt, heavy on casual psychedelic cool but tragically light on warmth and art-buyer chic. The gallery I knew was part of an art walk that'd been going on since Halloween and for some reason hadn't ended with New Year's. It was quieter and less disturbing than Dara on stage, so I went in.

"Can I help you?" I was asked before the door shut. The woman looked at my shirt, my jeans, my hair, and attitude, and came to the natural conclusion that I was homeless.

"I'm looking for something in contemporary space heater," I said.

"I'm sorry, you can't—"

"I'm with the *Daily Artist*," I said. "I'm on with my editor now. He's in Asia covering the Bladderbust Exhibit." I showed her the newest most expensive Apple phone ever made with a "Bangkok" over a foreign number aglow on the screen to prove I wasn't a derelict. Such a display meant I was either stupid rich and powerful or suffered from impulse control issues and poor money habits. You decide.

"Oh, okay," she said, brightening up like a lamppost at noon around here. "Here, have some cheese."

I smiled through chattering teeth but passed on the brie. Really? Brie? I found a welded horse head sculpture next to the heater vent in the corner particularly inviting and studied it in close detail.

"Okay, Fah," I said. "Who is this girl?"

"Her name is Sandi Wong. She's from Myanmar, formerly known as Burma."

"Okay."

"She is young and pretty and politically connected."

"To whom?"

"No one in power now."

"Burma is a military dictatorship, isn't it?" I remembered watching a documentary about it on Netflix, something about creepy tour spots.

"Yes and no. It's complicated."

"Do I need to know about that?"

"Probably," said Fah. "But you're the detective. You tell me."

I thought for a second. "No. No I don't." Confidence is my middle name. "Does she have money?"

"She stayed at this hotel," said Fah. "I gave her some. She flew to Utah to see old family and Sonny dance."

"Who's Sonny? A relative?"

"No. Famous."

"Sonny? Like Sonny and Cher? Someone's dealing with bad info here. Sonny Bono died to a tree-related skiing accident, like—"

"It's a party."

"Well, I didn't like his politics, and many people were pretty disappointed that he sold out the whole '60s inclusion, rainbow, liberal vibe thing to become a Republican bootlick congressman extending copyright law to benefit a few greedy corporations at the expense of the masses, but I wouldn't say there was a celebration when he died."

"In Utah!" he said.

"I think it was Tahoe, actually. California."

"No no no no no. Everyone knows."

"Know know knows what?"

"About Sonny dance with the red ford."

"Have you started an opium habit?"

"Flaner, you're pissing me off."

"Fah, old friend, bodyguard and drinking buddy, If I knew anything about a red ford and a son... Oh. Sundance. Robert Redford. The film festival. Ah. Gotcha. Okay."

"Sundance! Yes that's what I'm saying. You lose your language skills?"

"No comment."

"Sandi wants to be in movies. She went to Utah to meet people at Sundance."

The Sundance Film festival is world-famous and was happening now. I knew this. Not only was it on every newscast, newspaper, magazine, billboard, marquee and hip convo, it was one of the reasons Allie came up from Moab to be with me now, I recalled just then. The meeting with her agent was about that. We'd talked about it on the phone just yesterday. Nevertheless, my steel trap detective brain hadn't put the meaning to Fah's British accent. Score another one for detective insight. See why I was having issues? Sundance runs for a fortnight up the canyon from Salt Lake in a little stuck-up town called Park City and attracts movie folks from around the world. It's a big deal.

I felt a migraine coming on. Back into the phone, I said, "Do you have a picture of her, Fah?"

"Yes and other stuff. I'll send it to you."

I gave him my email.

"Sandi is related to General Tayza, U Tayza Min Ko."

"Oh, that guy," I said.

"You've heard of him?"

"No."

There was a frustrated gasp at the end of the transpacific connection. "He led a coup in a power grab in Myanmar. Look him up."

"Cut to the chase. What about him?"

"He lives in Utah now."

"Oh, of course."

"I need your help, Tony," Fah said. "This girl is special. She's a free spirit and lovely and lost. It'd mean a lot to me if you could find her and make sure she's alright."

"No promises," I said.

"Promise me you'll work on it."

"What did I just say?"

"I thought you meant her condition, not your work."

Trapped again. Bummer. "Okay," I said. "And Fah, I'm going to ask. Did you have an affair with this girl?"

"Why?"

"Getting the lay of the land, so to speak."

"Not me," he said. "I'm married."

"Uh-huh."

"Really, I did not," he said with just the right amount of indignation. "But she slept with other people. I could have."

"The one that got away?"

"No sex, but we talked for hours. If I had an affair with her, it was spiritual and emotional. Intellectual."

"Oh, well all right."

"Not really," he said. "It's just as bad. The wife isn't speaking to me."

"Did you buy your son a new car?"

"No," he said. "She feels a distance between us now. She says she doesn't know who I am."

"You told her?"

"She found us."

"Doing what?"

"Tai chi."

"I love that stuff, I get it all the time at Starbucks."

"Tai chi, not chai tea."

"Right."

"One's a physical meditation—"

"And the other is a hot delicious spicy beverage," I concluded.

There was a pause that challenged my confidence.

"Tony," said Fah. "I need help. I can count on you, right? You are good at what you do?"

Allie walked into the gallery then. She'd been to her car and was wearing now a coat with a fake fur collar. Tan and warm and upscale enough to make PETA people squint to make sure they didn't have to spit on her. She gave me a suspicious glance that was half curious, half welcome, half relief at finding me, half demand that I explain things later on, and half failed math class.

"I get lucky sometimes," I said.

I ENDED the call with Fah by assuring him I was good at what I did and he could count on me. It was a tough sell and felt like a lie, but Allie nodded encouragingly when I told him I was up to finding his missing friend and he said he trusted me. He might have been lying too.

The gallery lady offered Allie some cheese goo on a cracker. "It's garlic brie made in Cache Valley," she said. "By an artisan cheesemaker."

"Blessed are the cheesemakers," I said.

She nodded and moved away, not far, just a little space for us to admire all de art.

"Are you in the market for metal sculpture?" said Allie, appraising the horse head.

"Isn't everyone?"

"I could have one at the ranch."

"There it would be good," I said. "I think I'd rather have a movie poster."

"How about a photo of the Eiffel Tower?" Allie gestured to a large framed picture of just that, the world-famous Paris landmark at night, taken from a low angle and disappearing into an artistic vanishing point. "Oh. Yeah, I could—what the—Jesus."

My eyes traveled down the picture to the price tag: "$1,789—Nonnegotiable!!!" Three exclamation points.

"It's a photograph," I said. "Not even poster size. What is it, eighteen by twenty-four?" I pulled up a calculator on my phone and did some quick computations. "That's like twenty-four cents a square inch."

"Four point one four," said Allie, looking up from her own phone.

"Which proves my point," I said. "That's pretty pricey for a tourist shot."

It was a tourist shot. In the upper left-hand corner was an unmistakable fleshy thumb obscuring sixty dollars' worth of art.

"You like it?" Brie was back. "It's very avant-garde."

"Why?" I said.

Allie nudged me and murmured, "Don't make a scene."

How she knew I felt like making a scene is one of the things I admire about her. I didn't even know I was headed that way, but after her check, yep, I can say I was getting into scene mode. My personal insecurity, comedy show vibe, and new pressure at having cases was charging out toward my hatred of brie cheese and faux sophistication.

"I don't know," said the gallery girl. "But it is very *cool*, don't you think?" She used the word like she wasn't used to using it. Who doesn't know how to use the word cool?

"And expensive," Allie said.

"We sell two or three a week."

"What?"

"Don't make a scene," I whispered to Allie.

"Yes, it's one of our most popular pieces."

"Wait. You mean it's not even an original? Is it numbered, at least? A limited run?" I loved it when wonder entered Allie's brown eyes. They glowed with disbelief then, authentic, beautiful, and confused. Not as much as they have before, but the echo was there.

"Oh no."

"Then why is it so expensive?"

"Because that's what it costs."

"Everything is worth what people will pay for it," said I.

"This one's nonnegotiable," she said as if the note hadn't been clear. "It's actually one of our cheaper pieces."

"The frame's nice," said Allie.

"Oh, that's not included. That's just for display."

"I'm sensing you have a closet of these in the back."

"Uhm hum."

"Nice," said Allie.

"Let's go," I said. "Maybe we can catch the end of Dara's set."

"Must we?"

"We got our shots, we'll be all right, and I think we should leave."

I took one more look at the picture and noticed a signature in the corner, a stylized word that wasn't easy to read.

"Ba-rion," I said, sounding it out.

"That's the name of the artist," explained the gallery girl.

"First or last?"

"Avant-garde." She was getting a lot of mileage out of that.

"Does the author at least sign them all?" asked Allie. "Personalized signature?"

"Oh no. It's printed on."

"Why?"

I took the lead here. "Avant-garde."

"Uh-huh."

"I don't get it," said Allie.

"Nope," the woman agreed. "Cheese?"

"I'm not sure it is," I said. "We gotta go. Thank you."

Before we could get sucked back into the avant-garde world of gallery art, I whisked Allie back out on the cold street. I glanced at my watch. It wasn't even eight yet. Early for a Friday in any city, even this one. Randy said to expect him at eleven at the earliest.

We swam through the Fog® and re-entered the club. Luke, the bouncer, nodded us in as he held up another gaggle of kids at the door trying to enter the over twenty-one establishment. Luke was looking from their IDs to their faces and shaking his head. The gaggle—kids travel in gaggles—shuffled their feet and watched themselves do it, making sure they looked as guilty as possible.

The stage was empty. Dara was gone but not forgotten. Thousand-yard stares and an eerie quiet hung over the bar like PTSD. We returned to our booth just as Dara got back.

"It went well?" I asked her.

"I think so," she said.

Critter's mouth hung open. There was a subtle tremor that shook his eyes, and Garrett couldn't stop blinking. Perry's head was in his hands. Standard refilled his beer glass and downed it in one gulp before refilling it and going again.

"Sorry we missed it."

"Yeah, where were you?"

"Tony got another case," said Allie. "International intrigue."

Crossing the street, I'd given her a quick overview of who had called and what he'd wanted. Allie already knew about Fah. I'd told her the story before. She liked parts of it.

"Shit," said Dara as Standard drooled beer down his chin. "From unemployed to overworked in an hour."

"I feel a headache coming on," I said.

"Stay hydrated," said Allie, passing me my glass.

"That's beer."

"Utah beer."

"Right…"

I finished off my warm watery brew as a duet took the stage, a girl with a wooden flute and a pianist with an electronic keyboard on wheels. They were called Electric Joust and were on the marquee. They were the draw tonight. I didn't know them, but they'd been billed as 'fusion renaissance techno-dubstep.' Their first song brought up images of green-sleeved damsels traversing Jupiter and beyond the infinite with high blood pressure.

"We should go home," I said to Allie. "I want to be there when Randy comes."

"It's still early," said Perry.

"I thought you guys weren't communicating," said Dara.

"No. I like Perry."

"Randy, you idiot."

"Since when—"

"It's why we're here. Cheering you up, remember?"

"Right."

"The car was a dumb idea," said Standard.

"And don't go to the reunion," said Perry.

"And enjoy your work. You should be busy."

"Thanks, Critter."

"It doesn't matter if you suck at it as long as you enjoy it."

"You could have just stopped before that last sentence, you know?"

"You're a fine detective," said Garrett, giving his puppet a dirty look. "Chris Traard just has a PR person."

"You had to mention him," I said.

Chris Traard was another reason I was feeling low. Traard is a private detective too. He and I had nearly crossed paths a couple of times before. I always thought of him as an unimaginative dork, but a local paper, obviously starving for feel-good news or on the take, published an in-depth and glowing puff piece about him. It outlined his subtle and meticulous methods, mentioned how he was a veteran and past law enforcement officer, actually making detective before he went into "private practice," as he called it. He said he still helped local agencies on occasion. He mentioned several high profile cases where he'd worked and testified and managed to see justice done, prosecution and defense. "Persistence and discipline gets results. I dot all the i's and cross all the t's. I don't do shortcuts." I couldn't help but think that was a jab at me.

In a two-inch sidebar—because God knows why—they'd had a brief mention of me, the previously featured famous PI who'd made the paper before. They'd pulled a picture off the net somewhere. It showed me a food cart vendor spilling curry down the front of my Hawaiian shirt off a paper plate, half blinking, my mouth agape, possibly saying something like "shit" or "burger." Practice the faces you make when saying those words in the mirror. You'll see what I mean. This was on the same page as the official glamour shot of Traard at his desk, looking sternly at an opened file, three-quarter Nordic profile, clean shaven, American flag fluttering behind him, band music in the distance. The title was "This P.I. Stands for Action." I thought there was something racist and classist and political in it all. Curry-eating chunky hippy vs. ex-Marine cop. Who ya' gonna call? Traard's comment was a nice juxtaposition to the one quote the paper had from me—"I get lucky sometimes," a self-deprecating line taken out of context from an old interview.

Fuck.

I'm not sure that the old adage that any publicity is good publicity works in the age of social media. I didn't wait to find out. After receiving a flood of alerts about the article, reading it and melting down, in a rare moment of foresight and emotional self-preservation, I turned off the internet for a while. I didn't get many calls for new cases for that while. None actually. Not that I wanted any. Finally Moland reached out. Traard must have been booked up.

Allie put her arm around me, reading my thoughts and changing the subject. "Randy is staying with Tony while his ex is out of town," explained Allie.

"I didn't think you guys were getting along," said Garrett.

"We are," I said. "He's just a teenager."

"With a fucking fifty-thousand-dollar car," put in Dara.

"So...ungrateful?" offered Garrett.

"My headache's getting worse."

"Where is he now?"

"He could be in that gaggle of kids over there," said Dara.

See—*gaggle*.

The suspicious group Luke had held up at the door were miraculously in the bar now. They found a table and overcrowded it with chairs. A waitress was already there studying their IDs and glancing back at the bouncer, who shrugged. She took orders.

"No, he's not there," I said, but to be honest, they looked the same age as my son, and I thought I recognized one of his classmates. Randy's sixteen.

My headache tickled my temples.

"Honey, let's go home and cuddle," I said.

"Okay, Poopy," said Allie.

"Poopy? Pa-lease," said Dara rolling her eyes.

"That? That's what pushed you over the edge?" said Critter. "Poopy? That's your threshold?"

"Hey, guys, what'd you think?"

It was the comedian from before. The impersonator.

Dara opened her mouth to say something, but then flinched and let out a little yelp when Allie kicked her under the table.

"Good voices," I said.

"Allow me to introduce myself," he said as someone I didn't know. "My name is Mudd. Just kidding. I'm Henry R. Levinson, esquire. I put the levity in Levinson."

"Esquire? You're a lawyer?" asked Perry.

"No. A landowner. I share a house with my parents."

"Do you have a home loan?"

"Everyone does."

"So not a landowner," I said.

"Not even a little," said Standard.

He looked confused but pressed on.

"I'm sorry I missed your set, Dara," he said, already using first names. "I heard you're really good."

"Who've you been talking to?" asked Standard.

"Lots of people."

"Oh good," said Critter.

"I was going to do puppets," he said to Garrett. "But you know, they're kind of..."

"What?" said Critter.

"Cliché? Stale?" he said.

Garrett grabbed his wrist before Critter could get at the young guy.

"You guys are a hoot," Levinson said, sidling up to the side of the booth. "Mind if I join you?"

We all jumped at once.

"Oh, look at the time."

"I've got an anger management class."

"I'm being followed."

"We were just leaving."

"Let me bite him one time, that's all I ask."

Allie's phone rang. It was unmistakable. A custom ringtone of a cheetah purring and meowing. It sounded cute and alarming all at once.

"Terrance," she said.

Terrance was Allie's agent. Terrance found movie and TV animal work for Allie, taking a cut for dealing with Hollywood types. I didn't begrudge him a dime. Allie had an appointment to meet him, I remembered, but that was for tomorrow.

"Right now?" Allie looked at me with excitement and apology. I knew where this was going.

Being ever supportive, I put on a frown and moped.

She scowled and nodded with her ear to the phone.

"Hold on." She covered the mouthpiece.

"Now? Huh?" I said.

"Big party at Sundance," she said. "It's the final weekend."

I brightened. "That's convenient," I said, remembering Fah.

She shook her head.

"Just you, huh?"

She nodded.

"Great opportunity?"

"Yeah. You'll be okay, won't you?"

"Sure," I said. "I'll just have a mellow night with Randy. Do some bonding."

"Thanks, Poopy."

"Poopy?" said Levinson.

My snarling stare was cut short by my own phone ringing. Nothing special, just the loud old phone rotary ring that everyone uses. It's good and loud. Half the bar reached into their pockets. "Randy! Hey son, I was just—"

"Dad, I'm in trouble."

RANDY WAS into a collectible card game called Spells. It was his newest phase, slightly less expensive than an '80s cocaine habit but twice as addicting. Most people played for fun, and every game store in the known universe had Fridays set aside for local tournaments. Past those, there were regional, national, and world events. There were professional players that made money snapping cardboard, finding new ways to break the rules of the never-ending stream of new cards coming out. It was quite a racket. I have a collection of cards myself. I got into it for a while and collected every card in existence at the time, a few thousand, and then lost interest. I probably spent a couple grand on the game in college. The collection now is worth ten times whatever I spent. Everything is worth what people will pay for it.

Randy had called me from the Salt Lake events center, where he'd been participating in a regional Spells competition.

"Dad, I think I've been arrested."

"What? Why?"

"They say I was cheating."

"Who? What... What?"

"Dad, they got me in this room. A guarded room."

"I'm on my way."

"What is it?" said Allie.

"Don't know. But I'm going to find out."

"So...you're leaving...Poopy?" said Levinson as William Shatner.

"One bite. One bite!" Critter lunged at him but didn't have the reach.

"I'll come with you," said Allie.

"No no no," I said, surprising myself. "This is perfect. You go to your thing."

"It's a party."

"A party..."

"A big party at Sundance. With lots of movie people."

"A big party at Sundance..."

"I'll probably see Brad Pitt there and Emma Watson. Maybe Spielberg."

"Do you need a ride?" asked Standard.

"I've got a nicer car," said Dara.

"I'll carry your purse," said Garrett.

"No, my car's just outside," Allie said. "Are you sure it's okay, Tony?"

"Not as much as it was a minute ago, but it's not like I got an invitation."

"You could crash it," said Perry. "Claim to be someone's plus one."

"I'm not doing anything tonight," said Levinson. I think he was trying for Marlene Dietrich.

"Let me know what's up with Randy," Allie said and kissed me on the cheek.

"Okay," I said to her back as she rushed out.

"So how's that self-esteem problem coming along?" asked Critter.

"Great."

I got in my little green Prius and turned on the defrosters. The wipers left long frozen greasy streaks of hell-knows-what. When the heat melted it enough for light to pass through, I was moving. The events center wasn't far from the Cellar, and at that time of night downtown parking shouldn't be the nightmare it usually was. There was an underground place I knew that was close, and I angled for that.

I'd driven only a block or two before I was in Thick Fog®. I was anxious and in a hurry, but I had to go slow or risk splattering pedestrians. There weren't many places in the valley where people actually walked. This was one of them. It was eerie as all thick fog is, even if it's synthetic. Street lights glowed in gold, semaphores in puddles of green, red and amber. I fought the urge to use my wipers again as the film on my windshield turned everything kaleidoscopic. It was all messed up, illusionary, but there was a beauty to it. Just don't breathe.

The parking lot was littered with beaters, the kind of car a teenager reasonably gets for their first vehicle and drives into the ground through college. Randy's multi-coat cherry red Tesla was easy to find. I parked next to it. My headache was back.

I saw a marquee that directed me to the Spells tournament. I headed down the hall, but before I saw the crowd or heard it, I smelled it.

It is a terrible but truthful stereotype about gamers. They stink. Not every-one. Not all of them, but enough of them that there is an accurate cliché about the "geek stink." It's a smell of body odor, unwashed clothes, and Doritos.

It's an acrid funk shared by geeks of many stripes, video gamers, sci-fi con goers, and spellcasters, I discovered. It's the scent of basement pizza boxes, two-liter bottles of Mountain Dew and carpal tunnel syndrome. It's a smell I might have shared before I got married but hadn't known because somehow the carriers of this plague are immune to the eye-watering effects of it. That day I was not so blessed. I walked into the half-visible miasma unprepared, perhaps thinking some of the sulfurous outside air had leaked in, expecting factory soot and petroleum instead of athlete's foot and Mentholatum.

But I had my son to find. And so noble soul that I am, I ventured in.

I couldn't guess how many people were there, how many games were being played on how many tables, at least not in straight integers. Maybe in acres I could guess. Or hectares, but who really knows how big a hectare is? Or an acre? There were lots of people though. From wall to vanishing point wall, there were lunch tables set out in long rows, six players to a table, three games on each, players sitting across from one another. At least ninety percent were male. Maybe more. Body fat index was in the red. My appearance hadn't done anything to lower it. A stage was set up with a screen showing brackets and the time left in this particular round. As far as I could tell, they were about halfway through.

There were special games happening on the stage and cameras to film them. It wasn't like a video game, just a camera on a crane pointing straight down over the table. A small corner of the display showed heads and arms and cards turned at right angles. Dice and chits. Those had to be the premier games, those being played by somebody somebody else had heard of. In the one game, I quickly figured out who that somebody was. It had to be the guy with the Spells-sponsored jersey. The board had him ranked #1 coming in. His name was Dawane Osterlot. He was in his midtwenties, unlike his opponent, who'd had to have his mom drop him off. He had narrow designer glasses and a goatee that crawled down his neck under his shirt. His mustache was making an attempt to exist but hadn't decided if it had the time. He snapped his cards and moved his hands like a three-card Monte con man. The other kid, like I said, was young and looked well out of his league. He wore a middle school T-shirt that suggested he'd learned to play this once-fun, now hyper-competitive game, at lunch with his friends before geometry class. He probably wished he was there now. His hands shook as he played.

I moved toward the stage, thinking someone there had some authority to answer questions. The smell was everywhere, and I tried to remember to keep my mouth shut. Occasionally I'd walk through a cloud of nacho cheese or pepperoni pizza, but they were small islands in the sea of great unwashed.

I ran across people in bright yellow shirts with clipboards wandering between the tables, hustling over to someone or another whose hands popped up like sporadic geysers. I assumed they were judges, folks who could clear up some rule detail, who knew people who knew people and would be the kind of person I wanted to talk to. The stage looked crowded.

"Who's in charge?" I asked one.

"I am."

"So you're the guy who kidnapped my son and will now face federal charges?"

His horrified look told me he wasn't the guy in charge.

"Stage. The guy in the hat."

I completed my trek to the front of the room and found the guy in the hat. The hat was a fedora and would have made a complete stereotypical meme to match the smell if the man wearing it had the neckbeard of the reigning champion or been under sixty years old. His age spots were hidden beneath tanned wrinkles and over-bright teeth.

"Excuse me," I said. "I'm looking for my son, Randy Flaner. He told me he'd been kidnapped."

"What?" he said.

My comment drew the attention of the players but only for a second. A large man in a black button shirt and a Taser holstered on his belt bellied up to me like he was challenging me to sumo.

"Is this the rent-a-cop that's going to bankrupt this entire thing?" I said.

Randy hadn't told me much, but he had indicated that he was being held against his will. I'd seen no real cops and cheating at cards ain't a hangin' offense in these parts no more. I don't usually pull out the tough guy schtick, but in this crowd I thought I might dazzle them with threats outside their bubble, plus I was fueled by righteous parental anger.

"What?" said the hat. "Who are you? What do you want?"

Phones began to pop up behind me, like periscopes in a geek sea. Social media streaming cameras made the hat guy smile nervously and gesture for Black Belly to beat it.

"Come with me to the back," he said.

"I want to know what you've done with my son!" I said loudly, yelling really, turning my better side three-quarters profile.

"Follow me."

I did.

"Randy!"

"Dad!"

My boy leapt up and rushed for me. We spread our arms wide for a big hug, but he pulled up a step short and slid his hands into his pockets. "Hey, Dad," he said. "'Sup?"

Teenagers.

"What's all this, then?" I asked.

"He's yours?" said the hat. "He was caught cheating."

"And that gives you the right to—"

"I wasn't cheating." The indignant anger in Randy's voice was unmistakable. He nearly shouted.

There was time to come back to the imprisonment later, I figured. Randy was happy to have me there. I like my son a lot, love him even. A lot. He's going through some identity issues now, and neither of us is quite sure how I fit into his life now. Getting this chance to act for my son was not to be missed.

"Them's some mighty dangerous accusations you're laying out there, partner," I said to Fedora. The lawyer in me merged with a cowboy. "Who said he cheated and how exactly did he supposedly cheat?"

The big-bellied bully stun-gun-carrying guy slithered in.

Fedora exhaled deeply and I quickly scanned the room. There were boxes of cards, a trophy in bubble wrap, a life-size cardboard cutout of a four-eyed green wizard casting a yellow spell. One corner had a single chair and was separated from the rest of the room. The time-out corner. Randy had been there.

"I'm Evan Svenson," said Fedora. "I'm the organizer and company rep for this event."

I didn't recognize the flavor of his strong cologne, but my eyes found it only partially better than the floor musk.

"And?" I said.

"This is your son?"

"Yep." I puffed out my chest, putting it close to the level of my stomach.

"Would you like a soda?" He smiled warmly. My legal bluff was working.

"Cheating?" I reminded him.

"I didn't cheat," said Randy again.

"Of course you didn't. I just need to hear their misconceptions explained."

Without looking, Evan reached his arm out and the big bully meanie slapped an envelope into his palm. He opened it and took out two cards.

"We are a sanctioned event," he explained. "We feed into nationals and worlds. It's a big deal."

I stared at him as coldly as I could. Randy shifted his weight from hip to hip.

"Our rules are strict."

"You don't allow cheaters? How bizarre."

"Cheating comes in many forms," Evan went on.

"For fuck's sake," said I. "Get to it."

"Your son was caught using counterfeit cards."

"Forgeries?" I said.

"We only allow actual company-produced products in our tournaments. We understand that some of the cards can be pricey, but we have many different levels of tournaments to compensate for that. Proxies are banned and considered cheating."

"They're not proxies," Randy said. His face was red. "I paid real money for real cards."

Evan shook his head. He passed them to me. The first was called *Armored Yeti*, and it was a powerful card. A big monster. Bites hard. It was a game winner. The other was *Stringent Bolt of Pain*, and it too was a powerful card that *faced* an opponent—meaning it dealt damage directly to a player and not his pieces. Both looked like regular Spells cards. They felt like regular Spells cards. They had the foil emblem, the rarity marker, the signatures and backs. One was a little used, had some white on the edges like it hadn't been played in sleeves its whole life, but otherwise, they looked pristine.

I shook my head.

"The current meta uses both of these cards," said Evan. "That means—"

"I know what it means," I said. "It's what's being played right now."

"Do you play?"

"I used to."

"We should—"

"You're pissing me off, Evan," I said. "How are these proxies?"

"They're forgeries," he said.

"I'm being framed," said Randy.

"By whom?" I said, pleased to remember to use the objective case.

"Dewane Osterlot."

"Who?" Nominative.

"He's our reigning champion," said Evan. "He spotted the fakes during their game."

"On stage?"

"Streamed," said Evan.

"He must have planted them," said Randy. "He cheats."

"Now now," said Evan.

"That's my line," said I. I looked at the cards as close as I could in the weak light.

"They look kosher to me."

"We checked them. They are forgeries. Good ones, but they are not kosher."

"Cheaters will not be tolerated," said Black Belly like he was answering a drill sergeant.

"We've had some issues lately," explained Evan. "Some rather well-publicized incidents, and the company is sensitive."

"So you decided to make an example of my son?"

"Sure you don't want a soda?"

I squinted at him.

"Your son forfeits his professional points and has a two-year suspension," he said. "He cannot earn points or register for any tournament during that time."

"And he was publicly shamed on the internet?"

Randy ground his teeth.

"It is unfortunate that it happened how it did, but these are forgeries."

"How can you tell? How could Dawane Neckbeard tell?"

Evan took one of the cards and pointed to a corner. I shook my head. He produced a magnifying glass with a built-in light. Pretty snazzy thing, actually. He turned it on and gave it to me.

"The copyright symbol," he said.

I looked at the corner and saw 'Spells©' in the corner.

"So?"

"Look closer."

I squinted and stared, Then I realized there was a flaw. The circled C of the copyright symbol had a faint diagonal line through it. "Interesting, but that's an explanation, not an excuse. Who are you that you can arrest my son?"

"He wasn't under arrest."

"He came willingly?"

Evan nodded as convincingly as he could I thought.

"Didn't feel that way," said Randy.

"We were only escorting him out of the arena. We wanted to talk with him in private."

I looked at Randy. His rage was turning to shame, and I thought it was time to end this.

"Where can I find you, Evan Svenson of the fedora clan?"

He gave me his business card. I did not return the gesture.

"Let's go," I said.

We left the little room and I cast menacing squints behind me.

5

I FOLLOWED Randy's new ticket-me-please red Tesla back to my place in my little Prius. I felt like a tabby cat following a lion. He laid a patch of torqued rubber coming out of the underground garage. I made the incline alright with forty percent battery remaining. I lost sight of him at the top and drove for home, where I found his car in the driveway and the lights on in the house.

"Hey, Randy, are you hungry?" I called as I came in, but the screeching garage door drowned out any answer I may have received. Farther in the house, I tried again. "Randy?"

"I'm going to bed, Dad," he said from the hall. "I just want to sleep."

"Okay. See you in the morning."

I heard his door shut. I keep a room for Randy to use at my place for the rare times he stays the night. It is a bare guest room, less than an Airbnb, more than a closet under the stairs. He doesn't use it much. It was only because Nancy was out of town that he was here at all.

I knocked on the door.

"I'm sleeping!"

"Don't scream in your sleep." I opened the door to a dark room. "It scares the Republicans."

"Go away, Dad. Okay? I just want to sleep."

"I will, but I just want to say one thing. Maybe two."

"Get it over with."

"One. Chrysanthemum," I said.

"Nice."

"Two," I said, happy to hear a little smile in his voice. "This isn't a big deal. Don't let it be one."

"It is to me."

"Not even there."

"Don't tell me what I—"

"Sorry sorry sorry." Smile good and gone now. "We'll talk in the morning."

I heard him roll over, saw his head disappear under a pillow in the dim hall light, and left him.

Teenagers. Angsty teenagers.

It'd been a tough couple months with my son, I won't lie. His whole life he'd been a dream child, self-motivated, confident, smart. Good grades. Hip and techno-savvy; a pillar of his generation. Then all at once, he became angst boy. I suppose I have Nancy to thank, maybe, for his early ease. Though the light had gone out of our marriage early on, her ordered, practical, and sadomasochistic mind conceived to make us stay together until our son was fourteen before the divorce. That was Nancy. A divorce planned years ahead of time, date circled on a calendar. I went with it because I usually go with things. Randy had turned out okay, and Nancy was quick to point that out. Of course, he might have done just fine another way, but we'll never know.

Now, however, he is a different person.

I'm not blaming Nancy. Well, maybe I am. She is his primary caregiver now, and if not her, who should I blame? Me? Hormones? Society?

Okay, those are all pretty good suspects too.

Randy is taking after me in his recent ping-pong identity moves. I was famous for that before. Might be again. Randy went from honor-roll student in T-shirts and jeans to a Goth overnight with more attitude than appeal— thick eyeliner and black lipstick that went to his chin. I didn't even know Goth was a thing anymore. Before I could comment on it, though, he'd become a cowboy. How do you make that switch? He tapped his savings account for some three-hundred-dollar lizard skin boots and a two-hundred Stetson hat. Neither was broken in before he put a wave in his hair, joined the drama club and tried out for the school play, performing a faultless Porter in *Macbeth* but lost the part to a senior and only got Banquo. Banquo! A lead. Banquo—as a freshman. Sword fights, ghost. A great part. He was incensed at not getting the smaller part, quit and tried out for the golf team. Then the swim team. Then the e-sports team, where I thought he was back to normal, but nope. Before the team was even posted—him on the varsity list —he'd bought a pool cue and began hanging out in a bowling alley downtown. His wardrobe changed like a strobe light on a faulty circuit. His closet looked like a pawn shop. His teachers had mentioned it at parent-teacher conference, and Nancy had immediately gone out and bought more books about teenagers than Randy had costumes.

Hormones and Society—I'm bunching them together because I'm lazy— are, without a doubt, involved. Being a teenager is hard. We forget how truly miserable this stage of life is when we grow up. If we grow up. As our bodies push into maturity, flooding our blood and brain with chemicals Ken Kesey wouldn't have touched on purpose, we're also faced with social pressure long ignored and newly made by packs of other stricken teenagers. It's a gauntlet, a humiliating rite of passage. Just as we get interested in the opposite sex and get the equipment to make it work, our faces pop with zits, noses get out of proportion, voices crack and arms go gangly. If such a thing were done to my child by another person, killing them would be justifiable homicide. We just have to bear it. Yes, we. Randy has the worst of it, but the shrapnel isn't contained. Confusion abounds. I'm reminded of a piece of advice someone gave me when Randy was first born: "Eat your children while their bones are still soft." I thought they were talking about the terrible twos, but now I'm sure they were referring to adolescence.

Randy would be on my mind for the rest of my life. Even after he settled and landed and got through this hell, I would never stop worrying about him. That's the role of a parent. I'd keep bail money ready and a spare room for him until I was under the grass and he had a cowboy of his own.

The night was still early. I looked at my phone, hoping to find a message from Allie. Seeing nothing, I immediately slid into self-pity mode. I poured myself a glass of bourbon. Bourbon's been my drink lately. All the cool guys drink it. I flopped down on the couch, thinking of how this day was meant to end—*Mystery Science Theater 3000* rerun, cuddles, and quiet child-in-the-house sex in the master bedroom. Now my son was in a crisis, my girlfriend was going to parties without me, and I had taken on two—no, three—cases. After my second drink, I decided to do some digging into Randy's problem with the Spells tournament. That shark at the premier table looked fishy to me. An obvious suspect.

I pulled out my laptop, intending to look for videos of Dawane Osterlot, local champion, maybe find the video of Randy's match and see if I couldn't see him palming cards or something. Instead my email went into overdrive as my other cases, the real ones, the paying ones, filled my box with information.

I'd not been working for a while. That's a problem. I recognized it now with Allie's help. You've heard that when you have nothing to do, nothing gets done? Well, in my recent lethargy, I'd gotten something done. I got depressed and gotten in my head. Getting in one's head means taking inventory of one's life, in a bad way, reliving embarrassments and humiliations, double thinking every decision you've ever made. It's like that terrible hour of the wolf where you wake up at three a.m. to remember that time you tripped in junior high school and smashed chicken-fried steak on your shirt and had to wear it the rest of the day. Or that time you stupidly called a girl big because of her boisterous personality, only figuring out later that she took it to mean her hips. It was twenty years ago, but why let that stop you from reliving it? Work is important. Not just for money but for peace of mind because it keeps a piece of your mind occupied and away from that kind of shit.

When I was a kid, they asked me what I wanted to be when I grew up. I thought it was a shit question to ask anyone under the age of retired. Since I didn't know better, I said, "Happy," just like John Lennon. Maybe because of him. When that answer was kicked out I was told to try again. Unable to make such a decision then because I was a goddamn child, I said something along the lines of jack-of-all-trades. They let that one stand, probably thinking I'd grow out of it, and planned classes for me to try. The plan was that I'd find out I was good at something and be happy. In my head now, I think that there was a moment of failure. I should have said computers or fireman or haunted housekeeper and gone with it, followed it straight through, gotten a real job, security and such. I didn't have to like something to be good at it. Flighty, irresponsible, stupid, ugly, radioactive, smelly, cootie-ridden...my thoughts swirled in on themselves thinking of how at Randy's age I'd failed to go straight. Minus ten to morale roll. Fail. Take ten points psychic damage.

That winter had been bad on my morale all around. I'd been unable to lose weight, the one hobby I never seemed to master. I had a tummy. Nothing dramatic, but I knew it was there and wanted it gone. The inversion had dropped a level of chemical gloom no one could ignore, so I didn't. Add to this not keeping busy, an angsty teenager to fill my parent-guilt quotient, and a girlfriend who was so far out of my league I yearned to be a face on a milk carton, and you got Tony that winter.

And I get distracted easily.

I turned to the real cases and told myself that I'd be responsible and smart and together for a while.

The first message was from Bryan Moland, the fiancé who suspected his fiancée (extra e) of something untoward. Ick. The second of course was from Fah.

The new me poured a shot of Kentucky's best export over a glass of melting ice, watered it down with some soda water from a can, deleted fifty junk emails, and looked at the stuff from Thailand.

The missing girl was called Sandi Wong. I think Fah might have told me that already, but hell if I could remember. There was a photo of her with Fah in the hotel. I recognized the cool dragon-themed carpet. She was pretty. She was very pretty. Almond eyes, bright sly smile. Page haircut I fell in love with watching Bae Doona in *Sense8*. She had the unnatural air that comes from having a nearly perfectly symmetrical face. I held my hand up against the screen, covering each half in turn and squinting through bourbon-blurred eyes to verify. Fah looked very happy, maybe too happy. But I didn't judge. Much.

A photocopy of her passport didn't help as much as you'd think. I don't speak or read Burmese, so I made do with the few lines that had been translated to English. A bit of math told me she was twenty-three years old. There was something about the picture that bothered me. I couldn't put my finger on it, so I put my finger over it and saw again that beautifully symmetrical face. I didn't have access to the inside pages—the hotel just copied the first one, but Fah told me that Sandi had been traveling around Asia for years. She'd left her homeland, Myanmar/Burma (never really figured out which to use) four years earlier to see the world, possibly for political reasons. She'd told Fah that her family was related to an exiled ex-general who was now living somewhere in "Utah, United States." Sandi had indicated that she'd look him up while trying to be discovered on the snowy streets of Park City, hunting for casting directors and producers not named Weinstein. Stranger things have happened. I didn't know if she could act, but looking like she did, she probably wouldn't have to. Fah said she could act, though. He mentioned it. He was sure she'd be famous one day.

The exiled ex-general was General U Tayza Min Ko. Fah referred to him as Tayza, so I did too. I would have thought this a solid lead if Tayza weren't dead, but Fah said he was. He had a living son, however, somewhere in Utah, called Thiha Min Naings, referred to as Thiha, pronunciation unknown. Sandi was his cousin but they'd never met. The general left Myanmar when Thiha was just a boy. Since Sandi would be in the neighborhood, she thought she'd drop by and say hi. I wondered if, like many people unfamiliar with America and the West, she had misjudged the distances. Going from one end of this state to the other would be crossing a handful of international borders in Europe. But luckily, eighty percent of Utah's population lives along the Wasatch Front, a line of towns huddling the west side of the Wasatch Mountains, any of which could be reached within an hour from where I sat. Park City was one mountain over to the east, also an hour away.

I transferred all the information to my expensive new phone while wondering if she spoke with an accent, or if she spoke English at all. I had to assume she did. Other assumptions were that she was well-to-do, upper class, confident if not fearless since she traveled alone internationally as a twenty-three-year-old knock-out. I had to assume she was streetwise. She probably knew karate.

Fah said he'd driven her to the airport. She'd had five bags. After leaving her at the Lufthansa terminal a week ago Thursday, he hadn't heard from her. She hadn't said she'd call him or anything, he admitted, but he'd texted her and never got anything back. I called her number. It was a foreign extension. Lots of numbers. The voice mail was full.

I looked up Lufthansa flights out of Bangkok to Salt Lake City. No direct flight, but the website offered a few different choices for connections and arrivals. It was a good start. I toasted my success and could no longer taste the alcohol. Not a good sign.

I stared at Moland's email but didn't open it. Procrastination is my middle name, some would say my superpower. Others not.

I was pouring the last one because it was a Friday when my phone beeped. It was eleven o'clock. Allie was at a private party in a luscious mansion. She'd sent me a picture to prove it. Marble tile, ceilings higher than an opera house, beautiful happy people with finger foods and champagne flutes. A chandelier waiting to fall.

She wrote:

> Look who I found

Next picture was her being hugged by a man in said palatial estate, a selfie taken at Allie's arm's length.

I texted back:

> Who?

> Frank Tomas! From your high school. In for the reunion.

Oh, yeah, and I have a school reunion coming up.

I took a hard look at the man, his thin frame, sleek suit, warm grin, gold chain, hand around my girlfriend. I remembered him, and I hated him anew.

6

SOME PEOPLE FORGIVE AND FORGET. Others forgive, but don't forget. I forget but don't forgive. I will be pissed at someone for years but not know why. Seeing Frank Tomas in a picture brought up a bevy of bad vibes, but I couldn't recall specific reasons for them. He'd been popular in high school, and I wasn't. He was rich. I wasn't. He was homecoming king and in student government. I did a bit of drama and played Dungeons & Dragons in the library so I wouldn't have to ride the school bus where *Lord of The Flies* was replayed every afternoon as live theater. I'm not sure if our paths ever actually crossed outside of sharing a lunchroom or maybe a math class, but still, I feel resentment at just recalling those times and that guy. I seem to remember that he was voted most likely to succeed. I could look it up. I have my yearbooks around my house somewhere, buried in boxes of stuff I should have thrown away long ago. Finding those didn't seem like a bad idea just then, since the reunion was coming up and I might be going. I might not be too.

The bourbon and dread were catching up to me. As I drifted off to sleep that strange Friday night, I tried to focus on good memories in a warm bed but settled for passed out on a crunch couch.

In the morning I found a note on my laptop.

Went out.

I assumed it was from Randy, but he hadn't signed it.
Tasting my chia teeth, I texted him.

Sup?

I'm out.

Doing?

Stuff.

When will I c u?

I wanted to look hip by using text code abbreviations. I'm sure he was impressed.

Later.

Love you.

The ol' bait and switch with spelling it all out. No emojis here. Gotcha!
He didn't respond.
I relented and emojied. I sent him a heart for emphasis.
Nothing.
I peeled off my clothes that smelled like cheap comedy clubs and bad air. I climbed in my shower. Water is magical. A good long shower or a bath makes me feel like a new person. Maybe religions will pick up on that. Oh. They have.
Anyway…
I made a mental checklist of my chores, something Allie had been trying to teach me about. Organize…something. I dunno. I wasn't paying attention to the names, only the ideas. I'm an idea person.
I counted four cases now: missing Asian girl, local soon-to-be bride, chaos with cards, and since it was going to gnaw at my brain anyway, was I a fraud?
I texted Allie.

Sup?

Nothing.
She was probably asleep. It was still early, only eight fifteen in the morning and a Saturday. Who gets up that early?
Because I was a new man, at least while my breakfast cooked, I opened the stuff Moland had sent. There was a photo of the girl and her social media links. Her name was Madeline "Maddy" Smith. She was twenty-five years old, originally from Van Cleve, Missouri, wherever the hell that was. Probably Missouri. She worked from home as a bookkeeper. Her soon-to-be spouse, Bryan, reported that she was an only child with no living family. She'd served a Mormon mission in Milwaukee, Wisconsin, between high school and a short unfinished tenure at USC, dropping out to come to Utah last year. Her hobbies were homemaking and acting. She was part of a

theater company. They were to be married in three weeks and had met through an online dating service two months ago.

Two months ago.

Utah.

I made sure all the information was in my phone. I had plenty of memory for all the photos. I knew there'd been a reason for me to get the top-of-the-line maxed-out memory phone, some reason besides financial irresponsibility. Yep. Here it was.

There were fifteen professional engagement photos in different poses. They all showed him in a black tux and her in a modest wedding gown. It was long and white and sweeping, with a collar that went up to her chin. Long sleeves, which was good because all the pictures were taken outside in a canyon somewhere with snow banks and leafless aspens. Artsy, in a *To Build a Fire* kind of way. I always marvel at wedding pictures. *Oh look, here I am traversing an arctic wasteland in a wedding dress and who should I encounter but a handsome man in rented tuxedo. True Love!* The mountains must be littered with veils and cummerbunds, frozen bones, dead cameramen, and sure signs of cannibalism.

To get the taste of conservative kitsch out of my mouth, I drank three cups of creamed coffee and ate one big omelet consisting of cheese, ham, eggs and more cheese smothered in Tabasco sauce. After that, I set out for the airport.

I had a pretty good idea which flight Sandi Wong would have taken. Fah had told me she was wealthy. Wealthy people tend to value their time more than their money, so I looked for the fastest route, shortest layovers, fewest plane changes. There was only one that made sense.

I used to work at the airport. I used to work at a lot of places, but the airport was one of them. I still had some friends there. I no longer had my employee jacket that let me bypass security and sell dynamite on the tarmac, but I did know where the offices were and the general work schedule.

The lines to travel were thick and slow. The smell of missed connections and frustration wafted across the terminal buildings like a broken bottle of smuggled cologne in an overnight bag coming through customs. I crossed the main terminal and found my way upstairs to the offices. I was never popular with the bosses while I worked there, but after they fired me and I embarrassed them, I was actually reviled. But friends in high places never got me anywhere. Low places. That's where shit gets done.

I slithered into the main office, where a receptionist read a book behind a laminated desk. I knew the book. *What Immortal Hand*, an occult thriller. One of my favorites. Highly recommended. I knew I'd get along fine with this girl. She had taste.

"Hey there," I said. "Can you buzz Mittens up here?"

"Okay," she said.

Mittens was a baggage handler most days, but on Saturdays he managed the shop. It was a cushy do-nothing job; just sit in an office and drink coffee, watch Netflix and get overtime because it was cheaper than keeping the general manager's third cousin's nephew here on Saturdays when his time would be better spent studying for his history final.

My old friend poked his head out of an office and beamed at me.

"Tony, mon! How the hell are you?"

"Hanging low in the snow," I said and then flinched when I remembered we weren't alone.

The receptionist turned the page, totally caught up in the story. The book is that good.

"Come on back. We'll shoot the shit."

He pushed an unseen button, and a waist-high door swung open and I followed my old Jamaican friend down a beige hall. Before he could turn me into an office that had the rich invigorating smell of Colorado skunkweed, I stopped him.

"I need to look at some security tapes from last Thursday," I said.

"You on a case?"

"I am."

"Outstanding, mon, outstanding. Put that Chris Traard guy to shame."

"You saw that, huh?"

"No. No no...just heard about it."

"People are talking about it around here?"

"No no no no no. I forgot—I actually did not read it. Half asleep. Online. On a Saturday. Nothing else to do. Bored senseless. It was dumb."

"Oh."

"Good to see you," he said and slapped my back hard.

I let it go.

We walked down long windowless halls I remembered from my short stint there. I was acutely aware that I didn't have official clearance to be here now. It was committing a federal crime just being there. I clung close to Mittens who always had an aura of laid-back mellow that came from years of throwing bags into boxes and dealing with bullshit bureaucracies.

The TSA is a diabolic concoction originally meant to cut bullshit bureaucracy but then became one and worse. Think Darth Vader without the warmth. The job of keeping American airports safe is a joke so unfunny that I stopped doing jokes about it onstage. I used to but would often start crying in the middle of my set.

Having seen the work from both sides, as passenger and airport employee, I can tell you that what you suspect as a passenger is pretty much spot on. It's bullshit. It's security theater, a feel-good play of delay and frustration meant to further some authoritarian ideal of curtailing movement. Perry told me that, and I tend to agree. It has normalized oppression, playing on fear and dissuading people from moving around. If the extra bag cost and half-inch leg room upgrade didn't make you rethink your travel plans, the two-hour line for a cavity search might. I'm all for safety, but one has to agree that there has to be a better way. It's run by minimum-wage slaves who sometimes don't get paid, thus adding true injury to the insult of having to be the face of the demeaning shoe search and x-ray pageant. It's low morale, high stress, terrible pay.

These thoughts were forefront in my mind as Mittens steered me into the TSA security wing of the terminal.

"Yo, mon," said my friend to the guard at the door.

"Hey, Mittens," he said. "Tony."

"Hey...Bob," I said, reading the name tag. Thank God for name tags.

"Tony's gotta see some tapes from last Thursday," Mittens said.

"George is in today," said Bob.

"Still gonna," said Mittens.

Bob opened the door and we walked inside. It occurred to me that Mittens didn't have clearance for this room, either. He did, however, know Bob. I did too, apparently, though I forgot his name instantly and had to glance back and read it again, matching plate and face and trying to cement it in my medium-term memory at least.

"You're not supposed to be here," said George.

Then I remembered George—Georgie, a nickname his mother used at a visit once and he hated, so it had stuck. He was a rare animal, a longtime TSA employee. He'd been a longtime employee when I was here, which meant he was longer-time now. Math. He was an asshole as well, someone who enjoyed hassling people, not so rare in that and this job. He always made me think of the old adage there's nothing worse than a little person with a little power. He'd gotten grabby at the pat-down station and was moved to wands until he poked a guy "accidentally" in the balls and put him on the floor. He was made a permanent x-ray streamer. Now he got to sit in a room staring at a wall of flashing monitors on a Saturday, playing on his phone.

I knew this was going to be a conflict. I paused and wondered the best way to proceed. Should I kowtow to his authority? Play off his ego? Or treat him like the junior fascist he was? Why not all of it?

"I see you're still failing up," I said to him.

"What is that supposed to mean? I didn't do nothing."

"Failing. Failing up. I'm taking about your promotion. This new job. Perfectly aligned with your people skills." I gestured to the empty room.

"I never liked you, Flaner," he said. "And you ain't supposed to be in here. I could arrest you right now."

He stood up. I saw that he still wore a Taser on his belt. I'm sure that was a personal choice. What was he going to do with it in here? Jump-start the DVR with it? Still, I took note. I've been hit by those before. Not fun.

"Suspect arrived a week ago Thursday on United Flight 122 from San Francisco after making a connection from Bangkok. Asian girl. Five-foot-six.

Five bags. Probably first class." I made a point of speaking in monotone, as *Dragnet* as I could. Cable reruns used to be cool. I don't know if George had ever seen the old series or if there was just some instinctive trigger I touched by acting all cop-like, a sympathetic connection to his bully brain, but it had the desired effect.

For a moment his eyes went large.

"Wait," he said.

Fuck. His three brain cells had connected.

"You ain't a cop."

"He's on a big case. International intrigue," said Mittens.

"What's intrigue?" he asked, not surprising anyone.

"Secret," I said.

"And patriotic," added Mittens.

"I just need a confirmation she made the plane. That's all."

He squinted.

"Okay," I said and pulled out my wallet. I held up a twenty-dollar bill.

It took him a good long moment to realize what I was doing. A long awkward, stupid moment. Mittens and I shared several glances between us as we watched Georgie's face go blank for the slow movement of rusted sprockets in his head.

"Okay," he said finally. "What gate and what time Thursday?"

Mittens moved to a computer and quickly found the flight and gate. I could have done it, but I didn't have a login any more.

Or did I?

I stepped to another computer, flicked it on and waited for the monitor to come up.

Mittens, doing my work for me, read off the information to Georgie a few times until it stuck.

I typed my old scheduling password from the now-defunct Fly Away Airlines account.

I was in.

Shit.

I logged off again and put that little nugget of information into my data banks, if not for this case than a later one maybe.

"You guys still allow off-site call-in for scheduling?"

"What's that?" asked Georgie, squinting at a list of files scrolling in front of him.

"Oh yeah, mon," said Mittens, raising a suspicious eyebrow as I turned the monitor back off. "Outsourcing all that stuff lately."

"Doesn't surprise me," I said. "Lots of jobs can be done overseas now. Particularly if face-to-face contact isn't required. I glanced at the drooling ogre at the main station.

"Got it," he said.

"That was fast," I said, actually impressed.

"It's what I do," he said. "It's what I do."

Mittens and I exchanged another glance, then turned to the bank of monitors.

Eight of them flashed into replay mode, each showing a different angle or a different hallway, all at the same moment running simultaneously.

"That's the gate," said Mittens, pointing. "The plane was on time."

Three minutes later, people poured through the door into the terminal. First class was let off first, so we didn't have long to wait.

There she was—unmistakable page-cut hair, seductive figure, a Louis Vuitton carry-on swinging like it was empty on her arm. Since leaving Fah, she'd acquired a new accessory: a plump middle-aged balding businessman carried on her other arm.

7

THEY WERE touchy-feely all the way through the terminal. They waited together, practically sharing the same shoes at the baggage claim. Georgie had to dig a bit to find the exterior tapes, but he did, and we watched them come out of the terminal and, together, talk near a taxi stand, their breaths coming out in cold puffs as they laughed. Hand in hand, they boarded a car at the Ridez ride-share stand.

"I'll take my forty now, Flaner," said Georgie.

"Twenty."

"Forty. I had to search two banks."

"Hey, Mittens, you got a forty?"

"In the fridge upstairs."

"Money," said Georgie. "I don't drink on the job."

"Since when?"

He blushed and glared.

"Right, right. Hey, Mittens, can I borrow a twenty?"

My friend scowled.

"PayPal?" I said to Georgie.

"Okay."

Keeping my cash, I transferred the money, fascinated at the brave new world I was in—paying bribes by internet. At least I'd have a record for my taxes and expense report. Should I 1099 Georgie? That would be a dick move. I'd consider it.

Mittens wanted to hang out, chat for the rest of shift, another seven hours. I hadn't thought about my own insecurities in like an hour of sleuthing, and I knew I could prolong that by talking to an old friend over ganja and malt liquor. But I had to decline. We promised each other a good long visit in the future.

I left him and went to the ride-share line, looking for the silver Dodge Journey I'd seen pick up Sandi and Mr. Grope. It wasn't there. Of course it wasn't there. What the hell was I thinking?

I sat down on a bench to reconsider my life choices. That stupid Traard quote kept biting at me. "Persistence and discipline get results." It was a direct call to sit there and stakeout the stand until it arrived, however long it took. I supposed I could call the Ridez headquarters, if there was one, and try to get the information that way. A good bluff. I'd need some Rockford-level confusion and some luck—

Fuck—luck again. There it was. I relied on luck too much. What kind of a detective has luck written into their game plan?

That quick. Five minutes on a bench, and my stack came in. I had exposed myself as the fraud I was.

A silver Dodge Journey pulled up to the kiosk.

Holy shit, I thought. That was lucky.

I leaped up and ran to it.

"Hey buddy," said the driver, leaning in to talk across the passenger seat. "You in a hurry to go somewhere?"

"Are you available?"

"Yessir."

I got in.

I had used Ridez only once before, so wasn't overly familiar with the routine.

"You gotta request a ride," said the driver. "Hold on. Let me go off real quick. Tell me when you're about to request it. I'll switch on then and be the nearest driver."

"Pretty slick." I found the app. "It wants to know where I'm going."

"So tell it."

"Uhm, you gotta tell me."

"New in town? Whatcha looking for?"

"Take me to the same place you took this girl last Thursday." I showed him the picture of Sandi Wong on my phone.

"Eh…"

"I'm not a stalker," I said.

"No?"

"I'm a private investigator. She was with a big balding guy in a suit."

"Her husband?"

"No."

"Eh…"

"Okay, I know that sounds sleazy."

"Eh…"

"She's single. I'm working a missing persons' case. I followed her here, to your car, and then lost her. She's from Burma."

"Myanmar. They changed the name."

"Right. I need to find her and make sure she's okay."

The driver scratched his head and thought.

The car behind us honked.

He put the Dodge into gear and pulled out.

"So you'll take me?"

"Give me a second to think."

He drove the loop around Salt Lake's beautiful airport. I took in the never-ending construction, marveling at the early bloom of orange traffic cones, the state flower. He went back to the curb where I'd gotten in and stopped. My gut tightened. I opened my bank account to see how much I could BribePal this guy.

The driver—his name not to be mentioned, let's call him "Jay"—opened his computer and tapped keys. He radiated good nature. His smile was contagious, his eyes were full of that mischievous light children only see in Old Saint Nick's. Waves of contentment flowed like from a Buddha and put my teeth on edge. Such things are natural.

"Do you have a time?" he asked.

I averted my eyes and said, "About four o'clock. A few minutes after. They had lots of luggage. She had five Louis Vuitton bags. He had two Samsonites." Working at an airport, you got to know your bags.

I could sense he remembered them, but he didn't admit it.

I could bid $86.23 for an electronic bribe before I'd need to crash a credit card or transfer something. I doubted money would work on him, maybe souls or quests or something, but I was about to propose the eighty-six twenty-three when he said. "A hotel. They went to a hotel."

"Which one?"

"I'll drive you. Request the ride."

I woke up my phone.

"Downtown Merrill Hotel," he said. "That's where we're going."

"Got it. Ride requested."

He flicked a switch, and an iPad lit up on his console. A tap and a wink to me, he accepted the assignment.

"Good to go, buddy. Buckle up. Safety first," he said. "What kind of music do you like? I have some snacks up here if you want some. A cold Coke Zero or a Diet Mountain Dew. Free."

"Coke would be great."

"String cheese?"

"Sure."

He passed me the snacks and again circled through the construction zone we used as an airport and got on the freeway.

The haze was thick, and we passed through some fog banks, identifiable by the sudden white cloud appearing out of the rusty-gray ones.

"First time in Salt Lake?"

"I live here."

"Just coming home?"

"No."

"Wait… Did you leave your car at the airport?"

"Yep."

"Will you be needing a ride back?"

"Yep."

He reached into the glove box and gave me a business card with a phone number on it. "That's my personal number. Call anytime. Even if you just want to chat."

I took it, feeling warm and fuzzy. His contagious compassion spreading over his business card.

"And don't forget to leave me a review."

"And a tip?"

"That's totally up to you."

I munched cheese and sipped cold caffeine.

The Merrill Hotel wasn't the best hotel in the city, but it was in the top five. In my clothes, I would stand out like a cheeseburger in a salad. I didn't know anyone who worked there, and I doubt my twenty cash would let me see any records, at least not in the middle of Saturday afternoon. Maybe the night shift, but not then. Sundance was up the canyon, and the place would be full.

I could just go in and try to get lucky, but I knew the universe better than that. It was setting me up with this Ridez driver, daring me to roll again. I'd need to, but I'd had to shave the dice a bit first.

Seeing a box store off the freeway, I pointed. "Pull over there," I said.

"Sure thing." Blinker, checked blind spot, affirming look at me, and we were there.

"Wait here," I said.

"Will do."

"Are you always so cheerful?"

"Is it making you mad?"

"No, the opposite."

"That's the plan."

"I feel so manipulated."

I ran in and bought a cheap purse. It cost me my twenty dollars. I was now cashless, but I had a new handbag. And I could give to Allie when I was done. What woman wouldn't love a faux purple snakeskin handbag? The purple was real. The snake surely wasn't. I think it was pleather, but *real* pleather. Allie would flip over it. It would go so well with her…with her…

Oh well.

It's the thought that counts.

I climbed back into Jay's car and off we went to the Merrill.

"Nice ride."

"Thanks. It has a third seat in the back if I need it."

"Can I have another Coke?"

He squinted at me in the rearview mirror. "I don't know," he said but broke into a wide toothy grin. "Of course." He chuckled and passed me another can.

I slammed more cola and shook my head.

"What?" he asked.

"I'm just wondering how you've managed it."

"Being happy? It's all attitude."

"No, how have you managed to survive this long?"

"It's good for health."

"How about mobs of jealous pitchfork-wielding depressants unable to accept your existence?"

"Really?" His smile dampened just a bit.

"Can you wait for me?"

"Will you be fast?"

"This should be quicker than buying the purse. Oh, hand me your sign."

"My Ridez sign? I need it."

"I'll bring it back."

"This is a weird ride," he said but dutifully pulled his sign off a suction cup hook from his windshield.

"Do you regret it?"

"Oh, no. This is why I do this. I like adventure and love meeting new people. And being useful to—"

I bailed out of the car before he finished, before the cheer could erode my soul anymore. How can anyone go through life like that? The aura of that guy had threatened to suck the sarcasm and snark right out of me like a liposuction hose. No, thank you. I would resist to the bitter end. No Ridez driver was going to remove my dark superpowers.

I was considering getting a different driver for the ride back when I found myself standing in the lobby of the Merrill, distracted and drooling with human compassion residue, holding an electric Ridez sign and a purse too ugly to give to Goodwill. Combined with my choice of Hawaiian beachcomber fashion, I drew the attention of the staff right away.

"Can I help you?" It was someone official. Somebody in charge. The suit fit too well. His smug was a stink.

I quaked in fear, my usual lightning-quick wit eroded by Jay out in the car.

"I love everyone," I muttered.

"What?"

"No, no...uhm. I need to talk to the receptionist."

"Why?"

"I'm a Ridez driver." I held up the sign. It glowed in my hand. I flicked the switch to make it flash.

"You're picking someone up?"

"No."

"Dropping off, then."

"Missed again." I felt my power returning.

"What then?"

I held up the purse.

"Stunning," he said.

"Receptionist?"

I could tell I'd frustrated him. Other guests were eyeing us suspiciously. There was one dapper silver-haired guy sitting in an overstuffed chair reading a newspaper. If not for the modern magic of Lasik, I'm sure he'd have had a monocle. As he was, he glared down his nose as if taking aim.

"People actually sit in the lobby and read here?" I said.

"We have drink service in that part of the lobby," said the man.

"Far out."

I followed him across the marble floor to a long dark mahogany desk. His heels smartly clicked a pleasant call with each step, my sneakers squeaked a sickly reply. The acoustics carried.

Behind the desk was a professionally attired young woman. I couldn't place her age. Her outfit and bun said middle-aged, but her face and energy said barely legal.

"How can I help you?" she asked.

I held up the Ridez sign. It flashed in her eyes.

"I'm a Ridez driver."

"Yes?"

"Could you please turn that off," said the man.

"Oh, yeah. Sorry." I switched it off.

"I have this purse here. See?" I held up the purse.

"Very nice," she said.

"And?" said the man.

"I dropped a ride off here Thursday before last and the woman left this in my car. I just found it."

"I see."

"She arrived here at about 4:40. They checked in."

"Yes?"

"I was hoping to return the purse."

The man nodded to the girl who tapped the keys and drew her finger down a computer screen I couldn't see.

"They're not here anymore. They checked out the next morning."

"Well, can you tell me where they went? I really think the woman would want her bag back."

The girl looked at the bag and held back a frown.

"Do we have an address?" asked the man.

She shook the shock off and danced her fingers across the keys. I noticed a wedding ring on her finger, big-ass diamond, sparkly and new. Too big. It got in the way. A newlywed. Give her a couple years, she'd drop that rock off her hand like…well, like a rock.

"Yes," she said.

"And?" said I, stealing the man's catchphrase.

"And we'll send it on," said he.

"No."

"No?"

"No," I said. "Hell no. I'm not parting with it until I put it in her hands."

"Why not?"

"Because there's money in here. I'm not handing this to you people to pass on. You'll filch the cash and blame me. Nossir, that ain't going to happen. Plus I need a review."

"Please… We are the Merrill."

"No!" My voice echoed off the marble and into the faraway halls. Mr. Newspaper squinted again.

"And there might be a tip?" said the man.

"Just because I don't work in a big plush overpriced stuck-up hotel for the oppressing one-percent oligarch villains of the world and make an honest working-class living with what resources I have is no reason to deny me—"

"Fine, fine."

Faces appeared in the nooks and crannies, hallways and doors of the lobby. The acoustics carried. Nothing like a little socialist outrage to rattle the lackeys of the ruling class. Viva la revolución!

The man waved his fingers impatiently at the girl while glancing around for the ghost of Che Guevara.

"We have a billing address," she said. "The room was charged to KimCo. Mr. Smith."

"Smith?" I said. "Sounds like a—"

"A what?"

"A good upstanding name," I said lest they realize that Mr. Smith was probably cheating with Ms. Wong, and Mrs. Smith, formerly Miss Right, might be rightly pissed to learn about Ms. Wong in a suite used for only a few hours. The man, manager, concierge, rich-suited fellow— whatever— might realize that he was exposing a prominent citizen to possible scandal and rise to the imagined standards of his four-star employer and stop me.

The girl passed over a scrap of paper with the address on it.

I scooped it up with a "Thanks" and was out the door before the final s had finished its slithering echo across the lobby.

8

JAY TOOK me to my car. I left him a five-star review, tipped him well from my credit card, and put his number in my phone. If I ever needed a grotesquely cheerful ride somewhere, I'd have a contact.

KimCo was a construction company, and the offices were closed on the weekend. I'd found them on the internet on my phone, waiting in line to leave the parking lot. The president looked like the guy I wanted. Mr. Archibald Lewis. Lewis, not Smith. <gasp>

I called Allie as I got on the freeway. Hands-free. I was safe. She didn't answer. I wondered where she stayed the night and nearly crashed into a fuel truck.

"There is no sense following up KimCo," I said out loud. "Not until next week."

"Good thinking," I agreed. "At least you've confirmed Sandi Wong arrived as intended."

"Yes. That was some good sleuthing."

"You got lucky."

"Who asked you?"

"Just saying."

"Well stop saying."

"Don't be so sensitive."

"You don't be so sensitive."

"I know you are, but what am I?"

"Shut up."

"So mature."

"I said shut up!"

I drove on giving myself the silent treatment until I didn't know where the hell I was going. My instinct had kicked in, and I was on the freeway taking me home. Visions of naps and overeating danced through my head, a depressant's paradise.

I took a different exit. And found a coffee shop for some double-shot caffeine super-energy, brain-disciplining elixir.

I grabbed my computer and went inside for some free Wi-Fi.

The place was crowded. I'd have preferred a booth, but those weren't available. A bistro table with a wadded napkin under the base to level it was my portion that day.

My computer linked instantly to the internet. I'd used this café before. I sipped a cup of hot coffee-flavored cream. With Splenda.

There are lots of jobs that have been threatened or flat-out destroyed by the information superhighway. Encyclopedia salesmen are gone. There's an exhibit at the Natural History Museum with a Fuller Brush Man, a species who'd been hunted to extinction by chain stores. Private investigator is definitely on the endangered list. Anyone can find out so much about anyone else these days that it's a wonder I still make a living doing this. I do actually, or rather, I have. I could. I am. I will. I must. I must I must, I must develop my...wait.

Where was I?

Right. PIs. Private detectives, a.k.a. "sleazes" or "snoops," secured such sibilant sobriquets by slithering through sour shrubbery, sitting salaciously and sadistically spying like unsated satyrs upon the secrets of sinful sweethearts, swerving spouses and dishonest associates, through swaths of swinging lace or slits in sliding shades, to snap and sneak and subsequently gossip pernicious slander, slashing asunder lifestyles and existences like stray hissing snakes.

Much of what I do can be done at home by anyone with the internet.

I closed my thesaurus and brought up social media.

Remember when people were afraid the government would implant chips in their heads and track their every move? Yeah, about that. We now pay for the privilege of carrying a tracker in our pocket, posting updates and pictures with gross regularity. We've become a post-privacy society. What would the world need with a PI when you could Google everything, and everybody has happily put it out to find?

You only need someone like me if the person you're interested in doesn't have an internet footprint.

I'm talking about Madeline Smith. Maddy. The fiancée the fiancé wanted me to look in to. Moland, Bryan, must have done the same search I did and found it strange enough, or rather vacant enough, to call me in.

Randy had told me that his generation had fled Facebook once mine discovered it. That made sense. He used Twitter for his news and picture programs for his friends. Still, he had a Facebook profile in case he needed it.

I had one too. I did nothing with mine. Allie had one and did enough for both of us. She said it was about marketing. I'd thought it was about keeping in touch with friends.

"Maybe once," she said. "Now it's a commercial wasteland. Everyone's selling something."

"Not everyone."

"They're selling themselves if they're not pitching a product."

"If you're not the consumer, you're the goods?"

"Yeah. Even if all they post is weight progress pictures or vacation updates, they're pitching themselves, looking for attention."

"Don't forget about vague booking, posting something alarming without explaining what the hell you're talking about."

"Always worth a bunch of likes."

"I could use it for my business," I'd said. "Like you do."

"You could."

"No, wait. That's not a good idea," I concluded.

"Why?"

"Two reasons. One, my business is secret. I'm undercover sometimes. Fame is antithetical."

"Not really. If clients don't know who to call, who are they going to call?"

"And the second reason," I went on, "is that I don't have the energy."

"No argument there."

"Whoa, whoa, you are not allowed to agree with me on that kind of thing."

"Social media is a soul sink, a black hole of spiritual decay."

"I meant I'm lazy, but let's go with yours."

My eyes grew moist thinking how Allie and I used to be so close. How for a brief wonderful moment we'd been lovers and friends, how she'd completed me. For a while, a short, short while, now she was gone, jet-setting with new and better lovers at Sundance because I'd deceived her into—

"Oh, for fuck's sake!"

The entire coffee shop went quiet and turned to look at me.

"Did you see the shit coming out of Washington?" I said.

They all nodded understandingly and went back to their lives.

I shook off some self-destruction and went back to social media, but it was another avenue of self-destruction. I found myself looking up Francis Tomas. His profile was sickening. He had pictures of cruise ships and white beaches. Bikini-clad companions and a red Ferrari. He lived in Los Altos, California, a suburb of San Francisco in the "Bay Area." He was single. Divorced. Self-employed. Supported Greenpeace.

Fuck.

His newest photo album was from the party last night. Thirty-six snaps, mostly selfies, five with my girlfriend. No #MeToo hoverhands happening there. He was touching her, her arm, her shoulder, her waist.

Double fuck.

Allie wasn't the only person I recognized with him. Allie's agent, Terrance Rowski, was in the background, giving business cards to anyone with an empty hand. I saw more movie stars than I could name, two directors I could, and a plethora of over-tanned hardbody beautiful people who'd stepped out of a magazine to enjoy the martinis. The house of course was something out of Gatsby, the clothes out of Vogue. Just to rub it in, I glanced down at the hibiscus blossoms, palm fronds, and parrots on my own shirt. It would be camouflage at a Jimmy Buffet concert. In Salt Lake, in the winter, it was a statement. At the party Francis and Allie had gone to, it'd either get me thrown out as an obvious impostor or proved I was the most powerful person in the room who didn't have to give a shit about fashion, depending on how I sold it.

Allie of course looked fantastic. Flannel shirt, jeans. Hair straight as new spaghetti, eyes to wander in. She looked so at home, it was unsettling, and once again my insecurities stirred like a non-Bond martini before a gunfight.

Maddy.

Back to Maddy. Madeline Smith. For Bryan Moland. Stay on target...stay on target. Get to work, Tony. Be useful. Stay busy.

I texted Allie.

> So...where did you spend the night last night?
> Asking for a friend.

I waited for an answer. None came.

Mad. Mad. Maddy—Focus. Distract.

She was twenty-five years old, which was on the high end for the anti-Facebook crusade Randy had explained, but it was still possible. Her profile was new. Only a few months old. She'd come very late to the scene. Social media isn't for everyone. I hate it. Hate hate hate. I hate it as much as rich California fuckers touching my girlfriend. Maybe not that much, but you get the idea.

I reread the report Bryan had sent me about Maddy. She worked from home as a bookkeeper. Okay. Such a job wouldn't necessarily mean she'd need to have an internet presence. I searched Twitter and went ten pages deep on Google. Now there's some dedication and discipline. Nada.

What nagged me, though, was that she was an actress—an amateur, but an actress nonetheless. IMDb hadn't heard of her unless she was a Bond girl to Roger Moore and did Hammer flicks in the seventies. Actors lived on publicity. It just didn't gel that an actress would forgo the narcissistic world of social media.

I finally found her mentioned in a newspaper from the month before, a play review for *Damn Yankees* at the Timpanogos Theatre of Living Arts in Provo.

> *Dressed in modest yet suggestive clothing, she'd dazzled the audience with her portrayal of "Lola" the devil's home-wrecker.*

There was a picture of her. I remember the part as being all fishnets and bodice. But not there. A dress to her knees, bobby socks, covered shoulders —Utah County is a trip. The paper said that the next play would be *Flower Drum Song*, starting this week. *Flower Drum Song* was another archaic Rodgers and Hammerstein musical from the 1950s. It would probably be picketed for being too ethnic for Provo and too sexist and racist for the rest of civilized humanity. I had the movie on DVD at home. It came as a double feature with *Mama Mia*. Everyone loves Abba. *Flower Drum Song*, maybe not so much. I'm not sure about how racist it is. The movie famously features an all-Asian cast and is as accurate as any 1950s whitewashed popular art piece could be, i.e., not too much. The sexism is unquestionable, but again it's a reflection of those good ol' days when women weren't really allowed to wear slacks and measured their worth by marriage. Maybe it would go over well in Provo after all.

In any event, I figured I'd go see it. The question was would I go stag or not.

Still nothing from Allie.

I texted Randy.

> Sup?

Five minutes, nothing. Browsing new shoes.

Text to Randy.

> I'm still paying for part of your phone service. Sup?

Nothing.

Immediate response.

> Where are you?

Out.

> We could save money by changing your data plan.

I'm at the Spells tourney.

> What? Why?

Hanging out.

> Are they being nice?

Sure.

> Want to go to a play tonight?

Which one?

> Not Hamilton.

No.

> When will you be home?

After.

> 2 GB is enough data for anyone.

I don't know! After the finals. I want to see it.

> Okay. Love you <3

<3

I'd like to think he was being genuinely sweet with the heart return. We've been exchanging hearts since he got the phone. Randy told me that I was being too gushy after a friend saw such an emoji from his dad.

"It's sign of life," I said. "A heartbeat. I'm asking if you're alright. Just send me a heart back and I'll know everything is fine."

"Oh. Okay."

"And I love you."

I can still see the eyes rolling back into his head at that as he turned and went into the house. His mother's house. This was before he got his new car. He drives himself now, and I see him less than ever.

Oops.

Which reminded me, the first Tesla payment was coming up.

Oops.

Randy on my mind, Allie on my mind, all the ways I'd failed them on my mind, I switched to mindless internet browsing for a while. Allie said that it's a kind of drug. An addiction. The internet, the time sink, the instant stimulation is numbing people, she said. They just read bullet points and not stories, they look at cat pictures and comics and feed on vapid unnuanced sound-bited information streams. I saw an article about it that might have said something similar, but I'd only read the headline.

I searched for Dawane Osterlot, the local Spells celebrity who'd accused

Randy of cheating. I found a live stream of his current game. He was still undefeated in the tournament. I watched the feed. A camera angle above the table showed the board state, and another camera showed the players' faces now and again. Someone who knew what they were looking at could follow the action, but I couldn't. I understood the game, but they were using newer cards, and I didn't know what they did. I noticed again how Dawane moved his cards. He had the hands of a magician, a crisp dexterity that to the initiated signaled sleight of hand. A magician's hands. A dealer's hands. A cheater's hands.

As I fantasized about exposing the cheat on live internet stream, exonerating my son in the process, beating a confession out of the hustler with a black flashlight for setting up my innocent boy, Dawane reached across the table and shook his opponent's hand. He'd conceded. He'd lost. He was out of the tournament, beaten by a clean-cut blond teenager in a polo shirt and braces.

Huh.

The brackets were updated. Dawane was out and would be sitting at the analyst table for the finals, still hours away. He hadn't even made the quarters.

Huh.

I hate it when suspects don't behave the way I want them to.

Okay. I'd touched three of my four cases so far how about the big one? Fah had mentioned that Sandi Wong was going to meet with a fellow countryman, a relative. I dug up the name and looked up General U Tayza Min Ko. He had a Wikipedia page. Damn.

I'd heard that in the past, in the misty days of yesterday, the 'Who's Who' were listed in books. There's a Sherlock Holmes story where the good detective looks up some notable person and sees a bio complete with family lines and all achievements in a dusty leather-bound tome surely distributed at some secret gentlemen's meeting, handshakes and spankings. Things are more egalitarian today but also more exclusive. The web can offer information, but the place to be, the place that shows you've made it, whatever 'it' is, has to be Wikipedia. I've always wanted a Wikipedia page.

General U Tayza Min Ko had one. He probably had several. International figures have to be served up in multiple languages, right? I was sure he was big in Myanmar—if they had internet and their own Wikipedia. Oh look, they did. No help there, though. I still don't read Burmese.

Reading through the general's English details, I see that the "it" he did was try to overthrow the government in a failed coup fifteen years ago. It threatened for about a month, and then he fled the country to exile, eventually settling in the United States after being granted asylum as a political refugee. The story mentioned he died in a car accident three years back with his adjutant's son, Phyo. His own son, Thiha Min Naings, had been badly burned but survived the same crash.

Thiha didn't have a Wikipedia page, but I gathered he'd been born just before the coup, which would put him around sixteen or seventeen years old now. Randy's age.

I was moving to old news sites, following up on the accident to find the general's general area, when my phone chirped. A text flashed on the screen. *Unknown number, could be Francis Tomas.*

It read:

Look who I'm with—Your Allie!

9

LIKE I SAID, I have issues with Francis Tomas. I'm not sure what started it, but I'm pretty sure they revolved around jealousy, or envy, if you want to be technical. Envy is when you covet and want something someone else has. Jealousy is when you're afraid of losing something you have. Before that text message, I would have said my feelings toward my old high school classmate were all envy. Seeing him brag about having my Allie slid me fast and sure into jealousy. Bright green glowing jealousy with a side order of orange rage, taupe disappointment, and a thick yellow insecurity sauce for dipping.

"God fucking dammit!"

The café again fell silent, again pointed to me. A young husband and wife were at the counter waiting for hot chocolates with three young children. They stared at me in horror as if I'd just said my profane thoughts out loud.

Oh.

"Shit," I said. "Sorry. Sorry. I uhm... Did you see that sportsball score? Wasn't that something?"

Before they could register confusion, which was better than outrage, I suppose, my attention was pulled back to my phone where a bubble ellipsis flashed, indicating another message coming in. I sensed a photo en route. I was right. There was Allie again. I noticed this time that she was in a new place than the night before. Not the party house, but someplace out of town with the right clear natural morning light. I couldn't read Allie's expression. Was it surprise? Shame? Astonishment at what she'd had versus what was available?

The scene was a luncheon, a floor filled with white-clothed tables and uniformed waiters. I saw mimosas and steepled napkins on china plates.

Silverware that would be polished, not recycled. Crepes and eggs Benedict. Chocolate-dipped strawberries and lemon cheesecake. Upscale casual outfits. Pretty people. Lots of them. The ones in the picture were all looking the same direction as Allie, something interesting happening behind and above the photographer. Allie looked at the camera, that haunting expression on her face. I couldn't see Francis. I figured he'd taken the picture.

I looked at her face and tried to see what she was trying to tell me. It had to be condemnation. There was a sternness in it, a meaning. A goodbye.

Not knowing what else to do or say, I drank deep of my tepid coffee hiding in sweet cream. I texted only a question mark back, playing dumb, buying time.

Francis replied, *Look*.

The fucker was really trying to rub it in.

I couldn't… Couldn't. I just couldn't.

My eyes unfocused and my mind spun. How big of a fraud must I be that one night away from me with some rich good-lucky successful guy could rip Allie from me. I think I'd just answered my own question.

"Fuck fuck fuck fuck!"

A barista with a buzz cut, stenciled blue eyebrows, gold nose ring, and a sleeve tattoo of skulls and bloody knives up her arms appeared at my side. "Maybe you should go," she said. "You're scaring the customers."

"No, it's okay. He obviously felt threatened by me too. See? Because why else go to the trouble of making a point like this? Yes, it's sadistic, yes it's cruel, juvenile, puerile, senile, even penile perhaps, but doesn't it show a certain obsession with me? Hrmmm? Don't you think?"

"Maybe you should see someone," she said.

"Fuck that!"

"Sir."

"No, I'm going to fight for her. I've got worth. And if I don't, I'll get some."

"Can you please stop swearing and yelling?" she said, blushing and biting her lip.

"Flaner?"

I looked up. There was Henry Levinson, the "comedian" from the night before. The guy who did impersonations.

"I thought that was you. Trying out a new routine? Might not want to do it around here. Family folks, you know. Blue ain't cool." He said the last bit like it was a public service commercial slogan. "Just say no." "Blue ain't cool." "Buy bonds." "Don't litter." "Surrender Dorothy."

"You don't need to curse to be funny," Henry said. "There's only one way you can make people laugh—happiness. If you're full of joy, the audience will be too."

"You're full of it, alright."

"Darn tooting."

"Did you just say 'darn tooting'? With a hard G?"

"Darn tooting I did." Big grin.

Henry was just the tonic I needed. I might be questioning myself, but I was sure that I knew more than this kid. I'm not saying I know everything, but I know some things. The bright side of age is experience. Sure, there are facets of my life I continually second guess, but my bullshit detection was not one of them, and here was a slick of it running down the leg of some snot-nosed, G-rated, would-be comic child. Laughter comes from pain. It is as near a scream as you can get without crossing over. Healthy people seldom make good comedy. Happy people seldom make people laugh. I assume there were exceptions, but I sure as laugh-track-pablum-crap-pretend-comedy knew it wasn't the only way, or even the most common way. Or the best.

I was just about to unleash a scathing, curse-filled cathartic but possibly misaimed rant at Henry based on the word tooting with a hard G when I noticed the barista's worried eyes. The one family was gone, but new kids were streaming in. Some peewee girl's basketball game had just let out, and the place was full of red-jerseyed prepubescents requesting strawberry steamers and cocoa.

"I gotta go," I said.

"Let's hang out sometime," said Henry.

The barista's eye twitched.

"Somewhere else," I said.

She nodded.

Outside I felt better. The incident, some might call it a scene, a crisis perhaps, had passed, and I'd whiplashed through my insecurity with righteous indignation and authentic longing. I didn't know if it would last, but I was reminded of a great quote: "Before you diagnose yourself with depression or low self-esteem, first make sure that you are not, in fact, just surrounding yourself with assholes."

For a moment anyway, I'd found anchorage.

My phone rang. It was Francis Tomas.

The tooting rant I had ready wouldn't translate to Francis. I'd need more time to plan a takedown of that guy. A bit more information too. I was an assassin planning a kill, searching for weaknesses and brewing poison.

The call went to my voice mail.

I thought of Allie and for a terrible, backsliding moment wondered if she wasn't an asshole too. I shook that off. I'd need to talk to her, figure things out. I was willing to forgive. Wasn't I? I'm a jealous man.

Needing to move, I did a staggering full pirouette in the cold morning air. I might have made three of them, in fact, arms spread wide, hands twitching like I was shaking dirty water off them, siphoning the muck out of my imagination out with it. I remembered my confidence in knowing something about comedy, remembering, if only emotionally, that Francis

Tomas was the dick, and thinking that I was actually making progress on my cases.

I was doing it. I was somebody.

Inside the coffee shop, eyes stared through the glass windows. Children pointed, laughed and spun in gleeful imitation. Parents moved to stand between me and their kids. The barista was on the phone.

I dangled my car keys as proof I was leaving and possibly not homeless. I couldn't think of a gesture that could convey sanity. If you can think of one, let me know.

I drove to the Salt Lake Events Center to see how Randy was doing. It was time to dad.

The parking was worse than I expected. Salt Lake City proper has terrible parking. I might have mentioned this already. It's shit. If I did, it deserves another mention. There'd been some hubbub about the death of the inner city a while ago, and new trains were put in to help, along with a big controversial mall owned by the LDS Church across the street from their temple that is so upscale and expensive, so out of reach for the vast majority of humanity, that it has become a tourist attraction to gawking vacationers and a punchline to the locals.

To match the mall, and possibly to fill it with customers, the church—or rather some arm of the church—it gets hazy here—built a huge high-rise luxury apartment building where you can shell out seven figures for a condo with a view of the temple. These things did little to revitalize the city since they were too expensive for people who actually walked to nearby places. I avoid downtown like the wasteland it is. Overpriced, bum-ridden, cold and commercial. Full of soulless banks, towers of offices full of soulless executives, few places to sit and a critical lack of bathrooms. Worst of all is the parking. If they wanted to rejuvenate the city, all they needed to do is recognize the ridiculous lack of reasonable parking. The inconvenience, expense, and hassle of ticket-happy meter maids in glorified golf carts getting paid, I swear, on commission is enough to rattle the most civic-minded civilian. Utah is a suburban community. We have other malls—more convenient, reasonably priced malls. Granted, not all of them have a Porsche dealership on the second floor, but I'd take free parking over the moral police anyway.

Moral police, you say?

Yes, those rumors are true. The church, or whoever runs that big mall downtown, has its own security, and they follow anyone they suspect of anything. PDAs, public displays of affection. Kissing will get you tossed out, to say nothing of busking, protesting, loitering, smelling, or being Black. Think "conservative thought police." There've been complaints about profiling in the mall. Having been followed around for an hour by two ranger-hatted zealots for wearing a tie-dye shirt and sandals last summer, I can personally affirm it's not the place for me.

Still I had to park there.

The events center parking was blocked off for construction or repair. The smell suggested a sewer leak, but it could have been the tournament. I looked for a meter, but they were all full. Fools. The city, in their infinite wisdom, removed all coin-operated meters and replaced them with central computerized torture devices that only accept credit cards or something from a proprietary phone app. I've tried to make them work. They were a nightmare to use. App or no app, the menu to pay makes you have to endure a tutorial to park your car. Who needs that kind of aggravation? It means that there's only a certain demographic who can park in the city—technologically savvy people with stupid money and high patience. There are a few of them, apparently, all here today, of course, but those meters send a clear message from the city: Don't come here.

I took a ticket from the machine, watched the arm go up, and pulled inside the mall's underground parking lot. Ten minutes and two levels later, I had no idea where I was in relation to the events center, but I had found space by a flashy Jaguar diagonally parked across two places. I parked parallel to him and wondered if the Jaguar had access from the trunk. With a cement pillar on the other side, he'd need it if he wanted to leave before me.

It was petty and mean-spirited, but after cruising around the exclusive smog-filled Salt Lake downtown, I figure the guy was lucky I didn't fire-bomb his ride. I assumed it was a he, I imagined a he. It was a sports car, a kind of mid-life crisis compensator, third-wife bait kind of thing. Could have been a woman. Maybe she got it in her third divorce. Seriously though, if you feel you need to take two places to protect your car, you're a special kind of jerk, one who values your things over other people's needs. My parking was social justice, and I gave him three inches of driver door to work with. The pillar gave him six.

I found an elevator, noting my parking place by number, color, animal, quantum spin, and zone, finally just taking a damn picture of the sign, and rode up to the mall. It took me ten minutes to orient myself. I could have just asked the ranger who'd followed me at a not-so-discreet distance from the moment I got onto the floor, but I was afraid I'd say something that would get me in trouble. Lord knows I wanted to. The cool I'd developed momentarily after seeing Henry and justifying Francis' torment had melted beneath urban frustration.

The ranger boy followed me all the way, leaving me only when I exited the building. His job done, his senses keen. I didn't belong there. I hadn't even browsed the Porsche dealership, let alone buy a five-hundred-karat emerald pendant from the kiosk in the food court.

Outside air was acrid and dark. It looked like one of those pictures you see from Beijing that you're told is Beijing because all you can see is terrible smog. It was like that. Exactly like that.

I tucked my face in my T-shirt and crossed the street to find Randy at the Smells tournament—I mean, *Spells* tournament.

10

SOMETHING HAD CHANGED. There was a discernible difference in the atmosphere. It smelled fresh and clean. I found a building calendar of events to make sure the tournament was still here, and it was. I sniffed the air. Nothing. Which was good—no, better than good. I had expected to drop from the proverbial pot of smog into the fire of body odor. Nothing.

I expected to see an empty room, but the tournament space was as packed as it had been the day before. The scoreboard showed they were on the round of sixteen. Thirty-two players still in the hunt for a gold trophy, but cards slapped every surface, every chair a butt.

There's something about this game. People play it for fun, not just for competition. That's something you don't see in other sports. You don't see defensive tackles going out to the yard and bashing neighbors, you don't see tennis phenoms asking their friends for a pickup match after going five sets on clay. Score one for cardboard and non-physical activity. As long as there was space, carbs and caffeine, game on. The earlier tension I'd felt was gone too. Competition lowered, everyone just played cards. I suddenly wished I'd brought a deck. Looking for Randy among the tables, I overheard such things as, "Keep playing that deck until the combo triggers. I want to see it," "Great move!" and "You can have that spell back. You didn't see my board right." It was very friendly and warmed my heart, then I heard a discouraging word. "Get that fuck out of here!"

The mismatched sentiment drew my attention. A kid, probably around nine, looked sheepish and afraid as a group of older boys—they were all boys—surrounded the table. The boy had played a proxied card. He'd taken a cheap jank common card and pasted a picture of another card over it. It was not a forgery. Even a non-gamer could tell it was not real—curled edges, smears, bad paper, low dpi—but it also wasn't the actual card. That was where the rubber met the road. Fun as this game was, there came a time when the collector stepped in because allowing anyone to play a proxy card devalued the entire collection, the entire economy. Some cards, for rarity and power, were literally worth more than their weight in gold. Many times more. I have some. They're cool. Sometimes I weigh them. 1.814 grams, if you're curious.

The boy apologized, scooped his cards and without even offering a handshake, scurried away.

I was surprised Randy had been welcomed back.

I texted:

> Where are you?

Still at tourney

> Where at tourney?

Are you here?

> Yes

Why?????

> Why not?

Long silence.

I sent:

> You've got to be within earshot. Listen for your name while I shout it out.

E-22

Came the quick reply.

Navigation banners hung from the ceiling. I hadn't noticed them before, probably because of my watering eyes, but the whole room was set up in a grid pattern with columns of letters and rows of numbers. I quickly saw E-22 and set out.

The smell was definitely gone. It was a little unsettling, in fact. I was really curious about it, but I knew asking about it would be ill-mannered.

"Why doesn't it smell today?" I asked the first judge I saw. Why let manners get in the way of knowledge?

"We chased those guys out. They were DQ'd for stench."

"That's a thing?"

"DQ. Disqualified."

"I mean the purpose. For stench. That's a thing?"

"You know it."

"How many?"

"Two."

"Just two?"

"It doesn't take many unwashed idiots to foul the air."

"Why did it take so long?"

"It didn't."

"I was here last night at nine and the funk was thick."

"They were gone by then. The air just hadn't circulated."

"When were they ejected?"

"Four or five. Why?"

"OSHA inspection."

I could tell he was trying to read my identity through my Hawaiian shirt. If he weren't in the yellow vest, a responsible rules judge here, he'd have known I was joking. Something about a little authority sucks away all humor and imagination.

"Just two?" I said.

"Just two."

I left the judge, trying to remember chemistry classes, rates of decay, atmospheric dissipation rates. I fantasized about two smokestacks somewhere in the valley coloring the air slate gray and rust with yellow-vested judges driving them away.

E-22.

Randy didn't look up from his game. I know he saw me, but he was making a point. Not sure what it was, probably a warning not to embarrass him.

"Hey, Randy, remember me, your father?" I said, just to explain my presence to the gang.

He held up one finger, indicating I should wait while he pondered a play.

"Are you Randy's friends?" I asked the group.

There were three guys there besides my son. I've noticed something about teenagers. While they are usually embarrassed by their own parents, other grownups are okay. Psychologically, I think it's because they see adults who are not their parents as members of the group they're trying to join. Randy sees me as retrograde, that which he is leaving; his friends know me, if they know me, as a cool grown-up.

They introduced themselves. We shook hands. Randy cringed.

"I'm Oliver Evans," said one of them. "I'm in Randy's art class with Mr. Smith. Kevin is too."

Kevin said, "Sucks what happened to him yesterday."

"Doesn't look like it's a lingering problem," I said, gesturing around the room. "You're all still here. Having fun."

"They get it," said Oliver.

"Get what?"

"The oppression of intellectual property rights. Art and ideas should not be contained. It is capitalistic oppression and has to be fought."

"Oh, that. Yes, of course," I said. "I'd like to sign up for your newsletter."

"Shhh," said Randy.

"It's not chess, dude," said his opponent, a skinny kid named Hugh. "Cast or pass."

Randy studied his cards as if cramming for a test. I knew my presence had something to do with it.

Kevin went on, "Yeah, but Randy can't play tournaments again for, like, forever. He had the best chance of all of us."

"He has the best collection," said Oliver a little sheepishly.

"You guys know anything about it?" I asked.

"Like what?" said Kevin.

"Like how Dawane Osterlot could have slipped the bogus cards into his deck."

Kevin shook his head. Oliver eyed the pizza stand in the corner, dug into his pocket but came up empty.

"That's what must have happened," said Kevin. "That cheating bastard."

Randy didn't react, and this made my stomach lurch. I realized that I had yet to question the most important witness of the card caper—my son. Now wasn't the time. See, I can read a room sometimes.

"You guys trade cards or just buy them?"

"And buy and sell," said Oliver.

"Speak for yourself," said Kevin. "I haven't had a card leave my collection in a year."

"I like to sell the best cards. They're overvalued," said Oliver, studying Hugh's board. "I can pull a rare from a booster, sell it back to the shop for more than the rest, usually even for enough to build a whole new deck from the extra."

"Then why do we never see new decks, Oliver?" said Hugh. "You've been playing that same lame roaring bear deck for a year."

"Don't be dissing my bears," he said.

"Shhhh," said Randy.

"Dude," said Hugh. "Do I have to call a judge?"

"I'm just..." He trailed off. I could tell he was distracted, worried, upset, mildly verklempt.

"Who wants pizza?" I said.

"You buying?" said Oliver.

"Sure."

All hands went up.

I left Randy to take his turn, maybe finish his game without me there worrying him. His worry was my worry. He was hiding something. Maybe it was just his teenage angst. He'd withdrawn between character shifts in the past, not talking to anyone for days before emerging from his room in bell bottoms or with textbook knowledge of boson theory. I could be seeing that. Then again, maybe my son really had cheated and he was ashamed now.

I'd come to make sure he was alright. Even in the face of his distraction and discomfort at me showing up with his friends, I had to think that he was. He'd gotten back on the horse. The official Spells organization might be mad at him, but his friends, the only ones who really mattered, were fine with him. If they'd ribbed him about it, it had already happened and been endured.

I liked that. I liked Randy's friends. To me, anyway, they were the most relatable group he'd brought home in a while. He'd known Hugh since middle school and Kevin I'd seen at the house a few months before. They dressed like teenagers, not fashion victims, and I could totally relate to their interest in this game. Randy had grown up with games, video games mostly, and this was a healthy, albeit expensive evolution of that. Tournament play showed ambition. Parents love it when their kids show ambition. My question now was had that ambition been so powerful that my boy had resorted to cheating?

Was it cheating, though?

The strange economic burden of the game offered an unfair advantage to wealthy players. It occurred to me that it was therefore a kind of microcosm for capitalism like Oliver had said. If nothing else, it was a good life lesson for living in the United States. American Dystopia 101. One could make the argument for equity and justify proxies on the basis of financial advantage. That would be bad for the company, though, and I'd seen first-hand that they were serious about keeping that part of the game pure. The room was full of zealots who'd bought into that and now had a financial as well as emotional investment.

Economic theory was full on my mind as I shelled over thirty dollars for a six-dollar pizza and carried it back to the table.

"They took credit cards," I said. "Lucky for me."

"Thanks, Mr. Flaner." They dug in. Even Randy took a piece.

I'd cemented my position as a cool dad, at least with Randy's friends.

"I'm going to poke around," I said. "Catch up with you all later."

"Bye, Mr. Flaner."

"Bye."

"Bye, Dad," said Randy.

"He speaks."

And glared at me.

I winked at him.

He rolled his eyes.

I smiled.

Our ritual complete, I headed toward the stage, leaving Randy to his peers.

Parenting is hard. They don't tell you how hard it is do and then how hard it is to *not* do. Well, maybe they do—did—but I hadn't listened if they had. My usual story. I learn things the hard way all the time. This was one of them. My boy was breaking away. He'd always been independent, and I'd always been...well, me—a distracted half-child, never an authority figure. I'd been honest in my ignorance, clear in my confusion, and obvious in my incompetence. That my son was as awesome as he was had to be a sign of divine intervention or proof of the power of hands-off parenting. Helicopter couples behold my power and weep! Weep I say! I, in the meantime, wept for a different reason; seeing my son growing up. I choked back a tear, humming *Cat's in the Cradle* through quivering lips while I snaked through the tables to do what I could for my son.

The stage had another show match in progress. They looked like average players, not showboaters like Dawane Osterlot, intense and nervous at their moment of internet streaming fame

Dawane was sitting at a side table behind a microphone with another man. I couldn't hear what they were saying. If I had to guess, I'd say Dawane was a color commentator and the other guy was the play-by-play. A true sporting arrangement. I wonder if they had replay. How would that work with a card game? "Here's Jeffery pulling a gem from his hand and tapping Bob's minotaur." "Ouch." "Let's see that again." "Look at that wrist action..."

The one thing I saw though was that Dawane was enjoying himself. He smiled and joked. He was comfortable there. He was not the intense pressured player from the day before but a respectable expert sharing his insight. It occurred to me that this is probably the best thing a player could hope for as a career move after tournaments. This idea rested uneasily as I saw Evan Svenson, the organizer in the corner. The big burly security guy was in his cage somewhere.

It was clear Evan recognized me because his face flushed under his fedora and his smile dropped to the floor like the One Ring. He pretended not to see me.

I waved until I got his attention and continued waving, harder, even jumping up and down after he had obviously recognized me, until he was about to yell something in a loud, probably get-me-thrown-out-of-here-on-my-ass kind of tone with lewd language yet to be determined, when he finally waved back and signaled me to meet him behind the curtain. Glancing across the long room, as I followed the man backstage, I caught Randy looking at me. He wore an indeterminate expression.

11

"YOU WERE ABOUT to do something unpleasant out there, weren't you?" said Evan. "I could see it. You use embarrassment as a weapon."

"And sarcasm. Don't forget that."

"What do you want, Mr. Flaner?" Svenson said. "I thought this was dealt with."

"I want to know where the counterfeit cards came from," I said.

"Ask your son."

I squinted.

"You haven't even asked your son yet? Get your act together, man. I thought you were a detective."

"You've heard of me?"

"I saw the story about Traard. You were mentioned."

"Nothing that a good libel attorney couldn't fix."

"I want to hear what you have to say about it," I said, then added, "First." The guy was beginning to get under my skin.

"He was playing a game and Osterlot caught him with fake cards," said Evan. "He called a judge over and he was DQ'd. That means—"

"Dairy Queened? You bought him ice cream as an apology?"

"Disqualified." I was now under under his skin. Even playing field.

"Could Dawane have slipped a card from his deck into Randy's? He's a pro, you know."

"Pro what?"

"Shyster."

"I heard that."

Fuck. Dawane was right there in the entranceway.

"So you admit it?"

"What?"

"I see how you move your cards. You're a professional. You can do slides, false shuffles, crimps. Deal from the bottom of the deck, the top, middle— wherever you want. You can jog reverse and force. Palm and seed. I'd hate to play poker with you."

"Evan...?"

"This is Mr. Flaner."

"The detective?"

"You saw that Traard article too, huh?"

"Who's Traard?"

Huh.

Evan said, "He thinks you palmed a card into his son's deck yesterday. The kid that was DQ'd for counterfeits."

"Get real," he said. "We weren't even playing the same colors. My deck was inspected and clean. That's some libel right there."

"It's only libel if it's in print," I said. "This is slander."

I wasn't helping.

"He's right," said Svenson. "We inspect all the decks before the tournament. Your son's included. His card count and deck list didn't change. He had those cards when he checked in. He came with them. They just weren't caught until a match."

"Someone could have gotten to his cards and traded some out."

They both stared at me like I was an idiot, and I kinda felt like they were right.

"Unlikely?" I said.

"Unlikely," they agreed.

"But?"

"But they'd need to know his list, which isn't shared publicly unless they win. And they'd need to have access." Svenson was counting off details on his fingers like he was walking a toddler through the steps of making a PB&J. "They'd need to have access to superior forgeries."

"Good players are also aware that their games will be scrutinized," said Dawane. "It's suicide to even try."

"But...but..."

Svenson tipped his hat down a bit. "Only you are saying Dawane did anything. Your boy didn't accuse him."

"What did he say?" asked Dawane.

I shuffled my feet.

"You haven't talked to him about it?"

I scowled.

Dawane shrugged. "The copies were good. If I hadn't known what to look for, I'd have missed them. Really top-notch. If it weren't for the ego signature, I bet company execs couldn't have picked them out."

"They got by the first deck inspection," added Svenson.

"But you just happened—wait. Ego signature?"

"Yeah. The copyright symbol on the front of the card. It's altered. I'd run into them before at the Grand Tennessee event. They're still popping up. Not much—one or two at most. Until here."

"Here?"

"At this tournament we've found eight forgeries," said Svenson. "By far the biggest concentration so far."

"It's easy once you know what to look for."

"The copyright symbol?" I remember Evan showing it to me before.

Dawane nodded and casually leaned on a table. His cool was back. It was discouraging and made me feel like a fraud, a false witness at least.

"So you DQ'd eight people?" I said.

"Seven. Your son had two cards."

"Bully for us. Any connection?"

"They're all local to this area," said Dawane.

"Did they all play Dawane?"

"No," said the champion calmly. Too calmly.

"If you find out where they came from," Svenson said, "we'd be interested to know. There are crimes involved."

"Is Randy in danger?"

"Not from the company," said Svenson. "But the feds might. Intellectual property laws."

"Really? It's that big a deal?"

"There was a shop in China that was mass-producing copies. That was a big deal. We got them shut down somehow. Usually it's small stuff, kids with a scanner, but this new ring is just too damn good. Again, if there hadn't been that mark, it would take a scientist to detect the difference. They even got the foil hologram right."

"Scary good," said Dawane.

"But if you know what to look for, it's easy to detect?"

"Might need a magnifying glass, but yeah," said Osterlot.

"Why do it, then? Why would a forger leave such an obvious, albeit tiny, flaw?"

"It's a black eye for the company," said Svenson. "They're rubbing it in our faces."

"I'm sorry, Mr. Flaner," said Dawane. "Your boy seems like a good guy. He just got conned."

"But you...you...you..."

He waited.

"How are you this comfortable in your skin?" I asked him. "Really."

He seemed to know exactly what I was talking about.

"The stress is off," he said. "Now I can sit back and just enjoy the game."

I stared at him.

"I have to get back, Mr. Flaner," said Svenson. "Good luck."

"It's pissing me off that you guys are so nice," I said. "I want that on the record."

"You got issues." Svenson opened the curtain for me to go.

Dawane looked at me with infinite compassion, a bearded Buddha sympathizing with my suffering.

It was all I could do not to punch him in the face.

I have issues.

I left.

Back on the floor, my phone rang. Blocked number. Another one of those insufferable omnipresent robocalls. I declined the call as usual, cursing the FCC for letting this shit happen, and texted Randy.

> I'm going to leave. I'd like to talk to you tonight.

> Don't you have a play or something?

> Oh right. Wanna go?

> No.

> Well after that.

> I might have friends over.

I paused feeling thwarted and unloved. Issues.

I relented.

> Okay. TTYL.

> TTYL

> <3

I could feel the eye roll.

I second-guessed myself all the way back to my car. Had I come on too strong with Randy, pushing him for a conversation after he knew I'd just talked to the Spells guys? Did it smell like a parent meeting after the teacher conference? I think it did. Fuck. No wonder he was ducking me. It wasn't like that, I just wanted to ask about the cards. I wasn't going to accuse him of cheating on purpose even though he was acting suspiciously.

A new ranger escorted me to the parking garage, actually riding the elevator down to my level. "Nice day, isn't it?" I said.

"Yes, it is."

"Would you help me carry my abortion signs up? I'm meeting people, my husband and his bondage buddies. So much leather you'd think you were in a gay cowboy saddle shop."

His eyes went large. See? A little authority, and all sense of humor is just leached out of your skull.

"Don't worry," I told him. "We're *for* abortion. We want them to be required, actually. We're thinking of drive-through clinics in Provo by next year."

He reached for his walkie-talkie as the elevator door opened.

No one had answered him yet as I got in my car and drove away. Somewhere in the depths of moral police headquarters, a screenshot of my face in that elevator was being printed and pinned to a bulletin board of known troublemakers.

It's the little things in life you have to enjoy.

Another blocked call. Straight to messages where the "delete all" button awaited.

I didn't have a destination. I was thinking of lunch and also of Dawane. It was hard not to like the guy. He was confident. Confidence is very attractive. He could have been faking it like the rest of us, or I'd just caught in him at a zen moment. We all have those once in a while, but no one who isn't a moving beam of light ever maintains it for long. Still they happen. Moments of peace, transient wisdom, and comfort where we shine with calm understanding of ourselves and the universe. It pisses people off, so it usually happens in ashrams and prayer circles where sudden violence is frowned upon.

What really got to me was that he'd heard of me and not through the stupid Traard article. That little moment actually zapped me, stupid as it sounds. My issues include grabbing at straws because sometimes those straws can be buoyant, if only for a little while. Hey, it's better than drowning without a fight.

Issues.

My phone rang again. Blocked number. I reached down to send it to messages but hit speaker instead.

"Fuck," I said.

"I heard that," said Allie.

"Hello?"

"Tony, don't ignore me."

"Who's this?"

"I knew it. You're mad."

"Oh, is that you, Allie? How you been?"

"Dammit."

"Kinda what I'm thinking."

"Tony, I lost my phone. So if you've been calling it, that's why I haven't answered."

I hadn't tried to call her. Though I did send a text. Didn't I?

"You didn't try to call me at all, did you?" she said.

"How's Francis?"

"Ehhhg," she said. "Tony, did you even listen to the messages?"

I knew where this was going. Once again, I'd been betrayed by my own paranoia.

"I've been busy," I said. "I'm on four important cases at once."

"Four?"

"The missing Malaysian girl, the fiancée, Randy's cards and where to hide Francis Tomas' body. The last one is a work in progress."

She sighed.

"Where are you?" I said.

"I'm still up in Park City."

"If you lost your phone, whose phone are you using now?"

"It's Elizabeth Porter's."

"Elizabeth Porter, from *Beacon of The World*?"

"Yes. She was nice enough to—"

"You're hanging out with an Oscar-winning actress?"

"We're at a bruncheon."

"Bruncheon?"

"It's a lunch-brunch buffet."

"My head is spinning."

"Yeah, mine too."

"Is Francis there?"

"No."

"But you spent the night with him." Tactful as ever.

Heavy sigh over the phone. "Tony, some girls would find it cute that you get so jealous. I do a little, but it's also infuriating. You and I are practically engaged."

Now there was a loaded sentence.

"He sent me a dig on his phone. What was I supposed to think?" said I.

"What dig?"

"He sent me a picture of you and said, 'Look who I'm with—your Allie.'"

She laughed.

"You don't know the history Francis and I have," I said.

"You have a lot of childhood enemies, don't you?" She was referring to what's-his-name down in Moab.

"Maybe."

"He says he hardly remembers you," she said.

"I feel much better now. Thanks."

"Tony, I sent you that picture. 'Your' Allie was my signature, not his dig."

"Hold on."

I pulled into a ubiquitous Utah 7-Eleven and scrolled through messages.

"It's not a selfie," I said.

"No, Francis took that picture for me. Did you look at it?"

"Yes. You look lovely."

There was another sigh, softer and sweeter than before. Someone in the background spoke over a public address system.

"Look in the background, you oaf. It's Kyi Tun and his ward."

"Who?"

"Didn't you say that your missing Malaysian girl was coming to meet some general in exile?"

"Yeah."

"That's the general's adviser, Kyi, and his ward, the exile's son. The general died a while back."

"Oh...?"

"They're here at Sundance," she said. "I met them and put it all together."

"How?"

"I Googled it. That's how my phone was dead when I lost it. Aren't these the people you're looking for?"

"Maybe."

"Well, there you are."

"Are they at the bruncheon now?"

"No, but they're hosting a shindig later—cocktails. I know where."

"How soon?"

"In about ninety minutes. It's all on the messages."

Silence.

"Well?" she said.

"Where's Francis?"

"How the hell should I know?"

"Where'd you sleep last night?"

"Dammit, Tony."

"Just say it. You know where my mind has been."

"I love you, stupid. I stayed with Terrance. It's all in the messages."

"With Terrance?"

"He has a suite. I had my own room. He's my agent, you know."

"Right." I tried to visualize Allie and her agent making out in a honeymoon suite with mirrors over a heart-shaped bed because that's where my mind wanted to take me. Dumb mind. I couldn't see it, though. I knew Terrance was gay.

"You have ninety minutes," said Allie. "Get up here."

12

PARK CITY IS a unique place in Utah. Its history is at once interesting and infuriating. It is held up as a den of sin one minute and a paragon of the arts the next, an example of the pluck of western migration and the sleazy underside of the same.

Indians found the area first, but in keeping with American tradition, no one outside of a history lecture gives them a second thought. I'd like to think, though, that they were nice, pleasant people living in harmony, subtly feeling the coming shitstorm beneath their feet, and hitting the trail before the whites came and gentrified everything.

As far as the world is concerned, the first time the area existed was shortly after Brigham Young led his exiled cult across the Wasatch Mountains to settle a valley far enough from civilized eyes to carry on their cultish behavior. I'm not judging. That's what happened.

The Salt Lake Valley, before the Mormons came in 1847, was probably best known for being one of the problems faced by the infamous Donner Party, who passed through the area with much trouble and delay in 1846. They had to plow through forests, rappel up and down cliffs, forge rivers, and then cross a lovely, blinding arid salt flat. Precious days were lost, which translated into one of the worst disasters of American history. Hardly a ringing endorsement for travelers, unless you're looking for privacy. Welcome Brigham's band.

The area now called Park City got its name from Parley Pratt, an early Mormon apostle, who called it Parley Park City. Though the mountain pass up there has kept his name, Parley's Canyon, the Parley part was later dropped from the city as a historical retcon. The town was established as a racket, and that's bad PR for a religion. Here's what happened. You've seen it in movies, read about it in Michener's *Centennial*, but you never believed it. I'm talking about some jackass putting up a toll booth on a western trail. That's what Pratt did. And not a funny one like from *Blazing Saddles*—a real, armed stopping station that preyed on the '49ers rushing off for some California Dreamin' and all the short-cutters looking for new lands to breathe free. He made a fortune. The Parley Park City was a place for his goons to stay in between extorting travelers.

Thus was the foundation of the city established.

There was something called The Mormon War, which gave us another Western tragedy—the Mountain Meadow Massacre in 1857. Look it up for a good time. This happened just after the less famous but equally icky Utah-related horror show—the Handcarts disasters of 1856, where bunches of folks froze, starved, ate dead people, and were finally rescued only to have their plight forgotten as quickly as nineteenth-century PR could invent the memory hole.

When the Civil War happened, the Union thought the Mormons might go with the Confederates, and there was good reason to think they might. The Union set up a garrison of soldiers in a fort above Salt Lake City where the University of Utah stands now, cannons pointed downhill, to "protect the mail." Yeah, tensions were high then. From this garrison at Fort Douglas, in 1862, a certain Colonel Conner lit upon an idea. He sent soldiers into the hills around Salt Lake to prospect for precious metals. Having seen what Sutter's Mill did for California, turning a once-tranquil area into drunken anarchy, he thought to do the same to Utah, a noble effort to water the heavy Mormon population with fortune-seekers who probably wouldn't be Mormon. Parley Pratt was dead by then.

His men found silver outside of Park City and, like a true prophet, Colonel Conner's vision came to pass. The valley just over the mountain from the City by the Salt Lake became a boom town right quick.

Brothels and bars and more damn money than anyone should have a right to popped up like Junegrass. George Hearst, father of Randolph Hearst, of the later Patty Hearst set, bought a particularly rich vein of silver for $27,000, a fortune back then, which yielded $50,000,000 worth of silver—an amount of wealth so big, so disgustingly huge that even today when billionaires buy entire governments wholesale, it's a big deal. Susanna Bransford Emery Holmes, known as "Utah's Silver Queen," made $1,000 a day in 1894 from her interest in the Silver King mine. That's about $30,000 per day today. Meanwhile miners died by the dozens, wages were shit, hours were long, misery was high, and liquor prices were just barely afford-able enough to get them back into the holes the next day. So, you know, capitalism at its finest.

The place filled with sinners, alright, but the worst ones were in mansions and penthouses in distant upscale communities, sapping the area of resources, holding down the unions, drinking champagne out of slippers while nursing all the deadly sins—greed, sloth, and gluttony surely in the forefront.

God took note and burned the whole town to the ground in June 1898. The first place in the state to have electricity and phones hadn't leveled up their housing stats past clapboard and oily rags. Two hundred of the town's 350 buildings became charcoal. The town had 10,000 people then, mostly dirty lonely imported miners. Naturally, the first structure rebuilt was a saloon. In eighteen months, bricks were discovered, and the town was rocking again.

Mining continued but slowed. Ore prices fluctuated. The United States got off the silver standard, and new regulations about how to store dynamite were enacted for obvious but tragically late reasons.

Proper people down the mountain avoided Park City. There was work there, but also Gentiles, what Utah Mormons called non-Mormons. Also Chinese railroad workers who didn't go home after the Transcontinental Railroad connected up on Promontory Summit. Worst still was all the booze. Lots of booze. Oh, and hookers. Lots of hookers. Park City had the best red-light district between Cheyenne and San Francisco, outside of Ogden, where the railroad went. Ogden was a happening place too. Also shunned.

With all the fun people were having in Park City, it was only a matter of time before some upstart dickhead had to mess with it. This was done in 1917 with The Great Experiment. Unable to wait for Prohibition coming two years later, Park City banned alcohol just to get an early start. Morale went decidedly down. There were ugly riots and strikes for a while, but by 1921, of the city's twenty-seven original bars, people could get drunk in only twenty-six of them. Park City became the original home-brew haven—hipsters take note. Bootlegging was a growth industry. More fortunes were made on the livers of the working class. Sex continued to be profitable until 1955 when a big raid finally shut down the red-light district. By this time though, all the mines had shut down and the digger Johns had hit the road. The inhabitants left behind started calling Park City a ghost town, which is never a good look on a real estate listing.

Then came skiing.

God help me, I'll never understand skiing.

"Hey let's strap boards to our feet and race down a mountain."

"Won't we get hurt?"

"Snow is soft."

"Not always. I'll break a leg."

"Probably. Let's go!"

"Ahhhhh!"

Snap.

"Isn't this great?"

"My leg is bent funny. I can't feel my fingers. Or the tip of my nose. Are those wolves?"

"We'll make a fortune on this!"

And they have.

I have tried to ski, and I didn't like it. Could you guess? Other people have had a bad time too. There're lists of people who've died skiing. Not just professional skiers who are like professional base jumpers, I guess, relishing the misery for some kind of adrenaline rush, but people who have non-arctic lives. There was Mieczysław Karłowicz, a Polish composer who in 1909 got an early start at getting killed with boards strapped to his feet. The afore-mentioned Sonny Bono died skiing. One of the Kennedys, Bobby's son, died in Aspen. Liam Neeson's unforgettable wife Natasha Richardson, a great actress in her own right, died during her first lesson. And those people who didn't push up snowflakes still get cold and injured and insulted with three-digit cost passes, unfathomably long lift lines, twelve-dollar cocoas, and parking hassles that make a two-hour crowded, slushy bus ride become a reasonable alternative to your warm familiar car.

Crazy. But it was a thing. It *is* a thing. It's the thing that saved ghost town Park City from Superfund obscurity and created new ways to build fortunes on suggestible simple folk.

Like all modern American success stories, there's an element of govern-ment assistance involved. In 1963 Park City got $1.25 million dollars to build a ski area. That was a lot of money back then. It bought a gondola, a chairlift and two J-bar lifts. Rope tows weren't a thing yet, I guess. And so the ski craze began.

Winter sports as a whole are in the same category of skiing for me. Except curling. That's cool. Not only do people like doing them, but more of them like watching them. Jump ahead to 1995, when Utah is awarded the 2002 Winter Olympics. Park City would go on to host about 40 percent of all the sports.

And then there's the Sundance Film Festival.

For a fortnight every year, the town goes from expensive and exclusive to a celebrity-strewn melee unapproachable by regular human beings. It becomes the center of the entertainment world. Paparazzi stalk the alley-ways, movie stars sip lattes and wear fur hats. Lines for new movies stretch out up and down the hilly Main Street like Depression-era breadlines from four in the morning until curtain with Q&A to follow. It's a party. Getting selected to show at Sundance is in itself an accolade, worthy of a gold laurel emblem on a teaser. Independent movies are bought by big companies. Reputations are made and restored. Hollywood is there, but mostly it is for the independents, which is cool. Robert Redford started it, with a grant, and it's been going gangbusters for decades with no end in sight. It's spilled the banks of the little mountain town, and many of the movies are now shown in Salt Lake City venues.

Now the erstwhile ghost town is the hottest property in the state, if not the region. You might have to go San Francisco or Manhattan to pay more per square foot of floor. Real estate prices made mining look like a hole in the ground. Even before the five rings were flying over the town hall, Park City had become a snobbish, expensive, exclusive enclave of well-to-dos, people who want to get out of the valley smog, separate themselves from the rabble by distance and tax bracket. The Olympics made it worse. Sundance cemented the barriers. Today locals can no longer live there. It's just too expensive. Service people commute to work, some from as far away as Salt Lake City—fifty minutes down the once-tolled pass. Some from farther still. The problem is spreading, too. New developments and towns are popping up in true Utah-sprawl fashion. The little sleepy town of Heber, seventeen miles down a newly widened highway, is now a rich paradise of million-dollar mansions whereas when I was growing up it was known only for its dairy products.

Park City's wealth and affluence drew another wave of non-Mormons to the area, Colonel Conner's vision revisited in sequins and celluloid. There's sin still happening there. The usual seven, but it's quieted down under the cover of power. You can get drinks there and drugs and sex and ski in between movies, orgies, and harassment-suit moments. You can also buy a twenty-thousand dollar eighty-inch wire sculpture called "Ares" from the window of one of the many many many art galleries along Main Street. Chartered flights to Cannes are included with the price of dinner, and you can find a friendly Panamanian banker's home number on the bulletin board at Starbucks.

I don't get to Park City much. It's physically close but emotionally distant. Maybe once a year I make the trip. I'd never been to Sundance. I was filled with trepidation as I exited I-80 onto Route 224, heading for the haughty hamlet. I'd slid into historical sarcasm as a defense mechanism during the drive, burying my guilt at not trusting Allie or even listening to my messages before then. Everything was there, timestamped and sweet— her losing her phone, the Burmese lead, the staying with Terrance, the figuring out that I was being a baby and ignoring her. Thanks to Parley Pratt, Colonel Conner, and Robert Redford, I didn't get into my head again until I was three miles out of the city center, stuck in bumper-to-bumper stalled traffic, praying for a parking place this side of Wyoming.

> I may be late.

I texted Allie.

> Don't be mad. I'm trying.

I waited for a reply that didn't come. It took me a few minutes before I remembered she'd lost her phone.

13

I LIKE to think that there are universal equalizers in the world, things that bring high and low into parity. Death is one. So is traffic. When I crossed into the actual city limits I found myself sandwiched between a snow-white stretch limousine and a yellow Maserati mid-life crisis, the X99 Ego Boost. I couldn't see into the limo for all the smoked windows, but in my rearview mirror I saw a tanned silver-haired man grinding his capped teeth and pounding his steering wheel as we poked along at bursts of two miles per hour between long stretches where my hybrid turned itself off for idling. I imagined the people in the limo were all drunk and having unprotected sex with many partners. Why else have a limo? But my mood was closer to the teeth grinder. I had no way to contact Allie, and I was late and getting later, all the while stalled and staring at the ass end of a boomerang-antennaed limousine.

Finally, I made the left off the main road, skirting the worst traffic and finally, eventually, getting to the gate of the country club where the cocktail party was being held.

The man at the gate scanned down a clipboard for my name and didn't find it. He saw "Allison Braise +1" and "did me a favor." I was let in, and a parka-clad valet signaled me up.

I got out and remembered it was winter. Though the air was clear and the sky bright, two things not happening the other side of the mountain, it was a million degrees colder. Clouds, even mercury-infused smog clouds, hold heat. Nothing of the kind here. I felt my cheeks redden faster than that time I trumpeted gas at the yoga class—*Forward Farting Dog* for the win.

I jogged into the airlock as the valet drove my car away.

Inside, my poor choice of clothing was again evident. It was an afternoon cocktail party, so evening gowns and thousand-dollar ties weren't decking the halls. Instead, it was tasteful sweaters and turtlenecks, jeans and cowboy boots. I was lucky I had pants on. I remembered my previous idea that my Hawaiian shirt could be construed as eccentric, an affectation of the half-mad all-powerful producer, and decided to go with that. Confidence sells. Though inside I knew I was a fish out of water in an airplane trying to land the thing from the toilet, I put on a facade, an air, a mask of competence. A cocky, stuck-up don't-give-a-shit attitude slid me in without a second glance from the help and drew appraising eyes of the guests.

I was surrounded by pretty people. Hundreds and hundreds of them. This event was big. Cocktail parties usually mean intimate. This was grand, some might say monstrous. I recognized half the faces and most waistlines, gaunt expressions, and cheekbones from entertainment. Most I knew from before the camera, some from behind. A German director held a steaming cup and talked to a supermodel who'd taken her shirt off for a cup of tea. There were also people with similar body mass indexes to me. Those had to be producers, money of some kind. I nodded to a group of them by the hors d'oeuvres table and they nodded back. I was a goddamn master of disguise.

I asked for a tea from a passing waitress who could appear in *Vogue* and was brought a Long Island Iced Tea. Bonus. As I milled around the room, peeking into adjoining ones, admiring views out huge windows, I realized I'd been too quick to brand the group. There was a good collection of people wearing crap clothes as well, younger than me, but just as crappily clad. Either they were chic trendsetters or they were new filmmakers trying to get noticed. There was also a pretty good contingent of local dignitaries: a mayor, the lieutenant governor, a police chief, and rich people who got buildings named after them. There was also an Asian pair, Thai, I would say. One was in a suit worth more than my car new, and beside him a teenager with burn scars down his neck.

The man looked excited. He smiled and nodded to a bearded fellow who, from five steps away, I heard was an up-and-coming stuntman. "I'm an up-and-coming stuntman," he said. Beside him was a woman who looked oddly familiar. But then again, everyone in the room looked familiar. Beside her was a slender moppy-haired guy with huge black-rimmed glasses and a goatee. I figured him for a movie critic, or he played one in a movie. Maybe he was staying in character, waiting to do a DVD commentary after the party.

The older Thai hung on every word the stuntman said, nodding big-eyed as he learned how to fall off a horse. I could teach him that. The other Thai, the young one, looked ready for a nap.

I scanned my notes, gave the pronunciation of foreign names a good solid guess, and went over.

"Hey, are you Thiha Min Naings?" I said brightly.

He corrected my pronunciation. I tried again. He tried again. Once more for the Gipper from both of us, and we surrendered. "Call me Thiha," he said.

"I'm Tony Flaner," said I. "You're just the person I was looking for."

A man appeared at my elbow. A big man. Six and a half feet if an inch. He wore a suit with a bulge and waited for instructions. He was not Thai. The red hair and beard gave that away. His hands flexed in and out, massaging his caber toss callouses.

"Hi," I said. "I'll have another one of these." I handed him my empty glass.

He didn't take it.

"Master Thiha?" he said.

The boy was about to speak when the other turned to the conversation. Gone was his smile, replaced now with a look of suspicion and caution.

"I am Kyi Tun," he said. "First Adviser to General Tayza."

"I heard what happened," I said. "Tragedy."

"Yes," he said.

"Are you still grieving?"

"One never gets over the loss of a child, nor a nation over the loss of a great man."

"Your son?"

"He died in the crash with the General. Only his son, Thiha, escaped."

"That's rough."

"Are you a reporter?" asked Thiha. He looked interested now.

"No. I'm Tony Flaner."

"Is that a title?" asked Kyi Tun.

"No, it's my name."

"What do you want?"

"I want to first give you guys my condolences. I have a son too," I said to Kyi. I reached out to put my hand on his shoulder in a friendly condolence kind of way, but the big guy who wouldn't take my empty glass took my arm and lowered it smartly back to my side.

"Asian etiquette," explained the adviser. "We do not touch."

"Yeah. Human contact is icky," I said.

"What do you want?"

The hero/stuntman flowed into the crowd networking and chasing babes, unwilling to play with the Scotsman. I looked to see if Allie was on his path. I had yet to find her.

"I'm a friend of... No. I'm looking for someone."

"Who?" said Thiha.

"Why?" said Kyi.

"Her name is Sandi Wong. A friend of mine is worried about her."

"Who's your friend?"

"A butler in Thailand."

The two exchanged looks.

"A friend of Sandi's. She arrived in Utah last week Thursday and was supposed to visit the festival and drop in on you guys. She's Thiha's cousin from the old country."

They looked at me with blank, unreadable expressions. They'd seen through my disguise and knew I didn't belong here. I could just hear the order forming to have me escorted out into the snow, where the wolves feed on failures in tropical shirts.

"My friend is worried about her," I said. "Has she contacted you?"

"No," said Kyi.

"No?"

"Tony Flaner!"

Hearing that voice was like a punch in the yarbles while a bucket of cold prom blood dropped from a height. Like waking from a nap and realizing you're back in high school. Without pants. On exam day. No pencil, but copious explosive diarrhea.

"Is that Francis Tomas?"

"You remember me!"

"Fuck."

He waited for me to finish, thinking that was the beginning of a longer statement. I hadn't meant to append it, but everyone was staring.

"Fuck...fuck yeah, I remember you."

He smiled with bleached teeth. He'd forgotten to fasten the top three buttons of his shirt, and I could see gold chains glistening against his waxed hairless chest. He winked a Botoxed eye at me and stabbed out his hand for a shake.

I shook.

I could feel the Burmese contingent retreating.

"Hey. Here," I said to them. "Take my card. If she shows up or contacts you, can you let me know?"

Kyi nodded to the big bodyguard, and he swallowed my card into his palm before following his people away. He didn't even read it. It was one of my new ones: *Tony Flaner. I solve mysteries so you don't have to. Layaway plans available.* I hadn't gotten a lot of use out of them, to be honest, and still had a box on the shelf. I was drunk when I ordered them. Layaway was a dumb idea but a good conversation starter. No one remembers the days when K-Mart ruled the strip mall and you could buy luggage slowly over the course of a year. Layaway really didn't translate for services. That's an installment plan, right? But like I said, I was drunk when I ordered the cards one night. I also got a full set of designer spatulas then. They arrived in the mail just in time for weekday pancakes.

"So you never got out of town, eh, Tony?" said Francis.

"I did. I do. I am. I have a place down in Southern Utah."

"Warm down there, but not as nice as California. I tell you, the only thing better than the weather in California are the opportunities."

"Gold in them there hills?"

"You know it."

He actually slapped me on the back like we were old friends. I think he loosened a filling.

"Can't wait for the reunion," he said. "You are going, right?"

"I may have a conflict."

He looked at my clothes, hair, waist, shoes, soul, and raised an eyebrow.

"You should go. See the old gang."

"My gang was different from yours," I said.

"Of course they were." He slapped me again.

"Seen Allie around?"

"Yeah, she's here. Only the best people got invited. He gave me another sidelong glance. Are you a member of this club?"

"No."

"Then you ponied up the four figures for a ticket?"

"I was invited."

He looked shocked. "By who?"

"Whom."

"Always the smart-ass." A third slap and I was ready to burp.

"Allie."

"What is she to you?"

"My..."

"Whom?"

"What?"

"Just teasing you, old man. She said you guys were dating but haven't formalized anything."

"I hear you got married but divorced," I said, remembering his Facebook page.

"So you have followed my life," he said with an air of smugness that fit well in the room. "Traded her in for a better model and then thought, why settle at all? Life is too grand for limits. Got a big bank account and no chains. The good life." He raised a champagne flute to toast Fate's unfair favoritism and flagrant injustice. I'm sure that's what it was.

"Well, I gotta mingle," Francis said. "Schmoozing with the talent. Might invest in a new Australian drama starting production. It's about a boys' school with a tough headmaster who's secretly writing a romance novel. It's called *Boys in the Bush*.

"Really?"

"Ground floor."

"Oh look—a distraction!" He turned to see and I dodged behind the first corner that gave me cover.

In the next room were more who's whos. Out the window, I could just imagine the Grinch on Mount Crumpit strapping an antler to a dog.

"Tony!"

"Mary Lou Who?" I said.

Allie looked at me weird, then a smile creased her face and her heart grew three sizes.

"You made it."

"Hi." Reality and imagination were conflicting, and I was trying to read deceit and rejection in her face.

"You're an idiot," she said.

"You know me…"

She kissed me. On the lips. A real good one. Long and lasting. It drew looks, stirred longings and not just in my pants.

"The Burmese guys are here. Have you found them?"

"Already talked to them."

"Did they help your case?"

"They hadn't heard from her."

"So nothing?" She looked disappointed.

"No. That's big. It's a narrowing clue."

"Oh." She smiled proudly. "I'm a good sleuth-helper," she said.

"My gorgeous operative."

She smelled my empty glass.

"A little early for this, isn't it?"

"They gave it to me. I guess I just project alcoholic."

"I can't have any," she said. "I gotta be on my game."

This was her thing. This was important to her. Here she was rubbing elbows, trying to make a living. Schmoozing. Working.

"How's it going?"

She shrugged.

"What?"

"CGI is putting me out of business. Why pay me to train a cat over three years when you can have someone in Bangalore spit it out photorealistic in a month."

"So it's a bust?"

"No. A lot of people want me to train their pets."

"Does that pay?"

"With these people?"

"They all look phony to me." I may have said this a little too loudly, but I'm sure they were used to it.

"Probably. But the money is real. They'll go to great lengths to look the part. Looking rich is halfway to being rich."

"Poodles?"

"Shih Tzus this year. And ferrets. Go figure."

"My weasel whisperer," I said and kissed her, feeling like myself again.

14

MY TIME WAS SHORT. Already the sun was set, and I had to drive back over the mountain again. The play I had to see for that other case didn't perform on Sunday. Doing so went against the county's venerable blue laws. I was in a hurry to finish that one up. It seemed like the easiest to deal with, and it was also the least appealing. If I included a ticket stub in my itemized expense report for her play, it'd show I was active, if not enthused.

Still, I was excited to be with Allie, and, let's face it, I was swimming among celebrities with the prettiest girl in the room. My ego swelled, my self-worth doubled, my alcohol increased. We talked with Terrance for a while, Allie's agent, at a booth in a restaurant. The entire building was open to the party, the restaurant was just one of the places to be. It was an important one, though, since it had tables. Papers were being passed between fountain pens, and fortunes were being made and lost, stars made and shot down. Next year's surprise hit was skulking in the shadows, and distribution deals across Europe were being set. There was an electricity in the room that went beyond the five mixed drinks in my system.

"This is too big," Terrance was lamenting. "It was half this size last year. They should have never sold tickets. Now every actor on this side of the Sierras is here flexing their muscles to directors. It's tacky."

"You didn't pay a grand to get in here, did you?" I asked.

"Me? Oh no. I get invited to these things. Agent is as powerful as producer to most of these people. We get more pitches here than anyone. It's why everyone's here. Well, everyone who isn't anyone already."

"You talk like an agent," I said.

He looked down his nose at me. "I'm offended."

"Do you even do people?" I asked.

"Actors? Heavens no, but don't tell anyone."

"Specialty placement," Allie said. "Effects specialists, transport engineers, translators."

"Animal trainers."

"It's a niche market," he said. "But damn lucrative. Don't tell anyone."

"Can you help me with my novel?"

"Only if it can be made to run up a porch, push a doorbell and bark on command."

"That'll need a rewrite, but okay."

"So no on the play?" I said to Allie.

"I can't. Sorry. It's the big weekend, and the play sounds so lame."

"Would be better with you there."

"Sweet," she said. "Here. Have some water. You've got miles to go before you sleep."

I poured a Pellegrino.

"Sorry, Tony," said Terrance. "I have to steal your girl away. We have two more of these things to do. Ryan Gosling has a new kitten. If I don't connect him with Allie now, how ever will he get it to stand on his shoulder while he rides a motorcycle?"

"How indeed."

The party was thinning out. The Myanmarans were still there, the adviser still engrossed in the moment. Thiha was folded into a chair, Scotsman nearby.

"You know those guys?" I said to Terrance.

"The highlander is straight," he said. "Not that I'd ever cheat."

"No. The Burmese."

"Mr. Kyi is a movie fanatic. He's bonkers for the industry. They say that's why he moved here, to be near Sundance so he could rub elbows at this kind of thing."

"Does he have money?"

"I don't know about him, but the family does. Lots of it. That little boy there, the cute one all tuckered out."

"He's seventeen," I said.

"Uhmmm."

"Stop it," said Allie.

"I'm playing my part," Terrance said, and for the first time that night, I saw a different side of him. It was a flash moment as if he'd broken the fourth wall with a glance. I laughed. It made perfect sense in this milieu to do what he was doing. It was expected. It got him where he was going. It was an act, and he was in character.

"Well, he inherited a fortune from his father after that terrible crash in New England."

"New England?"

"Yes. Virginia, I think. CIA land. He tried a coup back home, I hear. Not very effective at regime change but very much so in pocket change." He grinned wide at me. "You can use that in your stand-up act."

"I'll pass."

"Rumor was that the general was working with the CIA to have another try."

"Really?"

"A rumor," Terrance said. "Another rumor thinks the car accident that killed him and the adviser's son was a government hit."

"Theirs or ours?"

"Either. Both." He shrugged.

"How do you know so much about them?"

"Allie said you were interested in them, so I asked around."

I looked at Allie. She shrugged.

Feeling a need to blend in, I shrugged too.

"This is his party, you know. Big rental fee, all the best catering. He'll be out a pretty penny even with the thousand-dollar fee some people have paid. Still, it'll be remembered as the best party of the festival, if only for cost. There was another in the running. It cost more and had less clothing."

"It wasn't that one the other night, was it?" I said, about to throw up.

Terrance read me and put on a disgusted face. "No no no. That kind of party is only good for crabs and tabloid fare."

Allie, sensing me trying to shut down, said to Terrance, "You were talking about our hosts."

"Yes," he said. "The clan moved out here after the accident. Some say to get distance from the intrigue, others to get Hollywood without the smog."

"Which is it?"

"I don't know," he said. "I'm an agent, not a mind-reader."

"You're also a pretty damn good rumor gatherer."

"That's one of the powers of a good agent."

"How goes the work for Allie?" I wanted to bring her back into the conversation. We were here because of her.

"Splendid."

"Any movie stuff?"

"Not yet, but everyone knows her now. It'll all come together. I plant seeds today, reap the crops later."

"I did get a couple of training jobs," Allie reminded him.

"I'm not talking about that. I don't want a piece of those," Terrance said. "Not unless the animal lands a film. That's where I draw the line."

"Are you turning down a commission?" I asked. "I don't think you're right for the business."

"I'll tell you truth, Tony." His voice was low, and he was himself again. "Allie got me my start. She's the animals, but it's opened up robots, and logistics, and weird services no one ever thinks about. I'm doing fine. I can let a poodle get away. It's who I am."

"Shih Tzu," I corrected him.

"Up yours."

"And ferrets," said Allie.

"Oh. Sorry. Yes. And ferrets." He slurped ice water out of a martini glass with an olive in it. Another master of disguise. "Come daaaaarling," he said. "Our coach awaits."

Allie looked at me, sad. "Are you going to be alright, Tony?"

"I'll miss you."

"I'll keep an eye on her. Go see that abysmal play."

Allie kissed me on the forehead. I felt five years old, but it was a good five years old.

They'd stopped serving free cocktails, so I knew it was time to go too. I downed another water and made my way to the restroom for some final kidney filtering before heading down to Utah County and an abysmal play.

"Oh hey, hey, buddy." A young man with slicked hair and open shirt approached me while I was at the urinal. You're that one guy, right? I thought I recognized you. I was hoping to talk to you. Can I send you a headshot? You did that one movie, right? Man, that was so good. I loved it. Can I shake your hand?"

"Sure, let me just shake this off."

He waited. He beamed a smile and waited.

Too nervous, I couldn't finish.

"Have you finished casting that next movie everyone's talking about?"

"*Boys in the Bush*?"

"Yeah yeah yeah yeah! I'd love a part in that one."

"Well, I'm not the one—"

"I'll give you a blow job."

"What?"

"It's okay. It doesn't matter if you're gay or not. I am. Well, bi, so it's all good. I don't mind. It'd be an honor." He pulled a manila envelope out of the air. He might have been holding it, I don't know, my attention was distracted, but he handed it to me nonetheless.

"What's that?"

"My resume and headshot. There's also a DVD of my acting reel. And a thumb drive with the same. All there. I cut the scenes to only the ones where you can see my face acting, not just my junk."

"Uhm…"

"I did summer stock in Carmel and a skin flick in Toronto. I do my own stunts."

"And sex scenes?"

"Sure."

I zipped up. No point in giving myself a hernia. When I turned, he grabbed my hand and shook it. I'd just finished using it to shake myself, so the motion was familiar.

"Have your agent call my people."

"Yeah, uhm. I was hoping you could help me there," he said.

"Just tell them that I'm interested in you. You'll get an agent. They'll line up to have you when they hear about a possible part in *Bushy Boys*."

"*Boys in the Bush*."

"We'll see."

He nodded. He didn't strike me as the brightest light on the marquee, but I felt for him. Breaking into art is hard. Even with his hard body and, I'm sure, luxuriant junk, it was a tough path. Big dreams broken in missed chances and fickle fates.

"So, eh, where do you want it?" he asked.

"What?"

"The BJ. Gotta say thanks somehow. Make sure you'll remember me." He smiled broadly.

He was handsome, but I was with Allie. Also I was a fraud. Mostly, though, I was with Allie. "I can't," I said. "I have a touch of…eh… gonosyphiherpeaids. Just a little flare-up. Won't last long. Itching isn't so bad with the ointment. I couldn't risk your health."

"Oh, man, that's awful. I knew a guy that had that once. Thanks for telling me."

"Yeah, well. Stay off carbs. Bye now." I waved him to the door. Beaming, he exited.

I was washing my hands, holding a manila envelope under my arm. when the door opened behind me.

"I thought that was you, Flaner."

I didn't recognize the voice, but the crew cut clued me in.

"Traard? What are you doing here?" He looked exactly like his picture from the paper—same cut, same suit. Only the eyes of my detective rival were different somehow.

He stared at me. I wondered if he thought I'd draw a gun or turn into a sparkly vampire.

After a minute, he said, "Same thing you are. Working."

"Working or getting work?" I said over the Dyson Airblade. Those things are so cool. How'd we ever get by without them?

"What?"

"Are you on a job or looking to get one?"

He looked at me hard. I could almost hear the grinding gears behind his hard piercing eyes. Finally, after a good long pause where I just stood there, he said, "What are you up to?"

Seeing the man in the flesh should have put me into a cataleptic fit, frothing at the mouth, kicking at the air on my back, crying for my binky. Here was the man who'd made me question my profession, my skill, my success—hell, even my manhood. But I didn't feel that. Maybe it was the flattery of strangers wanting to love me in public—every comic's goal—or more probably the confidence that Allie had in me, but I felt fine. In fact, I felt better than fine. I felt frisky.

Chris Traard wasn't as tall as me, and let's not talk about weight. I was fun and cuddly, and luck or no, I was a damn fine detective. Allie said so, so it had to be true. Even if it weren't, I knew one thing clear as crystal at that moment: I wouldn't trade my hibiscus frond shirt for all the suits and ties in the world.

And—and here's the big thing—I could tell he was nervous. The actor showed more confidence than Traard did. He was intimidated by me. Me. From the cool stare to the long reaction time, to the tense posture, it was clear. He'd summoned the courage to come in here. He'd probably watched me for hours and only now got the spoons to face me. Alone, in a sex-cave restroom. Okay, maybe he didn't know about the sex cave, but he hadn't come to the table, hadn't talked to me in front of anyone. He didn't lean toward the stalls or the urinals, so if had business there besides me, it wasn't urgent.

It was a moment of clarity, a rare spot of certainty and confidence. I knew it wouldn't last, but I had it then, and damn it felt good.

"Hanging out with my girlfriend," I said. "I assume you're drumming up work. Playing off the newspaper thing."

Long pause. Really, a long awkward silence as if he were calculating vectors, planning the bishop swap eighteen moves away, downloading instructions to fly a helicopter from Morpheus at dial-up speeds.

"It helped," he said.

"Nice."

He stared. I stood. I shifted my weight to leave. He stayed like he was concrete bolted to the bedrock.

"Been passing my card out," he said. "I might be brought in as a script consultant."

"Spiffy."

Long pause. Agonizing. Then, "Plus it's good public relations to be here. Meet new people. Mingle. Get seen. Mingle."

"You know, Chris—may I call you Chris? I'm going to, so let's say you agree—I prefer to have the—"

"That's my name."

"What?"

He looked at me. Squinted. Then slowly, as if the words were being assembled IKEA-fashion in his brain and sent down a dumbwaiter said, "Chris. That's my name. Christopher Ogden Traard."

"Yeah…that's special. Good for you. What I was saying is that getting famous in our business doesn't always work out. You lose the option of anonymity. My clients appreciate that."

A look of surprise, horror and embarrassment crept onto his face slowly. Really slowly. Weirdly slowly.

"Are you all right, Chris?" I said. "Someone give you some bad acid?"

He looked at me with shock now, fear. Slowly...slowly.

"Yes," he said. "Help me."

"Really? Wait. Don't answer that. We don't have time. I'd talk you down, but I have places to be."

"Can you get me out of here?"

"Are you serious?"

He nodded immediately, which was startling after the three-day conversation so far.

"Someone slipped you something?"

"Something."

"I'm going to Provo," I said. "Square capital of the state, conservative and uptight."

"That's where I live."

"Of course it is. Come on."

15

CHRIS TRAARD WAS NOT an ideal traveling companion. He was silent, sullen, introspective and then all of a sudden would scream about jellyfish in the engine. It made the drive a little tense.

"Who gave it to you?" I asked.

"Could have been that one guy. Or the other."

"Nice work, detective. Anything more you noticed?"

"They both had pants."

"Well, that narrows it down."

"Look out for the petri dish!"

"Petri...what?"

"Aghhhhhh!"

I slowed to under-freeway speed, and the threat passed, on the right side apparently.

He was incapable of telling me where he lived, so I asked him for his wallet.

"Why?"

"I need to buy a burrito."

"Oh, okay. Here."

I found his address on his ID and calculated the added time of pouring him into a Utah County suburb.

"Whatcha' working on right now?" I asked him. "Anything interesting?"

"Betelgeuse."

"Star or ghost?"

"I shouldn't have taken that drink. I didn't even know the guy."

"Peer pressure's a bitch."

"Mingling."

"Mingling. That's a great word."

"Mingling. Mingling. Mingling. Mingling."

"Yeah…"

And so it went into Utah County.

I took the southern route through Provo Canyon, faster with fewer visions of highway robbery. I kept Traard as calm as I could, playing a little Grateful Dead to help him through and mellow the ride. I was paying a debt. Others had done the same for me. Maybe Traard would one day repay the favor for someone. Might happen.

His house was a simple stucco rambler in an undisclosed cul-de-sac of Utah County. A woman ran out of the house. Unbeknownst to me, Chris had been texting her the whole time.

She rushed to the car, a phone in her hand, barefoot in a pink floral housecoat. "What does he mean the slush is whistling to him? And who's Jerry?"

"That would be Garcia. Can't speak to the slush. Help me get him inside."

"Is he hurt?"

"Someone slipped him a mickey."

"You?"

"Me?"

"I recognize you, Tony Flaner. What did you do to my brother, you jealous slob?"

"Have we met?"

"Chris told me all about you. He said you'd try something like this."

"He said I'd deliver him home from a bad trip I had nothing to do with?"

"I should call the police," she said.

Traard clung to me like I was a life raft. His legs were rubbery, but his fists were iron clutching my shirt.

"Listen, lady—"

She slugged me then. In the belly.

My words were added to the smog in a burst of clouded-white anguish. I doubled over.

She'd surprised me. If I'd expected the blow, I'd have tensed my twelve-pack abs and absorbed it like water into a sponge. But I hadn't seen it coming.

I examined the salt on the driveway for a while, Chris Traard challenging my balance.

When I found more air, I said. "Lady, take him."

"Where? To the hospital? We know where you live."

"That's creepy," I said, trying to push Traard on the woman. "He doesn't need a hospital. That won't go well. Just stay with him."

"Put him to bed?"

"No. Stay up. Watch movies."

"What?" She finally peeled him off me.

"He'll be fine in a couple of hours. Fifteen maybe."

"Flaner, we'll get you for this."

I staggered back to my car. I think she'd bruised a kidney. "You guys spend a lot of time talking about me, do you?"

"You're the worst. You'll never be as good as Chris."

"I admit I can't take a punch, but I can go to a party without pissing myself."

She stared at me, and then her eyes traveled to her brother's crotch, where wetness spread down and steam rose from that.

"Have a good night." I left them like that.

The drive with Chris had sobered me up. The water helped. And the weird bathroom thing. Traard's sister's sucker punch rounded it out perfectly. By the time I pulled into the parking lot of the Timpanogos Theatre of Living Arts in Provo, I was sharp and breathing normally.

The Timpanogos Theatre of Living Arts was a converted church. Not a Mormon church, but something else. There are other churches in the state, but not many. The competition is fierce. This one had a bell tower up high and plenty of parking. For the space it was a natural and organic mutation from theism to thespian.

Perry was waiting for me in the lobby.

"Where are the others?" I asked him.

"They wouldn't come."

"Their loss."

"Garrett and Critter have a show. Standard says local theater is one step above busking, and Dara let loose a tirade of hate against the play and its writers so awful that I could hear the NSA people on the line gasping in horror."

"You're making that last part up. I hope."

"Yeah. The tirade happened, but the NSA only listens."

"It's a good line, though," I said.

"Eh."

He handed me a ticket, and after buying a five-dollar popcorn, two four-dollar drinks and a three-dollar candy bar, we went inside. The ticket was cheap. They had to make rent somehow.

I'd invited my friends to the play once Allie said she wasn't available. I considered going alone, but as my mood was so much better than it had been, I decided to make it a party. I shouldn't have been surprised it was only Perry who came. My friends were like me. Flaky. Still, I was a tad disappointed. My new positive outlook hadn't reached them yet. Perry would do. Paranoid and schizoid as he was, he was still the most relatable of the bunch. With Perry, I had the cover of an evening of art with a peer. Going to a play alone is kind of sad and could be suspicious. Whenever I see someone eating alone at a nice restaurant or buying a single movie ticket, with or without extortionist concessions, I always feel pity for them, particularly if it's a date movie.

We found our seats five minutes before curtain. The house was practically full, only sixty seats or so, but still I was amazed there were so many people. I remembered that there'd been a positive write-up in the paper about the troupe, which couldn't have hurt. Plus it was a Saturday night in Provo, which is famous for not having a nightlife. This G-rated entertainment was just the ticket, a wholesome counterpoint to the graphic violence and adult situations being shown to packed houses just over the mountain in Park City.

The lights went down and Perry handed me a program.

I stared at him. "Now? Now you give me this? Just when the lights go out?"

"If you don't want it—"

"I'll keep it."

We sneered at each other as the music started. It was a good moment.

If you've never seen *Flower Drum Song*, I don't know if I can recommend it. On the one hand, though the music is not as good, *Flower Drum Song* is less scary than *Reservoir Dogs* for the average playgoer. It's the story of Chinese Americans working through love and cultural clashes here and there, old and new. Question of appropriation—I mean *assimilation*.

In the '50s, it was a deal. It's had revivals, but it's one of the harder Rodgers and Hammerstein's to bring back. The issue, beyond the cultural, is one infamous song. *I Enjoy Being a Girl* is a cute, bouncy number, a showstopper if done well. It's also so full of stereotypes and vapid femininity that it'll make your vinegar curdle if you don't immediately remind it that this is seriously flawed and dated fiction. Even then, your balsamic may need a few months of counseling.

In the scene before the song, there was a kerfuffle in our audience. It began with a stirring, a movement, three women whispering and digging into their bags. It was met quickly by the appearance of two ushers, one on either side of their section who, with flashlights shining into their three faces, asked them to step out.

"Please come with us, ladies," said an usher.

The flashlights were the only light in the theater, and everyone could see the outrage on the women's faces. One bent over and pulled out a roll of paper and tried to get the others to grab on. The one in the middle did, but the end was blinded. An usher grabbed the paper out of their hands and crumpled it up behind a flashlight beam but not before I, and probably most people, saw crossed knives beneath a green planet, making the female symbol look dangerous and astronomical at the same time. As for the writing, I didn't catch the whole phrase, but I could guess what the gist of it was by the word "objectifies," which was in the middle. Oh, and their chants were kind of telling too—"Women are people not objects!" and "A woman is a whole without a man!" They probably should have workshopped that last one.

They got through two rounds of the two slogans before they were led out in front of dancing flashlights.

After a good pause, the music came up, and the play resumed. I wondered if the scene had been staged. A little theater in the theater? A social commentary from the management in the face of retrogressive social portrayals?

Nope. That was made clear a minute or two into the restarted play when one of the protestors burst through and screamed from the doorway. "This whole show is a fucking disgrace!" The expletive was the clue. Real protest, real anger, real language. She was really dragged away this time.

And then came the scene with that song.

Knowing it was coming, reminded by the protest, I steeled myself by concentrating on the actress, the very Madeleine Smith I'd come to stalk who was playing Linda Low, she who enjoys being a girl. The actress entered in a bathrobe, her hair up in a towel and performed the song honestly and enthusiastically.

Like the rest of the cast, her Asian heritage didn't extend east of the Caucasus. The photos in the program made that clear. More paste than a pawnshop. The stage makeup, however, was excellent if not a little offensive. The whole cast had donned narrow eyes. I think it's a trick done with Scotch tape, but almond Asian eyes abounded. Their speech patterns were also, well, fabricated, some better than others, from canny to caricature. The production was good in a small theater kind of way, with revolving sets, decent sound and projection, nice choreography and color. A festive wholesome show from a bygone era that left me a little flat. I think they'd have been better off if...or maybe...hell. I don't know. How do you put on a definitive Chinese play without a single Chinese player? Should you try? Should you not? What are the PC rules here? Better to not give the culture some light or give it one like this? Did this do more good than harm?

These questions rattled me throughout the play and distracted me from my job, which was to see through the actress telling me about her pearl teeth to a fiancée who didn't have social media.

The intermission came and went, and Perry spent it in the bathroom, hopefully with less excitement than I'd had in my last visit. I read over the program.

Madeleine Smith—"Maddy" to her friends—had a surprisingly long list of credits. She'd done theater in California, Arizona, Idaho, and Colorado, but mostly, and lately, up the state of Utah—St. George, Panguitch (yes, that's a real place), Cedar City, and now Provo. South to north. This didn't jive with what Bryand Moland had told me. Padded resume? It said she worked with "small companies," but her roles were pretty substantial, at least to the ones I knew. She'd been Lady Macbeth, and in *The Sound of Music* she'd played Maria, Julie Andrews' role. She had a strong voice and could sing. Her Chinese accent was not cringe worthy even while dancing, and I seemed to remember a mention in the paper that she'd pulled off a New York borough accent for *Damn Yankees*. She was young, pretty, athletic. Accomplished. Attractive. Probably had a great personality, but I'd have to find that out for myself.

The lights flashed, and Perry came back to his seat.

"There's a party after the show," he said.

"Cast party?"

"A little bigger. I got invited."

"How?"

"I was recognized."

Remembering my previous conversation, I said, "You know, in my line of work, that's not always a good thing."

"Don't get jealous."

"I'm not. I don't. I'm saying—"

"I've just had more shows than you."

"I'm good."

"You are good. And people will come to recognize that. You'll be famous one day."

"I mean, I'm good with not being recognized in a bathroom. I don't like scenes in bathrooms. It gets weird."

"How weird can it get?"

I was about to tell him when the second act began.

More of the same, but I relaxed and let myself get caught up in the story, the music, the dancing. I ignored how the bawdy pieces at the nightclub had been sanitized to pablum. Not a bare shoulder in sight. I stopped wondering if there'd be political fallout for a show that centered around illegal immigration—"wetbacks." There was innocence to the show that fit well with the venue. Welcome to Utah County: set your clocks back seventy-five years. It helped that it was an earnest production. You could see the budget limits, but it was good. The actors were decent, Maddy being the highlight.

After the final double wedding fix, out of nowhere, there was applause and curtain calls. Flowers were presented to the leads, bouquets for the women, single roses for the men. What's up with that?

Perry and I lingered in the auditorium.

"The party is here," he said. "In the theater. I was told just to just hang around."

"Perry, I shouldn't have to tell you this, but it would be better if you didn't mention I was working a case tonight."

"Is this the fiancée or the Thai girl?"

"Burmese. But the other."

"Are you trying to be confusing?"

"A little bit. Zip it."

"Zipped."

When everyone was gone, half the house lights went dark, and we gave each other an appraising look.

"You look marvelous," I said

"Indeed," said Perry.

Rock music rose from backstage and behind us in the halls. Laughter echoed untraceably.

"I'm feeling like we should look out for falling chandeliers," I said.

"Don't be melodramatic," said Perry and led the way into the wings.

"You want to see melodrama?" I said. "I bet you ten bucks there's more drama backstage now than there was on stage during the show."

"It was a musical comedy."

"Chicken."

"Actors are just like regular people."

"Meaning they're just relaxing after a hard day's work? Nothing weird? Nothing special or weird?" I said.

"Exactly."

"Put up or shut up."

"Ten bucks?"

"Bwock, bwock."

"Fine. I'm the judge, though."

"There won't be any doubt."

"Pfft."

"Sucker."

16

PERRY SHOULD HAVE KNOWN BETTER, but he was blind to it. I'd been the same before Allie clued me in. Doing stand-up, I'd hung around show people. I'd been numbed to how stupid and petty and shallow the industry can be. Allie'd noticed it and reminded me. She said something like, "I can't believe how stupid and petty and shallow show people can be." She pointed out the visiting magician melting down in his dressing room because there was a typo on the flier that had filled the house. A contortionist was chugging laxative because she felt bloated before the show. She would later dash off stage mid-splits, never to return. Barry, the owner, was stealing tips while keeping a Las Vegas agent on hold for ninety minutes. My friends weren't immune. Dara was high-maintenance and toxic. Standard was a stuck-up pencil with flesh wrapped too tightly around it. Garrett should be committed, and Perry had been on several occasions. I pointed out to Allie that I was the exception to prove the rule. She gave a me wry smile. Just that day, I'd told her how untalented I thought I was at everything I did in my life and was seriously contemplating becoming a hermit in Peru and had already requested a brochure.

Having just come from the big-boy table of acting parties, Sundance schmooze on Burmese bucks, I had a pretty good idea what to expect backstage at this shindig.

We followed the music backstage to the suite of dressing rooms past the props and costume rooms. One of the actors, the one who played Wang Ta, the romantic male lead in the play, was sitting on an upside-down five-gallon orange Home Depot bucket bawling into his hands. His fingers were caked with grease paint and one of his slanted eyes had popped open to reveal a bloodshot orb of utter despair and pain.

"What is it?" asked Perry.

"I can't believe how low-energy I was. And on a Saturday!" He dropped his head into his hands and bawled long snotty gasps.

Perry handed me ten dollars, and we went deeper in.

"You're freaking me out a little, dude," I said to my friend.

"Really? Man, that sucks. Why? I've been strictly on my meds all week."

"That's it."

"Oh."

"Perry White! The famous insane ultra-talented voice of rebellion in Utah, our own wonderful comedic genius, Perry White!" We'd entered a hallway framed with people. The entire cast was there and bunches of others I assumed had been in the audience. Matching the face of the speaker to the program, I saw that it was the director, Ortwin Bishop, who'd given Perry his great introduction. Ortwin, what a name. Everyone turned to look at my semi-famous companion and clapped. "And friend," said Ortwin, gesturing to me.

Remember when I was saying that I was again feeling good about myself, that I had found a zen place where I was okay with my place in the world? Yeah, about that. It's one thing to feel that you've been overestimated and feel a fraud because of it. The flip side is when you don't get the recognition you think you deserve. When you are underestimated, or in my case, completely unrecognized.

I know what you're saying: "Tony, didn't you just tell two other characters that being recognized is not good for you?" So what if I did? Mind your own business and stop eavesdropping.

It's all situational. What got caught in my craw this time was my Perry envy. Although I am a detective now, I still do my fair share of open mic. Comedy has been one of the few hobbies of mine to last longer than seven months. I've defined myself by it longer than the sleuth thing. I've been around. Among people who know the local scene, I am known. I'm not as big as Perry. He actually makes a living doing it, but I'm somebody.

And I've been a famous detective. I've been in the papers—online and real paper, on TV news. Podcasts.

Yeah, I know. Self-pity. Stupid, shallow, and jealous. And I was there on a case, undercover. I'd extracted promises from Perry about my anonymity. I was well-positioned, but I was insecure. Perry smiled and waved and gave me a sidelong glance, sensing the slight I felt. When he was pharmaceutically balanced, he was a very shrewd customer.

"I'm Tony Flaner," I said before I could stop myself. "I'm a private detective. Perhaps you've heard of me. I'm here on a case."

Perry's eyes rolled.

If I could have turned to rubbing alcohol and soaked the carpet, I would have.

All eyes now turned to me. The conversations and joviality evaporated faster than my dream of isopropyl.

A consummate showman, Ortwin quickly regained control. "Well, we're glad to have you."

"It was a great play," said Perry. "Really fun."

"Hear! hear!" I said, raising my fist like some kind of agitator beseeching revolution.

"You're not helping," Perry whispered to me.

"I can't stop."

The sad sounds of the male lead crying behind us continued through an awkward moment of raised voices down the hall.

"I want to see her," a man's voice said.

A woman halfway between me and the new tumult looked around, made eye contact with me, and ducked into a dressing room. It was Madeline Smith.

"Tell her it's Glenn. Glenn Abergast. From Ephraim."

I thought I recognized someone. Not the guy down the hall, whom I couldn't see, but a closer man. I'd seen him before. My mind felt dull as a Ginsu bowling ball until I realized I'd seen him at the Sundance party that night. He was the guy in the thick-framed black glasses.

We made eye contact. I didn't see recognition in his expression. He might not have seen me at the party. There were too many better-looking things to gaze upon. The crowd shifted, and he disappeared behind a wall of heads, the throng if you will, which is never to be confused with a thong. I learned my lesson about that last year at the arts festival.

Ortwin worked his way down the hall toward the guy calling himself Glenn, and, though I couldn't see it, I could hear muffled sounds of eviction. A door opened, sucking cold acrid smog inside the hot hallway. Then it shut, and my ears popped.

I took advantage of the distraction to distance myself from Perry. Not everyone had been close enough to see me—the hall wasn't raked like the stage—so I tried to blend in near the dressing rooms.

"You were great," I said to one of the actors. "Do you consider yourself an actor or a dancer first?"

That did it.

Nothing gets show people talking like talking about themselves. I hear it's the same for writers. Want a writer to talk for hours? Ask them about their writing. You'll need duct tape and a leaded sap to shut them up.

Before the actor who'd done a soft-shoe solo had taken his story past the ballet lessons his aunt Connie had made him take, the hallway was again a lively party. Non-alcoholic bottles of sparkling juice were opened and poured into plastic cups and passed down. I got grape.

"To mid-run!" toasted Ortwin down the hall.

Toasts and drinking but no halt to the conversation. It took awkward moments to do that, and luckily they were out of those at the moment.

I'd lost sight of Perry and was looking for an exit from the dancer/actor who hadn't made the career move to one or the other yet, feeling that dance was more pure but acting more lucrative, when someone knocked into me and I spilled my purple drink.

It was a classic spill—a straight splash onto my crotch and then a linear soak down my inseam. I'd had practically a full cup. I stood there looking like I pissed myself and had an infection so bad they'd name it after me.

The perfect excuse.

"I gotta go," I said to the actor/dancer/chatterbox, pointing at the spill.

I moved down the hall to the door where Maddy had gone.

There is a special kind of vibe to a party that is standing room only, even if it's artificially created by throwing it in a hallway. Belly to belly, hip to hip, personal space was out, and touching was in. Familiarity was the keyword. I figured there were fifty to sixty people crammed there, down several confluences of backstage corridor.

I saw Ortwin, the director, and he saw me and moved away. I sensed skeletons in his closet. Everyone's got something to hide, and skeletons rattle at drafts. Pleased with my detective wisdom, I wormed into Maddy's crowded dressing room with renewed aplomb and soggy berries. Note to self: keep a change of pants in the car.

The heavy-framed glasses guy stood against a wall, eating cheese pieces with toothpicks off a paper plate. Maddy was at a makeup station, covering her cheeks in cold cream. Another woman stood behind her, over the chair, holding the actress' hair off her forehead. Madeline's hair was much shorter than her program picture, which was shorter than the photo I had of her from the engagement sitting. She'd donned a page cut in keeping with the role she played on stage. The color too was different. She'd dyed it black. The program had her as blonde, the engagement picture, a redhead. The two women were chatting like old friends.

"The floor supervisor threatened to put me back on at a register," the friend was saying.

"That would suck," said Maddy.

"I warned him."

"Didn't you get moved over as part of a raise?"

"Yes, when they moved me from part-time returns to full-time. It was a 'positional promotion' instead of money. But of course that was six supervisors ago. They don't remember."

The glasses cheese-eating guy turned a shoulder to me and tried to find something interesting to look at on the wall. He found something. So did I.

There on the wall was a photograph of the Eiffel Tower at night. It was the exact picture I'd seen in the gallery the day before. The one I couldn't believe anyone in their right mind would pay eighteen hundred bucks for.

There it was. Signed the same. Same finger blob in the corner. In a simple poster frame with glass. Right out of the gallery.

"Do you know how much that's worth?" I asked the guy.

"Priceless," he said. "It's art and a landmark."

"No," I said. "The picture."

"No idea."

"Costco will blow up any photo to that size for like, forty bucks. Less if you have a coupon."

"I see."

"But that one retails for $1,789—nonnegotiable. Three exclamation points."

"Uh, what? Okay. I really don't know; it's uh…" He paused to think. I guess I'd rattled him with the price. It had rattled me. "…Maddy's." He pointed to the actress. "A gift."

"Maddy!" I used the guy's gesture as an introduction and stepped up to her at the makeup table. "Wow. You did a great job."

She studied me in the mirror and then glanced at the man I'd been talking to. I didn't see his reaction, but thought I saw a shadow pass over her face.

"You're standing in my light," she said.

"Oh."

"I thought you handled the disruption very well." I stepped out of her light.

"She's a professional," said the woman, holding her hair.

"I'm Tony Flaner," I said, waving. "I'm a comic up in Salt Lake."

"He hangs with Perry White," said the guy. "Detective for hire."

"Consulting detective, PI, sleuth, or gumshoe, just don't use the other."

"Sleaze?" said Glasses Guy.

"And you are…?" I asked the question in a way that left no room for him to ignore it. I drew it out until there was only silence in the room.

"I'm Enzo Powell. Maddy's manager."

I then turned my gaze, wide and expectant, to the girl holding the actress's hair. Unable to shake my gaze, she said. "Kelly Gibson. I'm a friend of Maddy's—her best friend."

I remembered seeing her name in the program. "Did you do the makeup for the play? Fantastic work."

"Thank you."

Turning back to her, I said, "So, Maddy. You know Glenn Abergast?"

She knew the name. I couldn't read her exact reaction beneath the thick cold cream, but I knew she was about to lie to me.

"No," she said. "Who's he?"

"A fan."

"Like those crazy women," said Maddy. "Only wrong chromosome set."

"Name doesn't ring a bell?"

"Every name rings a bell," she said. "But placing them is harder."

A commotion in the hall made everyone turn. I was jostled and pushed and returned the favor as everyone looked.

"Fire marshal..." came the first fragment. "...pancake..." came another. "Now. Sorry. Come on."

Ortwin stuck his head in. "You all have to leave. The feminists called the fire marshals on us. We're too crowded."

"Pancakes?" I said.

"Yes."

"What about them?"

"The pancake house on Eleventh. Some of the cast are going there."

"Free pie if you order a meal," added someone.

"And one of our sponsors," said Ortwin. Ortwin...still can't get over that name. "Everyone not on the program or part of the production has to leave now."

"Or?"

"You'll be arrested," said the director.

Kelly looked at me, Maddy looked at me. Enzo looked at me. Ortwin carried his news like Paul Revere down the hall toward the exit after he stopped looking at me.

"See you guys for pancakes and pie?" I said.

"Too tired. Another time," said Kelly.

"Nice meeting you," said Maddy, behind a mask of white cream.

"I'll see you again sometime," I said.

A crack, momentary but clear. She didn't want to see me again.

17

I HAD A COAT, a simple yuppie parka-like thing Nancy had given me for Christmas. It was blue nylon and had horizontal bands of down that made it look like a spacesuit. I didn't think much of it until I was sitting in my cold car in the parking lot, shivering like an idiot in the dark, before I remembered I had it with me. I climbed into it and waited to get warm in the cold and dark, very cold and, okay, only kinda dark—there was a weak streetlight over the theater's parking lot.

Perry had left in his own car, disappearing into the darkness like his fears. I dug out my phone and found that Randy had texted me.

> Staying at Kevin's tonite.

The message was hours old. It had come in just when the lights had gone down for the play. I hadn't noticed it, because unlike the jerk in section A, I'd turned off my phone for the performance. I also didn't get a visit from the usher in the first act after I couldn't believe that Andrea and Scott were dating again. Has she lost her mind?

I was pleased he was set up for the night, but I couldn't help feeling like a failure when I realized I'd had the bit in my teeth with my detective thing, and my son, my boy, my trusting ward—the sixteen-year-old child I was watching this weekend—hadn't entered my thinking recently. A good father would have known his son's movements down to every stoplight in his overly expensive car. He'd have made sure, at least, that he was tucked in while chasing actors in smog-filled Utah Valley.

After pondering, typing, deleting, typing again, deleting again, pondering more, I finally texted back:

> Cool. I'm on a case. A couple actually. See you tomorrow. Have fun.

Kk

came right back.

> Be safe, be smart

No reply, so I sent a heart. <3

Eye roll emoji. I didn't know that one existed. It's good to learn new things.

The place had cleared out quick after Ortwin's threat. About fifteen minutes after the bulk of the parking lot emptied, there was another wave of exits. The cast and crew going to pie, I figured. Maddy was not among them.

Now, forty minutes after that, with my windows fogged to oblivion, my socks bags of ice, the lights finally went out in the building. Through the freezing greenhouse of my windshield, I saw four distorted figures emerge. Three of them went to a silver BMW I'd spotted when I could still see through the windows. The other went to a truck. Headlights came on and I ducked, hoping my car wasn't too obvious. I listened to the crunch of frozen gravel beneath German wheels and then poked up to see the truck heading one way and the Beamer another.

I fired up my little car, wiped the glass with a wad of napkins from the door pocket, then put the defroster to maximum and the car into drive and followed, discreetly, the BMW.

The Saturday night streets of downtown Provo belied the city's population. This was actually a good-sized city by Utah standards. But now tumbleweeds, if they weren't frozen in place, would still need Tinder to hook up. I contemplated that joke when the BMW turned into a residential area not far from the university; that would be BYU, not the U of U. Big difference.

My phone beeped, and I glanced down at a text from Randy.

Hey J, sup?

The BMW pulled into a little house that looked to have been built between the Second World and Korean Wars but was still more modern than its neighbors. I noted the street was not the one Bryan Moland had given me for Madeline Smith's home address.

As I racked my brain for Urban Dictionary recollections to decipher Randy's cryptic message, I watched as Maddy, Kelly, and Enzo left the car in a carport and strolled into the house. Maddy used her keys to open the door. I noticed Enzo was carrying a green bottle that looked like real champagne.

> Hanging out at Kevin's. No parents.

Okay.

> You there Jelissa?

Jelissa?

> Who's Jelissa?

I texted. I considered waiting for more intel, but Randy would figure out he was texting the wrong person pretty quick and I didn't want to be *that* guy.

Long pause. Then:

> Sorry wrong thread.

> Jelissa?

> A friend.

> No parents?

> I'm okay. I'm safe and smart.

> Hurm...

Then he pulled a cheap shot. He texted:

> <3

I wrote:

> Be careful

> Always.

> Kk

Trusting your child is part of parenting, I decided, and I didn't press the Jelissa issue. Jelissa, Ortwin...only in Utah.

I parked down the street and got out in casual burglar mode. No one walks in this state. People get in their cars to fetch the mail at the end of their driveways. Joggers appear only in certain gentrified neighborhoods at certain times. This certainly wasn't one of those areas, and the subzero smog freeze sure as shit wasn't the time. If anyone saw me outside, they'd know instantly I was up to no good.

I skulked the shoveled sidewalk, skipping over frozen dog turds until I could duck into the carport behind the BMW. People do garages now. Much harder to get into those unless you have an off-the-shelf replacement garage door opener set to the default code. Then, however, there could be the noise of an opening door because no one has heard of grease for the springs. I know. My garage door wakes the neighbors and sets the dogs to barking.

The side door where they'd entered was up three cement stairs, behind a screen door. A small window in it showed dim light. This was once the secondary or servants' entrance, depending on your snobbery. Now, being by the carport, it was the main entrance. No one had even shoveled the snow to the front door.

An archaic waist-high chain-link fence cordoned off the backyard. A little gate with frosted metal ornamentation matching the screen door showed signs of recent use; lots of footprints giving me cover as I slipped in the back.

I heard laughing from inside. Voices, rising and falling.

I kept close to the house, keeping my shadow out of existence.

There was a large single window edged by ochre drapes. Yellow light poured out of it onto the trampled snow.

The backyard was large by modern standards, which meant bigger than a park strip. There were a row of trees I suspected bore fruit in the summer and a garden surrounded by another chain-link fence. The snow in the garden was pristine, the rest of the yard was trampled and kicked up. Winter volleyball game?

Another bout of laughter pulled my attention to the house.

Squatting low and keeping the snow crunch to a minimum, I slinked to the window and slowly peeked inside.

It was a bedroom, and through an open doorway, I could see down a hallway. Enzo was pouring real bubbly into water glasses and handing them off to the girls. The bedroom itself was lived-in. The bed was unmade, clothes were tossed about in dormitory disaster dressing. Bras hung on the closet doorknobs. The closet itself was packed with clothes, piled high in shoes. The dresser had bottles of unctions no man could identify.

I ducked as Maddy moved down the hall into the room and plastered myself flat below the window.

My feet were freezing. The short drive from the theater had barely managed to defrost the windshield. My feet were low on the menu. I kept as still as I could, blowing breaths out of the side of my mouth like a smoker trying not to offend a date.

"Let Barney out," I heard someone call.

There was a back door a few yards away next to a large doghouse.

A doghouse.

I heard chains rattle and bolts slide back and dreamed of friendly quiet Labradors and blind chihuahuas.

The door opened, and a squat pit bull waddled outside and headed for a tree.

I froze, freezing as I was, and watched the dog do his business, his nose pointed toward the neighbor's house, where I saw the snow had been worked away to the bare ground by a pacing animal.

I considered warming myself with my own bodily fluids when the dog turned and saw me. I could see it clearly in the light from the house. I was in shadow, so it took him a moment to figure me out. When it did, a low menacing growl escaped his mouth, and he squared his square head at me. Then came a definitive bark, loud and evil, a challenge—a warning turned starting gun as the beast sprang at me.

If I had to have a pet, I'd say I'm a cat person by nature. They mind their own business and as long as you remember to feed them once in a while, they're easy to deal with. Allie has explained to me how humans domesticated dogs while cats domesticated us. Cats serve no function beyond fluffy self-guided furniture. Dogs, however weirdly bred and mutant, are actually useful. The American Indians used them to pull loads before mules and horses arrived, and ancient hunters harnessed their instincts to help wipe out whole species, but mostly today they are guards, loyal biting sentinels, better than a state-of-the art burglar alarm and, depending on the breed and temperament, can wipe out whole bloodlines with ripping incisors. Such was the dog that shot at me like a fanged guided missile.

Mike Hammer would have punched the dog, taught it who was boss. Columbo would have tamed it. Phillip Marlowe would have shot it even though Chandler would have gotten a lot of hate mail about it. Even before John Wick, it was a well-known trope—never kill a dog. My own personal brand of hearty detective had me running like a shitting rabbit, but since my body shape was closer to Poirot's than Magnum's, I ran badly, and the dog was on me after two steps. He jumped at my neck mid-bark and got a mouthful of nylon and goose down. I heard jaws snap shut as he ripped my coat apart like a weed-weasel sliding down my back.

He bounced off me in a cloud of feathers, rebounded once, spit twice, and was at me again.

The beast's flying weight had pushed me forward into the gate, and I folded myself over it head-first just as Cujo's cousin nipped and, blessedly, missed my frozen toes.

When I say head-first, I mean it. I tried to catch myself on the pavement, but my sleeve caught on the fence. It ripped away but not in time to catch the fall. I landed on my left cheek, scraping it open on frozen forty-grit as I forced myself to somersault into the parked car, which naturally, in keeping with recent events, had an alarm that filled the air with sirens and flashing lights.

I slumped away at a trot, trailing a line of feathers and blood spatter toward my car, wondering why the dog didn't just leap over the fence and kill me then and there. I'm not sure I would have resisted. It would have just deserts for the shit job of sleuthing I was doing.

I got to my car just as three figures turned the corner of the driveway onto the sidewalk. Enzo pointed. Kelly squinted. Maddy stood akimbo. All three glowed malevolently red in the flashing tail lights of the startled luxury car, which I realized then was wildly out of place in that simple neighborhood.

I turned on my brights to blind them with halogen power and slammed into reverse. Okay, you can't really slam a Prius into any gear. You got this little tiny direction lever on the dash that encourages you to hold your pinky up when you touch it, but you get the point. Using my rear-facing camera, I clumsily but speedily reversed down the block and then around it to where I couldn't see my pursuers. A quick turnaround and I was blazing out of Provo at midnight, five miles per hour above the speed limit. Yeah, I was a rebel.

As I was getting on the freeway and my feet were finally getting warm, I became aware of the pain on my scraped face, and, horribly, I felt wet at the back of my neck. I reached back and touched the spot. I pulled my fingers to my mouth expecting to taste hot coppery blood. Nope. Cold dog slobber.

18

MY DETECTIVE INJURIES are usually internal—a personal failure, my feelings hurt. No wait. See what I did there? I was about to opine about poor me and lie to do it. Let's face it. If you've followed my career up to this point, you know my injuries are usually on the outside. Shot, stabbed, blown up. The inner child was fine, the middle-aged guy, not so much.

Before I crawled into bed that night, feeling alone in my house where I usually live contentedly alone, I had to shake my head at the crap trying to seep into my brain. I focused instead on my facial road rash. It had scabbed over by the time I got home, down feathers weaved in for added strength. I put a bandage on it anyway. Well, more like a bunch of them, a matching weave of little finger Band-Aids, which I criss-crossed over my face like an idiot trying to darn a sock.

I was surprisingly tired. I attributed it to actually doing something that took me off the couch and into the orbits of other people. Taxing, am I right?

I found my bed unmade but soft.

In the morning I woke, showered, fished the Band-Aids out of the drain, and got dressed. It was still early. Ten o'clock.

I thought about Randy and the mysterious Jelissa, kinda hoping, kinda fearing how my son's night went. He knows about the birds and bees. He's an internet kid. So he's seen things we people wouldn't believe, but still, I think he's a good kid. If anything, he's shy around girls. I bet it took him three hours to muster the courage to mis-text her to me.

On the other fronts, I had some good things going on two of my four cases. I had a line on Maddy, a little validation of Bryan Moland's fears. The strange house was not as damning as the liquor that went into it. Moland was a straight-laced Mormon. He mentioned he and Maddy already had a date to marry in the Draper Temple, a rite in the Mormon church reserved only for the most devout members. Among other things, to be worthy, one has to pay ten percent tithing, attend church, avoid premarital sex, and stay the hell away from alcohol. Last night, I'd seen a glass in Maddy's hand. It might just be a small secret vice that I myself have, one she was getting out of her system before the nuptials, but Moland might think it was a big deal. I'd have to take my own morals out of it, but If I found nothing else, I could at least relate my perilous adventures as a Peeping Tom.

On the bigger case, I was developing a timeline. Sandi Wong had arrived in Salt Lake, checked into a hotel with a "friend," and then left the next day. Where she went was what I needed to know. Nah, no actually, keep it straight, Tony. Where she *is* is the issue. See? Coffee. Makes my mind...uhm. You know—not dull...yeah...the other thing. Stabby. No. No...sharp! That's it. Sharp.

My next step there would be to talk to the "friend" tomorrow. Her Burmese family said they hadn't seen her, and it made sense. They were knee-deep in Sundance. I doubt she'd have found them at home last week, and without contacts or tickets ahead of time, the chances of her running into them at the festival itself was slim to none.

Munching on a protein bar with my second pot of coffee-flavored half and half, I fired up the old Macintosh and surfed. I couldn't find an address for Kyi Tun or Thiha or General Tayza. I tried about every permutation for the names I could think of, but my Google-fu was not up to the task of dealing with the complexities of Burmese naming chaos, so I wrote it off as good security on their part. They were exiles after all.

I texted Allie.

> Miss you!

Who this?

> Cute. You got your phone back!?

Lucky for you. I could have been a serial killer.

> That got dark.

I have a day full of parties. Terrance got us into the big show tonight.

> What show?

Awards thing.

> Cool.

Are you okay?

I took a selfie with my scabs and sent it to her.
She said:

> What the hell???

> Are those feathers?

I ate dog spit too.

> Did the Burmese do that to you?

No a mock-Mormon mutt.

> What?

Another case.

She said:

> I'll try to be home tonight.

> Probably late.

You're going home????? :-(

> Your home!

:-)

> <3

Stay away from Francis.

> >8-\

Oops.

Have fun!

But not too much.

> Grrrrr.

Remember when people actually used the phone function on their phones? Called people? How ancient that seems now. Why have actual communication when you can hunt and peck on a keyboard scrolling for emojis?

> Love you.

> Love you too.

I left it at that.

To be honest, if I hadn't been on my computer I'd probably have called Allie. Randy hates it when I call him, but my girlfriend is worldly. I saw her use a rotary phone once. Really. Rereading what I'd just sent her, I cringed to see my insecurity forever recorded in writing. Call next time.

I texted Randy:

> Sup?

> Chillin'

> When coming home?

> Later.

Text or voice, pummeling information out of a teenager is never easy.

> Where did you get those fishy Spells cards?

> I dunno. Around.

> Who's Jelissa?

I'd put Randy in a spot. He'd already used his one brush-off allowed each conversation to dodge the Spells information. Now, he was faced with talking about his personal life. Check. He went for the easier out.

> Most cards came from Little Wars. Legit.

I knew he knew I didn't know what he was talking about. He was doing the angsty teenager thing, minimum data for minimum interference. I Googled, though, and found it, a game store. There was the address. It was in a strip mall in Murray. Ha!

He said:

> You're not going over there are you?

> I might.

> Please don't.

> Why?

Just don't.

Who's Jelissa?

I could hear the grumble across the internet.

It's no big deal. Tournaments are dumb anyway.

Dodged again.

Love you.

TTYL

I considered putting mysterious Jelissa on my list of cases, but I had four more than I was used to, and I was already interfering with my son's life with one of them. I'd let him come to me when he was ready. This proud bit of adult parenting wisdom didn't come easy. Or too quickly. I Googled the name anyway and was offered corrected spellings for Melissa, Jennifer, and Ava. I left it alone.

Feeling the motivation only Colombia's finest free-trade brew can give, I did a quick search for Abergast in Ephraim.

They were both real names. Abergast was ancient from a time when people had buckles on their hats. Ephraim, for the non-Utahn, sounds like a fictional place where cultists still wear hats with buckles on them. It's a real place, no buckles, but still culty in the Utah-culty kind of way —conservative, Mormon, and well off the beaten track of freeways, airports, and twenty-first century culture. It is about as centered in the state as a mathematician could devise. Its claim to fame is Snow College—home of the Badgers—educating four thousand motivated students wanting to get their degrees and return to civilization as soon as possible, or at least a place where the sidewalks aren't rolled up at curfew. Maybe a place with dancing. Electric lights. Two horses. I'd never been to Ephraim, but I had a good idea what it was about. Ephraim is named after a Bible character famous for being a son of another Bible character.

It would take my day to drive down there and a week to recover from the culture shock, so I let my fingers do the walking. If you got that last reference, you're old.

I found a number and called the only Abergast I could find there.

"Hi," I said. "I'm looking for Glenn. Glenn Abergast."

"He ain't here."

"Do you know how I can get a hold of him?"

"What's this about?"

"Kinda personal."

"Hey, buddy, we all got burned by that. Glenn's broken up. Don't you go poking his pain. You'd have been out the stuff anyway."

My mind went to drugs. Whenever I think of teeny tiny little towns and wonder what people do there, how they fight the isolation and boredom, I always go to drugs. I go to drugs over other things too, like slow weeknights and vacations. Sometimes for concerts.

"Does he have a cell phone? I'd like to call him."

"Him or Tiffany?"

"Him."

"Is this about the stuff?"

"No no. I'm good. I just got back from Denver."

"He's up in Salt Lake, I guess."

"Do you know where? How about that phone number? Does he have a cell phone? Do you know what a cell phone is? It's like a cordless phone with really big range."

"What are you talking about?"

"It's complicated."

"Who are you?"

"Oh, I'm sorry. My name's Tony."

"So?"

"So...you asked."

"Uh-huh."

"Does the water there taste like pencils?"

"What?"

"Glenn's number," I said. "You were about to give it to me."

"You got a pen?"

"I do."

"Was that what you meant about pencils?"

"Yes. That was what I meant."

He gave the number, and I thanked him.

"It's not his fault," he said. "It's hers."

"What is?"

"The trouble."

"What trouble?"

"You really don't know?"

"No. That is why I asked."

"Well, it's not my place to talk about it."

"Are you from Ephraim originally?"

"Me and Glenn born and raised here."

"Brothers?"

"Better than that. Missionary companions. I'm housesitting for him while he's gone."

"You go to Snow?"

"No. I got a job. I'm a mechanic."

"Ah, I see," I said.

"I hear what you're thinking. Not to brag, but I made a hundred and twenty-three thousand dollars last year, after taxes. I bought the shop and eighty acres for a ranch."

"Oh. Well, good you don't brag."

"What do you make?"

"Gotta go. Bye."

That got weird. Should I rethink my vision of Ephraim and small towns in general?

Nah.

As I called the number I got thinking about drug deals, who Tiffany was, and how anyone turning a wrench could make so much money in the middle of nowhere.

"Hello?"

"Hi, Glenn? Glenn Abergast. My name is Tony Flaner."

"The detective?"

"You've heard of me?"

"From last night."

"Well, okay. Could be worse."

"Weren't you also mentioned in that great article about Chris Traard, super detective?"

"You saw that down in Ephraim, huh?"

"It went out on the wire. Our paper picked it up."

"Your paper picked it up?"

"My family owns it."

"Well, you should do a follow-up," I said.

"You know how to get a hold of Traard?"

I ground my teeth and took a deep, calming breath.

"I'm calling about last night," I said.

"What about it?"

"Why were you at the theater? Was it Madeleine you were trying to see?"

"That's kind of my business, isn't it?" His tone had gone from plain to defensive. Maybe hurt.

"It's all right," I said. "I'm a detective."

"How does that make it alright?"

He was quick.

"Can I buy you a cup of coffee?"

"I don't drink coffee."

"How about a burger and a milkshake? Two straws."

"I have to go to church," he said.

"You're driving back home?"

"Visiting one up in Alpine."

Alpine is a little stuck-up community between Park City and Provo. Very conservative, very wealthy.

Should I rethink calling every community I can't afford to live in stuck-up? Nah.

"You're staying at a B&B?" I asked.

"We have a house here," he said indignantly. "Goodbye, Mr. Flaner. I'm not in the mood."

"Meet me at a game store called Little Wars at two this afternoon. It's in Murray. We should talk."

"You know her?"

"You want to talk about it?"

"I gotta go," he said and hung up.

I began to see why the younger generation didn't like phone calls. I'd talked to two men from Ephraim today, and I'd misread both of them. The first one was obviously my own prejudice, but come on—six figures for spark plugs? Who saw that coming? Worse was Glenn Abergast. I expected a yokel there too, a potential drug dealer. Instead I think I stumbled onto some kind of small-town aristocrat. His family owns a house in Alpine? He has two houses? That's something only a very rich or a very stupid person would have. I have two, and I knew damn well which group I was in. Glenn, I had to figure for the other. His family owned a newspaper. Nothing says money to burn like the money pit of print media. I sensed beneath his groomed face an emotional wreck of a man probably dealing with impostor syndrome, girl worries, and house payments. I hoped he'd come to the meeting. We had much in common.

19

LIKE CERTAIN OTHER COPYRIGHT-PROTECTED GAMES, Spells has the affectionate nickname of "cardboard crack," so I naturally lit upon it for a meeting with Glenn Abergast, whom I assumed was a drug dealer. It was all a plan. It had nothing to do with the fact that the tab for the store just happened to be open on my browser at the very second I needed a place to meet Glenn Abergast. That was just a coincidence. Totally.

I went to the high school reunion website page and saw a big picture of Francis Tomas right there. He was in between two starlets, a Sundance Film Festival photo backdrop behind them. The theme of the reunion was *What have you been up to?* The picture was Francis' answer. Which reminded me, it was garbage night.

Sundance was ending today. That was something. I'd have Allie back, maybe. I hoped. The thought of spending time with her was a good thought, and I focused on that while I tore black garbage sacks with pizza box corners and rolled the big lovely, life-saving garbage can to the curb. Okay, it was like twenty-four hours before it needed to be there, but it showed how ultra-responsible I could be.

I drove to the store with the windows open, trying to suck the down feathers out from last night, but catching a good plenty with my clothes, hair, mouth, eyes. White feathers whirled around me like I was in a Toyota snow globe.

I arrived a few minutes before my scheduled meeting with Abergast. I wanted to scope it out, work on the counterfeit case before refocusing an another. Two cases were paying; two were personal. I probably should have put the Francis Tomas case in the dumpster beside the pie boxes, between the coffee grounds and banana peels, but I knew it would eat at me until I could figure it out. I had the terrible feeling that what I was searching for in that case was not out there, but in here. The problem to solve was not a California success but a Utah failure. Me. The drive over to the store had me worrying I wasn't up to the task of any of it. When I pulled into the parking lot I felt like I'd been hit by a floundering freight train.

Murray is midway between north and south of the Salt Lake valley. It's eastish now because the west side of the valley only opened up for subdivisions in my lifetime. For a while Murray was dead center in the valley. It's where the hospital is, where the freeways cross. It contains State Street and Main. It had a reputation for being a rundown, crime-ridden, crack-house haven at one time, but now it's gentrified. The hospital helped that, as did active police and soaring land prices. Older people think of car lots when they think Murray, but most have all moved south now. It has a good indoor mall where ranger-hatted zealots buy their reasonably priced jackboots for work and leave other shoppers alone.

Little Wars Hobby & Card was not in that mall but another, one hearkening back to the crack house days. The strip mall showed age in its architect, which had studied the box store method of the seventies but flared creativity with higher eaves and pastel colors. Though recently renovated with new pinkish paint and a big sign proclaiming in twisted English its identity as "Murray Shop Place," it stank of low rent. Don't believe me? There was a karate studio anchoring one end, a nail salon at the other, a laundromat in between. There were, however, cars in the parking lot in front of the game store on a Sunday, a testament to location, product, and the relaxation of Utah's blue laws.

I know game stores. I haunted them as a kid buying the newest D&D books, board games and even Spells cards. Though Randy is in phases now, I have to admit he's often recognizable as a chip off the old block. I'd never been to Little Wars, but the name had an echo of table-top battle games where you move little painted men across felt, making laser sounds as you roll dice to determine the outcome of your turn. *Pew pew pew!* Good times.

My happy recollections of wasted Saturday afternoons were quickly erased by the pungent smell of eye-sizzling body odor. I'm telling you, folks, there's a stereotype about it for a reason. It was a tough call: carcinogenic city air or foul man-musk? Carbon fluorocarbons or crusty gym socks and urine stains?

I held in the doorway, contemplating the state of my lungs, when a guy behind the counter yelled at me. "Hey, in or out? You don't pay for the heat here."

He was late twenties, dark-haired, medium complexion, built like me with a little belly, in a black T-shirt and jeans. He wore a snarl on his lip, which almost sent me out to the two-pack-a-day "air," but I remembered I was on a case, and I was good enough, and gosh darn it, people liked me.

The second I was inside and the door shut, he turned his back to me and returned to a video monitor, where I could see he was playing a game with cartoon swordsmen and hoppity monsters with too many eyes. I wondered if theirs were watering too.

I slipped in between shelves of European board games and poker chip sets, slowly working my way inside.

Beyond the racks were tables with people playing Spells. About a dozen guys in six games were shuffling and turning cardboard in their own copyrighted world. An unused table had model terrain pieces. No battling there. I figured out why when I came to the wall of miniature army models. A single model, a lieutenant by the packaging, which stood about an inch tall with base, plastic, supplied unpainted and unassembled, cost fifty-five dollars. When I was playing, the piece would have been three ninety-five, and I'd have thought long and hard about it before slapping down my money.

"Who the hell can afford this game?" I muttered.

"They get ya by the short ones," came a reply. It was one of the players. A rare slender one, gaunt even, at a table shuffling cards. I couldn't be sure, but I thought that he might have a different odor than the others, a less objectionable one, but just as sharp. He had a black beard ending in a point and a see-through mustache on his lip. His dark hair was slick and pulled back into a ponytail.

"Winning?" I asked.

"Often."

"Did you go to the tournament?"

"I did."

"How'd you do?"

"Round of thirty-two."

"Win anything?"

"A box of boosters."

"Mulligan," said his opponent, looking at his cards before shuffling them again. A mulligan, I remembered, is when you hate your starting hand. Calling one gets a chance to reshuffle and draw new again. It's a do-over. The term came from golf, which was as close to an outdoor activity as ninety percent of Spells players would ever get.

"Why are you covered in feathers?"

"I got caught selling snake oil," I said.

"Where's the tar?"

"They're going green," I said. "Aloe vera paste."

"Ah."

"I'm looking for singles." In any other venue, I'd either be paired with another skier or get a phone number with stars by it. Here, it had a different meaning.

"Talk to Curt," he said and tossed a thumb to the guy at the counter.

"Hey Curt," I said. "I understand you got hot singles in my neighborhood."

"What?" he said. "What do you want?" With clear impatience bordering on anger, rearing up toward rage, he paused his game and turned to look at me.

"Spells singles?"

"I pay seventy-five percent of SpellsTracker's listing up to a hundred dollars, but I'm the final word on condition."

"I'm buying," I said.

"I charge ninety percent of SpellsTracker's listing, making me the cheapest store ever. There's my big-ticket selection." He pointed to a glass cabinet and went back to his game.

I squatted to look through the glass. He returned to clobbering a spider with a side of ham.

The cards in the case were all in clear sleeves with colored stickers on them, red, blue, green and yellow. I was going to ask what the colors meant when I saw the sign in the corner. *Red, heavily played. Yellow, lightly played. Green, near mint. Blue, Special—ask Curt.* Most were marked as yellow and green, even ones I'd have called heavily played. One card was held together with tape. That was the only red one I saw. I knew many of the cards from my days of the game, when my ever-changing hobby had me piling and filing cards in my living room. They were dear then, not plastic lieutenant dear, but still wallet busting for a starving college kid. I could only imagine what they were now. They were stacked overlapping, so I couldn't see the corner with a possible ego signature on any but the top ones.

I straightened up, expecting Curt to be there waiting to get a card out for me, but nope. He was still clubbing away with a bone.

"Goddamn son of a bitch. Fuck!" Curt yelled. "Cheatin' shit game fuck!"

My mind went to Dara, and I thought of hooking her up, but I was aware that much of the smell in my charred nasal passages was coming from him.

"Does the owner know you swear like that?" I said.

"I am the owner."

"How's the store doing?" I said, wondering how he was still open with such gracious manners.

"You buying anything?" He didn't say the words as much as spat them at me.

"My son says he bought some counterfeit cards from you. He was tossed out of the tournament Friday because of them."

"Get out of here," he said and pointed to the door.

"Bring out some cards. I want to look at them."

"I said get out."

"Listen, I'm not leaving until I get some—"

His face went cherry-bomb red and shaking, he walked into the back room. When he returned, he carried a double-bladed battle axe.

"Going to a cosplay?" I said.

"Motherfucker!" His eyes were wild. His fingers were twitching.

"Hey hey—"

"Beat it, dude," Bearded Guy said. "He's not having a good life."

I left just as Curt, aptly named, came out from around the counter. He lifted his weapon above his head and gouged off a piece of ceiling. Plaster rained on his head, getting into his wild red eyes. I noticed there were several previous gouges above him.

I fled.

He didn't follow me out, but the bearded guy did a moment later. He found me at my car just as a big Mercedes Benz rolled into the parking lot, driven by a clean-cut young man in a dress shirt and tie. It made slow circles around the parking lot, looking suspicious and suspiciously, but didn't stop right away.

"What the hell happened in there?" I said to the goatee.

"Curt sucks, but he does have the cheapest cards."

"Did you hear me mention the forgeries?"

"Yeah. Sorry about your son."

"Is that why they're so cheap? Forgeries?"

"No. Bulk. He buys crates of the stuff and has a hot online store with fair prices."

"But the counterfeits?"

"He'll buy anything from anyone. There's this one kid who I think is raiding his father's collection, bringing in sweet cards about once a week. Way out of his bracket. But Curt buys them, no questions asked."

"So that's how he stays in business. It's not his friendly customer rapport?"

"He used to be real nice once, when he first opened. Then he realized he had a job. Success is killing him. Poor guy."

"Poor guy with a battle axe."

"Yeah, bad day. His manager was supposed to come in. But blew him off for skiing. He's behind on his orders, and that new game is kicking his ass. Tough on him. Try to see his side."

"That would be the side with the wooden handle, yeah?"

"Yeah, but he has his good side too."

"Is that what you came out to tell me? That Curt is really an okay guy? Don't press charges? Stay off Yelp?"

"Yeah, that, and something else."

"What?"

He glanced at the car just parking in front of the Clean Jeans Coin-Op Laundromat and sidled in real close to me. I recognized the scent now. He said, "You want to buy some drugs?"

I BOUGHT an eighth of homegrown Mary Jane to do the guy a favor. The market for closet herb had been seriously cut by the legalization of recreational pot in Colorado. I'm all for supporting local business, so I did my part and slipped the baggie into my pocket just as the car pulled up to the curb, selfless hero that I am.

"Mr. Abergast?" I said, approaching the car.

"I wasn't sure this was the right place. Seems kind of seedy. Aren't those crash pylons?"

I looked at the curb in front of Little Wars. There was indeed a row of five three-foot-high cement pylons. None of the other stores had them. I'd seen them before in front of banks, payday lenders, jewelry stores, and computer shops, but never for a game store. They were meant to stop crash-and-grabs, that lovely fad of driving a stolen car through the front of a store and snatching everything you can before the cops show up. I remembered how expensive some Spells cards were—in the tens of thousands of dollars for the right one in the right set in the right condition. Smell-challenged Curt, I decided, wasn't as crazy stupid as he acted. It helped explain the battle axe too—not swinging it on me for taking up floor space, but for having it in the shop in the first place.

"Should we go inside?" He opened the door to Little Wars.

"I don't think that's—"

A gush of stink pushed Glenn Abergast backward like a fire hose.

"Oh my gosh," he said.

"Like crusty gym shorts and urine puddles."

"I was going to go with hobo's jockstraps and fish curry Dumpster."

"That's good too," I said. "Really good, actually."

"What was that?"

"Gamer funk. They sell it in aerosol cans."

"For what?"

"Girlfriend repellent."

"Really?"

"No," I said solemnly, shaking my head in shame. "I was making a joke. Sorry, Glenn. Don't take it too hard."

I could see he was confused.

"I'm confused," he said.

"That's one of my superpowers. Your resistance has been compromised by olfactory assault. Let's go over here."

I opened the door to the laundromat and was again hit by a wall of smell. They were every bit as strong but not nearly as offensive. Soap smells— clean, floral, sanitary. Bleach in a spring meadow. Visions of snowy hills like in the commercial. Stuffed bears plummeting into towels, happy mothers sniffing sheets. It was better than the game store, but I'm not sure it was any healthier. Hey, what if the laundromat pumped its air into the game store? Would the two ends of the spectrum meet and counter each other, leaving bland but breathable atmosphere? Or would they mingle and create a new malaise, a fresh-scented toxin reminiscent of troll farts in Rivendell? Something to ponder. Maybe there's a patent to be had.

There were two people inside the laundromat, both sitting in front of industrial dryers that could hold La-Z-Boys. One was a frazzled new mother rocking a baby on her lap, her hair six kinds of disarray, makeup more an afterthought than a repair. She looked up at us with red sleep-deprived eyes that begged for death. The other person was a twenty-something man, not too unlike the guy who'd just sold me pot. He wore trendy jeans that looked like they'd been fed through an Arkansas combine and left in the sun for the harvest season. He had a faded logo T-shirt under a blue sweatshirt. Apple, with the colored stripes. Old school. Narrow glasses, earbuds, eight o'clock shadow and a venti caramel mocha if I could decipher the Starbucks code on the side of his cup. He looked at me like I'd just stolen his last chalupa.

I led Glenn to the washing machine side, and we sat down.

"So you're rich?" I said.

"Is that what you want to talk about?"

"No. Well maybe. Sure. No. No. Let's not. You're good-looking too. Do you know that?"

"I'm confused."

"Welcome to the laundromat."

"Still confused. Did you call my mission companion?"

"I called the number I found for you and someone not you answered. He said he was your mission companion and told me how much he made a year."

"That's Jerry. He's sensitive about money. He's always compared himself to me."

"Since you're rich?"

"My family is."

"And you're part of the family?"

"Yes."

"So, using the transitive property of mathematical but not financial equality, you are rich."

"I guess I am," he said, almost ashamed. "Big fish in a little pond."

"Ephraim?"

He nodded. "We're an original pioneer family. I'm kind of the black sheep."

"Are they cutting you off?"

"No, but they raise eyebrows at some of my choices."

"Like what?"

"Well...hey. Why am I telling you any of this? It's none of your business."

"It's okay. I'm a detective." I gave Glenn one of my business cards, and it seemed to make him feel better.

"Tiffany," he said.

"Who's Tiffany?"

"My fiancée. My ex-fiancée," he said.

He looked over my shoulder and out the window as confusion returned to his face.

"What?" I said.

"That car has circled the parking lot like six times. It was across the street at that taco place when I came here."

"You circled the parking lot a couple of times."

"I was thinking."

"Maybe he's thinking too. Ever think of that?"

"What, uhm, okay. Sure."

Me the detective. Ever alert as a squashed moon pie, I hadn't noticed the obvious blue Honda circling my location like a starved buzzard. My lead had to point it out to me.

"You alright?"

"I'm not a fraud," I said.

"What?"

"Uhm...so, Tiffany?"

"I met her at a church event. An ice cream social for the singles ward."

"In Ephraim?"

"Yes. Back home. She was new in town. Working at the grocery story. We hit it off right away. We were so perfect together."

"Back up. At the theater last night—"

"I was there to see Tiffany."

"You mean Madeline?"

"Same person."

"How?"

"I guess Madeline is her stage name. Her real name is Tiffany. Tiffany Jones."

The blue Honda cruised close past my Prius.

He looked at me earnestly, clasped his hands together and looked even more earnest. "Have you ever been in love, Mr. Flaner? Love...love...it's so...lovely."

"Yes," I said, weeping inwardly for Keats. "Yes, it is."

"We were perfect for each other. We would hold hands in the soda shop and go for walks in the park. We'd talk for hours. We wanted the same things—marriage in the temple, big reception, kids, grandkids. We picked the date."

"How long between when you met her to when you were engaged?"

"Oh, a long time," said Glenn. "Four weeks."

"That's a long time?"

"Jerry got married two weeks after he got back from his mission."

"Four weeks would look long compared to that. How old are you?"

"Old. Twenty-four."

"And Tiffany?"

"Twenty-five, but the age difference didn't matter. We were so compatible."

"How could you tell?" I knew they hadn't had sex. Temple marriage and timing put that right out. How anyone knows they're compatible with a lifetime mate before fondling each other's naughty bits is beyond me.

"We liked the same china pattern."

"Of course."

"We picked all new housewares—bathroom, towels, even new furniture."

"You didn't have all that?"

"She was okay with the house but wanted to put our own touches on it."

"The house?"

"We have a little five-thousand square-foot place in Ephraim."

"On ten acres?"

"Twenty."

"Ah, well, it's always rough when you start out." I wondered what the world looked like from his wealthy watering eyes.

"Jilted you at the altar?"

"Yes." His lip quivered when he said it.

"Another man?"

"She said it just wouldn't work. She said it was all me."

"That's a new angle," I said. "And you got saddled with all the stuff, chairs and china?"

"No. That was all part of our registry."

"Uhm, so uhm…can I, uhm…ask you a personal question?"

"Isn't that what you've been doing?" he said.

"Actually, you just spilled everything and I was here to catch it."

"What's the question?"

"How much money did she get from you?"

"Nothing."

"Come on."

"A few dinners. A trip."

"A ring? I bet you gave her a nice ring."

"She gave it back."

"Wait…"

"If she'd have married me, she'd have been well off."

"Only if she could be satisfied with a small barony."

"We would have been happy."

"Your family has position?"

He nodded and wiped snot on his sleeve.

The Honda pulled back around.

"What was your missionary pal talking about, then, when he said stuff?"

"The registry."

"What about it?"

"There's a mix-up with it all. Macy's problem."

"What problem?"

"Returns. I mean, there were eight hundred twenty-six invitations sent out. Of course there'd be confusion."

"You know that many people?"

"My parents do. They reached out to everyone in the ward and the next one over and the next to that. You know. A wedding. Ephraim was small, and the whole town was invited."

I had visions of Don Corleone collecting envelopes at his daughter's nuptials. I substituted weepy-son Glenn for naive daughter Connie and the envelopes of money for tri-folded ink-jet screenshots of items to expect from Macy's home delivery truck, but otherwise it was pretty close.

"Is your father's name Don?"

"Yes."

"Don Abergast?"

"Yes."

"Powerful man, does favors for people, speaks funny?"

"He had a stroke, but he's healing nicely. His personal secretary, Tom, helps him."

"Hagen?"

"No, Olsen."

Pretty close.

"So, how does your family feel about this whole thing?" I said.

"To be honest, they're relieved." He sniffed and wiped tears.

"Vengeful?"

"What? No. Heck no."

"So why are you chasing her?"

"I told you. Because I love her and I can change—I will change. I want to change for her. Have you any idea what I mean?"

"I wish I didn't," I said.

The Honda pulled up behind my Prius and stopped. A door opened. A hooded figure got out and crouched behind my car.

"Okay, what the actual hell?"

I got up and left the laundromat. Glenn was crying, the mother staring, the hipster was staring malevolently.

"Hey, buddy!" I yelled.

A head popped up between the two cars.

About ten yards away, I hesitated, unsure what I was looking at. The figure hovered like a meerkat panning for hyenas. The head bobbed and shifted, twitched to me, until mirrored aviator sunglasses aimed into my soul. Reflective even in the smog, they hovered over a big bushy black beard and mustache, all framed under a ball cap beneath the hood.

"What are you?" I said.

My words spooked it. It spun around and leaped into the Honda. Gloved hands gripped the steering wheel as the car lurched into gear and then screeched away, leaving a black skid on the pavement and burnt rubber stink to mix with its cousins in the gloom.

"Huh…"

I heard noise behind me. Glenn was getting in his car.

"Where are you going?"

"I've got things to do. I'm led by my heart. She is everything."

"Dude, you need to get laid."

"Shut your potty mouth!"

And with that the Ephraim heir pulled away just as the Honda had— skid, cloud, stain, and gone.

"Huh…"

I scanned the parking lot, looking for ideas when a first-generation silver Prius pulled up in front of the game store's columnar barrier, and a tall lanky guy with long gray hair pulled back in an elastic got out and stretched.

He looked familiar to me. I felt that under different circumstances I'd know instantly who he was, like running into your favorite grocery store checker in the sex shop.

He bent his neck back and forth, working out a crick, I supposed, and then walked up to the door, opened it and went in.

A half second later, he was outside again, rubbing his eyes.

An intrepid adventurer, I saw him take a deep breath of brown air and go back inside.

I coughed and cleared room in my own lungs for new atrocities and heard steps behind me.

"Why you standing in the middle of the road, dude?" said the hipster from the dryers.

"It's where I stopped. Since no one has driven me down, I figured I had time to decide my next move."

"You have a way with people. Two cars screamed away from you like a bat out of hell."

"Maybe it's the shoes," I said.

He looked at my shoes. I watched the store.

"There are feathers on you."

Through the store window, I saw the gray-haired man talk to the owner, who looked pretty peeved. No axe, but red-faced and jerky motions.

"I saw you do a drug deal out here," the man said.

I dropped my chin to my chest and tried to remember if the county jail served creamed beef or turkey surprise on Sunday nights. I guess I wasn't the only one who'd figured out game store parking lots were good for drug deals.

"I should have known better," I said. "Low rent strip mall parking lot, store based on addiction. If I were a cop, I'd stake it out too. Got your quota yet?"

The gray-haired man exited the store, holding a white cardboard card box.

"And buy a can of Lysol!" he yelled back.

Like a robot, Curt the storekeeper rose from his chair and went into the back.

"You want to get involved in that?"

"No way," he said. "Curt's crazy."

I remembered reading that cops are not actually required to protect people. There was an incident in a subway where two cops watched a guy get stabbed and did nothing. Eye-opener, that one.

I turned my open eyes to my companion.

"Can I see your badge?" I said.

"I don't have a badge. I'm not a cop. Wait. Are you? You have to tell me if you are."

"I don't think that's true, but I'm not a cop, take that as you will."

"I didn't think you were. Those feathers."

Curt emerged from the back room not with an axe but a blue aerosol can. He raised it over his head and spun a circle, spraying into the air.

"Huh..."

The silver Prius backed out, pulled away, and joined traffic in a sensible, electric way.

The hipster cleared his throat again.

"What is it you want?" I said.

"Like, uh...I saw you buy drugs out here before."

"And...?"

"You want to buy some more?"

I DON'T KNOW what I'd bought. The dryer-fresh hipster swore it was organic and botanical, but it looked industrial. It was a beige powder in a small plastic Ziploc bag, the kind that cheap earrings from Amazon come in. It could have been a crushed pill, could have been distilled from a cane, it could have been the ashes of a phoenix, but he swore it was fungus of some kind.

"It's from Chile," he said with a wink. "From high in the mountains. You get it?" He nodded knowingly.

I nodded in agreement. "Absolutely not," said I.

"Yeah…"

It was cheap. A couple sawbucks, more support for the local economy. And it was organic. Go Earth.

When I got in my car to leave around five, I got a text from Randy.

Can you pick me up?

Where are you?

Kevin's.

Send address.

He did.
I said:

Wait

> Where's your car?

I don't know.

> What?

I don't know.

> What???

I said I don't know.

> Where did you last see it?

In front of the hospital in a handicapped stall.

> I think I know where your car is.

Yeah

> Why were you at the hospital?

Visiting someone.

> Who?

Someone.

> Jelissa?

He texted me Kevin's address again.

> I'll be there in twenty

Said I.

Here was a new twist to the day. My son had managed to get his fifty-thousand dollar car towed by parking in what is probably the only illegal spot in the state on a Sunday.

New mystery.

I kept a belated eye open for blue Hondas as I drove to pick up my son. All had been clear as I pulled into the driveway of a modern stucco McMansion, sure no one had followed me. Pretty sure. Kinda.

I honked the horn to let Randy know I was there. When the door didn't open, I honked again. Then, for variety and to make sure they didn't mistake me for a traffic accident, I did shave and haircut. My little car has a cute little voice, I thought.

The door opened, and Randy stepped out looking enraged and humiliated. My parental defenses kicked in and I wanted to jump out of the car, storm up to the house, and kick the shit out of whoever had done that to my son. I would actually never have done that, not my style. Maybe hurt their feelings, but you get the idea. Instinct.

When I caught my son's eye, I knew my fury was misplaced. He was pissed at me.

"Dammit, Dad. What is wrong with you?" he said, slamming the door as he got in.

"Yeah, I got this injury here on my cheek doing detective stuff. See the feathers? It doesn't hurt now, though. Thanks for asking. How was your night?"

He snapped his belt on and crossed his arms over his chest. His eyes were fixed out the front.

I backed out and aimed homeward. We drove in silence for a while. I tried a couple of sure-fire conversation starters. "Come here often?" "Sure is a lot of weather we're having." "How about that sports team?"

He put in earbuds, and I was exiled to the silent zone.

I didn't know what we were fighting about. The clue was "what is wrong with me?" The list was too long and, recent feelings aside, I wasn't then in the mood to inventory all my faults.

We pulled into the garage, and he was inside before I'd unbuckled.

I found the door to his room closed. I knocked on it. I knocked harder.

"The door's locked," he said. We had a rule that if someone's door was locked, they're to be left alone. It was a throwback to sexy days with his mother but had turned into a useful space-creating ritual.

"Sorry. I didn't check," I mumbled, testing the doorknob. Yep. Locked. "Are you going to want dinner?"

"Ate at Kevin's," he said as curtly as you please.

I wanted to ask about the car, Jelissa, what specifically I had done to piss him off, but figured those topics might be too heavy through the sacred locked door. "You going to bed then?"

"Uh-huh."

It was damn early for bed, but time is relative, and my relative needed space.

I felt I couldn't leave without at least a little more information. "How are you getting to school tomorrow?" A tactical question, not about the missing car but also not about the missing car.

Low and mumbly from behind the barrier, "Can you drive me?"

"Sure thing."

Silence.

I left him alone.

I called Allie. Called—no text this time.

"Oh, hey, Tony, I can't talk right now" was how she answered.

"Okay."

We hung up. I hadn't heard anything in the background but sheepishly remembered that she was at an awards dinner tonight.

I texted:

> Love you.

> Love you too. See you tomorrow.

> Tomorrow? I thought you were coming tonight!!

> Can't :-(

> Shit.

> Sorry.

That one hurt. I was really looking forward to seeing her, to talk though the Randy angst if possible, bounce clues off her, do the beast with two backs, but alas, such was not to be.

I forced down this new disappointment with all the rest, real and imagined, and told myself to adult up.

I poured a stiff bourbon, splashed it with club soda for plausible deniability, and ordered two pizzas—one for me, one to lure my son out of his cave.

The bourbon tasted good, refreshing, but I wondered if I couldn't be improved with the little baggie from the laundromat.

I sat down for some cerebral work, using Poirot's little gray cells to suss shit out.

The big case was totally stalled, and I couldn't think of anything to do until I visited Archibald Lewis tomorrow, a.k.a. Mr. Smith at KimCo Construction, last person I know to have seen Sandi Wong.

I'd fucked up the Spells cards case by pissing off the easily piss-offable owner of the store. I would have liked to have examined all his big cash cards in the display for possible forgeries, knowing what to look for. It might have given me an excuse to use the oversized magnifying glass Allie had given me for Christmas à la cartoon Sherlock Holmes.

Allie.

The name summoned a sigh and another drink. The baggie was empty. There were pale dregs in the bottom of my glass.

Oh yeah...

Allie had her own life and career, and what she was doing now—networking, mingling even, God help me for imagining it, innocent flirting—was part of it. This was not about me. My disappointment was selfish. I could see that. It preyed upon my insecurity, so...yeah, I was in familiar territory.

Another drink and I turned to the ugly case that had the most traction. Madeline Smith, a.k.a. Tiffany Jones.

Using my superpowers of internet, I found Tiffany and Glenn's Macy's cached wedding registry page. It was formidable but now off-line.

Just for fun, I searched Madeline's and Bryan's. Theirs was active and also at Macy's. I noticed many of the same things on both lists. The same pattern of Wedgewood china, the same stand-up mixer, the same top-of-the-line hoover vacuum. Couches were a little different, throw rugs a different pattern, but the mahogany four-post bed was the same.

I realized then as I poured another drink that, depending on my client's jealousy tolerance, I probably had enough reasonable doubt-destroying evidence to torpedo the nuptials. I surfed over to the theater page as my ears began to ring.

I poured more soda, stirring the grit up from the bottom. A little chalky.

The ringing grew louder.

My hangover was getting an early start. It switched to thumps, knocks, and banging.

I closed my eyes, trying to settle my fogged mind. I'd had half a fifth and some soda water—oh, and specimen unknown. So this was not wholly unexpected, but it was early.

I covered my ears and was surprised to learn that helped. Ever the detective, that was my first clue.

I turned to the entranceway. It was good and dark outside. I think it had been for a while.

"Tony? You there? Dude…"

I stumbled to the front door and opened it.

"Tony," said the man at the door. "Did you fall asleep?"

I looked at the pizza guy, remembering his name from many previous visits. "Cassidy," I said. "Damn good to see you. How'd you know to bring pizza?"

"You ordered it."

"Ah, good thinking." He pushed his way past me and put the pies in the kitchen. "You should just leave a key out here for me."

"No way," I said. "I am the soul of responsibility."

Cassidy helped himself to a beer out of my fridge.

"Is this enough monies?" I said, offering him my cash.

He plucked a couple bills off the stack and stuffed them in his fanny pack. At least, I hoped it was a fanny pack.

"Take it easy, Tony. No driving tonight."

"I'm in for the duration."

"By the way, there's a car parked up the street with a guy in it."

"Blue Honda?"

"Yeah. Friend of yours?"

"Let's find out."

I followed Cassidy to the door, or rather I leaned on him as he shuffled forward. He pointed up the street, and, like on cue, lights popped on and a car screeched away in reverse.

"Huh."

"Huh what?" asked Cassidy.

"I know that move," I said. "I did it last night."

"Putting a car in reverse? Pretty expert."

"Did I tip you?"

"Oh yes."

"Remind me not to next time."

"Bye."

Cassidy got in his beat-up POS and left me on the porch.

I waited for a minute to see if the Honda would come back, if Allie would appear, or the world end. When none of that transpired, I was drawn back inside by the seductive scent of jalapeño and onion pizza.

———

"Dad, come on. We'll be late."

I rolled over to see Randy standing in the doorway of my room. He was dressed and stressed. I was half in my clothes, half in a knot, with no recollection of what happened after that first slice of pizza.

"What happened?"

"Don't you remember?"

"Yes, of course I do," I said. "I just like asking questions everyone knows the answer to so no one is threatened."

"You drank. A lot. You surfed for hours. You ate pizza. You threw up a little."

"I think I remember that," I said, feeling the acid-peeled enamel-less patches on my teeth.

"You poured yourself into bed, and now you're waking up. You almost got one shoe off, but not the other. That's why your pants are bunched up like that."

"Good. I'm caught up."

"You said you'd drive me to school, remember?"

"I do."

"Come on, I want to get to class early."

"My boy, the scholar."

"Ehhhh. Dad, don't pressure me."

"Don't be so sensitive. Or loud. Do I have time for a shower?"

"A quick one."

"Go get a piece of pizza for breakfast."

"It's gone."

"Oh." My Randy bait had worked, apparently.

"There're some waffles in the freezer."

"I know."

"And a fresh bottle of syrup in the pantry, Mr. Attitude."

He left my doorway in an angsty huff.

"Hormones," I mumbled.

"I heard that."

"And?"

"I don't want to be late."

I got ready as fast I could, brushing my teeth twice and medicating with Advil.

Randy was waiting for me in the car. His face was bent over his phone.

"Did you vacuum the car?" I asked.

"You did."

"Where's my purple pleather purse and bisexual actor envelope?"

"I saw them in the freezer."

"Really?"

"Yeah."

"Did I have fun?"

He shrugged and I pulled out of the garage. The door shrieked in metal pain.

"It's not even light out," I said.

"It's winter, Dad."

"What kind of villains make people get up before noon?"

"We don't all have your life."

"What's with all the snark?"

"I thought that was funny."

"Did you? Did you really? Did you workshop it? What were the focus group scores?"

"Okay. I'm sorry, Dad."

I didn't ask him what for. I was happy just to have that much and used it to heal up all the little teenager stabs he'd thrown me.

"So I'll need to pick you up after school too?"

"One of the guys can drive me home."

"Tell me about your car." I'd waited as long as I could.

"I screwed up, I guess. I parked in the wrong place. It got towed."

"That was pretty dumb," I said.

He glared at me. "I'll handle it," he said.

"When?"

"When I handle it."

"You're doing it again, Randy."

"I'll handle it."

We pulled up to the curb. "Love you, kid. Have a good day."

"Thanks. Love you too."

Just as the door shut, I asked, "What did I do to piss you off, by the way?" I rolled down his window. "Yesterday."

He looked around as if seeing who was listening and then slumped back.

"You don't honk your horn like that."

"You don't?"

"No."

"I was supposed to come to the door?"

"Hell no."

"I'm lost," I said.

"Text, Dad. Just text when you're outside. It's how it's done."

He turned and, lowering his head, went inside.

I waited a moment, stunned. Someone behind me honked to go.

"Text me, you jerk!" I screamed out the window before pulling forward.

As I was turning out of the parking lot, a phone chirped.

Swerving to miss an elm that jumped right out in front of me, I fished Randy's phone out from under the seat. A text appeared.

> **Meet me in the prep room at lunch.**

It was from Jelissa.

22

THE MESSAGE DISAPPEARED, and not having Randy's code, face, or retinas, I couldn't bring it back up.

I might be too old to know that honking is an affront to the new generation, but I did have an inkling of the panic my son would go through when he realized he didn't have his phone. Is there a better example of modern terror than the sudden soul-puckering sweaty panic that comes from reaching into your phone pocket and coming up empty? Adrenaline rush, accusations, a new dialogue with God in the quest for our lost bionic selves.

I found visitor parking right up front. The student parking lot extended to the horizon behind me. From there came shambling shapes from the gloom, shuffling for the school like zombies smelling brains. It's not often I get such an apt metaphor as that, so I was feeling good when I went inside.

"Hey," I said to the woman at the office. "I'm Tony Flaner, and I need to see my son."

"Classes haven't started yet."

"Okay. Can you look up his schedule? I'm sure I'll find him chilling in his homeroom. Probably doing homework. He forgot something and he'll want it."

"His phone? He's not supposed to have his phone in school. Some teachers confiscate them. It's in the school contract everyone signed. Students and parents." She squinted at me through her glasses. "You're not bringing him a phone, are you?"

"No," I said. "His insulin."

Her face went flat. She tapped a keyboard.

"Art with Mr. Smith. Hall C, room 102."

"C-102. Got it."

I'd been to the school before for parent-teacher conferences, a complete waste of an evening where I stood in line for three hours to talk to a teacher who confirmed that everything I saw online was accurate. "Your son was tardy twice, absent once and got a B+ on the last quiz." Egads! The only revelation was that the teacher had lost most of her hair and all her smile since the official yearbook photo was taken.

The halls were filling up with half-asleep teenagers moving in slow waves and ripples hither and yon. The density wasn't thick enough for actual class, so I knew I had some time. When school was in session for real, the waves would be walls of people. Utah invented then perfected the concept of school overcrowding. The state has a birthrate of a third-world nation and the infrastructure to match.

The C hall was the arts hall. It sloped downward to the near basement, reflecting the employment future of those who chose this path. I found the room and peeked inside. There was my son and his friends, and there too was the guy I'd seen at Little Wars the day before, his gray ponytail elasticized back on his head. He was chatting with the boys.

I slinked inside. I can be slinky when I need to be.

"The facade has fallen," he said. "They were much better off working in the shadows, but once they got the reins, their vile evil greediness was clear to see. Tax cuts could have been shared with the middle class to hide the real winners, but noooo. In these last days of empire, the emperor walks with no clothes, and we all have new glasses to see it."

They were in a circle, Mr. Smith the teacher at the head like a kind of guru. He saw me.

"Don't I know you?"

"Yes," I said. "I'm the mixed-metaphor police. We need to talk."

He looked confused, then laughed bright and loud. "Sure."

Randy stared at me with wide, accusing eyes. Rage and embarrassment. Another fatherly faux pas. I dug into my pocket and passed him his phone. His hand dropped to his pocket, and sweat burst from every visible pore, his eyes went wild, crazy, panicked; he was about to scream through gnashing teeth, cursing the god who made him, but then smiled gratefully on my outstretched hand.

He brought up missed messages and eyed me askance. I ignored it.

"You're Randy's father, right?"

"Right."

I moved away from the group and encouraged him to follow me. I think he understood. My dad aura was disrupting my son's coolness chakra.

The classroom was actually two classrooms combined. Half had tables with computers on them but big enough to actually open a book on and write. On the other half was a collection of 3D printers and copiers, scanners, gizmos and gadgets and all types of technological art machines. A plotter was silently roving over a piece of paper the size of a twin sheet with an orange marker. I watched its robotic arm return to a bank of pens, drop the orange and collect a blue, return to the piece, drop, and draw again.

He saw where I was looking. "The plotter's awesome, isn't it? Slow as shit, but nothing beats it for what it does."

"What does it do?"

"Plots."

"Ah," I said. "You're Mr. Smith?"

"John Smith," he said, saying each word like he was taking a mallet to a peg, "but my buds call me Hunter."

"Named after Hunter S. Thompson?"

"No."

"Would have fit," I said. "Do you always host a before-school radicalization course?"

"We usually just bullshit while we play cards. No games today, though. Just heard about the tournament. Bummer."

"You play Spells?"

"Hell yeah."

"And talk politics?"

"The struggle continues," he said. "My family passed it to me, I get to pass it to the next generation."

"Your parents were radicals?"

"Altamont survivors."

"Altamont wasn't political," I said.

"Well, it was the '60s. The good ideas from those times are due for a much-needed comeback."

I thought I caught a grin on my son's face as he gazed into his phone.

I recognized the kids he was with. It was the same group from at the tournament. Oliver, Kevin, the other one. They looked like normal kids, not trendsetters or fashion victims like my son had gravitated to all year. I wondered if they'd followed him to all those dark corners of cliques or if this was a new old group. Kevin had been around a while, but I didn't remember hearing his name from Randy recently. Of course, I hadn't heard many details about anything in my son's personal life recently, either.

"You must be everyone's favorite teacher," I said.

"I am who I am."

"Is that stuck-up?"

"Fuck no."

"I bet the kids love all the casual swearing."

"That they do," he said.

I couldn't help but smile. "You'd have been my favorite teacher."

"What I mean is authenticity. That's what I meant by I am who I am. Authentic. Once you're comfortable in your own skin, you can't help but shine."

"Who sent you?"

"What do you mean?"

"Nothing," I said, wondering which god, from which pantheon, for what reason, had sent this hippy mystic to tell me to chill out.

I said, "I'm surprised you don't get in trouble for so openly talking politics."

"Oh, it's happened. Parents, am I right?"

"What happened?"

"Complaint. But I am who I am."

"How does that shield you in this state from angry caregivers?"

"I bring more than just my charming personality."

"You bring authenticity?"

"Exactly."

"Just that?"

"And this lab." He gestured to all the machines.

"Yours?"

He nodded and moved around the desk. It was overflowing with paper and projects, a half-framed fractaled LED portrait of Karl Marx in psychedelic colors marked with an A+++, a stack of laminated membership cards for the Wandering Dwarves AD&D club, complete with photoshopped pictures of kids in armor, ability stats table, and watermark. Hunter fell into a plush non-school-issue office chair and tossed his feet up on the only open space on his desktop. He signaled me to take the chair opposite, an antique eclectic paisley padded thing that wouldn't have looked out of place at a Victorian séance.

I sat.

"I gotta be me. That's why I became a teacher, man. To share the gospel."

"Go on." I steepled my fingers and channeled Freud.

"I was a rebel growing up."

"Unlike now?"

"I grew up around flower children. I can't tell you how many times I was dragged to see the Jefferson Starship or marched carrying a sign I couldn't even read yet. So for me, then at that time, with those parents, I turned right."

"Egads."

"Exactly. Corporate shill. Joined a rogues gallery of villainy. Made buckets of money, but man, was it not who I was."

"What turned you around?"

"Necessity and chance."

"And non-answers," I said.

"Exactly. I threw off the tie, tossed the gun—"

"Gun?"

"Did I not say a rogues gallery of villainy?"

"Why, yes. Yes, you did."

"To make my soul complete, I had to bring my knowledge and experience—"

"And money?"

He smiled broadly and nodded. "Randy said you were quick."

"He did?"

"Yeah. It's why I'm telling you this."

"Go on."

"He says you're going through an identity thing. He believes in you. He thinks you've found your calling and you're questioning it. Don't listen to the critiques, good or bad. Be yourself. Follow your soul."

"He talks about me?" I looked across the room at the gang over there laughing. I hadn't seen a smile on my son's face for a while, I realized. I felt a little melancholy.

"There you go, see? You're feeling left out. But it's alright. He's stretching his wings. He'll take a walk around the block and come back to you."

I suddenly felt very exposed. Here was a stranger who was obviously an important confidant in my son's life, and I didn't know he'd existed an hour before.

"He's a really good kid. He's got a great heart. I do everything I can for my kids, and so does Randy."

"Like what?"

"Like sharing lunches and rides and stuff."

"What do you do?"

"I give what I can," he said, smiling. "Teach gospel and spend time with them."

"I figured you for acid trips, not the guilt variety."

"Sorry, man. No no no. I'm not judging. I'm just telling you that you've done great with Randy. He's a self-affirming growing man. Making his own decisions, doing it with a good heart."

"Why were you at Little Wars yesterday?" I said to get back some control.

John "Hunter" Smith's face flushed. "You following me? I ain't a perv."

"Didn't say you were. I saw you there."

"Why were you there?"

"Following up on the tournament shit," I said.

"Of course. The detective." There was something in the way he said that. For the first time since he'd opened his mouth, he sounded false.

"That sounded kind of false," I said, ever the poker player.

"Randy mentioned you were a detective. Said a newspaper article pissed you off."

"You read it?"

He abashedly nodded. "We can't gauge our success by measuring others'."

"You left the corporate world to become a teacher or a therapist?"

He laughed and dug something out of his teeth. "I get to do both. Keep the art program top in the state with my state-of-the-art toys. I get away with a lot of things as long as it's all on the down-low." He winked.

I shook my head.

"Listen, Tony—can I call you Tony?"

"I've already started calling you Hunter in my head," I said. "Only fair."

A shadow in his eyes.

"Aren't we friends?" I honestly thought we were.

"Yeah, but only call me that in private. It's got baggage."

I shook my head again.

He winked and nodded knowingly.

Still confused, I said, "Sure, call me Tony."

"By all accounts you've been a really laid-back dad."

"All accounts, more than Randy?"

"Fuck yeah," he said. The F bomb made me look around. If anyone heard it, it had bounced off. "Randy's friends dig you, too. You're a hero to them."

"Now you're blowing smoke up my ass." I said the whole phrase out loud and clearly to show that I too could swear with sangfroid.

"Eh eh," he said. "True story, man. Cross my heart."

I didn't know what to say. My eyes scanned the walls for some inspiration. There were lots of pictures, abstract, classical, photorealistic. Photos—

"Damn," I said. "You too?"

"What?"

"That fucking Eiffel Tower picture is following me around like a blue Honda."

"I'm not familiar with the simile, but isn't it awesome?"

"You know what those go for?"

"$1,789," he said.

"You must have a lot of money."

"Have had," he said, looking at the machines. "Reserves are a little low now."

I admired the thumb smudge in the corner of the picture. "Is it a gag?"

"Yeah," he said, admiring it. "Do you get it?"

I racked my brain, suddenly confronted with the possibility that there was more to this touristy picture than met the eye.

"1789...the year of the French Revolution?"

"Give the man a cigar."

"And people pay that, just for the pun?"

"It's more than that."

The class was filling up, and the kids' conversations were now loud and boisterous. The sleepers had awakened.

"What?" I said.

"It's against the law to take pictures of the Eiffel Tower at night. It's copyrighted. The artist is sticking it to the man. Intellectual property is capitalism at its worst."

The bell rang. Classes were starting soon.

I stood up, remembering P.T. Barnum's axiom about birth rates, and multiplied it by Utah. "I should go and let you do your teacher thing."

"It was nice to meet you and have a rap. You got a great son. He's growing now, rebelling against…"

"What?"

"Whatever. Hang in there. He loves you very much. He's got to find his own identity, and the only way to do that, as you know from all your jobs, is by trial and error."

He gave me another wink. I was beginning to think he had a neurological problem.

I waved to Randy, who deigned to drop his chin in acknowledgment and thanks.

Mr. Smith shared a glance at Oliver, who then caught my eye and blushed.

"Okay, class," said Mr. Smith. "Open your textbooks to chapter eighteen, *Bourgeois Representation of the Working Class in Nineteenth-Century Art*."

23

I WASN'T USED to being up so early. My mind was groggy. My body under-caffeinated. I was hung over. With this list of ailments, I did not want to dwell on the strange meeting with Mr. Smith at school. I did want to consider that he was now my son's adult mentor and not me, nor think what it meant that my son had spoken highly of me to him. Confusion. A new layer of impostor syndrome or old-fashioned fatherly guilt and apron string cutting? With headache and heartache turning to hangry, I turned into a Denny's for some grub.

I promised myself not to think until I was fed while having as little human interaction as possible. I'd interacted a lot that morning already, more than any sane person should do in my condition.

The coffee was crap but abundant. The eggs were so good I ordered another round. Hard to screw up eggs over medium when you bathe them in so much Tabasco sauce they look like a Tarantino Western. Doubled up too on bacon and ham and the obligatory hash browns drenched in ketchup, another crime scene.

Slowly the feast brightened my senses. The sun rose to a respectable angle, and I figured I'd make the most of a Monday morning. I paid my bill, overtipped the weary war-torn waitress who'd dealt with a dine-and-dasher earlier.

Next stop: Archibald Lewis.

I wasn't surprised that the KimCo office was way out west in the developing areas. I expected a couple of double-wide trailers and a dirt compound full of heavy equipment. What I found was a cookie-cut model home at the edge of a fallow field growing plywood signs with spray-painted numbers on them. A Jeep SUV with a temporary license in its window was parked out front next to an aged Impala.

I got out and stretched, looked back to the city. From this distance and angle the gray-shit plateau of smog bisected the distant mountains like a hovering oil slick. Below was gray fog, the middle ochre ooze, but above I could see blue sky. It was hazy with some pollution run-off, like spilled sludge, but still there. It was nice to see blue again.

At the door I thought to ring the bell. It was a house after all, but the sign, *Come in We're Open*, meant I could go right in; they were open.

The door opened up to a hardwood entryway. I admired the crown molding, tasteful pictures on the wall, thick carpets, lights and even a lingering smell of fresh-baked cookies. Every trick in the real estate book was on display, but they weren't selling this house, at least not yet. They were selling snow and weeds with signs on them.

A young perky blonde woman greeted me from a room to the right, a sitting room turned office.

"I'm here to see Archibald," I said.

"He's in with a couple now. Would you care to wait?"

"Mind if I look around?"

"Oh, no not at all." She handed me a flier slicker than a crashed essential oil truck. It was full of architectural landscapes, floor plans, lists of included amenities, lists of optional upgrades. Prices noticeably absent. The house was small by modern standards but would have been a mansion fifty years ago. Three thousand square feet with basement—*Finished or unfinished—You decide!*

I followed voices toward the middle of the house to a slate-tiled kitchen where a man in a casual dress shirt stood in front of a big map of the field, outlining the lots and future shrubbery. He was talking to a young couple. They looked about twenty. She was very pregnant.

"Forget to spit out a watermelon seed?" I said.

They all turned and looked at me like I'd said something stupid.

"I need to talk to you, Archie."

"Do I know—"

His eyes went wide, filled with fear and sucked the color from his cheeks.

"Heart attack?" I said.

He tried to speak but fell into a coughing fit.

I opened cabinets full of brochures and office supplies until I found a bottle of water in the fridge. Should have looked there first. I gave it to him. He drank, coughed, spit up, drank and excused himself down another hall, where a fully furnished bathroom with custom brass fixtures and granite countertops surely awaited.

The couple stared at me like I'd done something to the guy.

"Hi," I said.

"Hi," said they.

"So...pregnant?"

She glanced up at who I suspected was her overly clean-cut, shaved, and still a little acned husband, as if looking for permission to answer. He nodded. She nodded.

"Looking to buy a house out here?"

The same routine. The same nods.

"Look," I said, pointing to the scratch on my face. "I got an owie."

They passed confused looks.

"You guys just get married?"

"Eight months ago," said the man. My ploy of pointing to my scab had won their confidence.

"Big Mormon wedding?"

"Two stakes."

"How many appetizers?" I am so witty.

"A hundred and fifty," said the wife.

"Much left over?"

"We ran out."

"I was eating éclairs for months after my wedding," I said, remembering how under-attended and over-catered it had been.

The map had about half the lots marked as sold. Even the duplexes were going.

Archibald returned, wiping his forehead with a wad of wet toilet paper. His expression was far from the excited face I'd seen on the airport video.

"Fall in?" I said. I was firing on all comedic cylinders that morning. Watermelon, appetizers, and TP—somebody stop me!

"If you'll excuse me," he said to the bewildered couple. "I have to talk to this man for a moment. Help yourself to some candy and some juice in the fridge."

I helped myself to a juice in the fridge and followed Archibald into another office, this one I think was meant to be an office. I'd have to check the blueprints. He shut the door behind us.

"I know why you're here," he said.

I flopped in a comfy chair across from his desk and took a swig of OJ. "I get that a lot. Everyone always thinks they know what's going on, but they never do. How about you let me—"

"It's about the other night with Sandi, isn't it?"

Orange juice dripped from my gaping mouth onto my shirt. I nodded and splashed some into my crotch. I swallowed the rest in self-defense.

"Do you know who I am?"

"You're Tony Flaner the detective."

"How do you know who I am?"

"Sandi mentioned you and after I left her, I looked you up."

"Why?"

"Because I'd done wrong. Because…because I had a suspicion that she was going to blackmail me, possibly with your help. I'd deserve it. And I was right."

"Wrong!" I yelled so loud he jumped. I heard the sound of something breaking in the kitchen. Probably a plate.

"She mentioned me?" I said.

"She said you were one of the people she wanted to look up in Utah."

"Who was the other?"

"Her cousin in Park City."

"She told you about that?"

"Yes," he said, now guardedly.

"You looked me up, huh?"

"Many people consider you the best detective this side of the Mississippi."

"Don't believe—Wait? What?"

"Listen, I want you to know that I love my wife," he said. "She's the world to me. I don't know what got into me."

"Who said that about me?"

"I named my company after her. Everything I do is for her and the kids."

"Was it online? A blog? A spoof site?"

"I've never done anything like that before. I felt sick the next day."

"Did you see the write-up about Traard?"

"What? Traard? Yes, I saw that."

"And?"

"And…she bewitched me. She was short on money and traveling on a friend's credit card. She was so full of life and fun."

"Do you have links?"

He took a deep breath and creased his forehead like a washboard. "Mr. Flaner, why are you here? Just say it."

"Here?"

"To see me?"

"You? Yes. That's my real intent. I need to talk to you."

"Did Sandi send you?"

"No."

"She's not blackmailing me?"

"Would she do that?"

"Things were too good to be true. One's mind can run amok."

"That it can," I agreed. "A friend back in Thailand asked me to find her. She hasn't contacted him since she arrived."

"I haven't seen her."

"You're the last person I know who did."

There went the color again. There came the fear. I offered him orange juice.

"After… ehm. In the morning, that is," he said after a sip. "I drove her to her cousin's house. I left her there."

"You just dropped her in the road?"

"No. I pulled up to the house. They have a big shelter over the door like a hotel. She got out, knocked on the door. It opened. She waved me goodbye."

"Could you find it again?"

"I have it on my GPS."

"Show me."

Archibald Lewis pulled out his phone and tracked down the address. I copied it into my phone and got a route that would take me a little over an hour.

"Did she seem welcomed at the house?"

"Oh yes," he said.

"Did you see anyone there?"

"There was this big Scottish-looking guy. Doorman or something."

I ground my teeth a little and smiled.

"Why are you smiling?"

"Lies lead to truths," I said.

"Are you going to tell my wife?"

"About the Scotsman? I doubt it. If she asks, and the conversation is flagging, I suppose—"

"About my one-night stand?"

"Oh, that," I said. I looked across the table at the sweating man. I have a very low tolerance for infidelity, but this still pulled my pity strings. I hate domestic cases, and I reminded myself I was not being paid to punish Archibald Lewis. By the looks of him, he was doing that himself anyway.

"Tell me about Sandi," I said.

"Energetic. Free spirited."

"Did you pay her?"

"I gave her some cash, but she never asked for it."

"Nor did she turn it down."

"She told me on the plane how by being friendly and alive—that was her word, 'alive'—made her friends. People would give her things, just for her energy, she said. For her stories. She could weave a tale and put herself in it. She convinced me she was at once a Burmese princess and a ragamuffin beggar before we landed."

"If she was broke, how'd she fly first class?"

"A sheik gave her the ticket," she said. "She'd told him she needed to get to America to flee the secret police. She could tell lots of stories."

"Did she say she was an actress?"

"She told me she wanted to be one. She told me she'd story her way into Sundance and get a role or her name wasn't—and then she giggled."

"She didn't tell you her name?"

"Sandi."

"Sandi Wong," I told him.

"We had a fun night. It wasn't just…you know. We laughed and talked and told stories. She performed a comedy monologue from some old English play. We talked books and movies. It was…great."

"You sound like you're in love," I said.

"It was like being with a great and interesting friend. Her confidence and pluck was intoxicating—not that I drink. That much. In public."

I finished the orange juice and tossed the empty at his garbage can, missing it by a mere four feet.

"You strike me as a man who has enough guilt right now," I said. "Be good and stay out of trouble and the universe might forgive you."

I took one of his business cards and replaced it with one of mine.

"She really is something else," he said as I was leaving. "I can't imagine anyone with a heart not being charmed by her confidence and verve."

"Verve?" I said.

"It means vigor."

"Vigor?"

"Vim?"

"Zest, zing, zap?" I offered. "Let me guess, you're writing sales brochures?"

"Yes, how'd you know?"

"I'm a detective."

"Okay." I could tell he wanted me to leave. He was a little embarrassed he'd kept me in his life with a vocabulary lesson.

"Goodbye, Archibald. I'll call you if I need you. You call me if you think of anything else."

"Like what?"

"I don't know. More synonyms?"

24

I WAS HALFWAY out of the valley zipping to Park City with a head full of accusation and worry when I realized I hadn't gotten an answer to who in the hell was saying nice things about me. What kind of treachery was this? When was the last time I Googled myself? In any other century that would be the dirtiest thing ever said. Now, it only highlighted my insecurity.

I texted Allie:

> I'll be in Park City in half an hour

I'm nearly at your place now.

> Shit.

Shit. Why are you going to Park City?

> Case.

Good for you!

I promised:

> I'll try not to be long

I've got things to do. I'm fine.

> Yes you are.

:-)

I'd been sitting on my ass doing nothing for weeks, missing my out-of-town girlfriend, and the weekend she visits, she gets called away and I fall into a well of work. I had to think the two things were related. Blue balls of responsibility? Maybe, but Allie always brought out the person I wanted to be, the person I was afraid she thought I was. After this long she'd had plenty of opportunities to see me as I thought I really was, slovenly and insecure, and yet she still liked me. That was proof of something, right? Maybe her insanity?

Strange that I was excited to confront the Burmese guys. Allie was on my mind, and I could feel the tides of self-doubt churning about, but the impostor syndrome was in decline for sure. I felt the old detective drive firing up. There are clues, and then there are clues. Information is one thing, nice in its own way, but discovering a lie—hell, that's red meat to a sleaze like me. Yeah, I'll own the title. People call us sleazes because we work with all the sordid stuff they leave behind. We don't make it. We treat it. We're like doctors. Yeah, just like doctors. Goddamn do-gooders, that's us. Do-gooders who get beat up a lot.

I had the bit in my teeth now; I had all the signs of progress. I'd been attacked. By a dog. But that counts. Even though it was on another case. Someone was following me, and I'd found a lie. I didn't know what it all meant, but I was stirring pots. Detectives are like cooks that way. Doctors who cook. Okay, the metaphors were weakening, but I was feeling good.

I also had a strange memory of solving the fiancée case. A fever dream from my laundry-drug stupor? Probably, but I took that as a good sign anyway, a positive affirmation that I could and would figure all this shit out. Can a man ask for anything more?

He could, but I'd take what was offered.

Siri directed without fail to a neighborhood in the hills, wooded and smelling of too damn much money. Ten? Twenty-million dollar homes? I'll never know.

Around a bend and up a hill, I came to a pair of pillars and a plastic white fence that would outlive the planet. No gate and a short driveway. I parked under a hard awning, just like Archibald said. Siri told me I'd arrived. I liked Siri's optimism.

I'd expected a house with Asian influences: pagoda roofs, ponds full of koi, frozen this time of year to be chipped out in April with hammers. A dragon or two. What I got was a big tasteful Western American house, with lots of yard and four garage doors. A mansion, but still it looked like a house, just a big one. It was a story taller and twice wider than the nouveau riche Utah standard. Unremarkable except for its size, which wasn't apparent unless you took it all in, which was hard without a drone.

Note to self. Get a drone.

I walked up to the door full of confidence, a detective with a purpose. I rang the bell and knocked too because just standing there seemed like a waste of time. Might as well get in some cardio.

The door swung open, and the big Scotsman stood staring down at me. I'm not a small man, six-foot-two before shrinkage. It was a strange sensation to look so far up at anyone.

"I don't remember you being so big," I said.

He raised an eyebrow. "Can I help you?"

It was the first time I'd heard him speak and, will miracles never cease, he spoke with a Scottish accent!

"Toss me a caber and slather me in haggis," I said as my way of endearing myself to him. "I've come to see the family."

"Are you expected?"

"You know...I might be."

"Who may I say is calling?"

"Whom."

He stared. Endearment over if it had ever been.

"Tony Flaner."

Now I might have been paranoid, or filled with wishful thinking, but I almost imagined, kinda thought, just maybe, there was a tick of recognition under his red eyebrows when I said my name.

"We met, sort of, at the party last night," I said.

"Wait here." He closed the door.

I stood there feeling awkward and so did some more reps on the door, changing it up a bit—left hand, right hand, fast, slow, *shave and a haircut, Ave Maria*. When the door opened again I was just about to riff into *In-A-Gadda-Da-Vida*. It would have been epic.

"The master doesn't know you," said the Scotsman.

"Then let's get acquainted." I ducked in under his arm. Like I said, I was feeling my oats.

"So where is the Myanmaran man?"

The inside of the house continued the theme of modern American classic, shifting and uncertain. Comfortable and welcoming, upscale furnishings but not a museum. Rich carpet, crown molding, wrought iron chandelier and gray slate tile. It was upscale with character by virtue of all the framed movie posters. *Casablanca, Alien, Citizen Kane, True Grit* (both versions), *The Arrival*. I had a flash of Archibald's model home and just then I had another flash. A big one. A bright burst of sensation. A spectral constellation of flickering sparks, drawing me to sleep.

Yeah. I'd turned my back on a goon. I'd grown softer. Not having a case in a while, I somehow had re-imaged the world had become Mayberry, where imported muscle, even when challenged, would never coldcock a cocky dick like me in the back of the head. I mean, Scotland. It's still Britain, right? Rabbit punches are most surely not cricket. But of course, I'd trespassed into a house of a family chased out of their country for not towing the line. Why expect their hired henchmen to play by the rules? Are there rules?

There's a long noble line of detectives who get bashed unconscious on a case. Jim Rockford of *The Rockford Files* couldn't go a week without a concussion. I'm sure the script said "knocked out," but make no mistake, the only way a person is actually knocked out is if they have a concussion. A *concussion*. To have been accurate, James Garner should have been a drooling chew toy by the final season, but Hollywood sugarcoats those things and makes aspiring detectives feel overconfident to turn their backs on bruisers. There could be a lawsuit there.

———

I woke up slowly in an Asian temple. The smell of exotic perfumes, incense of forbidden orchids and joss sticks floated around gold-leaf ornaments of serene seated men, suggesting that I was dead and had been following the wrong mythos my entire life. Buddha for the win.

"He's waking up," said a voice.

"Oh, good," I said, reaching for Nirvana. "Enlightenment."

"Not that kind of waking up," said another voice.

I rolled over and saw three figures across the room. One was sitting in a tall ornately carved throne-like chair, a red cushion under his ass. That was Kyi, the dead general's adviser who'd thrown the party I'd crashed. Behind the chair stood the kid, Thiha, if I remembered the name right, the general's son. He stood three-quarter profile to hide his scars. Behind them both, holding me in a red Scottish stare, was the brute.

"What's its name?" I said, nodding to the big guy.

"Stewart," said the man, making the name sound like one syllable.

"Tell Stert to watch his shit. He's lucky I had my back turned."

"What would have happened if you'd been facing him?" said Kyi.

"I mighta ducked, I don't know. It's a shit scenario any way you look at it."

I pulled myself up to sitting. I was on a settee, a matching piece to the chair. I'd been reclining Buddha-like, just with a sack of ice on my head.

"Who do I thank for the ice pack?"

"Yourself," said Kyi. If I understood the situation right, the real power in the house was the boy, Thiha. He was the general's heir. Kyi was just the help. He was obviously in charge, though. It smelled like a regency.

"I said the ice pack, not the wound."

"That was me," said Thiha. He glanced at Kyi's chair as if he'd stepped in something.

"I appreciate it," I said with a smile to Thiha.

Turning my face back to Kyi, I melted the smile into an accusative stare, complete with squinting eyes and a lip twitch. "Do you always welcome guests this way?"

Kyi looked shocked. "This is America. You're lucky you weren't shot."

"For wanting to see you?"

"For breaking into my home."

He had a point. America was the gun death capital of the whole fucking universe. War zones have fewer casualties than suburbia USA on any given day.

"Well...I guess, then...thanks? Let me just get my eyes to focus concurrently and I'll write you out a check."

"A check for what?"

"For your hospitality."

He looked confused.

"American isn't your first language, is it?" I said.

"I am very fluent, in English."

I shook my aching head and readjusted the ice pack. "American. Specifically the dialect of sarcasm."

Stert snarled at the jibe. He got it. Thiha's eyes went big. Kyi's eyes went small. Emoting all around.

To show how cool I was, I took my eyes off my captors and scanned the room. It was a sunroom—half greenhouse, half temple. Whereas the entry was movie-house modern, this was definitely Burmese. I could tell from all the gold cones and pokey bits. The gold Buddha sitting across from me, smiling serenely, looked positively serrated for all the edges and peaks on him, and the big-ass vase on the floor by the window with the needly nose cone could have launched for orbit with just a couple Estes Rocket engines.

Out the window I saw Utah winter scenery. Snow with brush fighting out. The sky was bluer than Salt Lake, so I had to figure I was still in Park City. I sure as hell wasn't in a hospital.

"Why am I still here?" I said.

"Instead of..."

"An emergency room."

"Or jail?"

"They have aspirin there too," I said, glaring at Stert.

Thiha got the hint. "Go get him something," he said to the beast.

The big man paused for a second to finish his stare and then left the room through a clashing Moorish door.

"It would be an international incident," said Kyi.

"For a couple aspirin? Jesus, good thing I don't need an antacid."

That got him. His placid face flushed, his jaw quivered. He was angry.

I'd like to think that pissing off people was a secret detective trick I'd learned, a way to measure my adversary, to know their emotional limits and so use it against them, but truth is I do this to everyone I don't like. It's a gift.

"Not the aspirin, you...Mr. Flaner."

"Ah, you were about to insult me. That was close. Could have been another international incident."

Thiha stared at me with either awe or horror. Kyi took a deep cleansing breath and put his smug smile back on.

"Thiha is the heir of the great General Tayza," he said.

"Tayza the exile?"

"Tayza, heir to the throne of Burma."

"Tayza the dead guy?" Okay that was cold. His son was right there.

Kyi's anger lowered to a dull dangerous boil. Not good. I like people pissed and stupid, not pissed and plotting. I shut up for a second. It wasn't easy. Is never easy.

"Among some classes," Kyi said with all the aristocratic hate he could slide into the sibilant word. "Thiha is now the heir to the throne."

"You're a prince?" I said to Thiha.

The boy blushed and gave me a half-nod, half-bow.

"Neat."

There was a long pause as if they expected me to say something more. It was hard, but I kept my mouth shut for a couple more seconds. The silence was too funny.

Stert re-entered the room and offered me a couple of white pills with his catcher's mitt of a paw. I swallowed them with a pull from a green fizzy Perier bottle.

"Did you use a blackjack or a purse on my skull, Stert?" I said. "Asking for a lawyer friend of mine."

His lip curled up in a snarl.

"Come away, Stewart," said Kyi. Thiha shifted on the balls of his feet. For being a princeling he was a very American teenager. I remembered then that he'd grown up here. He was three when the general had fled his country, twelve when the fiery accident killed his father and Kyi's son, Phyo, and given him those nasty scars he tried so hard to hide.

"Stewart is a necessary part of our household," said Kyi. "We have security. Thiha has enemies. You need manners."

"Hey, I'm not the one beating up strangers."

"What do you want, Mr. Flaner?" said Thiha. "Why did you come here?"

"Remember me from the big party?"

"Vaguely," said Kyi.

"Remember I asked you about something?"

"Vaguely."

"Well, you lied to me. Exactly."

25

THAT HAD BEEN my big line. I expected more than a cold stare from Kyi.

"Ah," he said after a good long awkward moment. "You are a detective."

"And what are you, exactly?"

"A guardian," he said. "And that is why I lied to you."

I smiled. It was accidental. I didn't mean anything by it beyond being pleased that the clue was actually right. I didn't relish the idea of hanging out with Guilt-abald Lewis in his field house again.

"How'd you find out?" asked Stert in Scottish.

Thiha nodded that he too wanted to know.

"My line is 'I'm a detective,'" I said with surprisingly good delivery.

Kyi nodded in appreciation of my brilliance, an understanding of my calling and skill. Or maybe he was admiring the barbed art.

Stert gave a loud Scottish sniff.

"You were saying?" I said, using my interrogation skills.

"I'm a guardian. Stewart is also a guardian. I think you'll appreciate how seriously we take security here."

"I already said thanks for not shooting me. How many times are you going to make me say it?"

I'd caught Kyi off balance with the callback.

Stert looked like he wanted to correct the earlier error with the shooting. Thiha was doing his best to look interested and doing a pretty good job of it, actually.

"So what happened?" I said. "I know she arrived, I know how, and at what time, and I know you let her in, or rather that orange troll did."

"We sent her away," said Kyi.

"Are you all sure you didn't bash her skull in first?" I said.

If looks could club someone, I'd have been hit again.

"When we found out who she was, we sent her away," Kyi said.

"She's cousin to the heir there of the heir of the thingy you said earlier," I said, eloquent as ever.

"No. She was an impostor," said Kyi. "She came under false pretenses for reasons of her own."

"She wasn't Sandi Wong?"

"That was her name," said Kyi. "But she was no relative of ours."

"Ours? Is that the royal plural or are you and Thiha related?"

Thiha looked shocked that I'd say such a thing. He exposed the burned side of his face to me. It was bad but not the atrocity he seemed to think it was.

"Since his father died, I've raised him like my son."

"Shit," I said. "I forgot. The car accident."

"I lost a child, he lost a parent. We've grown close."

I recognized fatherly outrage. "I'm sorry," I said. "I know I can be an ass."

He nodded, definitely in agreement that time.

For forgiveness and sympathy through guilt, I readjusted the icepack on my skull.

"So what happened to her?" I said.

"Stewart drove her to Salt Lake City and left her at a train station."

"There are trains in Salt Lake City. Story checks out," I said. "How long was she here?"

"An hour. We had tea, and after a bit of questioning, it was clear that she was not who she said she was."

"Do you know where she was going?"

"She mentioned something about doing some gambling."

"Any mention of Sundance? The festival was happening then."

"I don't remember. I might have mentioned it. I'm going to finance a film. It was on my mind."

"Oh yeah? What film?"

"I haven't decided yet."

"Isn't that the wrong way to go about it?"

"Why's that?" Kyi said, honest question in his face. Or he had gas. I dunno.

"Well when a non-movie type invests in a movie, it's usually because some director sold him on a concept."

"I'm becoming a producer."

"A producer?"

"Independent films. I love movies, and sitting on money seems like a waste. Good American entrepreneurship says to invest it."

I remembered the title everyone was throwing around at the party. "You wouldn't be thinking about going in on *Boys in the Bush*, would you?"

"You know it?" He seemed pleased.

"Everyone is talking about it."

"Yes, I'm very interested in that one."

"Would you take a piece of it or finance the whole thing?"

"It's only ten million. I'd take it all on."

"Yeah, with prices like that, why not do a couple?"

"What else am I going to do with the money?"

"Can't think of a thing."

The mood in the room had appreciably brightened. Kyi had blossomed once we got into movies. Thiha finally slid into bored teenager fidgets, but Stert stayed in character like he was auditioning to be a red-haired obelisk.

"Well, I'll just leave you, then," I said. "You guys are busy with all the security and stuff."

"Do you want to see my collection of movie memorabilia?" asked Kyi.

"Sure, I'd love to case the joint."

Like an excited child keen to show me his new finger-painted masterpiece, Kyi escorted me out of the big sunny day room into a dark hallway.

"No school today?" I asked Thiha.

"Uhm..."

"Homeschooled?"

"I don't feel good," he said.

"You do look a little green around the gills. Girl trouble?" I winked.

He hid his face from me.

"It's not a girl named Jelissa, is it?"

"Thiha," Kyi said to the boy. "You should go answer your mail."

"Fan mail?" I joked.

"We have supporters back home."

"Family?"

Some of the spring left his step. "Friends and some family," he said. "Thiha has a trust."

"Do you miss Myanmar?" I asked.

"We'd never go back there. We are done with it. It's a backward jungle. Here is where everything's happening."

I was going to point out that his opinion of Utah was far out of line from how the rest of the world saw the place but let it slide, allowing him some synecdoche for the country as a whole, or the Western world, or the good parts of the western world, or what we hoped the good parts of the western world would be.

Thiha walked with us into the hall and then turned off into a big office. It was another style. The house was full of changing decors, I learned. The entryway was Utah chic; the sunroom, Burmese temple; the study where Thiha was sent to his letter-writing homework would not have been misplaced in a medieval castle. The hallway was schizophrenic too, contorting and reflecting varying themes we passed, showing its confusion one minute with Roman arches, Egyptian columns, then sliding to near-black mahogany paneling, to paint, to textured floral wallpaper. Navajo rugs, Grecian tile, and then the remembered plush carpeting where I'd been clobbered earlier.

"I can't imagine a more expensive way to decorate," I said.

"Yes," he agreed.

I left out 'or the worst' because he'd already threatened to shoot me.

Thiha seemed like the only warm and loving person in the place, besides me. I was very warm and lovable. Most people thought so, I thought. Those people who didn't clobber me.

Kyi was rambling on about his great new find.

"I bid fifteen thousand dollars for the coat."

"A raincoat from *Groundhog Day*?"

"Yes, the one Bill Murray wore."

"Gotcha. Go on."

"Fifteen thousand. It was a major jump from the five thousand, and no one dared challenge me."

"eBay?"

"Southwick in Hollywood. They're always on the lookout for things for me. Let me know when something's coming up for auction so I can slip in and secure it."

"They saw you coming."

"No. I always bid anonymously."

"Security?"

"Unwanted attention is never desirable."

We'd left what I'd call the left wing and were heading now to the right wing. Lots of hallways. Lots of doors. Lots of rooms, I had to imagine.

"How many people live in this place?" I asked.

"What? Uhm. Just the four of us. Thiha and I, Stewart and Melecio."

"Who's Melecio?"

"Our cook and cleaner. A nice man from Cuba."

"Only four dudes in this whole big house?"

"When one desires solitude, it should always be available."

"Ten thousand square feet?"

"Twenty-one."

"Do you have a finished basement?"

"And two dining rooms, formal and informal, eight guest suites, a pool, and a gym." His voice was impatient, his mood souring.

"Who cares about all that, though?" I said. "I just want to see your memorabilia."

He led on, a bit warier than before. We came to a pair of double doors, which he threw open.

I'd expected a museum, glass cabinets roped-off displays with little cards naming and explaining every bit of trivia, but it was a closet of cardboard boxes. A big closet, but still, a closet filled with boxes. All had shipping stamps on them, some from far away, others as near as Amazon—a lot of those, actually. A place called 'Monsters in Motion,' another 'Hollywood Replicas,' slews of eBay shipping numbers; some better boxes had formal labels mentioning auction houses.

"I plan on displaying all this stuff one day," he said. "Now I'm just collecting it."

He showed me a box with a pair of shoes in it. Men's shoes. "From *Bullitt*," he said.

"Of course."

"And here's a lipstick from *Steel Magnolias*."

"Ah."

"A pillowcase from *Inception*."

"What a find there."

"An actual dial from the plane in *Captain America*."

"Which plane?"

"I'm not sure," was his reply. "I haven't seen that one."

He pulled out the gray raincoat, the new one that Bill Murray had worn. Maybe. It looked like a gray raincoat.

He beamed with each box he opened.

"Smell the leather of this gun holster. It's from John Ford's *Stagecoach*. Smells brand new, doesn't it?"

Looked it, too, but I didn't say anything. I had serious doubts about the authenticity of the collection, but Kyi's enthusiasm for it was unquestioned. He showed me stuff for at least half an hour. I tried not to glaze over, but it was hard.

"This is a lot of stuff," I said, wanting to go. "You got some history here."

"And more to come. What did you think of *Boys in the Bush*?"

"Provocative," I said.

"I haven't read the script yet, but it is the hot property. I just hope I don't get in a bidding war with that other producer, the one you know."

Mercifully, he was packing things and winding down.

I flashed back on that party. "Wait. Other producer? You mean Francis Tomas?"

"Yes, the man with two first names. He seemed very keen. He's one to watch."

Thiha appeared with Stert. Kyi looked at him suspiciously.

We stepped back out into the hall. It was a wide hall.

"Did the impostor girl tell you anything else on the drive over the pass?" I asked Stert.

"She was looking for a place to stay. I mentioned there were plenty of good places along the freeway."

Thiha cleared his throat.

"Yes?" said Kyi.

"I don't know what to say to the colonel," he said. "He wants dates."

"Tell him he should go onto Tinder," Kyi said and laughed like he'd just invented the goose. "I'll be along in a moment, Thiha. I'll meet you in the study."

With that, the young man turned and left us.

"Stewart will show you out. I have to assist Thiha."

"Thanks for all your help."

"Glad to be of service," he said warmly.

I handed him the ice pack. He looked surprised but took it.

Stewart showed me out.

At the door, I thought I'd see if my newfound bonhomie with Kyi translated to his goon.

"Say, what does your boss do for a living?" I asked.

"He told you. He's a movie producer."

"Right right right. I get that. Big movie fan. How does he, did he, will he, get his money? I'd like to get into whatever racket he's in."

He opened the door and gestured to me to leave.

I hesitated on the mat, rubbed the back of my head for effect and healing. It hurt like a son of a bitch. Note to self: don't rub cranial goose eggs. I looked up at the bruiser with big sad eyes.

He looked down his Celtic nose at me. I readjusted my estimate. He had to be six-foot-eight. I had to crane my neck to see up his nostrils. And this shit had to hit me from behind? I ground my teeth.

"Trust fund for the boy, and Kyi deals in collectibles."

"Trust fund baby, right. Think Kyi will make out on that coat?"

"Goodbye."

I waited for an answer.

He cracked his knuckles.

I stepped outside.

He stood in the doorway.

"Sap," he said just before he closed the door and locked it.

It took me eighteen miles toward home before I realized he was answering my earlier question about what he'd hit me with and not making a personal judgment about my intelligence.

Both ways pissed me off.

26

I DROVE HOME with a furrowed brow. I checked. In the mirror. Yep. Furrowed. All wrinkly as I dissected my life. I probably should have put on music, maybe some Death Cab for Cutie, that one about fires maybe, but instead I went over how stupid I'd been to let Stert clobber me. Right there was proof that I am not as good as some people think, whoever they are. Here was proof that I was a fraud.

The weird thing about it is, thinking about that moment wasn't the part that filled my guts with angsty churnings. Failure, my subconscious expected, hell, maybe even rooted for—treacherous subconscious. No, it was when the Burmese recognized me as a detective, when they admired that I'd found them. That's what made me ill. Couldn't they see that I'd just been flattened in their foyer? Who was I to earn any respect after that? I'd felt it a little in that room, under interrogation, but adrenaline indignation had shielded me then, and only now was the pain, both physical and emotional, settling in. It was a kind of delayed shock. I'd handled myself well enough in the lair, veiled shooting threats and all, so I was all confused again. I guess I'd done alright. Right?

I could take some comfort in knowing that soon I'd be with Allie.

I called her.

"Hey cutie-pie, I'm on my way home."

"Great."

"Is Randy home yet?"

"He should be."

"He's not there? Wait, are you home?"

"I'm at your place. Yes, but Randy went home."

"Eh…"

"Didn't Nancy call you?"

"She's at a conference."

"She came back early."

"And my son bailed on me to go to her?" Heavy sigh.

"Don't take it so hard. All his stuff is there."

"Someone could have told me."

"Your family has never been good at communication, Tony."

"Are you talking about the time I was an hour late picking you up or when I went on a trip and didn't tell you about it until I was on the plane?"

"Yes."

"Okay."

"It does give us the house to ourselves," she said.

The freeway became a parking lot of idling cars fouling the immediate air with new flavors of diesel disease as I neared the valley. I glanced at the clock. Evening rush hour had started.

"I may be delayed," I said. "There, I told you."

"Don't be too long."

I groaned.

We hung up.

Next call.

"Hey, Randy," I said. "So your mom's back, huh?"

"Yeah."

"You okay?"

"Yeah, I'm great."

The curt answers were not uncommon, but my heart was hurting a bit.

"Sorry I wasn't around more this weekend. Got lots of cases."

"Yeah, about that?"

"Let's do—"

"Could you drop the whole Spells card thing?"

"Why?"

"Just leave it alone."

"Any reason?"

"Skip it. Do your other cases."

"I'm trying to think of another way to ask you why you're asking me to do this," I said.

"It's...it's no big deal. I'm going to put it in the past."

"You're giving up the game?"

"I don't like tournaments," he said.

"The smell?"

"Part of it. Just drop the Spells case. Follow the other things you're doing. They're more important."

"I don't remember telling you what I was working on."

The guy behind me honked to tell me to fill the three feet that'd opened up between my bumper and the car's in front of me.

"They're real cases. They pay money, right? Don't you need money? Everyone needs money. Get it when you can."

"Huh…" I said, remembering his car payment coming due.

"Just leave it alone, okay, Dad?" he said. "I love you."

If I wasn't suspicious before that final endearment, I sure as hell was after it.

We hung up and I pondered his deflections and motives.

Another honk and another eighteen inches and I was on my phone again. With Siri's help I was on to a California number.

"Thank you for calling the Myanmar Consulate."

I listened to a long line of options, beginning with language selections but never came to a human operator. I played it twice and couldn't decide what button to push.

Traffic crept forward, the sky a brown haze, the road a lounge room of never-ending traffic cones and black exhaust-stained snowbanks. Flashing lights up ahead told me why traffic into the valley was worse than that going out. I bet it had something to do with following too closely. I sneered at the driver behind me.

I called the consulate again, scribbled info on a napkin.

The traffic crept along. I crept with it.

A complete shutdown as a fire truck wove its way through.

I had good bars. I tethered my laptop to my phone and found the old airline booking link in my address book. My password, as I'd tested the other day, still worked. I found the flight, picked the seats, and bumped two people who were probably jerks into standby.

Just as it was done, the traffic moved, and I was quickly home.

I opened the door and called, "Pack your bags, honey, we're going to Los Angeles!"

Allie stood seductively in the doorway draped in silky red negligee, stiletto heels. A rose in her teeth.

"What?" she said through the gritted teeth.

"Pack up. We gotta go."

"What?" she said again, the gleam in her eye fading.

"I'm being spontaneous." I extracted the flower from her lips with my own. "Aren't you always saying I should be more spontaneous?"

"No," she said. "Actually, the exact opposite is what I say."

"We have to be at the airport in thirty minutes."

"You're serious?"

"Bed and breakfast. Walk of Fame. Maybe Universal Studios. I've never been."

She let out a resigned sigh and followed me into the bedroom.

"You look nice, by the way," I said.

"Glad you noticed."

She stripped out of her lace.

"We can be there in thirty-five minutes," I said.

———————

We held hands as we boarded the flight in the nick of time. They were about to give our seats to some jerks waiting standby. We had only our carry-on bags and warm afterglows.

Once in our seats, Allie pulled a blanket over herself and cuddled on my shoulder. I felt a mile tall and too amped up to sleep, so fidgeted until we were airborne. Gear up, Allie turned the other way and slept against the window. I had the stewardess bring me a gin and Fresca and opened my computer for something to do.

I woke from sleep on an email I didn't remember writing.

Dear Mr. Moland, I am sorry to report this but it looks as if you're the targét of a ow gawer I ma snodrdnnkk.

The last time I'd used my email was when I was tying one on the other night.

Moland was the fiancé in the actress case. Was this why I thought I'd solved it? Because ow gawer I ma snodrdnnkk? It was a good hypothesis.

I stared at the words, trying to remember what I'd tried to say. I finished my drink, trying to get into the right frame of mind, and ordered another. Since we'd gotten a free upgrade to first class, the drinks were free.

I brought up my web browser and found a cached page of Macy's wedding registry. I hit the back button but got the dreaded no internet connection screen.

"Excuse me," I said to the stewardess.

"Same again?"

"Not yet. This is going to sound stupid, I mean, we're like a thousand feet up, but can I get internet?"

"Thirty thousand," she said. "Do you have a credit card?"

"Yes."

"Then you can get internet." Being as I was in first class, she walked me through the plane Wi-Fi system in a jiffy.

"Wow, how cool."

"Yes."

"Is it expensive?"

"Oh yes."

"By time or data?"

"Both."

She pointed to a widget on the sign-in screen that would show me my time and data along with a running total of what the charges were.

"We had to install that for parents. You can ration it in the settings."

"I'm good," I said. "Don't tell Mom."

As I said that, I watched time tick away. The data hovered at zero, but the cost spun up like the national debt monitor.

"Anything else?"

"Yeah. Bring me another."

Using my browser history, I investigated my own investigation. I'd visited the Macy's registry page many times, searching on different names.

I'd done many Google searches too and more importantly, a graphics search. I'd pulled Maggie's picture off the playhouse website and found the same one used on an old page in St. George that advertised *Death of Salesman* last year. The picture was over a different name, Jennifer Young. A search on that name found she'd been engaged to a nice kid named Peter Harmon before she left him at the altar. Peter was the only son of a very well-to-do Mormon family down south, a very similar person to Glenn Abergast and also Bryan Moland, I noticed. I now had three names for the girl, three big Mormon weddings all torpedoed at the last minute.

I found each wedding registered at the same store, the big Salt Lake City Center Macy's. The one in the scary mall with thought police. It was the best general store in the state, high-end stuff. I found that I'd spent a lot of time going through the registries, trying different names. I did the same again now, at great financial distress. In the course of forty minutes, I found two more possible pictures of "Maddy Smith" with soon-to-be jilted young well-to-do Mormon men. She was Noel Carson from Pensacola in Vernal, Utah, and Yvette Miller in Pocatello, Idaho, origin unstated. She looked different in each picture, but the list of requested gifts were practically identical. Each had a mention of an imminent temple sealing date—sealing means "married" in Mormon—and a reception at a local church.

I could see the con, but a few details were missing.

I found that I'd gone on Facebook. I'd again scoped out Francis Tomas, searched out his friends. I visited Allie's pages, her personal one and her business page. I'd looked at Nancy's—my ex-wife's—page and saw her with a handsome man with good teeth in a big ballroom, laughing and holding up drinks.

We're divorced, I reminded myself, but my lizard brain wasn't having it.

I leaped off that page quickly to land on my own and realized I was dolefully unrepresented. The last thing I'd written on my wall was that night.

Can't bleve how smartt I ma whn drunk1 #amsleuthhing.

Good stuff for future clients to see. The last update before that was Thanksgiving. A picture of stuffing. Woo-hoo.

I poked around, looking for a delete button for that post or maybe my whole profile, when I saw I'd searched some other familiar names. Three people from *Flower Drum Song*.

First was Ortwin Bishop, the director of the play. I'd searched him hard but found only that he loved theater, lived in Provo for his day job as a computer analyst, and wanted to get back home to Grand Rapids.

Next up was Enzo Powell, Maddy's manager. He'd moved around a lot. He'd lived in St. George, Ephraim, Vernal, and Boise, Idaho, within the last two years. He had pictures with his friends who were untagged, but there was Madeline Smith in his arms, there was Noel Carlson in a kayak beside him, Tiffany Jones on a hiking trail with a granola bar.

I remembered the next name, the other drinker in the house. Kelly Gibson. Her page was cached in my browser's memory, so it popped right up rather than the slow dial-up disgrace I otherwise endured, so maybe I saved a couple dollars. Win!

Kelly had fewer pictures than Enzo, but there was Maddy again. It was a picture from *Flower Drum Song*, backstage, maybe the very night I'd been there. The date showed it was. *With my best friend*, was what it said. Facebook was unable to offer the face a name, so I called her Maddy.

The seat belt light came on, and the pilot told us to prepare for descent, turn off all electrical devices, and return our seatbacks into a righteous and upright position, implying certain death awaited us all if any failed to comply.

Before closing my Macintosh and waking Allie, I noted where Kelly Gibson worked. For five years she'd been employed at Macy's department store, the big one downtown in Salt Lake City, in registry and returns.

27

I WASN'T KIDDING about the bed and breakfast. Using money I had no business spending, I'd booked a two-hundred-dollar-a-night love nest with a view. We picked up a rental car that smelled of talcum powder and vomit and boarded the late-night LA freeway like we knew what we were doing. With Siri as our copilot, we headed into the hills.

It was dark and late, but I was excited. Not only had I had sex in recent memory, I was also on an adventure with my best bed-buddy. And, I'd broken a case. I brought Allie up to speed on my progress, what I'd found, what I suspected, and some of the other stuff including Randy's strange behavior and the ulterior motive for the trip.

"I can write it off, see? I'm on a case."

"Shouldn't you check it out first with an accountant? It sounds like it all could have been done with a phone call."

"Nah. I got put on hold."

"Asking forgiveness instead of permission doesn't work with taxes."

"Don't be negative. I have Bryan's case busted open."

"How long did that take you?"

"I really should say I cracked it on Saturday, but I'll claim today because I was in a drug-induced stupor then. So three days."

She sighed and smiled.

"What?"

"You run rings around Traard with your efficiency."

I wasn't happy to have his name brought up, but I did see the point.

"But…" she said.

"What?"

"You're not going to make much money on this one. Three days won't make a car payment."

"It's okay," I said. "Randy got his car towed."

"And that means you don't have to make payments?"

"Huh…"

"We're here," said Allie, looking up from her GPS.

It was storming. California has winter too, I guess. I planted a kiss on Allie's mouth at the door. It would have been a magical moment if the rain had been warmer than single digits Kelvin.

"Mr. Flanders?"

"Flaner."

She looked confused.

"It's us."

Halfway behind the door, slumped over a bit, gray hair and ashen face, the old lady looked us over and said, "You're wet."

Allie picked up the line before I could. "Yes," she said just like Janet. "It's raining."

We both looked behind us, waiting for the lightning flash that would illuminate rows of motorcycles. It didn't come.

"Well, I guess you better come in," said the woman.

"I guess…" said I.

She showed us to our suite. It was smaller than I expected, but the view was interesting—rain-soaked and black but with lots of lights that suggested there was life out there somewhere. Nice.

She told us the rules, warned us about the yellow cat who stole things and the gray cat that hid in luggage. She gave us a key to an outside door, had us sign a guest book and finally took her leave. The minute she was gone, Allie and I peeled away our clothes and spent eight minutes on the bed. I guess I was tired from the last time.

We fell asleep cuddled up, listening to the rain and watching the lights through the window.

———

Dear Mr. Moland, I am sorry to report this, but it appears as if you've been the target of an elaborate and practiced con game.

The letter began. I listed the clues I'd found, including hyperlinks and photos before summing it all up.

The game was to get well-connected Mormon men engaged, ones from wealthy families in wealthy areas with a huge circle of wealthy friends—big Mormon wards where everyone is sure to send a gift—and then send them all to a single bridal registry at Macy's. The wedding would be canceled at the last moment, and your Maddy would return the gifts for cash with the help of a cohort at the store. I am convinced this is the situation. You may look at the information and gather different conclusions, but I doubt you will. I'm sorry. I don't think this is the answer you wanted, but it probably isn't far from what you suspected. If you want to take this further, I don't think it would take much effort for law enforcement to follow this trail as I did and make arrests. The amount owed me and the remittance address are below.

The payment, as Allie had mentioned, wouldn't cover a single car payment for Randy's towed Tesla.

"It's a great letter," I said to Allie. "Thanks for the help. Works much better without all the swearing and references to *Aladdin*."

"You're welcome." But she looked pained.

The letter flew out my computer into cyberspace with a friendly swoosh.

"What is it?" I asked.

"So let me get this straight," said Allie, putting down her coffee. "A stranger offers you a bag of some unknown drug and not only do you buy it on the spot, but you run home and take it that night, with your son sulking in the house, while you're working?"

"You make it sound like I was being irresponsible," I said. "Look what it did for me. I cracked the case over a pizza."

"Ignoring that you then forgot you had, I suppose it is something. A worthy bit of sleuthing. Congratulations, you moron."

She kissed me. "And the big case?"

"Not as good," I said. "Hoping to get some answers here. I'm working on weak information."

"Did you try to do some research on the computer?"

"I ran out of drugs."

"Phone calls?"

"And lose a romantic weekend?"

"Touché."

We finished our breakfast, a real English thing, with eggs, bacon, beans, sausage, more bacon and tomatoes, real cream butter so rich I put some in my coffee and on all four of the pieces of toast I had, leaving off the orange marmalade because I don't know what those chunks are in there. My body is a temple.

At Allie's insistence, I told Randy and Nancy where I was and what I was doing.

> In California. Working on a case.

RANDY

Kk

NANCY

I was just there

Why'd you come home early?

Have fun.

I showed the exchange to Allie. "That's a new way to say 'mind your own business,'" she said.

"That's what I thought."

"Okay, Sherlock, put that away. Let's go get some clues."

Allie was excited to be part of the investigation. She'd been asking for months to join me on a case. It hadn't worked out before. Now it was.

The day was bright and warm, at least by our standards. There was a layer of smog over the city but nothing like we'd left. I remembered a time when LA was shamed into cleaning up its air and had done it. If only such things worked in Utah. But, alas, Utah is a shameless state, at least at the legislative level.

How does the song go? 'LA is a great big freeway'? Yeah, that's it. Spoken by the incomparable Dionne Warwick over fifty years ago in *Do You Know the Way to San Jose*. It is still the quintessential description of the city for me. Disneyland is an island in a sea of freeways, the beach the edge of them. Some neighborhoods, I'm told, have flavor, conclaves of peoples with real identities—Mexicans, Koreans, Blacks, and whites making a community out of the geography, but from the freeway you only get billboards and brake lights.

It was still morning when we joined the flow toward Wilshire Boulevard, the famous street where the embassy was.

"Consulate of the Republic of the Union of Myanmar," Allie corrected me.

"Rolls off the tongue. I can see why they dumped Burma."

Allie scrolled through her phone, excited to be here. I watched the traffic, excited to be moving at all.

"It's not good over there," she said. "Military rule. Check out this picture of their parliament. All uniforms. More generals than...than...help me out here."

"More generals than a Napoleon party? Nuremberg icebreaker? An LDS General Conference?"

"That last one is best, but few will get it."

"Know your audience."

Allie read on. "There's a facade of civilian leadership," she said. "A president, but the military can veto anything and...eek."

"What?"

"Reports of genocide."

"Eek," I agreed. "Coups?"

"Lots of them. It's a kind of national pastime."

"See anything I can use?" Our exit was up ahead. Siri reminded me to get in the right lane.

"Be on guard. Be polite. I doubt they'll have a sense of humor."

"Would I do anything to embarrass myself or my country?"

"What's plan B?" she said. "For after you get us thrown out?"

"Phone. I'll change my voice."

She chuckled as we followed Siri's sweet voice into urban sprawl.

"When are you going to tell me about Sundance?" I asked.

"Not much to tell."

"Tell me anyway."

"I saw your friend again."

My breakfast shifted. "And?" I said far too cheerfully.

"He hit on me."

I ground a molar to a new plane. "You're attractive and wonderful. He'd have to be a fool not to."

Allie, Allison Braise, really is gorgeous. She has hair straight as a pencil, hazel eyes, a bright smile. She wears an even tan that she earned by being outside. Her cheeks glow red from wind and warmth in equal glory. She has a grace, an authenticity, that moves her beyond shallow looks to the true beauty of a real person. It's the kind of vibe the girl next door gives off but without the passivity. She was my first love, and I still had to pinch myself whenever I remembered we were a thing.

"I think it was personal," she said. "I didn't want to tell you."

Still smiling hard, too hard, my eyes watering from the strain, I said, "Do tell."

"It's nothing."

"Go on. I'm good."

"You should drive through the intersection. It's a green light."

"So it is."

"You're sweating."

"So I am."

"It's no—"

"Go. On."

"The weekend was really fun. I wish you could have been there for more of it. Lots of interesting people. I got a couple good leads and two solid jobs. Good business—"

"Francis Tomas, please."

A car behind me honked because I hadn't accelerated past five miles per hour. I went to eight.

"He wanted to know about you. He asked about your successes."

"What successes?"

"Everything. Personal, money, career. He kept coming back to me with a new angle, a new way to probe about you."

"Huh," I said. It was becoming a catchphrase.

"Then when I said you'd divorced and we were dating, he moved on me."

"How hard?"

She sighed. "Very hard."

"And you...?"

"Were flattered."

"Just as an aside," I said. "Is there anything like a barf bag in your door pocket?"

"Nothing happened," she said.

I knew that would be the answer, but the fear of it had focused my insecurity to a boiling point, and my breakfast beans were making a comeback.

I swallowed and forced the smile on again.

"Put away that fucking smile. It's creepy. So fake."

"How long did this go on?"

"It began at one party and then he followed to the next. He wouldn't leave it alone."

"Did you encourage him?"

"Once I realized what he was doing, I most certainly did not."

"But he kept at it? He must have had some reason to think he had a chance."

She squinted at me. "Tony, don't be an ass."

"I'm just asking for the sake of conversation. Lots of weather we've been having."

"The parties were full of girls, actresses wanting to sleep with him."

"Why?"

"He claimed to be a producer."

"Is he?"

She shrugged. "Terrance didn't think so. He thought he was a poser, but he talked a good game. Dropped things in casual conversation like how his Maserati is being shipped over from Tuscany next month, number six of only one hundred in existence, and how he was at the governor's inaugural party and gave a toast at dinner."

"Which governor?"

"He didn't say."

"But he kept fishing for you even after dropping chum like that?"

"I don't want to sound stuck up, but yeah, that's what he did."

"And you think it had to do with me?"

She nodded. "Creeped me the hell out."

"Not doing much for my calm, either."

"Terrance finally rescued me and kept him at bay."

"I owe that guy."

"No. I do. You were never in danger."

"Sorry."

"It's okay," she said. "It was weird, though."

"I haven't thought of that guy in decades, and now he's all up in my shit."

"Hey...don't call me shit."

"Did he get all up in you?"

"Of course not."

"Then I wasn't talking about you."

"Yes, you were."

"Really?"

"Yes."

"Okay. But it's a little freaky."

"I thought so, too."

"One thing, though," I said. "He could have been after you because of you. Don't sell yourself short. That's my job. You are gorgeous."

"Thanks."

I can give the advice, I just can't take it.

The tall Equitable Building loomed up to the right. We turned the block and found parking for only ten dollars an hour and got out to find the Consulate of the Republic of the Union of Myanmar. Word on the marquee said it was on the fifteenth floor.

Allie slipped her hand into mine and kissed me.

"He never had a chance," she said.

"I gotta put a ring on it," I said.

"If you think you must, but I'm committed already."

"You mean you should be."

"Nah. You make me laugh."

28

I WAS of two minds about what Allie had told me. Emotionally, it was troubling, but intellectually it was really cool that we could talk about stuff like that. Guess which side rode up with me in the elevator?

On the fifteenth floor, we found the consulate. I've been to embassies before, but nothing as small and casual as this one. Where were the armed guards? The bullet-proof glass? Magnetic surveillance? Orbital mind-control laser relays? It was just an office. It could have been an office of a big import/export business with a penchant for iconic decoration. There was a receptionist at a desk. A door behind her. A flag and pictures of people I assumed were the government. In a waiting area several Asian people sat quietly, thumbing through newspapers written in a script only Tolkien admired.

As we stepped up to the desk, I finally saw a guard. He was in full military uniform. Hat and medals. A pistol at his hip, white-gloved hands. He stood in a vestibule beside a glass door that I suspected was tougher than it looked. It was a consulate after all. Like an embassy, but not in Washington.

"Hello," I said. Always a good way to start.

"How may I help you?" responded the receptionist.

"I'd like to talk to the cultural liaison."

"The what?"

"No, uhm. The political liaison."

"Who?"

"The ambassador. Yes. That's who I need."

"We have a consulate, not an ambassador. This is a consulate, not an embassy. The embassy is in Washington DC."

"Consulate then."

"We do have one of those," she said.

"Neat."

"Do you have an appointment?"

"Do I need one?"

"Usually, yes."

"But today's my lucky day, right? How cool is that, Allie?"

"Very cool."

"Not that cool," said the receptionist.

"I think you have a tourist missing," I said.

"You think?"

"Well, I don't know."

"Do you want to make some kind of report?" she asked and thumbed a desk drawer of files digging for a form that I knew wouldn't provide me with any information.

"No. Not like that," I said. "I want to talk to somebody about it."

"Is it an emergency?"

"Uhm. Could be."

"Call the American police."

"I don't—"

"Can we get an appointment?" said Allie, coming to the rescue.

"What're your names?" she asked us.

We told her, filled in a basic form, and she told us to have a seat.

"Good thinking," I said to Allie. "Beating them at their own game."

"Be careful," she said. "I bet there are listening devices and cameras everywhere."

I looked up at the ceiling and saw three cameras. Glancing back down the hall, I saw two more.

"What gave it away?" I whispered.

"All the cameras with microphones everywhere," she said and winked.

I kissed her.

"Bet we won't get in today," she said.

"We'd have been sent away if that were true."

"Betcha."

"You're basing your opinion on past experiences. Never a good guide."

"Betcha," she said.

"Betcha." We shook hands.

I was thumbing through a travel brochure about the wonders of Asia when the receptionist called us up.

I beamed at Allie.

She stuck her tongue out.

At the desk, the receptionist said, "There is somebody you can meet with on Wednesday at six o'clock in the afternoon."

"That's evening. Nearly night. And that's tomorrow."

"Yes."

"But that's a day away."

"First available appointment. Would next week work better?"

"Who is it with?" asked Allie.

"A security man."

"Can we instead see the—"

"No."

"Okay," I said. "I guess we'll see you tomorrow."

As we got to the elevator, Allie said, "I win."

"What do you want?"

"I've always wanted to see the coast highway. Let's go to San Francisco."

"Really?"

"Be there by dinner."

"Okay," I said. "Now who's spontaneous?"

We retrieved the car, found the 101, and sped north.

I've heard about the wonders of the Pacific Coast Highway, and I'm sure it's very beautiful—in the summer, but this was winter and a storm was here, so it looked like just another dreary coastline to me. Not that I've seen many of those—a couple on the BBC and black-and-white late shows with forlorn women looking seaward. Besides the darkness of the water, the threatening clouds and rain, there was little to recommend us to stop and linger along the way, so we made good time.

And we had a good time. Seven hours in the car with Allie was just what I needed. With the sex out of the way for a while, we could concentrate on getting reacquainted. I know there's a point in every relationship where long silences are normal and serene when conversation lulls because each knows the other that well. We weren't there yet. We were giddy to chat and tease and play and listen to music and talk politics and movies. The time rushed by and I only had to pull over twice, once for gas, once to catch my breath after laughing so hard.

We called our LA B&B saying BRB ASAP, OK?

Allie found us a room in the middle of The City by the Bay. "My treat," she said. "I got a nice advance from a director's wife to train her pet."

"Shih Tzu?"

"Ferret."

We got in before six o'clock and thought to see some of the sights right away, but the storm had beat us there. The city was a gray smear beyond the car windows. The cold and damp seeped in between the layers of our clothes and chilled us in places Utah's dry cold never touched. I've always been a fan of this city, but I'd only been there once or twice before. Once for a week, once in a layover. Maybe twice for a layover. San Francisco is an icon, an echo of the '60s enlightenment movement, gay rights, good music, and pirate culture going back to the first days. Earthquake bait, freezing fog that's there so long it gets mail delivered, and now a cost of living so high that people are fleeing it for Manhattan to get a little rent relief. A recent blight of homelessness had manifested itself as a plague of used heroin needles scattered in the streets with a kind of Biblical feel to it—locusts testing the ground before an invasion. Minefields of dog mess were compounded by human additions, and the seafood just wasn't what it used to be. At least that's the buzz on the internet lately. I kinda suspected such bad PR didn't make a lot of sense. Knowing that it was a nexus of smart people, I wondered if it was a misinformation campaign, meant to keep people away and maybe roll in real estate prices.

"That's tin-foil hat stuff," Allie said. "Where'd you get that idea?"

"Perry."

"I should have known."

We did one stop before the hotel because we found parking near Haight Ashbury. Once the rain let up, we figured tourists would be out. The locals already were. A little freezing rain is barbecue weather there. We passed people on bikes and walking their miserable dogs. Allie grunted in disgust as we stepped over piles of poo and hypodermic needles.

The famous home of the Flower Power movement was just a bunch of cool-looking old buildings with steep steps and bay windows. I tried to imagine the energy that had sprung from there, but in the rain I had only visions of Altamont and the receding wave Hunter S. Thompson had seen from that window in Las Vegas. Everything seemed dirty now and expensive and out of reach—a tourist attraction, historical monument remembering a time that had passed and now only echoed.

We browsed a couple of curio shops, more to get out of the rain than anything. Allie bought a tie-dye sundress so airy and light that it made me happy just thinking about it and excited to think of her in it. It would be half a year, I knew, before she'd be able to wear it outside of a well-heated room, but when she did, it'd be wonderful.

I bought some anti-war buttons, some for the old wars, some for the new ones, and wandered into a gallery with psychedelic prints for sale, spirals and patterns that seemed to shimmer as you looked. There were famous concert posters, Jefferson Airplane at The Fillmore, Jimi Hendrix, Janis. There were black-light posters that Allie talked me out of buying in bulk.

"Black light makes your dental work glow funny," she reminded me.

Then I found an old friend. That goddamn picture of the Eiffel Tower at night with a thumb in one corner and a price tag of $1,789—nonnegotiable!!!

"This thing is haunting me," I told Allie. "The gallery Friday, Maggie's dressing room, Randy's teacher and now here."

"We're just not in touch with art," she said. "I mean, besides the reference to the French Revolution, I don't get it."

"It's spitting in the face of the establishment," came a voice.

An older woman with silver gray hair whom we hadn't seen before came forward, pointing to the picture with a circling finger.

"How's that?" asked Allie.

"It's a copyright infringement to take a picture of the Eiffel Tower at night."

"Come on," said Allie. "Everyone takes a picture of it. You're telling me they arrest tourists leaving Paris?"

The woman smiled. It was a warm smile. She had good teeth. When her smile faded, her lips creased in wrinkles to match her eyes. She had no makeup. Here was a woman who didn't hide from her age, and as such, I had a very hard time guessing it. Sixty to eighty. Timeless.

"Night photos," she explained. "With the lights. The tower is public domain, but someone says they have rights to it lit up. If you buy a postcard of it like that, you're paying the copyright holder something."

"But not this one?"

"Oh no. This is pirated and proudly so."

"Did you know about this?" Allie asked me.

"Oh yeah," I said, concealing the fact that I'd only heard it that weekend. "Real scandal."

Allie shook her head as if trying to shake a fly off her nose. "But it costs a fortune. Hard to justify sticking it to the man when it's so expensive. Isn't capitalism the man?"

"All the money goes to the public domain defense fund."

"But first it goes to Barion," said Allie, pointing at the name. "He takes his cut."

"He swears he doesn't."

"You know him?" I said.

"Moved back east and got involved with some bad people there."

"Bad as in 'he's dead now'?" I said.

"I don't remember," she said, looking away.

"So how do you know that the charity is on the up and up? I heard that most charities—"

"I guess you're right," she said. "I really don't know." She moved to leave, some urgency in her step.

"Huh…"

"You should buy it, though. Great conversation piece."

"I don't have that kind of money to make a statement."

"What do you use money for then if not to make the world a better place?"

"Ouch," I said.

"I don't mean to judge," said she. "Forgive an old hippie."

"Forgiven."

She turned and left the shop, popping open a red umbrella just outside the door.

"That was trippy," said Allie.

I went up to the counter. "Is all your work by local artists?" I asked. For emphasis, I pulled out my wallet and shuffled my credit cards giving off the "I'm going to spend a buttload here" vibe.

He didn't seem to notice.

"Yeah," he said. "Bay City Brands." It was the name of the gallery. I saw it on a business card and slipped it into my wallet beside my nearly over-drawn Visa. He didn't care.

"But some of those artists are dead now?" I offered.

"Yeah, some are."

"And some have moved away from the city?"

"Hard to live here on what an artist makes," said he.

"But all themed for the city. How droll."

"Droll," he echoed, making me feel like the idiot I sounded like.

"Some have nothing to do with the city at all. Like that Eiffel Tower. That looks really out of place. Kind of puts the lie to your gallery. But Barion was from here?"

"Uh-huh."

"Where is he now?"

"Disappeared."

"How's that?"

"Orion Babbs," he said. "Look him up."

"How about you tell me?" I flashed him a five-dollar bill.

He almost laughed.

I pulled out two more singles.

He rolled his eyes. I thought of how Randy could learn something from this guy's eyeball technique.

The rain continued to pour down. No one was on the street, no one else was coming in.

The clerk sighed in defeat.

"The Babbses were part of the original Merry Pranksters," he said. "Orion was their kid."

"You ever meet him?"

"Nah."

"So what happened?" said Allie.

"He was a good artist. Got recruited into organized crime out of college."

"I don't remember that table at my recruitment day."

He smiled.

"So what happened?"

"To Orion?"

"No, to recruitment day," I said. "Was it budget cuts?"

He smiled again, wryly this time. I'd zinged him.

"Turned state's evidence."

"Prison?"

He shook his head. "Witness protection."

29

THE RAIN LET up as we checked into our hotel. We found our room, wished we'd brought a change of clothes, and then went in search of dinner.

Just at dusk we found a shorefront restaurant on the pier The Bay Barnacle Bistro. It advertised fresh seafood and a great view.

It was loud, crowded, high-volume seating but still romantic. Just out the window was the water, and there in the gloom, fog moving in like a curse, was the sinister Alcatraz Island. A homeless guy strolled up the boardwalk, wearing a garbage bag rain poncho. He paused, admired the view, zipped down his pants and pissed on a bench. But really, it was romantic.

Though the place felt like a tourist trap—its location could make it nothing else—we appeared to be the only ones. The rest of the clientele seemed local. None of them cared what it looked like outside, stark and menacing, and all had their noses stuck to their phones. I'm not saying tourists don't miss great sunsets and ambiance to their own personal addiction devices, but these seemed uniformly yuppie, rich, and well-acclimated to the shit weather and heart-stopping prices on the menu. They ordered reasonable portions and good wines. Every once in a while, one of them would look up, survey the other diners, pass judgment, and return their verdict in whispers to their companions.

I waved when it was our turn and got a turned-up nose for the effort.

"Somebody we know?"

"Entitled locals," I said.

Allie looked at them. "If I had to guess, I'd say they were recent transplants, here about five years, more than two, less than six. Make more money in a week than most do in a year. In technology. They're pissed off that tourists are cramping their style."

"But not real local?"

"Hell no. I know the type."

"Do tell," I said.

"We have plenty of people like them in Moab. Most are older, have less money, don't carry phones that haven't been released yet, but the mentality is the same."

She was right. Snotty girl had a phone that had been advertised but wouldn't be widely available for a week or two yet.

"Nice detective work," I said.

"I learned from the best."

"Poirot?"

She blew me a kiss.

I ordered Maine lobster, and Allie had Atlantic cod. The irony was not lost on us as we watched the sea outside our window.

We were working on some oysters from New Brunswick when a woman at the bar shut up the whole restaurant by saying loudly, "Oh my god, I think I used to date that guy."

Everyone turned to look. Everyone but a man sitting two tables behind Allie.

"Ooooo," she said. "I think he saw me." As subtle as an axe murderer.

All eyes shifted from her to the man who kept his face turned to the window, stuffing sourdough bread in his cheeks.

In answer to a question her companion must have asked, someone with a volume button, the loud girl said loudly, "From Tinder. He was weird. Into some real sick stuff."

The girl with the blushing guy stopped chewing and held still as a bunny in the lights of a Peterbilt.

"Gross stuff," Loud Girl said. "I mean, really."

I didn't think Valley Girl accents existed anymore, remembered only in '80s movies with hair scrunchies and Vuarnet sunglasses, but here it was.

"Spanking. I mean, who wants to be spanked? Weirdo."

The woman with the blushing man began chewing again, and I detected, possibly hoped for perhaps, the slightest smile tug on her lips. She put her hand on his and he turned to her with a sheepish smile and sipped a glass of red wine.

"He's one of the reasons I stopped using Ti—"

"Shhhhhhhhh," I hissed.

"Oh my God," she said when she realized I was directing it at her.

I got up, went right to the bar, bent down to her on the stool, leaned in close, and went, "Shhhhhhh. Use your indoor voice. Kay?"

"I never..."

"You should try it," I said.

She turned back to the bar. The snotty looks directed at me had changed to something between awe and amusement. The restaurant noise returned.

"We could try some spanking," Allie said.

It took all my superpowers to keep the oyster I was eating from shooting out my nose.

———

The next day we got a good start.

It was sunny and cold, but we were still warm from each other's company.

Enough said.

We grabbed food from a drive-through—breakfast sandwiches, curly fries, and espresso. I pointed the car south but also a little west.

Allie noticed when I passed the freeway entrance. "Where are you taking us?" she said. "Another surprise?"

"Los Altos," I said. "I've always wanted to see it."

"Los Altos? What is it?"

"A place. A suburb of San Francisco. We're nearly there."

"What's there?"

"Dunno. Let's see."

"But you've always wanted to go there?"

"Sure."

"That name sounds familiar," Allie said. "Where have I heard it recently?"

I squirmed a little.

"Why are you squirming, Tony?" Then I saw the light in her eyes. "Frank Tomas lives there. You're going to see what his house looks like. Tony—"

"He does? How do you know that?"

"He told me," she said. "He told everyone. I mean ev-er-y-one."

We passed Lincoln Park and were in the city.

"Did he tell everyone where he lived exactly? I mean, an address?"

"I'd think you had that already from your research," Allie said.

"I couldn't find it. Just the city."

"Why is he getting to you?"

"You know why."

"Oh, well, yeah. He's a douche. Don't worry. He said he was leaving Utah after Sunday, after your high school reunion."

"We're here. I'm curious," I said.

"Okay, but we're on a schedule."

Los Altos was a pretty town. You could tell it was originally agricultural but had been gentrified fast and well. The main streets were lined with single-level shopping with parking problems. Beyond the commercial areas, streets of suburban sprawl that would make any Utahn feel at home stretched out in organized tree-lined streets.

"There's a lot of houses here for sale," Allie said. "It isn't the season for that."

"Maybe California doesn't have a selling season."

"Spring is best everywhere, I hear."

"Me too."

"Mostly modest houses, old ramblers. Notice that they're all shown by appointment only."

"That says money."

"But lots of them," said Allie. "I bet some big tech company went out of business recently."

"That's a good guess," I said, wishing I'd thought of it.

"What's wrong?" said Allie. Man, she was quick to detect my mood. How could she do that? "Why the sad heavy sigh?" Puzzle solved.

"You're very smart. You've got a good eye for people. You figured out a real estate clue I missed and then used the clue to deduct a plausible theory."

"A clue? Really? I found a clue? Which case?"

"The uh...one you...never mind."

"Oh. The Frank Tomas one? That's at 'case level?'" She squinted at me. "Who's paying for that one? Besides me, I mean?"

"My insecurity."

"You're looking for failure. Stop it."

"It finds me. If I don't look at it, I can't hit the bowl."

"Hit the...?" She laughed. "Forget about that."

Not everything the night before had gone great.

"How are you going to know which house is his?"

"Names on mailboxes, but we really don't have time to drive the entire town."

"Good deduction."

"Look," I said, pointing to a car coming the other way. "A Utah license plate. A transplant, like you predicted. From Silicon Slopes to Silicon Valley."

Silicon Slopes is the nickname of an area between Salt Lake and Provo where tech companies—"Shit me a fishhead!"

"What?" screamed Allie.

"I know that car. I know that guy."

The blue Honda. A bushy-bearded face beneath a ball cap sat at the wheel. Behind reflective sunglasses, the driver slowed and tracked us as we passed each other. I tracked him right back and slammed the brakes.

He hit the gas.

I thought of throwing it into reverse and doing "a Rockford," a specialized bootleg turn made famous, if not invented and actually performed, by the great James Garner as everyman detective Jim Rockford in the famous TV series, *The Rockford Files*. It ran for—

"What does that even mean?" Allie said.

I started a four-point U-turn.

"What? Oh. That car's been following me from Utah."

"No, the fishhead thing. I can't even—"

"He's getting away." I cranked the wheel and after only three points was on his trail. "Did you see which way he went?" I said.

"He turned right at the stop sign."

I turned right at the stop sign.

Utah streets are in a grid. I could sense something of the like here but with sudden endings and meanderings. It made for a cozier neighborhood, dissuaded through traffic, but made car chases difficult.

I saw the tail end of the Honda disappear behind a hedge at a swerve in the road.

"If we get close enough, get the license plate," I said.

"We'll catch him," said Allie. "I believe in you."

I made the turn and stared down a street without a blue Honda in it.

I adjusted my speed. "You look right, I'll look left. Look in driveways, not just down streets. If there's a likely street that disappears around a corner, sing out."

"Laaaaa!" she sang.

On the left, I saw another. "Laaaa!"

"Tons of criss-cross streets."

"I thought California burned down. This foliage is a pain."

"I know," said Allie. "We should do something about that."

We cruised the streets for fifteen minutes and finally had to give up.

"Still believe in me?" I said.

"You know I do, Tony. You're not a fraud."

"How'd you know I was thinking that if I wasn't a fraud?"

"You have problems with logic, that I'll grant you, but not in hiding your emotions. Still, I'll bet a week of spankings you solve all your cases."

"Even the Frank Tomas one?"

"Tell me what you think the mystery is, and I'll tell you if I think you will."

"I think he's out to get me. I want to know why."

She pinched up her mouth in a thoughtful pucker. "Okay," she said. "Betcha."

Allie navigated us to the freeway leading us back to LA for the meeting at the consulate. My phone rang. Allie answered it. I was driving and being responsible. No, actually I was driving on unfamiliar and crowded freeways. I was pants-shittingly scared and concentrating hard not to take a wrong road, crash, run out of gas, or accidentally join a cult. The NuSkin billboard was eerie.

"Hello, this is Allie answering for Tony Flaner. Who is calling?"

"A real noir secretary," I said.

She listened.

"Uh-huh…oh…yes… No, I don't think you should…here's Tony."

She put the phone on speaker and held it up.

"This is Tony," I said.

"Mr. Flaner, this is Bryan Moland. I got your message."

"Oh, right. Sorry about that. I'm out of town on another case. I should have told you in person. Or maybe called you. My bad. I just thought you needed to know right away."

"I confronted Maddy about it," he said.

"Let me guess, she denied it all. You'll just have to take the data and make your own judgment. I know personal stuff—"

"No, she admitted all of it."

"Oh," I said. "A confession." I beamed at Allie, feeling some much-needed validation. Allie didn't return the glow.

"She says if I don't go through with the wedding, let her pull in the swag—swag, she called it swag—whatever is that?"

"It's slang for goodies. It came from either an old pirate idiom for treasure or a modern acronym for 'Shit We All Get' that conventioneers use to describe the stuff in gift bags."

"Mr. Flaner, she said if I don't go through with it, she'll ruin me."

"What? How?"

"She has some letters and personal things. Some photos."

"Were you a bad boy?"

"Mr. Flaner, please take this seriously."

"I am. I'm trying to ask you what's in the photos."

"We messed around. Nothing that technically would constitute premarital intercourse, but photos that would embarrass me if she sent them out to everyone on our guest registry."

"That was the threat?"

"Yes."

"Ugh." I understood Allie's reaction now.

"That…that can't happen," Moland muttered.

"I'll be back in town tomorrow," said I. "We'll go over options then."

"I can't let her do this to me."

"We got this, Bryan. Don't worry. Relax. Take a pill. Go to sleep. We'll talk later."

I think he heard me. I think I'd helped. I thought I left him in a calmer place. Going to bed, my only basis for thinking all this was that he said "okay" before the line went dead.

30

I RELAXED when the traffic did, and we made good time back to LA. The little rental car hadn't been able to catch a late-model blue Honda, but it did eat up carpool lanes with a certain panache.

"Just when you thought you'd finished a case," said Allie.

"It is finished."

"But..."

"What?"

"How devastating for him," said Allie.

"Yep."

"He didn't sound good," said Allie.

"Nope."

"Call him back."

"Go ahead." She dialed—yes, I trust Allie with my phone code. That's true commitment.

"No answer," she said. "Went straight to message."

"He's probably napping like I told him to."

"Would you be napping?"

"No. I'd be obtunded."

"What's that?"

"Flat on my back passed out, blunt to all sensation. I would achieve this with the help of some chemical assistance."

"Suicide?"

"No...don't say that," I said. "He's fine."

"He sounded rough."

I recalled what I knew of the man. Bryan Moland was a mature, upstanding citizen. Successful in all aspects of his life. All but one, I guess.

"Nah. He'll lawyer up. That's what he'll do. If he's not taking a Benadryl break right now, he's chatting up some high-priced mouthpiece."

"Is that what you're going to tell him to do when see him? You're going to tell him to get a lawyer?"

"What else?"

We arrived in time to go to our bed and breakfast for a change of clothes.

"We're leaving tomorrow," I told the landlady.

"You still gotta pay for last night."

"Okay."

"Just 'cause you didn't sleep here doesn't get you out of the cost."

"We get it."

"You had a reservation."

"That's how it works."

"I've already charged you for last night."

"That's fine."

"If I see you trying to reverse the charge, I'll get you banned from Airbnb forever."

"Didn't know you could do that."

"Just try me."

"We'll see you tonight."

"Charging you for tonight too."

In our room, Allie said, "She went Riff Raff to slumlord in a hurry."

"Economic anxiety."

———

We arrived for our six o'clock meeting at the Consulate of the Republic of the Union of Myanmar at 5:55 p.m. like a coupla bosses.

"Remember us?" I asked the receptionist.

"No."

"We have an appointment at six."

"With whom?"

"I dunno. You made the appointment."

"We're closing."

"Nooooo," I said. "No."

"What?"

"You told us to come back today at six o'clock. We're here at six. We want to see somebody. The ambassador. Yes, that's who we're here to see."

"The ambassador isn't here."

"Vice ambassador?"

"Legate?" offered Allie.

"Flaner and Braise?" she asked.

"That's us," we said together and then giggled because that's what couples in love do at times like that.

"Have a seat," she said.

The waiting room was deserted this time which made it hard to pick a chair. So many choices. The one by the plant? The one with more magazines? Armrests or not? Upholstery, leather, or pleather?

Before I made my move, Allie was already sitting down, browsing at a museum brochure. I considered sitting next to her, but the seat by the plant looked so inviting.

"Flaner and Braise."

Standing at the inside door was a man who we hadn't heard come in.

He was out of uniform but stood like he was used to being in one. He looked us over like a cop sizing up suspects.

"Follow me," he said with the foreign English accent that made Americans blush.

He led us into a little office to the side, not big, not important, but busy. There was no window, but it had two chairs for us in front of a desk piled with papers, magazines, newspapers, brochures, maps, and stacks of manila files with labels I couldn't read.

"I didn't do it," I said out of habit. "I'm innocent! Where's the fucking clock?"

"Right there," said the man.

"Oh. Yes. There it is. It's a nice one."

"It's atomic. Sets itself automatically."

"Very nice."

We sat down.

"I'm Sergeant San," said the man, offering to shake my hand.

I stood up and shook it.

"Police or military?"

"In Myanmar, they're much the same, but I'm a policeman."

"I thought I got the vibe," I said. "Chief of security around here?"

"Why do you ask?"

"I'm not sure you're the guy I need to talk to."

"I'm the only one available."

"Low on the totem pole, huh?"

"Seems so. Why are you here?"

"I told you I didn't do it."

"Yes…" he said, confused. "Uhm…who sent you?"

"I'll never talk!"

Allie put her head in her hands.

"What?" I whispered.

San looked to Allie for assistance.

She shook her head. "He gets this way."

"What kind of interview room is this, anyway?" I asked.

"It's my office," said San. "What's wrong with it?"

"There are no hooks on the floor for ankle shackles, none on the table for handcuffs, no two-way mirror to watch the torture, no obvious cameras or microphones to record my confession. The chair's too soft, you have a computer and here are more brochures advertising your lovely country. Is this some kind of new mental pressure tactic to get me to talk?"

"Is it working?"

"Yes!" I said. "I admit it! I cut the labels off all the mattresses. Not just mine, but the ones in the bed and breakfast this afternoon. The woman was rude. I needed vengeance. I have a string of labels on a wire I wear around my neck at night—a grisly warning for whoever fucks with me that I know all there is to know about natural fibers and stuffing contents. Washing instructions, countries of origin. All mine!"

"Tony? How do you stay in business?" said Allie.

"What business is that?" asked San.

"He's a private investigator."

"Stool pigeon!"

"So we're in the same business," he said.

"Maybe that's why he's acting this way," said Allie.

"Is he mentally deranged?"

"I think he's trying to make a point."

"And what point is that?" I said to Allie.

"I have no idea," she said.

"Ha! Neither do I."

"Is this a prank?" asked San.

"Nah," I said, relenting. "I like to get the measure of who I'm dealing with."

"A test?"

"Yeah," I said, leaning back.

He pierced me with his dark eyes and said, "You were pushing me to see how far you'd have to push me before I disappeared on you both."

I laughed.

He didn't.

I chuckled.

He stared.

Allie squirmed.

"You're...you're serious?"

"Gotcha." He laughed.

"Do you have a towel, or is this one of those super absorbent chair cushions?"

"You better not have."

"Tell him why we're here, Tony."

"I'm looking for a missing girl. I thought you might be able to give me some information."

"Who is it?"

"Her name is Sandi Wong," I said. "I'm looking for her for a friend."

I'd surprised him. "Sandi Wong?"

"You know her?"

"Who's your friend?"

"A Thai. You don't know him."

"Are you sure?"

"I hope not," I said. "You're beginning to scare me."

"It's the uniform."

"You're not wearing one."

"Yes," he said.

Allie swallowed and snuck a look at me as San turned to his computer.

"Is it always this tense?" she whispered.

"Until the beatings start," I said.

"Not funny."

San smiled.

I swallowed.

San's face was awash in blue light. We couldn't see what he saw, but it looked to have pleased him. "What do you want to know about her?" he asked.

"Is she related to the late General Tayza, dead, now deceased?" I sweated. A little late, I realized that people like San are the kind of people who can arrange car accidents for subversive exiles.

"She is not."

"Are you sure?"

"We know of all the General's family," he said, and I thought I saw him glance at one of his files.

"She claimed to be a cousin."

"Our records go five generations deep and six wide."

"Maybe under a different name?"

"All are accounted for."

"Any in the US?"

"Three, but none fit the girl's description."

"Wait," I said. "I didn't give you her description."

He turned the monitor to show me. There was the passport picture Fah had sent of her. I had it on my phone right now. "Someone else looked into this same claim recently," he said.

"And who was that?"

"Kyi Tun, former adjutant to General Tayza."

"Ah...no. That makes no sense," I said. "They're in exile."

"The general was in exile, but like you said, he's dead. Kyi is still a common citizen. The general's son is the important one."

"Keep your friends close and your enemies closer?"

"Anything else?"

"I've met them. They're paranoid. They think someone murdered the general."

San reached over for a manila file from the stack and opened it.

"The crash was suspicious, but I can assure you my government was not responsible."

"Was mine? Asking for a friend."

He flipped a page or two, traced his finger down lines and squiggles that I assumed were language, and said, "Investigating police thought it was a little suspicious. It was most likely an accident."

"Can you be more specific?"

"No. That's all I have," he said. "Except this." He showed us a picture of Kyi and a boy huddled together in the foreground, medical people working on the child, putting bandages on him. In the background was a smoldering car.

The picture was bleak, heartbreaking. Allie turned away and steer the conversation back. "What did they want with Sandi Wong?" said Allie.

"Same as you, checking her claim to be a cousin."

"What could she gain from that?" I asked.

San leaned back in his chair, relaxing a little. Some of the earlier tension evaporated.

"Money?" he said.

"They do seem rich."

"Do they?"

"Something about a trust fund for Thiha."

San went back to his folder. "Yes," he said.

"Big one?"

"Enough."

"Not telling, huh?"

"We try not to brand a son with his father's sins," he said. "The government has allowed a trust fund to be kept for the use of the child. Enough for college."

"College?"

"That's what it's for."

"They have a mansion. Kyi's producing movies. He collects shit off eBay like he's opening his own Planet Hollywood. Stert can't be cheap."

"What's stert?"

"Scottish bodyguard with no sense of humor or love of the spontaneous."

He looked again. "College fund. A small living allowance."

"Was the general rich?"

"He absconded with the money, but it was seized back after he died."

"All of it?"

"Most of it," he said.

Something there didn't track, but before I could put my finger on it, ask a question, or embarrass us again, Allie said, "So Sandi wasn't expecting money. Maybe she thought she really was a cousin."

"Probably just looking for a place to stay. I understand she's an actress and in town to meet people at the Sundance Film Festival."

"You know about that?"

"Everyone knows about Sundance."

"I mean her being an actress and visiting the festival."

"Oh. Must have heard it somewhere."

"Do you have a file on her here on this gorgeous mahogany desk?"

"No."

"How about under all these museum brochures?" I took one. *Ancient Art and Exhibits.* It was the same one Allie had found in the lobby. On the cover was a vase like the one I'd seen in Kyi's sunroom.

"No," said San. "No file. I'm sorry."

I stuffed the brochure in my pocket with one of San's business cards. I also helped myself to a couple of butterscotch candies in a bowl next to his paper clips.

"Anything else?" he said.

I unwrapped a butterscotch and rolled it against my teeth with a clacking noise.

Allie rolled her eyes and elbowed me. "We should go."

"The man asked me a question, I'm considering."

San went back to his computer. "Sandi Wong arrived in your country two weeks ago. Nothing else."

"Nothing?"

He grimaced. "She left Bangkok. Before that, she was in Hong Kong, mainland China, Myanmar. Taiwan, Myanmar. She travels."

"Family? Relatives?"

"None on record."

"You're a police state," I said. "With scary secret police who disappear people. You've got to have more than that. Where she went to school, what she reads, what to put in with her for a Room 101 visit."

"She changed her name," said San. "Does that help? When she was eighteen, she changed it to Sandi Wong."

"From what?"

"Chime."

"Chime Wong?"

"We don't have surnames like you do."

"Is Sandi Wong a rare name?"

"Absolutely not. Many of our people have taken Chinese names like that."

"It's Chinese?" I asked.

He rolled his eyes.

"How did you know who to look for if the name is so common? Airport records?"

"Kyi faxed us a copy of her passport."

I laughed.

"What's so funny?"

"Who uses a fax machine? Such a rube!"

He took a deep cleansing breath, part Buddhist, part anger management.

"I have a question for you," he said.

"I told you I didn't do it."

"You say you met Kyi and Thiha?"

"Yes. Yes, I did."

"This is very important. If you can't answer it, don't. If you lie to me, I'll know."

"How?"

He smiled, and a chill went up my back. Allie gripped my hand.

"Secret police," I said.

"Did either of them express a desire to return to Myanmar or strike you as political in any way?"

He held me in his steely eyes, but he could not kill the beast. That's how flustered I was—I was putting new lyrics to *Hotel California*.

"Actually," I said calmly and honestly, "Kyi said he wouldn't return home for anything. He called it 'a backward jungle.' He's head over heels in love with America and its movies."

"And the boy, Thiha?"

"Typical teenager. Sluffing school, doing homework, getting too much blue light after dusk. Some say it messes with your sleep patterns."

San held me in a hard gaze, not blinking, as if reading my soul. I matched him as best I could, trying not to blink either, meeting him dry eye for dry eye, but I couldn't keep up. I finally figured I'd blink for the both of us and went on a blinking frenzy making everything look like a silent movie.

The breeze must have finally gotten to him.

"Okay," he said, shifting a file from the top of his pile to the bottom. "Thanks."

"Let's go, Tony," Allie said, standing and pulling me up by the elbow. "Let's get some pizza."

"Want to come?" I asked San.

For a moment, I thought he considered it. "No, thank you."

A guard with an assault rifle escorted us out.

The receptionist was gone. The guard took us to the elevator, put a key in the panel, turned it, and when the door opened, he waited for us to get in. We got in.

"Why did you want that brochure?" asked Allie.

"This thing on the cover," I said, pointing to the pointy vase.

"What about it?"

"I saw one just like in Kyi's house. Guess how large it is?"

"Sixty-two point five centimeters," she said. "I read the description."

"Nope. It's about two feet."

31

WE HAD STREET TACOS, not pizza. LA isn't famous for pizza. Street tacos seemed more appropriate, plus I was beginning to worry about my bank account. Randy's first crushing car payment was coming out of it any day. I wondered if he'd fetched it out of impound yet.

> Pick your car up yet?

No.

> Why?

TTYL.

The tacos were cheap, so we had a bunch of them sitting at a plastic picnic table with built-in chairs. There were napkins, six different sauces, and three advertising tents in Spanish.

I munched my six-sauced tacos, mulling ideas. Cars cruised by in the darkness, slowing to peek out, see if they knew who we were, maybe wonder if we had drugs to sell or wanting to sell us some. Allie wouldn't let me even try to buy any.

The interview with San wasn't sitting right. I didn't know how, where, why, or even who, but after talking to him, I had logical connection and theory, but emotional disjoinery. The emotional would turn logical after a time, I hoped. Or it wouldn't and I'd forget it. I'd just have to wait and see.

Allie was quiet at first but finally said, "Did she deliberately lie about being a cousin?" She was doctoring her second taco with the green sauce, trying them one at a time like an amateur.

"Fah thought she was legit, but he might not have seen it. Abergast, the guy she had a one-nighter with, said she bounced from place to place on the generosity of strangers. After listening to San and the Burmese in Park City, that sounds right. A hanger-on. A wannabe."

"Which is it? Hanger-on or wannabe?"

"What's the difference?" I asked.

"Well, a hanger-on is like a groupie. A wannabe wants to be in the band."

"I'm not sure either fits."

"But you just said it."

"Well, she strikes me as a free spirit, using her charm to get what she wants."

"You said she wasn't a prostitute," said Allie.

"Not like that. More of an actress, playing parts in real life to fit the opportunities."

"Now you're making her sound like an improv prostitute."

"I see a low-level grifter, not out to bankrupt anyone or get rich, but getting herself invited to parties on yachts, guest houses—that kind of thing. Hang out for a while, then move on, maybe with some new scratch in her pockets from new charitable friends."

"She has a list of them," Allie said. "Fah, Abergast, Saudis."

"Each one in a position to help her. Hotels primarily. She's a gypsy, maybe."

"But she got busted in Park City."

"Yeah, there's that," I said.

"Where next?"

"Finish these tacos, catch a movie. Maybe see some sidewalk stars. Bed and a plane in the morning."

"Okay, but I was talking about the case."

"I knew you were. I'll let you know on that."

———

January is not the right month to visit California, but it was better than back home.

Psychically, it had done wonders for me. I'd got to spend time with Allie, and we'd had adventures and I got to write the whole thing off, include it on my expense report to Fah, who'd pay it in Saudi blood money. Allie made me feel not ten feet tall but loved and appreciated. She didn't puff me up with praise where my own inflated skull would carry me away in a breeze but instead grounded me like tent spikes in the wind. Gusts ripped and worried me still, but I had a grasp on it, and as we ended our trip, the occasional panic attacks of fraud syndrome were easily put down in her lovely eyes. It didn't hurt that I felt I was making progress. There, too, Allie deserved some thanks.

"Thanks," I told her the next morning as we settled into our seats for the flight home.

"For what?"

I smiled.

"You're getting mushy again, aren't you?"

"Little bit."

"You were a little mean, though."

"What?"

"Telling our B&B landlord that we might turn her in for not having mattress tags."

"She threatened to hold our deposit."

She kissed me.

Yeah, it'd been a fun trip.

Allie rolled over and slept. I was regretting how early the flight was. We had to be at LAX by three a.m. That was brutal. To combat my tiredness, I'd had a quadruple espresso in black coffee and could now hear the color blue.

Wired and wondering if I'd done permanent damage, I tried to remain calm.

Then we flew into the storm we'd met on the California coast heading to Utah now for some skiing, apparently. As a warm-up, it juggled our jet with turbulence that made my butt pucker and teeth grind.

In between buffetings, I busied myself on my computer, burning up hyper-expensive minutes watching cat videos and then, when I felt sufficiently guilty, actually doing agonizingly slow internet research to justify the line item on my coming expense report.

Thiha was a student at Park City High School. The school didn't have roster lists, but unlike many of his hip friends and my son, he had a lively Facebook profile.

I saw pictures of him on the slopes with friends, waterskiing last summer with his group. There hadn't been a lot of traffic recently, but there were no fewer than thirty posts telling him to get well soon and come back to school.

The last message he'd left was a week ago Friday, something about not feeling well and staying home. That was the day Sandi had visited the house. I tried to read something into that but figured his guardian had kept him out of school to enjoy Sundance. He'd been out of the school all that week. He still was out a half week after the festival had ended.

Huh.

Another message popped up.

"Heading to school. Hope to see you today, Thiha!"

It was a nice-looking blonde girl, Steffi by name. She was in drama club and had a one-eyed calico called Banjo she swore could tell the future.

Thiha was active on Twitter, or at least he had been before Friday. Nothing since then. His tweets were about bands and school, traffic issues leading up to Sundance, but none about the conference at all. Nothing.

Nada. No mention of the big party Kyi had thrown, no mention of meeting people, seeing flicks, being in the who's who. His friends didn't hold back. There were countless selfies with celebrities on the sidewalks of Park City, blogs about commercialism, links to IMDB pages. But Thiha had gone radio silent.

I zoomed in to a photograph of Thiha. The scars were visible, obvious, but didn't hide that fact that he was a handsome boy.

My detective brain tried to outline him for a police report. Five-eleven, black hair, brown eyes, Asian features. And that's when I stopped. I honestly couldn't add any more. I felt racist wondering how Asian detectives describe their perps. I had fallen for the cultural blindspot of not sensing the different features of another race. He looked like Kyi to me, and that made me ashamed.

I pulled up information on General Tayza, a photo from a news story, hoping to put him against Kyi to at least sense differences. I could see differences between the men—stronger jaw on the general, more piercing eyes, but beyond a different bone structure, square compared to Kyi and Thiha's oval, I was at a loss on how I'd fill out a report on these men so every Asian person on the planet didn't get picked up for "matching the description."

Seriously, I felt like a complete sleaze. Which, I remembered, was one of the many names of my occupation.

"Arrrghhhh!"

"What is it, babe?" said Allie, half asleep.

"Feeling like a loser."

"I will fuck you up," she said, half asleep. "Stop it."

She nuzzled up to my shoulder and went back to snoozing.

I found a website that showed the average faces of many countries. I looked at them—Thailand, China, Japan, Myanmar, Denmark, Hungary, Greece. It was a computer amalgam, a miracle composite that I tried to memorize.

I hadn't known Sandi Wong was a Chinese name. San had seen my ignorance of that as a defect. He'd been right. I needed some serious international education if I was going to keep taking cases from across the ocean.

"Return trays to their upright positions. We are approaching Salt Lake City."

Outside my window, I saw a miracle. The winds that had soiled my drawers on the flight over had blown the smog out of my city. Some other poor SOB was now breathing that shit, but my valley was as clear and beautiful as a dream.

I stared out my window, admiring the purple peaks in white linen that is the Utah valley on its best winter days. This was a best winter day.

I wanted to tell the pilot to circle for a while, admire the city, its geometry and beauty. I'd put the fuel costs on my expense report, but I didn't get the chance.

"Turn off all electronics," came the command.

"The valley is clear, bright, and windy," came the captain's voice. "It'll be a balmy sixty degrees when we land, but by tonight, expect snowfall. Welcome to Salt Lake City."

The wind was serious. We hit the runway hard. Allie woke up suddenly with a startled expression on her face. She looked to me for guidance.

"There's a thing on the wing," I said.

"Ehhhhg…" She slugged me.

We were home.

As we struggled to remember which one of the identical floors we'd parked on, struggling to verify that we had indeed brought a car there, I got a call from Thailand.

"Tony."

"Fah," I said. "I've been meaning to call you."

"You have? Why? You have news?"

"No. I was just wondering who you liked in this year's Oscar race."

"Have you found Sandi Wong?"

"No," I said. "That would have been news. I'm collecting leads. That's where I am."

"I have one for you."

"A lead? You do? How? Why? What?"

"I wasn't completely honest with you before," he said.

"Found it!" Allie pointed to my little green car with the "My Other Car is a Tesla" sticker on its bumper.

"You slept with her?" I asked.

"That's not important."

"Fah…"

"I lent her my credit card."

I took a steep intake of breath through my teeth, the painful hiss transferred across the globe.

"She didn't have one," he said.

"How much did she take you for?"

"It has a limit on it," he said. "A hundred thousand. She can spend no more."

"What is it?" said Allie, seeing horror on my face.

"Fah, you're telling me you gave this girl a hundred grand? How long did you know her?"

"Baht," he said.

"But what?"

"Baht, baht baht. Thai baht, not dollars."

I covered the phone. "What's a hundred thousand Thai baht in dollars?" I said to Allie.

She asked Siri the question. "Three thousand one hundred fifty-one dollars and fifty-one cents," answered Apple's robot. Allie held up the phone for me to see.

"Okay, that's not so bad. Flush with money. You were helping out a friend. I get it. What difference does it make what form it's in?"

"It does here," he said.

We threw our bags in the back and climbed into the car.

"How?"

"It's still in my name."

"Your wife found out?"

"Nearly." I could hear shame in his voice.

I considered telling him about Archibald Lewis and the cousin lie, but I wasn't ready for that.

"She's hardly used it," Fah said. "Actually only once."

"When?"

"Last Sunday."

"That recently?"

"A hotel in someplace called Sandy, Utah."

"That's in Salt Lake," I said. "Can you send me the address?"

"Of course," he said. "It is good news though, isn't it?"

"Too early to tell. Stay on the card, and if you see it again, let me know. That would have been a good lead at the beginning, by the way."

"I told you I gave her some money."

"But a credit card? A traceable credit card? Limit or not, you were taking quite a chance. She could have set up payments, hit you all at once, used your identity for personal gain." I paused after that. Emotion-touching logic. A connection.

"I wanted to track her," he said.

"Now that's just creepy."

"I know."

"Anything else I need to know?" I asked.

He was quiet for a moment. "I did sleep with her," he finally said. "And I think I love her."

"I mean anything I didn't already know."

32

I KNEW where to find the Drop Inn Comfy Quarters Inn in Sandy before I read the address from Fah's forwarded credit card statement.

It was the first real crumb I'd had since I'd left Park City. San had only backed up their story or maybe their motivation. I was happy to have something fresher than Stert's assurance he'd dropped her off somewhere.

"I'm wired like an auditing Thetan on an E-meter," I told Allie. "I'm going to follow this up now. I'll drop you off at my place."

"The hell you will."

"You want to come?"

"Of course I do."

"You're not sick of me?"

"Of course I am, but I still want to go."

"Could be dangerous."

"At the Drop Inn Comfy Quarters Inn?" she said. "I'll take my chances."

The Drop Inn Comfy Quarters Inn was just off the I-15 at what people in my neighborhood consider one of the four three-wrong ends of the valley, this one south, the others being north, west and center. Not quite past Point of Mountain, where the statuesque prison and gravel pit prepare you for Utah County, but close enough to be boonies. The Inn was a pimple of a hotel, a child of sprawl and freeway access. I'd never been inside it before, but I assumed it would adhere to the pattern of cheap, convenient motels everywhere.

We pulled into the parking lot just past seven in the morning, which, as you know, is one hell of a shitty time to be awake. I expected to find an empty lobby and a sleep-deprived night clerk with a meth habit. But the place was hopping with eager-faced women hustling toward the smell of an included breakfast in the back.

The clerk welcomed us warmly, "Welcome to The Drop Inn Comfy Quarters Inn of Sandy. Do you have a reservation?"

"Do we need one?"

"Today you do," she said.

"Why?"

"Full up. For the convention."

"What convention?"

"The International Needlepoint Enthusiasts Convention," said a big-haired Texas-drawling woman passing behind us. "INEC. It's a big deal. Never been to the Beehive State before."

The word beehive induced a glance up at her head and a low-rising buzz in the back of my throat.

Allie elbowed me before more could happen. "How lovely," she said.

"Best get in early if you want good seats for the demos."

"Oh, we will."

She headed toward the smell of coffee and—was that bacon?

I remembered there was a convention center across the way. This was one of the closer hotels to that. Now I had a little better understanding how it stayed open. Random travelers couldn't be enough to keep this and the hundred other motels like it open.

"Heather," I said, reading the clerk's name off her badge and showing I was good people. "Was it this busy over the weekend?"

"No. This is big."

"When did they arrive?"

"Monday. Most leave Friday."

"Not the weekend?"

"Gun show at the convention center then."

"Another one?"

"Every month."

"How was it a week ago? The week of Sundance?"

"Slow."

"Yeah, about that," I said. "Were you here Sunday before last?"

"Yes." I could tell she was wary now. The question was too pointed.

"Can I ask you about one of your patrons that night?"

"I don't think so."

"Can we make an appointment?" I offered.

That confused her and me too a little, I admit.

"Let me talk to my boss."

Heather excused herself into some back office, shutting the door behind her. We wandered toward the smell of coffee. My espresso buzz was still raging, but I knew that if I didn't keep the caffeine redlined, I'd crash hard sooner than later. I was trading a worse crash in the future for energy now. It's a common bargain among the chemically reliant. I'd made it many times.

There are cheap hotels, and there are cheap hotels. The measurement is usually age, decor and the free breakfast, if any, it offers. A full buffet was out of the question. That was reserved for nice places. The kind with star ratings and maybe a pool. Who can pay kitchen staff? There's a reason most cheap hotels sprout up next to Denny's and IHOPs. It's a courtesy. In places without such planning and luck, the standard for years used to be free coffee and a muffin. "The continental breakfast" it's called, though I honestly don't know on what continent that means breakfast. The English have a plate of food so big and varied for breakfast that it's the only meal they're famous for. The French have baguettes and sex. The Germans would no sooner eat a muffin for the most important meal of the day than they'd eat a bowl of rice, which I assume other continents do. South America had fruit involved, I was pretty sure.

I digress.

The standard was raised by an arms race of budget hotels like this one vying for vacationers, conventioneers, and racketeers who offered them state-of-the-art self-service hot food. Thus was born the *lobby waffle*, a hot made-to-order pancake with abs that guests make themselves on a complicated skillet thing with buttons. All the staff have to do is open a carton of batter once in a while, put out some butter and a bottle of syrup and wham! A hot breakfast. Bring the kids! Soon they invented ways to make microwavable eggs, bacon, hollandaise sauce that let a strung-out night clerk get a meal ready before the truckers got up. Civilization at its finest.

Allie and I hadn't eaten, or at least I hadn't. She might have had some gum or something, I'm not sure. I went straight into line and fired up the two waffle makers.

"We're eating here?" asked Allie.

"Oh, you want one?" I said. "You can have one of these, I guess."

She squinted at me. She was good at that. It's a female thing. Or at least a thing females I get involved with have in common. Or it's about pushing people's patience. We'll never know.

We hooked up with some pre-cooked bacon, some eggs that had never seen the inside of a shell, and some muffins, the old standby, while the waffle timer ticked down.

"Get us a seat," Allie said. "I'll wait for the waffles."

She'd chosen the easier assignment, to be sure. The place was packed with needlepoint enthusiasts. Most were women, well, all of them, really, but the ages ran the gambit from old to not so old. They occupied every table and most chairs. They ate and talked and glanced up at two flat-screens sharing news and morning shows. Blessedly the sound was off and subtitles on.

I saw a couple of women wiping their mouths, piling their dishes and collecting needles, threads, and wooden frames from around them. They were leaving. Before I could move in, though, a new cluster of three women entered the dining room and surveyed the scene. Their eyes fell on the table. They were shrewd ones, wise in the ways of crowded cafeterias.

The couple stood up, and I moved in.

Balancing two plates and a cup of coffee, I slid my butt on a still-warm chair, introducing myself thusly, "Good morning ladies, could I ask you to— Aaaaah! Fuck me sideways!"

I leaped up. My plates flipped out of my hands onto the table, floor, and nearby onlookers. Eggs, muffins, plastic forks—an exodus of protein and carbs. My coffee stayed closer and dumped itself straight into my crotch, giving me a stereo sensation of sudden, absolute pain. What is it with me and crotch spills?

I'd like to tell you how the audience reacted to my introduction— performers are taught to read the room—but I only had brain cells for my ass.

I hopped a step or two to a wall, giving the coffee a chance to run down my thighs, looking for new tender scorchable skin.

Allie rushed over. Waffleless, I remember.

"Tony?"

"My ass." I turned the other cheek.

"You sat on something," she said. "Hold still."

I felt the pain in my bum shift and burn. I screamed again. Nothing noteworthy. Maybe a fuck or two.

"I can't get it."

"Let me help," said one of the new women. She put down her purse and came up with a mini-Leatherman, one of those multi-tool things you get at Costco in industrial shrink-wrap. She kneeled down behind me. In the moment of stillness that followed, I saw a room of shocked and concerned onlookers.

The pain came back with a confirmed reservation. A digging and a fire. Then a quick slide and I knew at least that part was over.

I turned around to see the woman holding a three-inch steel needle in the pliers of her tool.

"Oh, there it is," said one of the women who'd been at the table. "I thought I'd lost that."

She stepped forward with an open napkin and the other woman dropped the dirk inside it. She folded it up, put it in her purse, and before leaving, said, "Sure, you can have our table."

"That was in deep," said Allie.

"Was it? I didn't notice."

"That was the bluntest needle I've ever seen. And maybe the longest."

"All good to know," I said, gritting my teeth and hopping on one leg. "Hey, I have an idea. How about we go get some tetanus shots after this?"

"What's going on here?" Heather had come in.

"That man sat on Hazel's needle," said someone. "He dropped his food, dumped coffee on his cock and spouted profanities. Hester pulled it out and Hazel left for the conference. Now he's thinking about getting a tetanus shot."

"That pretty much brings you up to date," I grunted.

"You helped yourself to food?"

"You didn't say we couldn't."

"The sign says the breakfast is for guests only."

"We felt so welcomed by your warm reception and friendliness that we felt like we were guests."

"We were hungry," said Allie.

"And I wanted coffee. It smells great. Really hot."

A teenager with a rag, broom, and dustpan appeared and went to work on the crime scene.

"Your waffles are done," said someone.

Heather raised an eyebrow. "We could call this theft," she said.

"Or we could call it waffles. It's not like we got to eat anything. The chair was booby-trapped. Which reminds me, when was your last OSHA inspection? Your insurance paid up?"

Heather cared about her job because the OHSA and insurance things seemed to get to her. If she'd just been a wage slave like the pimply kid with the mop, that would not have worked. Owners and managers or managers-to-be cared about such things.

I decided to change the subject.

I shifted my weight and regretted it. "So what did the boss say?" I checked to see if I was bleeding.

"He said to use my best judgment."

"Good," I said. "Let's limp over to your surveillance video and take a look."

"Wait a minute," she said.

"I just want to see the lobby. Not the secret hidden cameras you have in the suites and bathrooms."

"You're not helping," said Allie.

"It'll just take a second," I told Heather. "Then we'll…be…uhm."

My eyes had found one of the televisions.

As I stood there, careful to keep weight off my left leg, I saw a scene of a frozen field with a pretty blonde in a parka holding a microphone to her chin, chatting away.

The grammatically challenged chyron claimed *Body Found Dead*. The subtitles read, *Bob and Sue, police are saying it appears to be a homicide but will know more after an autopsy. In the meantime, they're asking any members of the public who might have information to come forward.*

Tiffany, do they know who owns the dead body?

Idiots shouldn't ad-lib.

Yes, Bob, they have. Tiffany looked surprised, then fumbled for a notebook and squinted to read it. *They are reporting that the victim's name was Madeline Smith, a resident of Provo.*

33

WE SAT in a back office with Heather, eating breakfast. We had waffles. The coffee was much better in a cup than on my penis, if you must know.

Allie and I had shared a look together when the news story ended and went over to basketball, always basketball.

"I'm a private investigator," I'd said, finally pulling rank. "I need to see your security tapes."

That's how we got waffles and a quiet room in the back.

My ass felt like I'd been bayonetted. Yes, I think I can say that. I have some experience there now. Allie had visited an ice machine and made me something to sit on. There'd been some blood but not much. A single hole in my jeans and a little blot that Allie said would be a memory before I forgot about it. Not sure what that meant, but she was trying. That left only the deep tissue damage in my gluteus maximus and possible needlepoint-related diseases, like tetanus, cross-stitch itch, and grandma funk.

"Here's who we're looking for," I said after we'd settled in.

Heather took my phone and zoomed in on the credit card receipt Fah had sent me. She went to her computer and brought it to life.

"You think it was a stolen card?"

"No."

"This is a missing persons' case," Allie said.

"Shhhh," I said to her. "We're detectives, not snitches."

"I can't know that?" asked Heather.

"Can you be trusted?"

"Yes."

"Then you can."

She flitted screens to icons and lists.

"Sorry," Allie whispered to me. "I guess I'm rattled."

"It happens," I said. "No biggie."

I was rattled, too, though. The newswoman's call for tips was aimed squarely at people like me, people who knew the deceased and knew a possible suspect who had reason to kill her. Those that had actually threatened her perhaps before disappearing.

I texted Moland while Heather searched.

Hey Bryan. Sup? Did you kill Maddy?

Strange how even in texts, I lack an internal censor.

I waited for an answer.

"Here it is," said Heather. "Yeah, I think I remember her. I was on duty then. She checked in at eleven o'clock for a single night. Paid with this credit card. It was foreign but checked out. No other charges."

"What do you remember about her?"

"One suitcase. She was pretty. An Asian gal. I remember telling her that Fah was a cool name. She told me that that was the name of her friend back in Thailand and that her name was Sandi. Yep. She checked in as Sandi Wong."

"What did she use for an address?" I asked.

"Bangkok," she said. "It matched the credit card, so all good."

"How did she act to you?"

"She was quiet. Only answered direct questions. She wore a hat that was cool. Fashionable. Said she was on her way to Las Vegas."

"Winter hat?"

"No. Stylish. Had a black veil."

She turned back to her records.

Allie caught my eye. "Murdered last night," she whispered in my ear. She had her phone open to a news site. "Not long after you talked to him."

"Fuck," I mouthed back.

"Fuck," she agreed.

"What's fuck?" asked Heather.

"Uhm..." began Allie.

"When a man and a woman become very friendly, and no one's watching, unless that's their thing, the couple might—"

"Never mind," said Heather. "Here." She turned the monitor so we could see the scan. "This is what she used for ID." It was a familiar picture—the inside of Sandi Wong's passport.

"Can you email that to me?"

"No."

"Why?"

"Best judgment."

"Did the curtain match the drapes?"

"What do you mean?" asked Heather.

"Yeah," said Allie. "What do you mean?"

"Did she look like this picture?"

"Of course," she said.

"Do those cameras in front really work or are they fakes?"

"Real."

"Video?"

Heather turned the monitor back and did her thing. "Now that we know when to look..." Her screen was a wall of files. "You're lucky you came when you did. Tomorrow these tapes would have been gone."

"You only keep them two weeks?"

"Five days," she said. "Big memory files. See? They're already marked to be overwritten."

"But you make backups?" I said.

"Not of the surveillance videos."

"Today's Thursday. Call up Sunday. Ahh!" I'd accidentally shifted on the ice, and my ass remembered its new hole. I thought it'd be numb by now, but only the surface was. The deep deep deep stab was still angry and would be for quite some time. It promised me.

"Honey—" I began, but Allie was way ahead of me. She handed me a couple of ibuprofen, well five, and I swallowed them with creamy hot coffee on a frozen butt. She took a few herself.

Heather gave me a look.

"It's not your fault," I said to her.

"No," she said. "It's yours."

"What?" I said. "What do you know about it?"

"I know better than to sit on a chair before making sure it's safe to sit on. If not a needle, then ketchup."

"True that," I said. "I have this learned lesson until I forget it."

"Here she is." She turned the monitor for us to see.

She expanded a little video box to fill the whole screen. Allie and I leaned in to get a better look. I winced, of course. I'd wince a lot in the coming days.

"There are two cameras," explained Heather. "I'll switch to the other when it matters."

The scene was of the lobby. It showed the door, the table of brochures, a nice plant, the hotel insignia rug, and the receptionist's desk. Heather appeared at it just as the door swung open and a figure entered.

We couldn't see her face, but clearly it was a woman. The angle was high in a corner, the kind of placement that would cover the most space with the least detail. She wore a plain coat and a red hat with an old-fashioned but stylish black veil.

She took a step inside and then took her coat off, revealing a red dress beneath it.

"I remember that dress," said Heather. "Very nice. It had a cool pattern in it. Silk, I think."

"Just the thing to walk the streets in," said Allie.

I gave her a crusty look.

Heather switched the view to a camera that covered the desk and cash drawer and the faces better. Another downward-facing angle but better and closer than the first.

"What are those cameras? Seventy-two dpi?"

"They were cheap," was all Heather would say.

The resolution was crap, but it showed what we expected. A young Asian woman with a single case checking in and then walking down a hall and disappearing into an elevator.

"Can you follow her up?"

"Nope," said Heather.

"Best judgment?"

"We don't have cameras up there. Or in the suites and bathrooms."

"Well, none that you know about anyway. Can you call your boss and ask if we can see his secret tapes?"

She glared at me. I shifted in my chair with a little scream.

"Any chance I can get a copy of what you showed me?"

"No."

"Had to ask," I said. "No biggie. I don't need them yet, but I'd recommend that you not destroy any of them."

"Why not?"

"Because if you do after I asked you not to, and this goes to the po-po, it'll look very bad on you and your boss and the whole franchise."

"Okay." She took a bite of her waffle. She was eating it raw like a cookie. The savage.

"Boss is your dad?"

"No comment," she said. "Anything else?"

I waited for her to save the files. She did.

"I think that's it." We got to our feet. "Thanks for breakfast."

"Careful, those calories can really get you in the ass."

"Hilarious!"

Out in the parking lot, limping to the car, I said to Allie, "Really, that was hilarious. I like her."

"You definitely have your own detective style."

"Is that good or bad?"

"I'd say freaking awesome. No one sees you coming. You got everything you came for, right?"

"And a deep subcutaneous stabbing."

"A good morning. What now?"

"New pants and a Band-Aid," I said.

We drove to my place as the traffic grew thick with rush hour. On the way, I had time to consider my growing list of injuries. It was important that I remember the old ones. It's so easy to forget the old favorites when you have new ones that make it uncomfortable to sit.

"I told you it could be dangerous," I said. "The life of a detective is one of danger."

"I can see that," said Allie. "You never know when you'll be stabbed. Or where."

The house was as I left it. I cruised around the block once, looking for a blue Honda but didn't see one. I did a mental calculation of how long it would take one to drive from Los Altos to Sugarhouse and had no idea. A long time, I figured.

We went inside and showered. "It's just a red dot," said Allie, inspecting my butt cheek. "No blood. Just a dot. And bruising. I don't think you even need a Band-Aid, though."

"Can you kiss it better?"

"No."

"Then I guess I gotta settle for a Band-Aid."

After fresh clothes, Allie made a few calls to check on her ranch, touch base with her agent who'd arranged for some dogs to be flown to Salt Lake on Sunday morning for her to take back with her. I made some more coffee and dug out a bottle of pain pills I had left from my many visits to the hospital. This one was from Canada, so you know it was good shit. I took it in preparation for the caffeine crash I was building up to. I had a Pop-Tart.

My phone rang.

It was the police.

Shit.

"Hello, I didn't do it?"

"This is Deputy Rogers of the Utah County Sheriff's Office. Is this Mr. Tony Flaner?"

"Who's asking?"

"I just told you."

"That may be true—"

"Do you know Bryan Moland?"

"Why?"

"Did you text him asking if he'd killed a young woman named Madeline Smith?"

"Who?"

"We'd like a statement from you."

Silence.

"You're the private investigator from Salt Lake?"

"Maybe."

"It would be a shame to have your ticket pulled for non-cooperation with the police," he said. "Not to mention criminal charges that might arise from withholding information in a felony case."

Allie came in from the kitchen with a Pop-Tart of her own.

"Yeah, that would suck," I said.

"Bad news?" she whispered.

I shrugged, nodded, shrugged again.

"We'd like you to come down," said Rogers.

"Where's Bryan being held?"

"Utah County Jail. Just booked him."

"Well alright, then. What do you need me for?"

"Come in and we'll talk."

"I'll have my lawyer schedule a convenient time. Is this a good number for you?"

It was. I hung up.

"You have a lawyer?" asked Allie.

"No."

"So it's going to take a while for your lawyer to get back with them to schedule a convenient time."

"It is," I said.

Allie smirked. I liked her smirk very much.

"So they arrested your client for the murder?"

"They did."

"Not surprising."

"I don't see him for it, though. We were going to talk."

"No offense, but sometimes you think too much of yourself."

I had to laugh. "Lately it's been the opposite."

"You think too little of yourself sometimes too."

"Oh…really?" I said. "Well…so do you! Ha!"

"You're sweet, but I got some bad news."

"A little more couldn't hurt."

"I've got to run back up to Park City. Terrance needs me to sign some things. He's leaving tonight. I gotta get this done."

"Let me go with you."

"Why?"

"It could be dangerous."

"You really want to sit in a car for an hour?"

"I gotta think."

"About anything in particular?"

"Yeah," I said, finishing my coffee and Pop-Tart. "I gotta think about whether I got Maddy Smith murdered."

34

THERE IS no official code of ethics for private eyes. There are warnings and lists of regulations that apply to us, helpful reminders not to get in the way of real police, but as far as how to morally conduct ourselves, that's left pretty much blank. Probably intentionally so. We peek in windows, embarrass people with dirty laundry and piss folks off by accident and design. Loose morals is in the job description.

I'd given up marital work for that reason. I felt sleazy doing it. I felt sleazy now. Part of it was that I had to wade into a con game built on trampling lonely men's hearts but also because the worst outcome that could have happened had happened. Maddy Smith was dead. I'd poked the jealous bear who'd sent me sniffing, and off he went. I should have known this would happen. I wanted to tell myself that I had a gut feeling that Bryan Moland was an upright fellow with a head on his shoulders who could handle an out-of-state impersonal email turning his life upside down, shattering his soul, embarrassing him, and then sending him unprotected into a snake nest to face blackmail threats. I'd not even ever met the man in person. All had been through email, texts, and phone calls. How the fuck could I ever conceive that I knew him and how he would react? I couldn't. I didn't. I was making shit up now to justify a horrible mistake. I'd wanted the case to be over. I'd been lazy. I'd been insensitive. I'd been a sleaze.

And now Maddy was dead, and I'd made my client a murderer.

There wasn't a court that would judge me as hard as I judged myself. This was business as usual for a PI. It would make an interesting plot twist in a book, but I knew I'd let everyone down. Marlowe would have known what to expect. Rockford would have gone in person, Poirot would have made a production of it. Me? I sent an email while on vacation.

Allie offered to drive and kept quiet as my little green electric car wove up the steep pass. I wondered where the toll booth had been.

From the effects of worry, guilt, exhaustion, and Canadian opioids, caffeinated as I was, I fell asleep.

I awoke in a half-neck knot with a drool puddle on my shirt. Somewhere close, possibly in my own head, someone was explaining to someone else, who was very hard of hearing, that there was a sale on chili dogs and ninety-six-ounce Thirst Stompers. Don't forget the gum!

I shifted my weight and regretted it. I kept forgetting that one muscle group was off-limits for a while, or at least needed special care. I threw my head back on the seat cushion and remembered that one area was hatching a Scottish hematoma. Just to round out my menu, I picked at the scab under my eye.

"You're awake," said Allie.

I opened the door, swung my legs out with some effort, tried to stand, and fell into an oil spot between gas pumps.

"Feeling good," I said as Allie rushed over to help me up. "A little stiff."

"God, Tony, you're a wreck."

I stretched. "I've had worse. This one is just such a pain in the ass."

"Cute." She returned to the talking gas pump and topped off the tank. I considered going in for a chili dog. I don't even like chili dogs.

"Are we nearly there?" I asked.

"There and gone. We're on our way home."

"What?"

I looked at my watch. Yep. It was eleven in the morning. Last I looked at my watch, it wasn't nine thirty yet.

"Well, glad I came," I said. "Want a chili dog?"

"Hell no."

"Good call. Gas station squirt chili has a reputation."

"Unlike their squirt cheese, hot dogs, taquitos, burritos, and pickled eggs."

"They have a reputation too, just different."

She put the nozzle back and chose not to get a receipt. The planet thanked her. The gas pump thanked her too at a volume that rattled my fillings.

"Are you feeling any better?" she asked.

"Warming up."

"I didn't mean physically."

"I know," I said.

We left it at that. After a quick trip to the bathroom to filter some coffee through my kidneys and buy a ninety-six-ounce Thirst Stomper, we were back in the car. Allie had to hold my bucket of Coke Zero while I got my seatbelt on.

We pulled out onto the street, went two blocks, and a silver Range Rover cut us off. Actually, it nearly took off our front end. Allie honked. A hand extended out the driver's window and offered us a one-finger apology.

Allie's cheeks went red. I tried to see the driver, but my humongous cup blocked my vision.

Another car cut her off, and then another.

"Your space bubble is too big," I offered.

"The hell it is. This place is full of assholes."

"Touché."

I noticed the Range Rover pull into a grocery store parking lot. Allie followed it in.

"What are you doing?"

"I'm about to teach some asshole some manners," she said.

"Assholes are immune from manners. Trust me, I know. That's why we're called assholes."

"Fucker flipped me off."

The big beast parked, and the driver's door opened.

"Hold it," I said. "That's Stert."

"Who?"

"The asshole who clobbered me."

"Oh, I can't wait to hear what you say to him." She grinned a vindictive grin. "You'll make his grandchildren weep."

"I'd rather not," I said, feeling the knot on my head. "What's he doing here?"

"Shopping."

"Let's follow him," suggested Allie. "I bet you can find some way to really cut him to pieces in front of the cashier. It'll be glorious."

"He carries a club with him."

"It'll be in public," she said. "Please. Defend my honor. And your own."

"Alright. Help me out of the car."

By the time we'd limped to the door, my muscles were warm enough not to put me on the linoleum like a sack of onions. We slid into sneak mode and hunted our prey.

We found him walking slowly down the main aisle, reading overhead signs.

"He sure is big," said Allie.

I pulled out my camera and took a picture of him. He had a small shopping basket on his arm. I figured I could burn him hard with *Wizard of Oz* memes if nothing else. Photoshop Toto in there with him looking up. Maybe say "If I only had a brain." Post it on his wall or Instagram. Burn!

He disappeared down an aisle, and we followed discreetly.

Nutter Butters were on sale. Artisan bath bombs could be had for six dollars a splash. A sign on the display warned children that they were not candy. They sure looked like candy. They tasted horrible, though.

Allie glared at me.

"Want some?"

"What is wrong with you?"

"The world may never know."

We turned an aisle and then pulled back quickly before he could see us. I stuck my phone camera around the corner and snapped picture after picture, hoping I had one of him squatting. Always good meme material.

I pulled my phone back and looked at the snaps.

There was Stert picking stuff off a shelf.

There was Stert putting it in his basket.

There was Stert looking back at the camera.

There was Stert walking down the aisle.

There was Stert.

"Hi, Stert," I said.

He looked down at me. I couldn't read his expression. Rage? Pity? Surprise? Embarrassment? Bowel blockage? Viagra withdrawal? Pre-teen puppy love? Really, it was hard to tell.

A low menacing Scottish growl rumbled from his torso. He moved his eyes to Allie and then to the row of cashiers.

"I see you chose the cost-efficient Tampex variety pack," I said. "Insert me questioning your manhood here."

He glanced down at his basket, looked back at us, and without another word, walked to the checkout.

"Really?" said Allie. "That's the best you got? Tease the guy about his purchases?"

"Okay. It wasn't my best but know the undercurrent."

"Which was?"

"He seems to be the kind of guy that would work on. A guy with issues."

She rolled her eyes. "Like?"

"Like rage, pity, surprise, embarrassment, bowel blockage, Viagra withdrawal, pre-teen puppy love? I'm not sure."

"You were scared."

"Could have been that," I admitted. "I did the best I could. Not everything can be gold."

A text popped up.

Missed call camera time. A message.

Stert went through the self-checkout, and after a quick glance back at us, left the store.

"I guess I could have said something," said Allie. "But you got me sneaking. Took the vinegar out of me."

I played the message and wandered down an aisle looking for ass-friendly mercurochrome.

"Mr. Flaner, this is Bryan Moland. I was arrested for…for…they think I did it. They think I killed Maddy. I'm in trouble. I need your help. Call me."

I thought for a second that he'd used his one phone call to reach out to me, but the call had come from his cell phone. That meant he was out and melting down. Made sense. Out, because people like him didn't stay in the big or little houses for long. Too much money and position. Suits were getting him out before the ink on his fingers was dry. It also made sense that he'd be melting down. It was terrible and wonderful to hear the emotion in the message. A broken man, fearful and sad. I liked that. I liked too that he called me.

"That was Bryan Moland," I said to Allie. "He called me. I think he wants me to find the real killer."

"Or he wants to buy you off so you don't go to the cops with the motivational evidence they're looking for."

"I want to think he is looking for a hero. You suggest he's looking for an accomplice."

"Call him and find out."

I was about to when my phone rang.

"Bryan?"

"No, Nancy."

My ex-wife.

"Hey, Nancy, how was your trip? Good to hear from you. I didn't think we were talking right now."

"The seminar was a bust, and no, I'm not talking to you."

"Sounds like you are."

"That car..."

"Is sporty."

"I've got to work late. Randy needs a ride home from school. Can you, pretending to be a responsible parent, pick him up?"

"Can I take him for ice cream?"

"Sure."

"How about a movie?"

"Okay."

"A shopping spree at Target?"

"Haven't you done enough, Tony?"

"Are we talking about the car again?"

"Yes."

"I suppose me picking him up means he still hasn't ransomed it out of the tow yard yet."

"That is correct. He says he'll do it himself. He doesn't want any help from us there. He said it was his mistake and he'll make it right. He's being very responsible. Unlike some people."

"Allie, Nancy thinks you're irresponsible."

"Allie's there with you?"

"Maybe."

"Put her on."

"Why?"

"So Randy won't be left at school all night when you forget to pick him up."

"When have I ever... Don't answer that."

I passed the phone to Allie.

"Fine, fine. Made some good contacts at Sundance. Got some work. Very exciting. No Tony was only there for a moment, just at one party. No, he didn't get thrown out... No... He's working now. He's on a case, a couple actually. The murder? How'd you know? Oh. Well, in a roundabout way, I guess... No. No. Nancy... No. That's not very nice; Tony is an excellent detective. Uh-huh... Really? Is that why you called? Oh. He'll be there. Nancy, you need to chill."

She gave me the phone back.

"Hi, Nancy," I said. "Allie says you need to chill."

I could hear her teeth grind.

"Why are you making me raise our son alone?"

"You won custody?"

"Tony!"

"I'm helping. I'm helping. I do everything in my power and more."

"Do less."

"You're talking against yourself now."

"A fifty-thousand-dollar car?"

"The car again. Do you want one? Is that what this is all about?"

"It's irresponsible."

"But you just told me how responsible our son is. Get your stories straight."

"You! You're irresponsible. What father gives his son that kind of machine for a first car?"

"One that cares very much about his son."

"Ahhhhhhhhhhgggggg!"

"You're really on edge, Nancy. Did something bad happen at the seminar you're trying not to think about?"

Long pause.

"What was it?"

"I don't want to talk about it."

"Tell me..."

She sighed and sniffled.

"I had twenty percent forfeitures on my last quarter's sales. Bank repossessions. I was used as an example of how NOT to match buyer with seller. They tried to block out my name, but everyone there knew it was me. It was humiliating."

"You closed for over half a million last quarter."

"They didn't last. But it made me look like a loser. A fake. A charlatan."

"They're jealous," said Tony.

She sniffled a little. "I gotta go. Tell Allie I was out of line. And Tony?"

"Yes."

"Good luck on your cases. I know you'll solve them."

"Thanks, Nancy."

I ended the call.

"She's one stressed gal," said Allie. I could see her ears were red.

"She apologizes," I said. "Told me she was out of line."

"She absolutely was. Do I want to know what she said?"

"The car and other things?"

"So no?"

"No."

She had a point about the car. It was a dumb thing to do. I liked that Randy was facing his own mistakes in getting it out of impound, but I didn't understand why it hadn't happened. Randy had money. He had savings. He had allowance. He had advances and loans. He was well-to-do. Hell, he owned a Tesla.

"You were going to call Bryan back," Allie reminded me.

Allie picked up a bottle of antiseptic and a sack of Nantucket cookies. My favorites.

"Hello, Bryan? This is Tony."

"I've had a heck of a time," he said. "I was arrested."

"I heard. Sorry, man."

"I loved her. I'd never have done that. How could anyone think I'd do such a thing?"

I winked at Allie. "I know you didn't do it, Bryan. You're not that kind of person."

"Thanks, Mr. Flaner."

"You want me to get right on an investigation to see what I can find out about it?"

"The police will do that. I'm innocent, so I'll be okay."

"Because of who you are—rich, privileged, Mormon, the whole nine yards—I'd agree. You'll be fine."

"Thanks."

"Sure you don't want me to look into it? Usual rates."

"Not yet. Not until we know more."

"Okay."

"But in the meantime, Mr. Flaner..."

"Yes?"

"I will pay you ten thousand dollars if you don't talk to the police."

35

"WHAT ARE YOU GOING TO DO?" asked Allie. She was driving again, and I was sitting on a leaking ten-pound bag of ice, pissed that I'd again been so wrong.

"Take the money and go to Aruba," I said.

"I can't. I have Shih Tzus coming Sunday and a ferret."

"I'll miss you."

She glared at me. "You bought time with the police. I assume that was to gather more information. So you'll dig some more?"

Once again, Allie had overestimated me. Once again, I felt like a poser. Feeling sickeningly sorry for myself and a bit cranky, I told the truth. "I put off the police interview for no other reason than I don't like going to police stations. There are cops there. I'm not a fan. My decision was strictly personal and selfish."

"I see we've dropped our panties and climbed up on the pity pot," she said.

"Maybe."

"Well, cut it out."

I folded my arms across my chest and stuck out my lower lip.

"We could call around in Vegas. Find Sandi down there," she said. "She's probably hooked up with a new sugar daddy and is living it up."

I wrinkled my forehead and stuck my lip out further. Allie was kind to turn the subject to another case, but in doing so she again highlighted my failure by stating the obvious answer I hadn't seen. I don't know what I was thinking, but it wasn't that.

"Maybe you should take over," I said. "I'll deal with the weasels."

"Tony, this is really unattractive."

"So now I'm ugly?"

"Stop beating yourself up."

"Maybe I will. Maybe I won't. Whatcha going to do about it?"

"What's eating at you?"

"I'm butt-hurt."

She laughed, and the sound of it brightened my mood. "Best use of the phrase ever," she said.

I shifted and hurt and put the ice on the floor and sat in a puddle.

"We gotta pick up Randy," I said.

"We have plenty of time. Unless he's getting out early."

"Usual day, I think, but I don't know."

I pulled out my smartphone to access the school calendar. It was harder than it sounds. They bury that shit on their website.

"All good," I said and then opened WebMD to investigate puncture wounds. I really didn't want to get a tetanus shot. I'd just had one. If I got a tetanus shot every time I was stabbed or shot, I'd have time for nothing else.

"Are you up for a drink?" I followed the links of symptoms. "Let's go to the Cellar and have a beer and nachos. Waffles and Pop-Tarts only go so far. I'm crashing."

"Shit. Were we in California this morning?"

"Uh-huh." I didn't like what I was seeing. "Let's go catch my breath. We'll sit in some low light with some lowlifes. Always good after a day like this."

"It's only afternoon."

"You're not helping."

The freeways were easygoing and downhill, so my car got a full battery, and we made good time. Breaking out of the canyon into the Salt Lake Valley, we were presented with a breathtakingly clear view. The wind had purified my city. It was gorgeous this way.

I give my state a lot of shit, because frankly, it deserves it, but looking west from the east bench on a crystal clear winter's day, blue sky and brilliant, the inversion just a bad memory, made me remember why I put up with it. It really can be a beautiful place.

My mood improved.

"How goes your WebMD search?" asked Allie as she took our exit.

"It's not good."

"Infection?"

"Cancer," I said. "WebMD is sure I have cancer."

"Neat."

In midday sunlight and in a crisp breeze, we arrived at the Comedy Cellar and found the parking lot not deserted. Not crowded but not deserted. To me, it was always more nightclub than bar, and I'm sure Barry would have preferred that, but the lack of places in Utah to get tequila shots at two p.m. meant that there was an afternoon business. Barry wouldn't miss a buck. The state is cheap, and getting anybody to pay cover to see a comedy show is somewhere between hard and a fool's errand.

We slipped in a back door because I was practically family after so many years of haunting the place, playing the place, embarrassing the place. The staff waved us in, and we went to our usual table. Dara was already there with Henry Levinson, the young kid who did impersonations. Both had half-finished martini glasses in front of them.

"Getting an early start?" I asked.

Henry looked up and smiled.

Dara looked up and blushed.

Dara's blushing made me pull up short.

My pulling up short made Allie walk into my back.

Her walking into my back made us both topple onto the floor.

"Cut those two off!" came the yell from behind the bar.

"We just got here." I pulled myself up.

Dara scooted a little away from Henry. Henry kept his stupid smile on his face.

Dara couldn't make eye contact.

We slid into the booth and waited.

"Hey there, Tony," Henry said as Ronald Reagan. "Me and Nancy were just here talking about a chimp I used to know."

"Lovely," I said.

"They're not really going to cut us off, are they?" said Allie.

"Let's find out."

I flagged down a waitress and ordered us a pitcher of beer and two cheeseburger plates.

"What brings you to these parts, partner?" asked John Wayne.

"We're searching," I said.

He didn't get it.

"We've been out of town," said Allie. "Got home this morning and have been running around ever since. It's been nuts."

"Doing what?" asked Dara, nice and calm and innocent as you like.

"Tony's cases. He thought he had one wrapped up. Well, he had, but then it blew up and now it's a murder."

"Wrapped up in a tuxedo," said someone who might have been WC Fields.

"Can you do anyone more recent than that?"

"Ringo and I were just down in a watery grotto," he said.

"George Harrison?"

"Yes!"

"You're very talented," said Allie, pouring her first beer. "Are you performing again tonight?"

"Not tonight."

"Are you, Dara?"

"Not until next month."

"Then why are you here?" I said.

"Hanging out," said Henry. "Absorbing the atmosphere. Dara's been giving me special tips." I closed my eyes, or I might have seen him wiggle his eyebrows. I don't know if that happened or not, but the chance was too great to risk.

Something didn't sit right. Actually, a lot didn't sit right, but there was something about Dara's questionable choice of mates that bugged me like a roach necklace.

Our food arrived.

Allie shared french fries with the others and pulled the pickles off her cheeseburger. I took them on mine and dug in.

Barry does a pretty good bar menu. The cheeseburgers are the closest thing to a real meal unless you consider jalapeño poppers, flaming shredded-chicken nachos, or a towering pole of onion rings part of a well-balanced diet. The beer was cold, the room dim, my date gorgeous, and my verbally abusive friend fidgety. The day was looking up.

After half my burger was devoured, reforming into a digestion problem my jet-lagged intestines would have to handle their own way, I turned to Allie and said, "I need to know more about the murder. That's critical."

"Go to the crime scene?" she asked.

"Don't even know where it is."

"Oh, that's right," said Henry. "Dara said you were a detective. That is so awesome."

"Dara, you talking about me?" I asked my friend.

She shrugged.

"She said you were the best there is. Said you'd solved some serious cases, and she'd helped sometimes."

"Really?"

"No," said Dara. "I told him you were a double douche with toxic shock syndrome sauce."

She was back.

I felt an overarching need to change the subject.

"I am not in the mood to talk to the police," I said. "Nor do I want to go to Provo right now. Allie, I want you to call the Utah County Sheriff, ask for Deputy Rogers. Pump him for information."

"Me?"

"He knows my voice. Just claim to be another cop. Or maybe a family lawyer. Get him confused. Find out cause of death, time of death, location, and anything else they have on Moland."

"No. I couldn't do that," said Allie. "I'm sweating just thinking about it."

"Is that about the body they found last night?" asked Henry. "I saw that on the news. They said they have someone in custody."

"Had," I corrected him. "He's rich, so he's on the bricks."

"So he didn't do it?"

Allie sucked air through her teeth. "Well…"

"I'll fucking do it," said Dara.

"No way," I said. "You'll fuck it up."

"Why the fuck would you say that?"

We all knew the fuck why.

"Utah County," said Allie, finding a way to put it politely.

"Oh. I can curb that shit. If I want to."

"Let me," said Henry. "Oooo ooo. Let me, let me!" He bounced in his seat.

"No."

"I can do this. I even have a character. Detective Mulroony of the City Police."

"Which city?"

"Whichever."

"Pass."

"I've used him before."

"How?"

"To get out of school."

That's what was bugging me. Henry's age. If I remembered rightly, he wasn't old enough to drink—wouldn't be for years yet.

"I've also used him to get out of a ticket once. Really Mr. Flaner, I can do this for you."

"Is that a martini?" I asked.

"Yes. The first one was hard to drink, but this one is much better."

"How'd you get it? How'd you even get in the door?"

"Oh," he said and winked. "I got that covered."

"Detective Mulroony?"

He reached into his pocket and pulled out a driver's license and passed it to me.

I inspected it and found nothing amiss. There was a picture of Henry Levinson. It looked to have been made that day—the hair was the same, the expression, the pimple.

"Where'd you get this?" I asked.

"A friend of a friend of a friend." He winked.

"Let me borrow this for a second," I said and scooted out of the booth.

"You're not going to narc on him, are you, Flaner?" said Dara. "Because that would be some first-class low-asshole fuckery."

"No, just want to look at it closer."

Henry watched me go. He downed the rest of his martini like it would be the last one he'd have for two years.

I found Luke, the bouncer, in the back unpacking liquor boxes.

"Barry around?" I said.

"Not until tonight. What's up?"

"Look at this." I showed him Henry's card.

He glanced at it. "Yeah, I saw that already."

"But you know he's too young to drink," I said.

"He was here the other night performing."

"Under special presenter license, I thought."

"What's that?"

"Isn't that a thing?"

"I don't know. Barry let him in before. He didn't drink then, but he was here. He shows today and gives me that, and it's all kosher."

"What happened with those kids the other night? You said you'd had a bunch of questionable IDs lately."

"I let most of them in," he said. "Two didn't know their birthdays when I asked, so they hit the road."

"So the IDs are fakes?"

"Too good. More likely they found a way to trick the DMV."

"Okay."

I went back to the table and found the three waiting for me with grins on their faces.

"What?" I said. "I didn't narc." Well, I kinda did, but not really.

Henry read off a napkin. "Madeline Smith's body was found in Eagle Mountain on the far side of Utah Lake, just opposite Provo. She'd been killed somewhere else and moved. Her body was discovered at two a.m. By smoochers. Kids looking for a place to fornicate." He winked. Dara gulped. "She was probably killed around seven p.m. the previous day. Cause of death appears to be a blow to the back of the skull. Possibly multiple ones. Bryan Moland, her fiancé, was arrested and booked but is out on bail. He has no alibi, and they're investigating for possible motives. They think this one is wrapped up."

"How did you…"

"Detective Mulroony," said Allie. "He pulled it off."

I stared dumbfounded.

"That quick?"

"He confused him," said Dara.

"I told him we had a similar killing in Ogden and wanted to compare notes before I talked to my lieutenant. A courtesy thing since we are both BYU alumni."

"You went to BYU?" I noticed the new martini glass.

"No."

"He was acting!" Allie waved jazz hands.

"He was really good," said Dara, giving Henry a playful grin and eyebrow wiggle.

"Did I solve your case?" he asked.

I sat down and munched a french fry. Getting information from cops is one of the hardest tricks of the trade. In the best scenario, the gumshoe has a

friend on the inside, someone with a badge who can let slip important information. Bribing is not out of the question, subpoenas are a last resort.
Tricking them, well—that's just perfect. It's the mark of a seasoned, smart,
effective PI. And that wasn't me. I'd asked Allie to do it, then Henry had
volunteered because she refused. I again felt like a fraud.

"Do you need me to call again?" said Henry, signaling for more drinks.
"To follow up on anything? Best have me do it before this next drink. They
go straight to my head."

And Henry had done it with a buzz on.

I sulked.

This is where my head was at. I knew it was wrong. I knew it was stupid.
I knew to stop it before Allie recognized what was happening and punched
me in the arm. Problem was that thoughts seldom overruled emotion, at
least not in my case, even when someone tells me "to get over it," which,
interested reader, has never worked on anyone for anything, so stop
saying it.

More drinks came, and I bottled my mood as best I could.

"Are you mad, Mr. Flaner?"

"You done good, kid. You done good."

Dara winked at him.

He chewed an olive.

"Let me see your license again," I said.

Dara's eyes narrowed.

Henry slid me the card.

I turned on my smartphone camera and used it to zoom in.

"Where did you say you got this?"

"I'd rather not tell you," he said after Dara kicked him under the table.

"No danger. I'm just curious."

"The night I performed when you and Allison left early, I ran into an old
high school friend of mine. He had a fake ID. I asked him if he could get me
one. He said he could. I emailed him a picture and personal details along
with a hundred-dollar e-payment, and next day it appeared in the mail."

"Could I talk to this friend of yours?"

"No."

"I think it's important," said Allie.

"Why do you think that?" he asked.

"I've seen that look in his eye before," said my lovely girlfriend. "He's
found a clue."

36

THE LICENSE TOLD me that Henry Levinson was 21 years old, 6'1" tall, 172 pounds, brown hair, brown eyes, didn't need glasses, would share his organs if he died in a way that make them useful, and lived at 2804 Hibiscus Drive in Millcreek, Utah, an older upscale neighborhood on the east bench.

It's called an ego signature. It's a deliberate mark left by a criminal at a crime scene to taunt the police and celebrate outsmarting them. Remember *Home Alone*? The Water Bandits always left the sinks running in the houses they burgled before Macaulay Culkin sadistically tortured them into submission and years of physical rehab and dark psychotherapy where daily electroconvulsive treatments only brought on flashbacks of bowling balls and visions of mute Indians. That's an ego signature. It's like signing a work of art, but in the case of forged driver's licenses, the signature can't be so obvious. It wasn't.

It was the C in the word Hibiscus. At first glance, you could think it was an ink smudge, or a trick of the light, but once I found it, I could see nothing else. There was a slight red line through the C turning the letter into the anti-public domain symbol I'd found on the counterfeit cards Randy had been busted with.

I pulled out my own license and looked at Allies' too for comparison. Dara told me to fuck myself when I asked to see hers. Though there were Cs on our cards too, nowhere was there a faint line across them like in Hibiscus. Further, the C in Millcreek was not crossed. Only the one, but definitely there.

I gave Henry back his card and didn't press him for his contact's name. He'd done me a solid, and Randy had asked me to lay off that case.

Randy.

Shit. Randy.

"What time is it?"

"About four," said Allie.

"We better go."

I dropped some money on the table. "Thanks, Henry," I said.

He, as some kind of New Jersey gangster, said, "Forget about it."

In the car, Allie asked me, "What does the stuff Henry found out tell you?"

"That he is better at getting information out of the police than I ever was."

"Oh, we're here again?"

"A little bit."

"And the licenses?"

"A connection, but not for my cases. At least not on the ones I'm working on."

"Which one aren't you working on? Moland? You think he's guilty now?"

"It looks bad for him," I agreed. "And I guess I should have called that inactive since I'm not actually working for him anymore unless I want ten thousand dollars to be a tampered witness."

"So...the Frank Tomas thing?"

"I almost forgot about him. I guess I'm not officially working on that one, either."

"Because you've come to your senses about him?"

"Which are?"

"That what he does with his life is no reflection on what you do with yours."

"But it is," I said. "He wants it to be. That's the kind of person he is. An in-your-face haha-look-how-cool-I-am guy who looks down his nose at everyone he can."

"That has nothing to do with you."

"And I don't know what to do there. Usually something comes along to tingle my little gray cells, but nothing from him."

"What about the blue Honda?"

"Oh. Yeah. Okay. I guess that counts. Wait, I thought you wanted me to forget about that one. Why are you helping me?"

"Sorry. You really should ignore Frank. Probably not go to the reunion Saturday if he's still in your craw."

"The reunion..." I moaned.

"So which of the cases you're not working on were the licenses?"

"Randy's counterfeit cards."

"Didn't he ask you to lay off that?"

"Yes."

"And you are going to?"

"Yes."

"Is that the game store he told you about?"

"Yes."

"Are you going to meddle in there?"

"Yes."

We pulled into the parking lot of Little Wars games. The guy from the laundromat was leaning in the passenger's side window of a white camper, talking with a shifty-eyed driver.

"Drug deal," I said.

"Looks like."

"Want some? It's wonderful stuff. It makes you work hard and fast and effectively and then erases all memory of you doing it."

"No, I'm good."

I was worried about Curt, the cranky shop owner. There he was behind the counter, still moving computer people around a bloody landscape.

We went in, and I leaned over the expensive rare card display and was surprised to see it nearly empty.

"Hey, Curt," I said. "Good to see you. What happened to all your rares?"

"Sold them all in a lot," he said, leaning back. A victory screen appeared on his monitor, and he let out a loud satisfied sigh. He looked at me and squinted. "Hey, I know you."

"You're not going to get your ax, are you?"

"What? Oh yeah. Sorry about that. You understand how it is."

"Game rage is a thing," I said.

"Yeah. I've been trying to beat that level for a long time."

I scanned the room for customers. There were a few games in progress—Spells, Settlers of Catan, some space opera thing that looked complicated. A mother with a stroller perused boxes for a party game that didn't involve drinking. The guy who sold me pot, a couple others.

"When will you be getting more?"

"Don't know. I have to wait for them to walk in. I buy most of my singles locally."

"Nobody's come in this week to move some?"

"No. Been really quiet. That happens."

"Give me six new booster packs," I said.

Allie raised an eyebrow.

"A peace offering for Randy," I said.

The computer screen flashed twice, went dark and then became a sad blue error message.

Curt gasped, stared at the computer in disbelief. Then he threw the cards on the counter and rushed to his keyboard. He frantically tapped keys, mashed chords, wiggled the mouse while chanting the mantra of the unsaved: "No no no no no…NO! Sonovabitch!"

The seasoned gamers saw what was happening and quickly left.

"Get out of here," I said to the woman with the stroller. "Now!"

She didn't understand but did as I told her, pushing the baby through the door as the chants rose in urgency.

"No no no no. What the actual…oh. Come on. Come on. Come on. No… It's a new computer. I had fifty hours in that level."

"I'll get those packs another time." I took Allie's arm and exited just as Curt staggered into his back room.

"No no no. Sonova… Sonova…" He was crying.

I was with Allie at the car when we heard the sounds of destruction. Blow after blow, crash after crash, cut after cut, from a heavy-bladed medieval weapon upon a misbehaving computer. It was called Little Wars, but from the computer's point of view, it was a big ambush.

The goatee guy from the store and the drug dealer from the laundromat stared at each other across the parking lot like two outlaws in front of a saloon.

Distant but approaching sirens scattered them away.

We took our leave as well. Besides not being in the mood to talk to cops, even those not investigating my clients, we were pressed for time. We were already late to pick up my son from school. Nancy would shit a brick if I was really late. She was looking for bricks to shit on me. She really took it hard that I'd so out-gifted her with our son at Christmas. She was jealous and threatened. Yeah, that was it, and not the ridiculously inappropriate present.

The parking lot of the school was eerily empty. I looked at my watch. We were half an hour late, and the place had emptied like a roach warren in dusk. A couple of kids milled around, talking, looking expectantly for late parents, hiding from the bullies lurking just off school grounds, waiting to beat them up. That was my school experience at one point. Seemed like an everyday thing, but Allie has since convinced me it wasn't.

None of the kids was mine.

We went inside, thinking my son would be there. It was a bright and beautiful day, breezy and clear, a storm coming but blessedly untainted.

He wasn't in the lobby. We went to C Hall, thinking he might be there playing Spells. He wasn't there. Mr. Smith—Hunter—was on his computer and waved to us as we approached.

"Tony!" he said, seeming genuinely glad to see me. "How are you? And this must be Allison Braise. Randy told me you were a looker."

Allie and I exchanged a glance. I didn't know what to say. I didn't know what to think. Which was creepier—that my son had told his art teacher about my girlfriend or that he found her attractive? WWOD—What Would Oedipus Do?

"Hi," said Allie with a wave.

"Whatcha doing?" I said.

"Seeing if I have enough in my account to buy a new ZX-2280," he said.

"You have a ZX-2280?"

"Yeah." Upbeat.

"And it's broken?"

"Yeah." Downbeat.

"Who bought the last one?"

"I did." Matter of fact.

"Not the school?"

He laughed. "Hell no. This is America. Starve the arts. If it can't be immediately monetized, it has no value. The district doesn't even pay for my paper clips."

"What happened to the old ZX-2280?"

"Wore out. It happens. But the cost of the alpha drum alone is as much as a whole new machine. Capitalism, am I right?"

"Sucks," I agreed. "Still, it'll be good to have a new ZX-2280."

"I love the ZX-2280."

"What is a ZX-2280?"

His mouth fell open and then turned to a grin. "Sorry. It's a multi-faceted, 2D foil printer."

I stared.

"It's that big gray-and-white one in the back."

"It's for class?"

"Yeah. It's our secret weapon to this year's state championship graphic arts gold metal. Count on it."

"We're looking for Randy," said Allie.

"He left with Oliver," he said.

"Shit."

"Shit why?"

"I'm late. His mother's going to chew my ass."

"I got the impression from the boys that they'd arranged it yesterday. He wasn't waiting for you."

"Oh," I said. "Relief or rage?"

"What's that?"

"I was talking to Allison. Should I feel relief that I didn't disappoint my son, or rage that his mother sent me to the wrong place, possibly to set me up for failure?"

"Let them balance out," she said. "Let's use Hanlon's Razor."

"Which one is that?" asked Hunter Smith, art teacher. "The one with the knot?"

"No. That's Occam's Razor. Hanlon's Razor is— " I cleared my throat, bit my lip, and looked at the ceiling to remember. "Never attribute to malice that which is adequately explained by stupidity."

"That's a good one."

"People apply it to Tony all the time," said Allie. "But he's often slow to implement it himself."

"Ouch."

"Yeah, ouch," agreed Hunter.

"It's a way to remind yourself not to get butt-hurt so easily."

"Are we talking about anything more than Nancy?"

"Frank."

"Huh," I said.

"He's not after you. He's just a braggart. Nancy's not out to embarrass you. She's flustered."

"Stop trying to confuse me with your logic and clear thinking."

"Sorry, master. I have overstepped."

Hunter clapped his hands. "I want to party with you two!"

"I guess I have to find out where Oliver lives," I said, dreading calling Nancy or Randy. Neither one was particularly happy with me.

"I know where he lives," said Hunter.

"You do?"

"Yeah."

He bit his lip and looked at the ceiling to remember before scribbling an address on a slip of paper and sliding it over to me.

"Blue barn-like thing," he said. "Chipping paint. Car on the lawn. You can't miss it."

"Thanks."

"Don't be judgmental," he cautioned us. "Some people live harder than others."

37

THE HOUSE WASN'T FAR, just a couple blocks. Walking distance from the school. We pulled up to the curb and saw it as described. Barn-like, blue chipping paint, a rusted car in the yard. What Hunter hadn't told us was that it had John Mellencamp's famous freeway running through the backyard.

"I'll go get him," I said to Allie.

"Don't want me to come?"

"He might be angry."

"Why?"

"It's a Thursday."

"Sure?"

"I have no idea. How does anyone know what will and won't set off a hormonal teenager?"

She nodded sympathetically. "There's a lot happening to him. School, girls, cars, hobbies, friends, hippie teachers."

"None of which I'm really allowed to help with."

"Giving someone space is still giving," she said.

Can you see why I loved this woman?

"I'll be right back."

The first scent of coming snow was in the air. Snow has a smell. In Utah, during the inversion, it's a toxic pants-moistening poison smell, but in nature, on a clear day with winds, it has a crisp smell of ice and talking snowmen. I decided to let it go and knocked on the door.

Oliver opened it.

"Hello, Mr. Flaner," he said. "Is everything alright?"

I took a deep sniff and said, "Tell me you're cooking with oregano."

"I am," he said.

"Oh, then everything's fine. I came for Randy."

"He's downstairs with Jelissa. I'll go get him."

"Wait a second, hold up," I said. The name required pause.

"Yeah?"

"Uhm, can I uhm?"

"What?"

"Come in for a second?"

"Sure."

He wasn't thrilled with the idea, I could tell, but being a polite boy, he let me in.

The place was more run-down inside than it had been outside. Worse, there were definite signs of hoarding. Piles of newspapers, magazines, and ten-cents-a-pound bulk paperback purchases still in boxes. Torn cushions and lawn chairs in front of a tubed TV. Bare bulbs sharing a light fixture with cracked bells. A smell of Spells tournament body funk mixed with a comforting aroma of cooking Italian food.

"Whatcha having?"

"I'm making some spaghetti," he said. "You want some? I can make more."

"No I'm—"

The sound of a sizzling fire yanked Oliver back through a door into a kitchen. I followed.

A pan on the stove had boiled over, extinguishing the gas burner.

"Never cover pasta," I said.

"I know. I was sloppy." He mopped the water off the stove and relit it.

The kitchen was in better shape than the living room. No hoarding, but definite poverty.

"You want a Coke or something?"

"Sure."

Oliver pulled a single can off an empty shelf in a tragically sparse fridge. Ketchup bottle, pickle jar. Pint of half and half.

"On second thought," I said. "I better not. It wouldn't sit well."

He put it back.

I helped myself to a chair at the little table. Oliver's backpack sat on the floor, where he'd been studying history in between sorting Spells cards. An accordion file folder marked "BILLS" was pushed to one side. I saw pockets for electric, gas, and sewer. "Due soon," "Can Wait," and "Emergency." The last pocket looked pretty full.

"Where're your parents?" I asked.

"Mom's in the hospital. Got hurt at work."

"Your dad?"

He shrugged his shoulders.

"Just you and your mom live here?"

"And my sister."

"Jelissa is your sister?"

"Yeah."

"Randy likes her." I didn't state it as a question, though in fact it was.

"Yeah." He poured a jar of marinara into a saucepan and stirred.

I saw on the counter several bags of groceries that looked to have just been brought in. From within one, Oliver pulled a package of sausage and set a couple to frying on a skillet.

"Three pans," I said. "You're really going all out."

"It's a simple meal but a great one. Just takes a little effort. These Italian sausages are the bomb."

"You bought all these today? I mean, all fresh ingredients?"

"I thought Mom would be home today, but they're keeping her another night. I'll make hot dogs tomorrow or something. She likes those better."

"You're very thoughtful."

He adjusted the flame. "I help out. I usually do the grocery shopping. I make a little money on the side cracking Spells packs and selling the good ones."

"I heard there was good money in that."

"Mostly eBay."

"But locally once in a while?"

"Saves on shipping, and I can move them faster. Also good for the bulk sales sometimes."

"Very entrepreneurial of you."

He salted the pasta, which was boiling again, stirred it with the same spoon he'd dipped in the red sauce.

"My mom lost a good job back in November," he said. "She's been trying to catch up with three until something good lands. My cards gave us a Christmas. That's when the auctions really go nuts. Grandmothers buying sets for their Spells-addicted grandkids."

He turned the sausage.

"Dad," said Randy. "What are you doing here?"

He looked horrified.

Beside him, looking curious, was a pale pretty girl with bobbed purple hair and a handful of my son's fingers. Her lipstick was a little smeared. So was Randy's.

I stood up.

"Your mom sent me to get you."

"Okay."

I picked up a stack of rare cards and inspected them for the tell-tale public domain clue. All clear.

"You get any of those counterfeit cards?" I asked Oliver.

"No," he said quickly. "I only buy sealed packs and sell in singles. Only those."

"Come on, Dad. Let's go."

"Don't you want dinner?"

The two hands had separated. Randy tried to hide his blushing face while she beamed hers.

"Nice to meet you, Jelissa," I said to her. "I've heard absolutely nothing about you." Randy said hello to Allie and sulked into the back seat.

It'll come to the surprise of no one that Randy chose silence as the sound de jour for our ride home. I'd overstepped my bounds by recognizing his love interest, seeing them hold hands, and then announcing that he'd kept her secret from me. The first two were obviously accidents, but I had to take the rap on the embarrassment issue. I'm like that. Those who are not loved are not teased. Those who are loathed are also teased, but I love Randy, and the little dig was as much a product of my own insecurity, my feeling of distance toward my son, as much a good line. I might be an adult according the IRS, draft board, and drinking laws, but I'm still petulant and act out when my feelings are hurt. My son pulling away from me most definitely fell into that category, and I'd acted according to my emotional age. not the number on the door sticker.

Which made me think of Randy's car.

I didn't bring it up. A small concessional apology for my misstep. I should have just allowed the silence to do its thing, but I can't stand awkward silences. It's why I'm shit in interrogation rooms. I see a vacuum of noise and have to fill it. It's usually not a problem unless someone's been taught how to exploit that, like interrogators.

"I saw Mr. Smith today. He's a hoot," I said.

"Yeah." The one-word answer was twice what I expected.

"I might be off base here, but I think he might be a socialist."

"Ya think?" Sarcastic bite.

We were nearly at Nancy's house before my mouth ran the embargo. "Jelissa seemed very nice," I said.

"Yeah."

"I like Oliver."

"He's a bud."

"His mom's in the hospital? That's why you were there?"

"Yeah. And she'll probably lose her three jobs. All minimum wage but still something."

"Ouch."

"This is what your generation has done to mine, by the way."

"I agree."

"It's time for a revolution."

"I'll be at the barricade with you."

"Don't tease me."

"Dude," I said. I always called him Dude when son sounded wrong. "I'm not. Shit's gotten shittier. Greed is a real disease."

He was quiet for a moment.

"Did you really like her?" he said after a minute.

"I did indeed."

I saw a twitch of a smile in the rearview mirror.

"She's poor," he said.

"Such things are temporary and unimportant. Don't you fall for the fallacy of judging people by their bank accounts. That's as shallow as it gets."

He nodded. "You sound like Hunter."

"He wants to party with Allie and me."

"Please don't," was his firm reply.

"Okay."

We pulled into Nancy's driveway. It used to be my driveway too. I could see no one was home.

It was dusk now. The sun drops fast in January, disappearing behind the western mountains long before the weather channel's official time of sundown.

"Do you need a ride tomorrow?" I dared a little movement toward the taboo subject.

"No. Mom's got me."

"Okay."

He took a step, then turned. "It goes both ways, Dad," he said.

"What's that?"

"People judging people on the wealth."

"I know."

"Okay."

"Bye, Randy," said Allie. "Say hi to your mom."

"Love you, son."

He waved and went inside.

Watching my boy walk up those steps in the light of a cool clear January sunset at "magic hour," as the film people call it, I was overwhelmed with emotion. I was also six ways to tired and had had one hell of a day. My mind was filled with facts and clues, ideas and suspicions, caffeine and pain relievers. It all swam together in deep, sleep-deprived pools of protein-gorged synapses, desperately looking for a nap to clean themselves in blessed REM. If you'd asked me then why I broke down crying in Nancy's driveway, I might have mentioned that she'd removed my favorite gargoyle from the porch, the one with the sleepy eye who kept bears away—guaranteed, but I suspected it was more than that. It was growth and potential, successes and missed opportunities. I realized in a flash at that moment that were no second chances for some things. To a parent's horror, I realized that most of the good or bad I would ever do in my son's life had already been done. It was a self-reflective moment, full of regret and triumph, loss and giving. I loved my boy, his ups and downs, his triumphs and failures. I ached for his heart in the throes of first love. I quaked as I thought about what he must see, the future, the choices, the changes ahead. I hoped he did not see it as I did then. It would overwhelm him if he did. What I saw then, though, clear as the valley after a windstorm, was my boy becoming a man, and I finally understood the noble and beautiful reasons he didn't want his car.

38

ALLIE DROVE US HOME, letting me have my breakdown. I fell asleep against the passenger side window, waking up to drool smears on the glass when she jostled me awake in my garage.

"I'm beat," I said. "Wanna go to bed?"

"Who says the art of seduction is dead?"

"Sleep."

She kissed me. "I know what you meant. Yes. I can't believe we're still functioning."

"You lasted longer than I did."

"Talk about a softball setup," she said.

"Egads!"

We shut off our phones, turning out of the world, and stripped naked, which turned on other things. Then we crawled under the covers. We topped off the tired tank with some wrestling, and then, with Allie in my arms, my son in my heart, and a world of clues in my melting head, I fell asleep.

———————

I dreamed of the beach but somehow it had turned, and I was in the waves. Laguna Beach, California. I know the place. The undertow. The riptide had me. A wave rolled over me in the dream way of weightlessness and I couldn't breathe. I tried to swim to the surface but my body was paralyzed. I searched for jellyfish, thinking I'd been stunned into catalepsy when Allie's scream woke me, and I smelled a pillow pressed to my face.

I didn't scream, but I grunted good and heavy and struggled for my senses.

My arms were pinned beneath the blanket. A weight was on my chest. Someone was on top of me and it wasn't Allie. I felt her beside me in the dark, shaking the bed, maybe pushing, maybe hitting.

The pressure relented. I caught a breath, and I heard a loud slap. Then Allie was still.

The pillow was back.

Before it covered me again, I saw the green numbers of my clock. It was 3:40 in the morning. I was going to die at 3:40 in the morning. I am not a morning person. Putting these facts together with a good dose of terror and righteous rage at whatever had befallen Allie, I bucked and kicked and wiggled and fought for all I was worth. When I grew tired, I pretended that I was at a Bible camp and the reverend had snuck into my sleeping bag. Now I had serious disgust to help fuel my fight.

My assailant pinned me flat. Between the pillow and pressure, I could not draw a breath.

Whoever had me was strong.

I tried playing dead. Limp fish, after a death shudder. Method acting.

Nope. The pillow pushed harder.

I screamed into it, "Move, Tony, you stupid idiot!" Which was a stupid thing to do. I didn't have the breath to spare for self-incriminations. If I lived, Lord knew there'd be plenty of opportunity for that.

The back of my hand found the alarm clock, and I made to grab it.

The pressure on my face relaxed a fraction, and I felt a hand grab my left forearm and smash my wrist on the end table before returning my hand back under the blanket and resuming my smothering. I hoped the sound I heard was my IKEA furniture breaking and not my bones, but I was worried. I was no match for this Swedish furniture. It'd taken me half a day to build the damn thing. I'd thrown away the instructions prematurely for reasons that probably went back to caveman days when Og refused to ask directions to the mammoth herd and had to eat roots for a week.

Such thoughts flashing through a victim's mind were not unusual, I thought, as another worthless, unhelpful thought appeared. I figured my brain was finding ways to distract me, to make my crossing of the rainbow bridge soothing and calm. A nice experience. Not the murder that was really happening. That was a nice thought, I thought. And thought maybe I should think of other things right then, like was my knee at the proper angle to test whether the attacker was a man or a woman?

Up came my knee and hit an ass.

No gender confirmation. No balloons of pink powder or cupcakes with blue filling. No crunch, no clue. I would think of them as "they" until I found out a sure gender. It was only right. Why should I treat strangers differently from my friends who choose a nonbinary identity?

Flashing on the idea that I was doing the killer's work for them by wool-gathering, I heaved up my knee and hit again, but this time harder. The pillow shifted.

I brought my hand up from where it'd been pinned beneath my thousand-thread-count duvet cover. It was nice, cream-colored, and smooth and soft. I'd gotten it on sale, so it wasn't as expensive as the one—

"Fuck!" I yelled with my last breath.

I was beginning to think I was drugged but then thought, in what I hoped was a cogent moment, that my brain was being tragically starved of oxygen and every time I moved a muscle, I sent necessary atoms to parts of my body that weren't thought. That was a good thing.

My left hand was unhappy but joined my right to pry the pillow loose.

The assailant shifted. Moved up on my chest. Fresh stale crotch air filled my nostrils. It was air, though. Is there anything more beautiful than stanky unwashed briefs stank air? I couldn't think of a thing at that moment.

I opened my eyes as my assailant pinned my arms under his knees. I suspected it was a him then because of the smell, size, and weight. I would confirm that later.

I gasped what I thought would be my last breath just as he readied the pillow for another go at my face.

He shook it, puffed it up, fluffed it, which might have given me the idea.

As the pillow came down toward my face, I took action.

I...

I'm not proud of it.

I almost left this part out of the story, but for honesty's sake, here it is.

He must have been in sweats. Loose ones. If he'd had jeans on, tight-ass-defining hip-huggers, it wouldn't have worked. I'd probably still have tried it, but the result wouldn't have been as effective.

I... Fearing for my life, left with very few options—still half-asleep and groggy, oxygen-starved from near suffocation—I... Out of ideas. I...

Yeah.

I...

I leaned forward and bit the guy's wedding tackle like I was a rabid wombat finding a bag of candy. Cadburys and Twix come to mind.

The effect was immediate.

A cry. Male and agonizing. The kind of sound no man should ever make, the kind of sound no man could ever forget.

I bit a little of myself at that moment, that part of me that united with all men, throughout the world and time, who know the pain of testicular mastication and penile aggression.

Perhaps it was that affinity, the fraternity of the vulnerable ballsack that kept me from using my full force and castrating the fellow then and there, spitting out his torn pants, musky boxer shreds, and former glory in a bloody splat on the floor. I think that thought crossed my mind and was instrumental in my not doing it.

I released them, and the echoing scream turned to whimper and quick movement.

I rolled over and gasped for air.

Coughing, I tried to yell, "I have a gun. Show yourself." It wasn't loud, but in the silence after that scream, you could have heard a nut drop.

I didn't have a gun with me, but I did somewhere. I'd have to look for it, maybe the basement. It was an effective half-truth, a ruse that told me my mind was working again. Coughing and gagging, I watched my assailant limp-crawl out into the hallway, and soon I heard a front door slam shut.

"Allie," I said, reaching for the light. "Allie, are you okay?"

She was face down. Her pillow caked in blood.

I screamed. Not that unspeakable bit-balls agonizing screech as before, but a similar one, an emotional one, the sound of someone fearing what they loved most had been taken. No second chances.

I turned her over.

"What happened, Tony?" she said, her eyes coming to focus.

I laughed. It was relief and joy and pent-up adrenaline.

She raised her head off her pillow and touched her face where blood was running out of her nose.

"Why are you laughing? And why does your breath smell like an old gym sock?"

My wrist was bruised and not broken. So said the nice EMTs. They wrapped it up and told me to have it looked at in the morning if I felt like it. Allie, they decided, had a broken nose and a possible concussion. They wanted to take her to the hospital. She resisted, but I insisted.

"You're new to this concussion thing," I told her, spitting out toothpaste on the driveway and refilling my brush. "Unless you try to sleep in a strange bed with people waking you up every hour to make sure you're not dead, you'll never have the whole experience."

She agreed to try it "for research," but the police wanted a quick word first. They had questions, like how did the guy get in?

"There was no sign of force on any of the doors."

"He definitely used the front to leave."

"Yes. We found some blood drops on your doormat."

I shuttered. Brushed harder.

"Could he have had a key?"

"I bet Tony forgot to lock the door," said Allie. He does that all the time."

"Did you, Tony?"

The policeman, Petersen, knew me of course. He'd been called out to my place more than a few times. Sometimes, though rarely, like this time, I'd called him myself.

"I might have forgotten to lock it."

Petersen, who like I said, knew me, rolled his eyes.

"Or he was a skilled lock pick," I offered.

"No new scratches at all on the lock."

"Then he must have had help from the inside." I glared at Allie, who gave me the finger. I was glad she was feeling better. She didn't look it, though. Already her eyes were bluing up. She'd have a couple of Grade A shiners by morning. Which was now.

I'm not a morning person.

They took Allie away, and Petersen walked through the house. He found no one but uncovered a ball-peen hammer beside my bed. I didn't own a ball-peen hammer. I didn't think Allie did, either.

"You working on a case, Tony?" asked Petersen.

"A couple." I brushed the backs of my incisors really good.

"So which one hates you?"

"No idea."

"You have an idea. I know you. What you mean is everybody hates you, right?"

"I could identify him, though."

"Why didn't you say that before? What's the description?"

"He probably limps."

"And…?"

I shrugged.

"So, a big guy who probably limps. That's what we got?"

"I hurt his balls."

"Got a good kick in, huh?"

I brushed my tongue.

He sighed. "Can you point us in any direction? For your own good?"

"Well, there's one thing you might check on," I said, working on the right upper molars.

"What's that?"

I'd thought about it since the attack. Who had the most to lose? It came down to Occam's Razor this time. The simplest, most obvious solution. It came down to Provo.

"One of my *old* clients"—I emphasized *old*—"is currently under suspicion for murder."

"What does he have against you? Too much oral hygiene?"

"I know things that can hurt his chances in court."

"Such as?"

"Such as, he had a motive."

"Anyone else?"

"Probably."

"Probably? Like probably limps?"

I nodded. "There're things I don't get yet. Things I haven't put together."

"But someone thinks you might have? Is that it?"

"Happened before."

"So someone's overestimating you?"

"What?"

"You'd like to think that, wouldn't you? You want to believe that your reputation is so grand that just being on a case would scare the ne'er-do-well so much that they'd try to kill you before you even knew why. So to be sure, the villain wants to kill you before having good reason to, on the off chance that you'll figure it out."

"Well…"

"Or maybe it's not even a case—yet. Maybe they're just afraid that you will, at some future time, maybe a year or two, be asked to look into this or that and to be sure, they'll kill you now. Such is your superpower."

"Now you're just being hurtful."

"Tony Flaner, big private investigator. Big name. Big nothing," he said. "Mr. Flaner. You're a lucky loser with visions of greatness. Next, you'll be telling me that time travelers are coming to Sugarhouse today because of the great threat you pose to their century."

Strange to hear my own fears pushed into my face.

"Did you get called here out of a movie, by any chance?" I spit more toothpaste and rearmed.

"Yes, as a matter of fact, I did."

"Did it have Bruce Willis in it?"

"Yes."

"Was it the one about the monkeys?"

"Tell me about the murder suspect who's suborning perjury," he said.

"Utah County sheriffs want to talk to me about him."

"That's out of my jurisdiction. Do you need a ride?"

39

I DIDN'T GO BACK to bed. I wasn't tired even though I knew soon the hideous face of dawn would creep over the mountains and fill me with anxiety. I've been conditioned to dislike the dawn. Not the sun, not the dark, not even dusk—dusk is cool. I love dusk. But dawn, I dislike. When I was young, I saw way too many of them on the way to school. Waking up in the dark, seeing nothing but blackness outside, staggering through shower and clothes and Frosted Flakes and then freezing my coccyx off waiting for an overcrowded child-filled mobile hellscape of middle school cruelty. The sun would paint the sky in a growing glow, usually in pinks and purples and oranges and red—for me forever, the colors of half-asleep, all-foreboding fear, smeared and surreal. I didn't like it. When I got older and could pick my classes, I was careful to avoid any that might put me under the gleam of the foreboding morning sky. Red sky in morning, Tony says fuck off. Clear morning, same. Then came work as an adult. All the old butterflies migrated back to my diaphragm from Mazatlan with the dread of new light as it was now coupled with the dread of a day at work. Work sucks. Every day, that coming light showed me the coming drudgery that eventually filled every job I ever had, reminding me of Aristotle's quote, which should be over the door of every factory and office in the world: "All paid employments absorb and degrade the mind." Though I'm sure there are exceptions, which I couldn't remember that morning after Allie got punched and I got nearly deaded, the rare and few sunrises I ever enjoyed were from among those that I stayed up all night for. Those that had rolled out of bed in the dark were all for shit. This particular occasion did nothing to change my mind.

The EMTs had slinged my hand. They'd offered to take me to the hospital with Allie, but it would be an extra charge. This is America, as Childish

Gambino so eloquently put, so I didn't trust my insurance to cover it. Maybe I'd see my doctor in the morning. He's writing a paper on dangerous occupations. He likes me.

I took a swig of straight bourbon, swished it around my mouth, gargled and repeated three times at the memory of the night's events. I smacked my mouth tasting bourbon, toothpaste, and musky undies. I took a couple shots to dim the pain in my hand. I made a pot of coffee and spiked it with another shot when it was done.

The fucking sun was beginning to rise.

My guts churned with memories of first periods and first shifts. To get my mind off it, I went to my favorite time sink. The internet.

I found a cute cat picture, one of those bald ones that look like a scrotum but playing with a catnip mouse. I stared at it and, naturally, flashed back on the evening, brushed my teeth again, gargled three fingers of Kentucky whiskey and changed tabs.

Allie told me she'd call later and told me to stay on the case, "to get the fucker," and like an idiot, I hadn't gone with her. This made me a poor excuse for a boyfriend. I realized I should get in my car and go to the hospital that instant, be by her side. Be the one who woke her up and observed her sleeping like a Minbari lover for three days. I shouldn't have listened to her. Who was she to tell me what to do?

Allie didn't play games like that, though. I did, not her. If she wanted me there, she'd have said so. She's like that. I love her.

Okay.

I closed my eyes and let the caffeine and Kentucky sour mash do its magic. For a little extra oomph, I threw in an Om or two.

I had hunches. That was a good thing.

They all pointed negative. That was a bad thing.

Push and pull is my mantra when I'm not using Om. Some things pull me forward, while others push me away. Usually I'm pretty good at recognizing them. Not this time. I had ambiguous butterfly-dawn-level feelings that I couldn't be sure weren't wrapped up in my own inadequacies.

I'd thought Bryan Moland incapable of violence. Yet everything pointed to him killing Maddy, bashing Allie, and attempting to murder me. Still, I didn't see him for it. Even after he asked me to perjure myself and probably broke in tonight, I had my stubborn doubts. There were a half dozen guys out there whom Madeline had conned. Hell, there were Provo feminists with a theatrical grudge. A long list of suspects for her killing.

For my attack, however, not so many this week.

I'd made a police report naming him, but it didn't sit right. I could do with fewer hunches and more facts, I decided, but I was my own worst enemy.

Sandi Wong was in Vegas. Why hadn't I made plans to follow her? I was on Fah's dime. I had the time. Allie was leaving Sunday.

Sigh.

Thiha was still not back in school. Nothing new on his page.

I searched Bryan Moland's social media. He hadn't posted anything since I'd told him about Maddy.

Randy had a rare update. His status was now "complicated."

I searched Frank Tomas and found him living it up at the Little America hotel downtown. "Waiting for the big party tomorrow." Shit, the reunion. Shit shit shit. He was excited about it. I could sense it in the twenty pictures he took of his food, or rather selfies with supporting entrée. Look, there he was, tanned and fit and grinning over a bowl of yellow soup. Whoopee.

I called the hospital and found out Allie was asleep.

I searched eBay for Spells cards, looking for forgeries, and found a hundred and fifty million auctions and gave up immediately.

eBay made me remember Kyi and his Hollywood collecting addiction. Recently, I've been meaning to pick up a pair of life-size Zanti Misfits. They would really tie the room together. I found a pair, but they were in shit condition.

Kyi had mentioned a Hollywood auction house. I finished my boffee (booze+coffee) and moved to straight cream and Joe, no kicker. After two more Oms, I found Southwick of Hollywood.

They had several interesting pieces. A Rolls-Royce Silver Ghost. A time-share in Bali. A jewelry collection with provenance. On the movie side, I found an MGM prop room lampshade with black tassels that looked nice. Dental tools from *Marathon Man* were surprisingly cheap. A sports coat like the one worn by Dustin Hoffman in *The Graduate* was surprisingly expensive. It was a knockoff, but whatever.

I noticed one name kept popping up: exile95.

It couldn't be.

I clicked on the name and found a list of public auctions he was currently involved in. Plenty, but none bank-breakers. Then I saw he also had his own auction running. I clicked on that.

It required me to be a member.

I clicked new member and filled out the usual internet infosteal, name, address, etc. I was Easy Marlowe of 221A Bakers Avenue, Cleveland Ohio, 44105. I had it memorized for just such an emergency. I used my spam Gmail address. Everyone needs one of those. Then the questions got strange. It asked my net worth and told me how to send in confirmation of said worth. I would not be able to bid on anything on the site until verified, but I could browse.

How nice.

I said I was worth ten million dollars and waited for a bot to call bullshit. It didn't. I got a confirmation email. I found it among a hundred offers for Mexican Viagra, hot single hookups, and *Snow Falcon Fanciers* newsletters. Never figured out that last one.

Back on the site, I was in.

Nine-five was the Myanmar telephone area code, by the way.

If I had any doubt who exile95 was, one more click put paid to that. There on the screen was the vase I'd seen in Kyi's sunroom. The picture wasn't from his home, though. It was the same as the one I'd seen on the brochure on San's desk at the consulate.

Eighteenth-century jewel-encrusted twenty-carat gold offering container. Sixty-two-point-five centimeters tall, with lacquer and bamboo highlights. One of the most recognizable pieces of art from the royal treasury. A personal possession of the great queen Supayalat.

I did some quick cross-tab checking and found out that Supayalat was the last queen of Burma. After her, they got coups and shitshows.

Back at Southland's, I scrolled down the auction and saw the current bid was $8,820,000 from a "verified bidder." American money. I checked. The auction would run for another week. As I watched it, it spiked to $9,010,000. Everything is worth what people will pay for it. There'd been eighteen unique bidders so far, many had bid several times.

Never underestimate the worth of memorabilia, be it a trench coat, dental tools, or an ashtray from a dead queen. Rich people would see it as an investment, inflation-proof as long as there are fans. And why not throw in a tax deduction? At the bottom of the page, I read:

All proceeds from this auction will be delivered to the Monarchy Return Fund. Thank you, brothers and sisters, aunts and uncles, friends of the Monarchy. With your help, we will soon be back.

Kyi had said, and Wikipedia agreed, General Tayza was a distant relative of Supayalat. I had to figure that Thiha could be the one who would "soon be back." At least I figured out where the money was coming from. A college fund couldn't buy you a spoon from *Breakfast at Tiffany's*. I wondered how much it cost to return a king to the throne of Myanmar? Would the vase be enough? Who sells that?

The internet showed me a picture of General Tayza standing rigid in his uniform. He was an intimidating figure. His eyes stared out at me. Supayalat had the same staring eyes.

I poured another cream spiked with some straight coffee and noticed the sun was over the mountains. If dusk had the magic hour, dawn has the fucked one, as previously explained. That time was over now. I was safe to look outside.

A blue Honda sped away from where it had been parked across the street as soon as I opened the blinds.

"Huh."

More information that didn't fit yet.

Clouds were forming. Snow on its way.

I recovered the brochure I'd taken off San's desk at the consulate. The vase was in a Burmese museum. I found it online and thought to use my new keen knowledge of the country's area code but didn't feel good about asking some poor clerk to make sure the vase was there. Had too much of a "is your refrigerator running" vibe to it. Luckily, I didn't have to. It was listed as part of the collection, but "not on display."

Huh.

Another click on the Southwick's page led to a letter of authenticity. It showed the provenance of the piece and included the museum. It was signed and had stamps on it. It looked kosher, though I had nothing to compare it to.

I tried to make out the signature, but it was one of those author-like ones that steal the whole page: Scott O. Ryan, esquire, was what I could make out.

Huh.

It could have been a coincidence, a slip of the hand who'd scribbled it, but the downstroke of the S in Scott crossed the C.

Huh.

Ethanol—and caffeine-fueled little gray cells spun with ideas—some real, some false. The whole just out of reach.

Hunches? Coincidences? Blue Hondas?

Moland.

The car outside. It had to be Moland. Returning to the scene of the crime, maybe coming to take another crack at me. Little backstabbing murdering fuck.

Magic electrons told me the remaining run of *Flower Drum Song* had been canceled. No reason given.

My hand hurt. My butt reminded me to look before I sat.

A small article in a Provo paper said Maddy had been hit with a blunt instrument from behind. I remembered the hammer by my bed.

Sigh.

Hunches can be wrong, I told myself. False sightings.

My phone rang, and I jumped like I'd been goosed by a moray eel.

It was Bryan Moland.

"Hi, fucker," I said. "Why didn't you just come to the door? We could have had a nice non-caffeinated, non-carbonated drink compound made with essential oils."

"What?"

"You left your hammer, by the way. What do you want me to do with it? Wipe off all the fingerprints and throw it in the river?"

"What?"

"Ha! Joke's on you. The cops took it."

"Mr. Flaner, I just called to tell you that I'm sorry that I asked you to lie."

"I bet you are."

"I confessed it all last night. They booked me for concealing evidence. I'll be out again this afternoon maybe, after another hearing before the judge."

Now it was my turn. "What?"

"The sheriffs might come to you for confirmation. Don't hold back. Tell them everything. I'm sorry I asked you to lie for me. That was wrong. I'm not that kind of guy. Not really."

"I never thought you were," I said.

40

BRYAN SAID that I was one of the few people in all the poop he was going through (yes, he said poop) that honestly thought him innocent. The echo was not lost on me.

"Do you want me to poke around a bit?" I asked.

"I do, but my lawyer may not."

"Have him call me."

"He mentioned subpoenaing you for the names of the other men Maddy had done this to."

"Subpoena? Why not just ask me?"

"He thinks you'll be a hostile witness."

"If he subpoenas me, damn right I'll be hostile. I'm hostile that he thinks I'll be hostile. Do you know what a rabid wombat can do to a man?"

"No."

"Well…you don't want to know."

We hung up, and I wondered who I was. The question was coming due. Allie was leaving Sunday. After that, I'd have no one to tell me to pull my head out of my ass. And Saturday, well, that was the reunion.

I couldn't think about it.

Back to the twenty-first-century distraction machine. We don't have Soma, but Apple does its best to give us a brave new world.

I Googled the vase keywords and description going twelve pages deep but couldn't find the auction listing anywhere publicly. Other Southwick's auctions were up top and proud. A six-word description taken from a new auction for a shoelace used in episode twenty-eight of season nine of *Bonanza* appeared on the first page twice. Kyi's auction was off the grid. I'd stumbled into the infamous dark web.

Get ready for a letdown.

Dark web is a really scary term that people like to throw around to defame the internet and spook people into supporting what Perry calls the "cyber-surveillance-censorship agenda." It conjures up visions of human trafficking, drug deals, hitmen for hire, and all notions of perversity functioning in the internet equivalent of bathhouses, bordellos, and backstreet bazaars. Nasty criminal internet destinations do exist, to be sure. They constitute the underbelly of the internet. However, that underbelly is just the underbelly and may or may not be part of the dark web. There is a difference. The dark in dark web isn't a moral judgment harkening back to colonial racist terms of good white/bad black, but a reference as to light, or how easy it is to see.

I blame Google. It controls internet traffic. Back in my day, I can remember where one moved from one site to another by links on that site, following a wave of information to unknown realms. Now few sites have links, and everyone just looks for what they want on the first page of the all-powerful search engine god that gives us doodles and creepily remembers our birthdays.

Google and other search engines send out bots to every electronic corner of the web and find pages and categorize them and rank them to be offered later. That's the bright web. A place the bots can see. The dark web are the places the bots can't see.

What can't a bot see? Anything behind a firewall or an "enter password" screen that locks it out. That's it. These sites not are hidden beneath some cryptic *Matrix* IP address. They don't need to be in a Slovenian basement or an abandoned oil rig. They just don't let the bots peek in. Thus, the only way to get to the page in question is to know where it is. Sometimes people share that kind of thing with word of mouth, like the Silk Road site, or sometimes it's a link on an auction page that's trying to keep out the riff-raff. I learned all this over the course of three hours and about a hundred texts from Randy at school who was surprisingly eager and fascinatingly fast at texting me all this.

What it all meant here was that the offering dish auction was by invitation only. It was listed nowhere on Southwick's public pages. Behind the firewall of a basic password, however, there it was, along with all the other high-cost or secret items for sale.

The day was really happening now—afternoon and racing toward dusk.

I went to fetch Allie. She'd called and said they were letting her go.

On the drive, I brooded over clues and plans of action. I had many of the one and none of the other. The first hadn't finished hardening, and the second didn't know how to speed it up. My problem was that I had too much going on. Too many cases. I had to think they were all still live, even though I'd figured out some of them, but until I actually did something performed the mythical plan of action that began this paragraph, I'd not have that all-important '90s New Age fad of 'closure.'

Jell-O was the closest thing my brain offered for a plan. I left it alone to harden. I put it all in the freezer and drove across town in a windy rain that promised to deliver the storm that had been promised.

I had Allie for today and tomorrow. That was something to think about. I'd miss her when she was gone. Our last hurrah together would be my high school reunion on Saturday.

It wasn't the same flutter of diaphragmatic butterflies as a cold winter dawn, but it wasn't far from it. I dreaded it. I looked at it like torture, archaic and punishing. The obvious choice would be to not go. Easy. Done. Forget about it. Take my lovely Allison Braise out to a movie or go bowling or get matching tattoos instead. Why was that so hard?

Randy once asked me, when we were arguing, how it was that I knew how to push all his buttons. I told him, "Because I installed them." That's kind of what was happening here. The peer pressure of those high school days was oppressing me from the past. My reputation and self-worth were still at stake. I cared what the others thought of me and knew what they'd all think if I didn't show up. It didn't matter that I couldn't remember more than a couple of their names or that I had gone out of my way to intentionally never think of most them ever again. It still somehow mattered. It was a waypoint. The end of a quarter. Time to see where we were. How'd we done. Who we were now.

High school hadn't been terrible for me. Lots of kids had it worse. Some I had helped to make it worse. There was that. I didn't want to look into Danny's eyes and see him recall the bullying I'd done to win the affection of another friend. I'm not happy about that. I didn't want to see Daren, who bullied me hard, even punched me in the face once. I didn't want to see Eliza, whom I'd kissed once and never talked to again because she laughed into my mouth. I didn't want to see a thousand faces who may know me, remember me, that I didn't know or remember, each of them comparing my current state with who I was then, weighing more heavily those earlier years than those few hours when we danced to old songs and shared family photos.

My parents had had class reunions with real regularity, ten, twenty, twenty-five, fifty years. Thinking of it now, reunions are archaic social media, an outdated live version of Facebook where you couldn't close the tab. Everyone would be judged. It was a test, a quiz, maybe a final exam for high school. Where had all that chicken-fried steak, trigonometry, and crepe paper taken us? Do we pass? Catching up was comparing lifestyles, careers, wives, and God help me, weight. Are we who we wanted to be? Are we who they thought we would be?

To get an early start on the festivities, I compared myself to Frank Tomas and came up short. He'd be the star of the show. I'd only been a jovial class clown; he'd been a big deal, famous, most likely to succeed. And he had. He was in town bidding on scripts at Sundance, living in Silicon Valley, waiting for his Maserati.

When Allie saw me enter the room, she shrieked. "God, Tony! What's wrong?"

"What?"

"You look like someone died."

"It's nothing."

"Okay. Good."

"I don't want to bother you with it."

"Thanks. Hand me that—"

"I mean, what do I care what others think of me?"

"Who?"

"Why should I have to compare myself to other people?"

"Oh, I see."

"So what if I haven't really found a calling yet."

"But you have."

"One that I was good at?"

"You are."

"Who am I fooling? I deserve it."

"Deserve what?"

"Everyone's scorn. It'll be good to finally stop pretending, to come out as the fraud I am. It'll be liberating."

"As a detective?"

"That and everything. I'll make a clean breast of it. I'll use it as a pulpit where I tell my entire group of peers—"

"High school classmates are no longer your peers," she said firmly.

"I'll tell them—don't interrupt. I'll tell them that I use humor as a shield."

"You think that's been secret, eh?"

"Allie, I don't—Oh no!" I hadn't even taken a good look at her. There she was, lying in bed, a big white bandage in the center of her face with two black eyes behind it. "I am so sorry."

I rushed over and tried to find someplace to kiss her. I settled on her forehead and the fingers of her left hand.

"I'm okay," she said.

"You don't look okay."

"I dare say I look better than you did when you came in."

"How do I look now?"

"Embarrassed."

"Good. The communication centers are working."

"Give me my clothes."

I helped her dress, and the nurse came in with a short mountain of paperwork. Instructions, prescriptions, bottles. Bills.

"Don't blame yourself for what happened to me," she said as we got in the car.

"I hadn't until now."

"Oh."

"Let's get you home."

"Is it safe there? Did they nab Moland yet? I'd like to file a complaint."

I pulled out onto rain-slickened roads. "They did, but he says he didn't do it."

"It had to be him. Who else had a motive? Hiding one murder is a pretty good reason to try another."

"Where'd you hear that?"

"You told me."

"I must have been drunk."

"Is he denying he attacked us?"

"He says that's not who he is."

"And you believe him?"

"Yes."

"Why?"

"There was an authenticity about him when he apologized for asking me to lie."

"An authenticity?"

"And an absolute inauthenticity when he asked me to be immoral in the first place."

"That's why you think it wasn't him?" I could tell Allie wasn't buying my hunches.

"There's another thing," I said.

"A hunch?"

"Well, no... Yes. Well, something else, too."

"Tony, you told me yourself that circumstantial evidence is evidence. To quote, 'If it walks like a duck, swims like a duck, quacks like a duck, has motive, means, and opportunity to kill another duck, it might be a murderous duck.'"

"This duck was in jail all night. He turned himself in around four o'clock yesterday, fessed up, including motive and was there all night."

"It could still have been him," she said after a while. "He could have hired someone."

"To what purpose?"

"To shut you up."

"After he'd told the cops everything I would say?"

I could see a pout under her bandages.

"Any progress on Sandi Wong?" she said after a while.

"I don't know," I said. "A hunch."

"What?"

"Not good."

"Tell me."

"The Jell-O isn't jiggly yet. How about a pizza?"

"Get it delivered. I don't want to see anyone. I don't look at all like myself."

I slammed the brakes and fishtailed into a curb. The Audi behind me was concerned enough to flip us off and honk as it passed.

"What's going on? Tony, are you okay? Are you having a stroke? Your face is all contorted. Does your arm hurt? Where's my cell phone?"

"Shhh," I said.

"Excuse me?"

"Shhhh," I said again, and for emphasis, raised one finger into the air. The universal "give me a quiet minute" sign.

"You scared me."

"Shhhhhhhhhhhh!"

"Sorry."

"Sh."

I was jiggling.

"I'll need to see it on paper," I said.

"What?"

"Shhhh."

"Erg!"

"Oh, and I probably need to do some crime."

41

ALLIE WAS PEEVED because I wouldn't tell what I suspected, or how I knew it, or where we were going, or why, or what was up with me brushing my teeth all the time.

We were hungry, so after phoning in Allie's prescriptions, we grabbed lunch and ate it while waiting in the pharmacy drive-up queue. We were behind three SUVs of homeschooling housewives. They were there to refill their Prozac, Ritalin, Diazepam, Ambien, Zocor, Adderall, Prilosec, Lisinopril, and Viagra—for the weekends—but no caffeine or alcohol. God forbid. All part of well-balanced suburban existence in the prescription drug-abuse paradise that is my home.

"Give me a clue," said Allie, washing down her pill with a strawberry shake when we were finally clear of the parking lot. I had vanilla, the king of flavors.

"I don't want to jinx it," I told her.

"There is or there isn't," she said. "There is no jinx."

"And you say I butcher movie quotes."

"You do."

"You don't have to go with me if you don't want to," I said. "In fact, it would probably be better if you stayed away."

"It could be dangerous?"

"This time, yeah. Actually. Yes. Don't go."

"More dangerous than your house?"

I had to think about that. "I don't know."

"Then I'm coming. If only for a chance to get you to tell me what's going on."

"You know what's going on," I said. "You just don't know why."

"And you do?"

"I have suspicions. I want to check on a couple things."

"We're going to OfficeMart?"

"I want a calendar."

The storm was easing into it. Uncertain rain, some wind, a flake or two. Churning gray skies. But the air was still.

Allie stayed in the car because of her bandaged nose and black eyes. I took my puncture wound, smacked head, cheek scrape, and minty mouth to the Day-Timer aisle and looked for a monthly pocket calendar. It being January, they had a big selection of expensive ones but a decided lack of inexpensive options. How inconvenient. I could either drop half a yard on a pleather-bound book, or go up to three months' salary and get an online subscription to *Organized Professional Weekly* with a new three-ringed briefcase.

I finally found a paper calendar for a sawbuck in the desk blotter section. It wouldn't fit in my pocket, but it might in the car. I paid for it on credit and found Allie applying makeup to her face when I brought it out.

"You don't wear makeup," I said.

She giggled. "I don't wear much, but I do. That you don't think I do is very sweet." She blew me a kiss.

"You don't."

"I do."

"I thought I knew you."

She toned down her black eyes with powders. "You think I'm a fake now?"

I smiled.

"What?"

"Here." I handed her the big calendar and a marker. "I'll drive. You write."

She enthusiastically took the material and readied herself to take dictation. She wore a mischievous little grin that I found adorable even though her bandage covered up most of it.

"What?" I said. The question of the moment.

"What what?"

"What what that smile?"

"You're going to give me clues, aren't-cha?" She slurred a little and grinned again. Her eyes were glassy beneath the makeup and bruises.

"What did you take?" I asked.

"Just my pills," she said. "What date are we starting on?"

"Go back two Thursdays," I said. "The day Sundance started. The day Sandi Wong arrived and spent a night with Archibald."

"Okey-dokaley."

"Sandi and Archibald. Write that then."

"Done," she said. "Wait, we're going to Provo? That's the fiancée murder case. Whattabout that?"

"We'll get to it. I just want to see everything spelled out."

"Hey, look," she said, pointing to the traffic. "A UDOT parking lot." She burst out laughing. "That's pretty good. You can use that one on stage."

UDOT is the Utah Division of Transportation. It's got issues. The twice-daily snarl they call I-15 is one of them.

"Yeah that's pretty good," I said.

We'd hit rush hour right in the teeth. The few miles from Salt Lake to Utah Counties would be a crawl and stop.

"Next?" she said, giggling.

"The next Friday, day after that. Sandi goes to Park City and is sent packing."

"I'll write Wong is all right." She burst out laughing again.

We inched forward.

"What did you take?" I asked. "Pill-wise."

She handed me the bottle. "Take four every two hours for pain," she said.

I read the label. "Take two every four hours for pain."

"Oops." She burst into hilarious laughter. "That's great!"

I knew the drug. Don't ask me how. She'd be alright. She wouldn't be driving but would have a fun time for the next few hours. She already was.

"Next?" She tapped the Sharpie on her tongue, leaving a big black mark. "Ick," she said and giggled.

"The Friday after that," I said. "Last Friday. Not today, but the one before. There." I pointed to the date.

"Got it." She drew a big smiley face on that day.

"Why'd you do that?"

"Because that was the day I came up, and you got all your cases."

"Right."

"See? I'm paying attention. Pull forward. You have three inches."

"You too?" I said.

She shrugged.

I pulled forward three inches.

"Now the Spells tournament was on Saturday."

"That's part of this?"

"No hints," I said.

"Okaly smokily."

"The party at Sundance," I said. "That's a big one."

"I knew it!"

"You did?"

"Nahhhh." She rolled down her window and yelled, "I am so high!" She had snow in her hair when she pulled her head back inside.

We filled out the calendar with important dates. When Sandi was seen at the hotel Sunday night after the Park City party. Also Little Wars with the previous suitor, Aberghast, a few hours before that. Monday with Archibald, the unfaithful builder, and a trip to Little Burma up in Park City. "Put a star on that one."

"I knew it!"

"Really?"

"Noh!" And she laughed and laughed.

California, Tuesday through Thursday last week. The consulate, San Francisco, Los Altos.

"Blue Honda?"

"Shit yeah. I gotta remember all the times I saw that."

"You should write it all down," she said. "It'd make a cool book."

"Ya think so?"

"I do."

Wednesday in LA, telling Bryan the scam, and that night Maddy killed.

Home again. Park City and Stert. "Yesterday," I said. "Shit, that was only yesterday?"

"Me getting punched on Thursday night or Friday morning?"

"Friday, I guess."

She wrote. The traffic moved.

"Hey, how come you didn't get hurt?" she asked.

"You screamed and saved me."

"Oh."

"Thanks."

"You're welcome. How did you drive him away?"

"I used my mouth."

She smiled. "You can talk your way out of anything!"

"Yeah…"

We took the exit and headed toward Maddy's secret lair. Allie added what I could remember of when I'd seen the Honda first. "The Sunday when I bought the drugs. Don't put that down! This could be evidence."

"Don't do drugs," she said, and laughed and laughed.

"Am I this much fun when I'm wasted?"

"Am I fun?"

"You really are."

"So are you."

"I'm driving," I reminded her. I had to adjust my position in the seat. My ass hurt, but the blood was elsewhere.

We passed the house and drove around the block once. The sun had set, and the snow was coming down. It wasn't sticking yet, but it was making plans. The freeway signs warned people not to travel if they didn't have to.

I parked the car a couple of houses down, facing it, and turned off the lights.

"Allie, I'm going to go over to that house on the left there, the dark one. I don't expect anyone to be there, except maybe a vicious, cold, emaciated dog."

"You're not serious?" Her eyes were big and unfocused.

"Nah," I said.

"You are zerious," she said. "Do you have a gunz?"

"Yes."

"With you?"

"Not exactly."

"Trunk?"

I shook my head. "It is somewhere in the house. But I won't need it."

"What do you want me to do?"

"Keep an eye out, and if you see danger, let me know."

"How? Honk the horn three times? That's a good one."

"Start with the phone."

"Oh, right."

I kissed her. She slipped me the tongue, and I nearly melted.

"That's not helping," I said.

"You kissed me. Okay, go go go. Do the detective thing. Hurry back."

"You know I will."

I left her in the driver's seat with a marker and paper. I figured she'd entertain herself for a while. I shouldn't have brought her. I was committing a crime. Once I broke into the house, she was an accomplice.

I did the deed through the side door. It wasn't locked. Provo.

I hesitated to turn on lights. I used my phone's to navigate. I wasn't sure what I was looking for, but I thought that if there was something, it would be here. The cops didn't know about this place. I'm not even sure they knew Maddy's real name. I didn't.

If anyone had been there before me searching, they'd done it by radar. Nothing looked moved or disturbed or out of place.

I bumped into a kitchen chair, which bumped into a cheap table that toppled a cheap empty champagne bottle to the floor, which alerted Baby Cujo in the backyard that life was in the house. Like a car alarm, the pit bull started howling and whimpering. I went to the door and saw snow falling heavily in big sound-absorbing fluffy flakes. The brutish vicious sounds of the dog were lost in the storm.

I was about to return to searching when I saw that his bowl was empty and he had no water.

This was the thing that had caused my facial laceration. Or was that me? He was scary that night, and a little now, but I heard plaintive howls, not warning barks from him. I took pity. He was just being who he was. He was the most honest player in the whole play, I realized.

I found a bag of dog food and opened the door.

He looked up and barked once as a watchdog. I kept moving forward, shielding myself with the fifty-pound bag of teeth-glistening pit bull chow.

He wagged his tail. I poured him a big bowl of food and refilled his empty water dish. It might freeze by morning, but he'd be good until then. I made sure there was a warm blanket in his little plastic house. I'd call someone in the morning about him and this place.

Back inside, I went to the bedroom where I'd seen Maddy before.

I opened her closet and poked around. Her clothes were there but also some costumes she'd worn in the play I'd seen her in. One from fan number, a red sexy thing and a pair of yellow danceable slacks. There were hats, silly, pointed things, some with lace. A bowler in the back. More shoes than any man ever owned in his life. She had a lot of clothes. I took a picture, thinking Allie, when she was sober, might be able to give me insight into her psyche by looking at the contents of her closet. Twenty-first-century tea leaves.

I opened a drawer and found Maddy's drawers. Her bras were still on the doorknob.

I slid my hand between the mattresses and came up pay dirt. I withdrew a manila envelope and dumped it on the unmade bed.

There were three thumb drives. One was marked "PH," another "GA," and the third "BM." I took them and would look through them later at home, suspecting what I'd find. The one marked BM I took to mean racy pictures of Bryan Moland. Just that, and hopefully not another kind of pornography.

There was a stack of IDs, driver's licenses and passports. There was one for Laurie Peterson, Noel Carlson, Yvette Miller, Dee McGrath, Jennifer Young, and Tiffany Jones—Abergast's once fiancée. They all had pictures of the woman Bryan Moland knew as Madeline Smith. They all, somewhere, had a C with a faint line through it. There were two passports. One in the name of Dee McGrath and another for Margaret Norton, I didn't have time to search those for the ego signature, but I saw that both had pictures of Maddy.

I felt a shiver in me bones.

It was my cell phone. Allie was calling.

"There's a blue goddamn Honda parked down the street," she said.

"I'm coming out."

I peeked through the window at the near whiteout, and I saw a figure dashing toward the house from the opposite end of the street.

I slipped out the side door and waited in the carport.

The quiet was complete in the falling snow. It was like wearing earmuffs. It was beautiful and serene. There was light, some reflected glow making the ground and the air practically iridescent. The kind of scene that makes you feel small and Christmasy. A Currier and Ives moment. A white gliding silence broken only by the sudden barking and hysterical screaming coming from the backyard.

My plan was to let the guy have the house. Once he was in, I'd leave. I'd already taken one bite out of crime. Not sure I was up to another one.

Before I could make my move, a screaming figure sped and leaped over the fence the way I had and smashed his face against the frozen concrete like me.

The sunglasses flew off. The fake bushy black beard turned sideways.

A familiar face looked up and removed his ball cap, showing a crew cut.

"Traard? Seriously, you? What the hell?" I said.

"Flaner, help me up. I've been bit."

"And you scraped your face. We're twinsies."

He had a tear in his pants that showed a pale ass. A couple of spots of blood where teeth had touched tush.

"Start talking, Chris. Why are you following me? I thought we were friends."

"You did?"

"No," I said. "I kinda hate you."

"Don't say that." His lip quivered. "You're my hero."

"Fuck off."

"No really," he said. "I wish I had your skill."

"I read your article. *Discipline*. That was a shot at me, Traard, and you know it."

"They took that out of context," he said.

"Uh-huh."

"I might have been jealous."

I shook my head.

"What takes me months of spreadsheets and observation to compile, you spit out in an hour with a hunch and a joke. I write blog posts about you, how you're the born detective—the artist, and the rest of us are craftsmen at best, fakers at worst."

"You wrote nice things about me on the internet?"

"Yes."

"Under your name?"

"No."

"Is that why you're following me? To see how I do things?"

"I was paid to follow you. I got the job offer a week ago Sunday."

"The day after the party? The day after I drove you home and poured you into bed?"

He nodded. "Good money. All expenses paid."

"They paid your expenses to California?"

"No," he said. "That was for a different guy."

"What did he want you to do?"

"You know I can't reveal that."

"Do it anyway," I said.

"A movie producer I met at that party," he said. "He wanted me to check out his competition. Background stuff on a guy called—"

"Francis Tomas."

"Yes," he said. Eyes big, cheek and forehead, I noticed, bloody. "I wondered if you were on the same case."

"What did you find?"

"My client has nothing to fear," he said and chortled. "Easiest five grand I ever made."

"And the guy—wait, five grand?"

"It was a good trip."

"Shit."

"What do you make?"

"Forget it. So you're saying the guy who sent you after Tomas was not the same as the one who sent you after me?"

"That's it."

My phone vibrated again.

"I think..." Allie giggled. "That someone else is coming over. Is there a party?"

I pulled Traard into the house and shut the door. We hunkered down in the kitchen.

"Do you have a gun?" I asked him.

"Three on me. Two more in the car."

"You've got issues."

The door opened and a female voice called out, "Poor little Bowzer-man, is the little poochy hungers?"

The lights went on, and Kelly Gibson stood staring at Traard's gun as we stood up from behind the table. Traard had a fifty-caliber Desert Eagle small-penis-compensator leveled at her.

"Put that away, Chris," I said. "I know her. She's a friend of... What was Maddy's real name?"

Kelly looked at me dumbly, wheels turning in her head.

Allie appeared in the door carrying the calendar, snow in her hair, eyes wild and excited. "I saw the lights. I figured that was my signal to come in."

"Allison Braise, this is Kelly Gibson."

"Hi."

"Hi."

"Kelly is—was—the bestest friend of..."

"Margaret Norton."

"Margaret Norton," I repeated.

"Should I write that down?" said Allie.

"Sure."

"Where?"

"In the margins."

"I'm sleuthing!" she said.

Kelly was young and wore her naivety like a badge. A little silly, a little selfish, a little stupid. A girl who made the wrong friends, maybe, got involved in the wrong stuff perhaps but would live to learn from it. Unlike some.

"You look sick, Tony," said Allie.

Two deaths. One and...

"You do, Flaner," said Traard. "Are you okay?"

I tried to measure how much of all this was my fault. Could I have done more?

"I think he's going to throw up," said Kelly.

"He's getting in his head," said Allie. "Tony...don't."

Could I prove anything? Could I guess where they'd...

"What is it?" Kelly seeped back

"Oh oh oh oh oh..." said Allie, a spreading grin on her face.

I checked my phone.

"Now he's smiling," said Kelly. "That's kinda creepy, all of a sudden like that."

"He's got it!" said Allie.

"He has?" said Traard. "He does? How? What does he have?"

"Kelly, I have one question for you," I said.

"Okay."

"Were you with Margaret last Sunday?"

She knew what I meant. She hung her head but nodded.

42

WE DROVE HOME in the thick of the storm. I white-knuckled the freeway at thirty miles per hour while Allie played with her seat belt for ten minutes and then suddenly yawned and fell asleep.

When I got home, I circled my block to make sure everything was clear, then I pulled into the garage and closed it. I carried Allie to bed and put her under the duvet.

I went to my computer and found Thiha's page.

I sent him a private message.

> I need to talk to you about Sandi.

About ten minutes later he messaged back.

> Yes. I want to talk to you too.

> When can we be alone? Your house? Tomorrow?

A couple minutes later.

> Yes. Tomorrow would be adequate at my house.
> Come at 9 in the a.m.

> Can't that early. Have busy morning. Make it noon?

> Yes. That will do. Come alone.

I closed the computer with a smirk. I made a few more calls, checked the locks three times, made a half-ass search for my gun, gave up, and finally crawled off to bed.

———

Utah is pretty good at removing snow from its streets when it wants to be. We've had a lot of practice and a shit-ton of salt thanks to a dead sea that smells like dysentery hog ass on its best days.

Next day, I drove up the canyon to Park City on clean dry roads under a blue winter sky. They'd been cleared, and the sun had come out to make them chalky white with dried salt. With the brilliant snow on the shoulders, it made sunglasses a must.

The traffic was light until I exited, then it was Little Sundance as weekenders rushed to the slopes to break legs, tear tendons, and justify their poor life decisions involving Gore-Tex and goose down. I counted three ambulances.

Once in Kyi's upscale neighborhood, I slowed and checked my watch. I was right on time.

The roads were clear, dry as bleached bone. Residential neighborhoods are low on the plow list. Leaving the house this morning, I'd had to force my little car through twelve inches for half a mile before I found wet asphalt on a main street. I was in a good part of town, but I wouldn't see curb for a day or two at least. Here, with easily three feet of fresh fall, the roads and sidewalks were clear as fresh Kleenex. I guess if you pay eight digits for a house and four a month to an extorting HOA, you damn well expect not to be bothered by a little thing like blizzard snow above seven thousand feet in the Uinta Mountains. I mean, really.

I pulled past the house and parked out of the way.

I left my sunglasses in the car and instantly regretted it. There is no easy transition from sunglasses to winter glare, and there is no glare like a winter glare.

Squinting so hard, I walked into a post, I stumbled up the salted walkway to the door where I felt for the jam, pushing every bump that could be a bell until I heard one ring inside.

I felt the door open—a gap—and I staggered inside.

"Close the door," I muttered. "So bright. The light, it hurts us."

The door shut behind me. I blinked until my eyes became accustomed to the light of the foyer. When I could see, I saw Kyi smugly pointing a gun at me.

"I'm here to meet Thiha," I said. "No need for that. I'm not a security threat. I have an appointment."

"Yes, you are," he said.

"Oh?"

"I have to confess, Mr. Flaner, I deceived you. It was not Thiha you were communicating with last night, but me."

"You impostor!" I dramatically pointed at him, arm shaking in faux rage.

"I'm afraid so."

"So you lied to me!" Hands drawn dramatically to my face, shock and wonder.

"You're being very dramatic, Mr. Flaner."

"Egads!" Jazz hands.

"What is going on? Did you not see I have a gun? You've been trapped."

"Curses!"

"Flaner?"

"I have to confess, adviser Kyi, that I suspected a trap, and I too have deceived you."

"You have? How?"

"I did not come alone!" John Travolta *Stayin' Alive* pose. Pelvic thrusts.

The door opened again and Allie pushed through.

"Hi," she said. I didn't like the look on her face.

"I got this, Allie," I said. "Trust me."

Stert was behind her, walking kind of bow-legged.

I remembered the taste of unwashed boxer shorts and uncircumcised Scotsman, and threw up a little in my mouth.

"Allie, come here," I said. "I need a hug."

"Sorry, Tony," she said. "I got caught."

"You done great," I said. "Perfect."

"Really?"

"Yep."

"I wish you'd tell me what's going on."

"I found her outside by the gate," Stert said. "I didn't see her get out of his car. I don't know how she got there."

"Ridez," she said. "Tony arranged it."

"I got an app." I waved my cool expensive phone. Stert ripped it out of my hand and threw it into the fireplace, where it shattered into high-tech confetti. I died a little inside.

"What an asshole," I said.

Kyi waved his gun and gestured for us to go into a great room, which was good because I'd noticed it before and wanted to go there now.

Stert stared at me with cold Scottish malice as he pushed us forward.

"What did you want to see Thiha about?" asked Kyi.

"Is he here?"

"Yes."

"Bring him out."

"Why?"

"I want him to meet everybody."

"Everybody?"

The doorbell rang.

"Yeah."

"Stert," said Kyi, sending the brute waddling away. "Not a noise," Kyi said to us.

"Or what? You'll shoot? That thing makes noise, you know."

"Why are you so confident?" he asked.

"Yeah, Tony. Why are you?"

Stert, big-eyed and squatty, came back in with two men in tow. Kyi hid his gun.

"Hey, glad you guys could make it," I said. "May I introduce Bryan Moland and Deputy Rogers from the Utah County Sheriff's Department."

"Why am I here?" asked Rogers. "This was supposed to be my day off."

"Crime," I said. "Probable cause."

"Flaner?" said Moland. "Glad to finally meet you in person."

"Hey, there. This is Allison. Isn't she cool?"

"What happened to your eyes?"

"That." I pointed to Stert.

Rogers looked him over.

The bell rang again.

Stert went to answer it.

"Rogers, why don't you go with him?"

He nodded and did.

I winked at Allie. There was some conversation in the foyer and then the sound of footsteps. Many footsteps.

Stert rushed back and said to Kyi, "A bus has pulled into the loop," he said.

"A charter," I explained. "Surprisingly reasonable to hire. I used a Groupon."

Standard, Garrett and Critter walked in first, Perry behind them, sulking and suspicious.

"These are my friends," I said. "Hey, guys. Where's Dara?"

"The fuck is this place?" came a familiar voice.

"There she is," I said. "She's a handful. The child with her is Henry Levinson. He's actually central to this whole thing."

"I am?"

I nodded.

More people poured in. "Kyi, you remember Terrance Rowski, Allie's agent, from your party. And Francis Tomas. Hey Frank."

"Flaner! How ya been? Hope life's treating you as well as it's treating me."

"Sit down, Frank."

Kyi and Stert shifted uneasily and kept their eyes on the policeman.

"Hey, everyone, this is Dawane Osterlot, Spells champion. He plays no part tonight, but he's actually a pretty cool guy and had a free Saturday."

"How is this helping my image?" I asked.

A girl walked in behind him.

"Everyone, this is Heather. Hi, Heather! She manages the Drop Inn Comfy Quarters Inn in Sandy. Good waffles. Hot coffee. Shit seating."

"Hi." She waved.

Everyone answered "hi" in unison.

"And here's Archibald Lewis. He builds houses and cheats on his wife."

"You said you wouldn't tell."

"Mittens here works at the airport."

"Yo everyone." He waved and smiled big. "Always wanted to be at one of these."

"One of what?" said Kyi.

"Now we have Glenn Abergast, the fiancé before Bryan Moland."

The two men squared off at each other but were pushed farther in by the steady stream of people still entering.

"Welcome the fatale groupies: Kelly Gibson, friend and makeup. Ortwin Bishop, director and choreographer. Enzo Powell, manager, promotion, and real love interest of the late Maddy Smith, a.k.a. Margaret Norton, a.k.a. Jennifer Young, a.k.a. et al."

They entered without making eye contact with anyone. I'd threatened them hard to be there.

"You all know Chris Traard, private investigator, but Mr. Barber from the Salt Lake Tribune is probably new to you all. Thanks for coming."

Traard stared wide-eyed at Stert, and I knew I was going to have a good time.

"Lastly...?"

Deputy Rogers looked out the door and nodded.

"Here's Jay, Ridez driver extraordinaire and on his arm Sergeant San of the Myanmaran secret police, fresh off a plane from Wilshire Boulevard, California. Swimming pools. Movie stars."

Kyi didn't like that. I liked that he didn't like that.

The room was packed now, everyone looking around, confused.

"Settle in, settle in," I said. "Only your household is left, Kyi. Bring out Thiha."

"I'm here," said the boy. I hadn't seen him come in. He stood in the hallway by the wall. Next to him had to be Melecio, the Cuban butler. He looked concerned and afraid, old and tired.

Traard raised an accusing finger at Melecio. "That's the guy who gave me the drugged drink at the party."

"Yes or no: meant for me?" I asked the Cuban.

"I was told to give it to the detective. How was I to know there were two? It was an honest mistake. Please, show mercy!"

"A nod would have been enough, but I see you went ahead and gave yourself a couple lines. Well, welcome to the Screen Actors Guild."

Thiha looked like he'd been crying. He also looked like he'd been slapped recently. Hard.

"Why are all these people in my house?" said Kyi, coming to his senses. I knew he would eventually. The shock of a bus full of suspects and side characters emptying into one's great room can only last so long.

"I'm glad you asked," I said.

43

"IT ALL BEGAN IN THAILAND," I said. "A friend of mine was seduced and beguiled by a lovely young woman out to see the world, funded by her charm and the kindness of strangers. Our missing guest, Sandi Wong."

All eyes on me.

"Crimes and lies, fakery and fraud!" Melodramatic forearm on forehead emoting shame.

"What the fuck, Flaner?" said Dara.

"Shhh, he knows what he's doing," said Allie.

"Since when?" said Standard.

"Shhhhh."

"A week ago Friday, I picked up the case of the suspicious bride and also the missing international tourist." I waited for the reporter to write that down, and when he didn't, I repeated it. "The case of the suspicious bride— I'll wait. Okay? And also the missing international tourist. Got it?"

The reporter nodded.

"I was feeling pretty poorly about myself," I said, assuming a pacing pensive pose of a thoughtful gentleman, hands behind back, slumped and shuffling. If I'd had a smoking jacket, it would have been perfect. "I had what is known in the business fraud syndrome."

"I've never heard that," said Traard.

"I think he means show business," said Garrett.

"All artists get it," said Critter. "It's part of the human experience. A self-doubting that all living self-conscious creatures share." He sagely nodded his head, his googly eyes rolling in their plastic housings, his felt fangs catching the breeze.

"Is this going to go on all day?" asked Heather. "I have a shift at five."

"Shhhh." Allie had my back.

"Was I who everyone thought I was?" I continued. "Did I deserve my fame? Did I deserve the scorn?"

"You're working on it," said Deputy Rogers.

"Shhhhhhhhhhh."

"These were the questions that dogged me as I asked the other questions, like where the hell was Sandi Wong? Where had she gone? Where was she now? Who was the last to see her?"

"Wait, you were working on another case at the same time as mine?" said Bryan. "That's double billing. Isn't that illegal?"

"No," I said confidently. "Pretty sure it's not."

"Humph."

"My soulmate, Allison, left me that night for Sundance, where she and her agent, Terrance, mixed and mingled and got a Shih Tzu of new accounts."

"You make it sound dirty," said the agent.

"I got into one of the ritzy parties the next night. A high-powered shindig hosted by our own Kyi Tun, adviser to the late General Tayza, ward to the general's son, Thiha."

Thiha shifted uneasily.

Kyi had his back to a wall. The gun bulged in his pocket. Or maybe he was just glad to see me.

"Say hi, Kyi," I said. "This party is for you."

"I want you all to leave," he said. "Now."

"But you asked me why we're all here. You all heard him ask, right?" Everyone nodded.

"Allow me to tell, and then we'll all leave. Heather has a shift at five."

"Seriously," said Perry. "It'll go faster if you just let him do it. I've seen it before."

"Thank you."

"Don't mention it."

"At the party, not only did I have a very awkward experience in a public restroom, but I met Thiha and Kyi and their asswipe there, Stert."

"Stewart," said Kyi.

"Say your name, Stert," I said.

"It's a Scottish name," he said. "Stert."

"One syllable. I rest my case."

He glared.

"Also in attendance was the incomparable Allison Brasie, Terrance Rowski, agent to the same, Chris Traard—that's important—Francis Tomas —not so much—and Enzo Powell with his thick black glasses. Everyone, except me, was there to make connections, get deals, make hookup for themselves or their clients."

I nodded to everyone for emphasis. I got a lot of blank stares back.

"After the party and the aforementioned bathroom incident involving a hot production property called *Boys in the Bush,* I turned my attention to the fiancée case." I pointed at Bryan so he wouldn't sue me. "I witnessed a local performance of *Flower Drum Song* down in Provo, where Madeline Smith played one of the leads. If you don't know the play, you're probably better off, but just so we're all on the same page, it's about Asian people—Chinese folks in San Francisco. All the characters are Asian. This being Utah and Provo, the least diverse city in America—there was a study—the cast consisted of white-bread WASP actors made up to look Chinese. Kelly Gibson there did a really good job creating the illusion."

I expected more from her after the compliment, but she was distracted by my gripping story.

"I followed Maddy after the show and found a secret residence Bryan, her betrothed, did not know about. You didn't know about another house she was renting, did you?"

"No."

"Ha!"

"What?"

"Just good to be right. I'd guessed that part."

"Go on," said Rogers.

"Inside, I observed Maddy with Enzo and Kelly and saw a different side to her. She was supposed to be a nice Mormon girl anxiously excited to be married in a temple. But she wasn't that. That was an act. She drank alcohol and kissed Enzo on the mouth. With tongues. She wasn't who we thought she was."

"Wait. So you solved the case last Saturday? And you still billed me?"

"Shhh." That time it was me.

He waited.

"I wasn't sure," I explained. "The next night—Sunday, a biggie—I met Glenn Abergast and got more confirmation that we had a serial bride."

The young man from Ephraim looked around with tearful doe eyes.

"That day I also bought some unknown drugs, which I took because reasons. In a haze, I put it all together about Maddy but entirely forgot it the next morning because of said drugs."

"What kind of drugs?" asked the deputy.

"Candy," I said. "A sugar high. Pixy Stix and Mountain Dew. Might have been a SweeTARTS involved. Don't quote me."

Critter rolled his eyes. It's what he does.

"Moving on. Sunday night, the day after the party, two things happened. One, a blue Honda started following me, and two, Sandi Wong was spotted at the Drop Inn Comfy Quarters Inn in Sandy. I knew about the first thing immediately, but it took a credit card trail leading from Bangkok to Zion to lead me to the video."

"He sat on a needlepoint pin," explained Heather. "And he spilled coffee all over his crotch. There was some worry about lawsuits."

"Wait, slow down," said the reporter. "I'm missing the dates."

"We have a calendar back at Tony's place we can let you have," said Allie. "I helped with it. I think."

"You did," I said.

"I was on drugs."

"What kind of drugs?" asked Deputy Rogers.

"Legal ones," she said.

"Monday, I find Archibald Lewis, the filthy two-timing now-guilt-ridden, embarrassed builder, who at the time I thought was the last person to see Sandi."

"I want to go home," whined Archibald.

"Archibald put me straight, though, redeeming all his earlier sins by proving that Sandi had come to this very house that very first full day she was in Utah."

"I'm redeemed? Really?"

"No."

"You skipped something," said Allie. "Kyi at the party."

"Oh, right. At that big party, I asked Kyi if he'd seen Sandi. She had told my friend in Thailand that she would look them up. You see, Sandi claimed to be the deceased General's cousin, which would make her, by virtue of the confusing cousin relationship tree, also a cousin to Thiha. Sandi also wanted to attend the Sundance Film Festival, fancying herself an actress. At the party, Kyi, Thiha, and Stert all claimed to have never seen her. But Archibald blabbed, and I'd caught them in a lie."

"Does my wife need to know about any of this?"

"Does she read the Tribune?"

"No."

"You're good."

"She had something about her," he explained. "She was..."

"I believe you," I said. "But I no longer believed these guys." It was hard to gesture to the whole household at once because Stert and Kyi were on one side of the room and Thiha and Melecio were on the other.

"Another trip to Park City and Stert clobbers me, from behind, when I wasn't looking, with a goddamn sap. He laid me out right there in the foyer."

"Assault and battery?" asked the deputy.

"Trespassing," said Kyi.

"When I woke up, I was in a nice sunroom down that corridor. Lots of great shit back there. Buddhas, ashtrays, jars—some museum quality." I winked at San. His face was granite. Secret Police, amirite?

"Kyi explained that he'd lied about Sandi because they were paranoid, thus clubbing two birds with one phrase, my attack, their deceit. He told me —and here's where we pay attention—snap out of it, Standard."

"What?"

"Kyi told me that they discovered that Sandi was an impostor that first day they met and so sent her packing, politely but firmly. Sandi Wong was an impostor. She was not a cousin to the general. She was, however, a real Myanmaran, and that matters."

San, the secret policeman, looked bored. It might have been jet lag. It could have seething rage for dragging him here from the coast on a red-eye flight.

"Kyi then showed me his expensive memorabilia collection. That, this house of kitsch, and the fact that he was bidding big bucks on the *Boys in the Bush* production told me, if I had any doubts before, that he had more money than he knew what to do with. I was told that the money came from Myanmar, a trust set up for the general's son. There is a trust, but not *Boys in the Bush*-big trust."

"We have friends back home and people all over the world who help us," Kyi said. "It's for the boy's future."

"Don't interrupt."

Kyi was no longer keeping an eye on the deputy. Now he stole glances at San.

"A trip to California and we met Sergeant San who, taking time from his secret policing, filled me in on Sandi Wong's deception."

"It rained a lot," said Allie. "But we got to San Francisco, too."

"And Los Altos, where that blue Honda was seen again. You want to take this part, Chris? I need some water."

He stood up and took a notebook out of his pocket. Melecio appeared with a glass of ice and a bottle of Perrier on a silver tray before he could start.

Traard gave him a dirty look and then said, "I was hired by the alleged Mr. Kyi Tan of…I guess you know where he lives. It's here. I was hired by Tan to investigate the alleged financial and social disposition of a one alleged 'Francis Tomas' of Los Altos, California, whom he said was in an alleged bidding war with him for the alleged rights to produce a movie. Allegedly."

I saw Francis, whom I'd blessedly forgotten about, wriggle in his chair, his grin sliding away.

"What did you find?" I said.

"Francis Tomas lives in a basement apartment. He works as a part-time caretaker at the Shady Time Motel and Massage Parlor in Oakland. His net worth is minus six-hundred thousand dollars if one includes overdue child support and alimony payments, racked-up credit card debts, skipped loans and recent dental bills."

"Behold a man who peaked in high school. Behold the panic of inauthenticity. Behold the poser, Francis Tomas," I said.

If Frank could make a more pathetic face, I couldn't imagine it. "I just...I just wanted...the reunion, you know?"

"I get it," I said. "Really I do."

"Can I be done?" asked Traard.

I nodded. "I forgot to mention that Sergeant San knew about Sandi Wong because Kyi himself had called the consulate the previous Sunday to check on her claim of kinship."

I looked around the room to see if anyone saw it. No one did.

"I didn't get it then, either," I said. "Instead, I remembered the fiancée con and stupidly called Bryan and told him how she and her cronies set up nice rich connected Mormon men to collect shower and wedding gifts only to dump them at the altar. Kelly here also works at Macy's returns in downtown Salt Lake City, the place where all the would-be weddings gifts were registered and where the gifts were returned for cash before Margaret/Maddy changed her name and did it to some other sucker."

Both Bryan and Glenn swallowed hard.

"Maddy/Margaret kept blackmail information in case the con was discovered, which it was. She threatened Bryan with it after he told her he'd found out, and, coincidentally, that night she was killed."

"I didn't do it."

"I know you didn't."

"You do?"

"I do. I'm getting to it."

"Any fucking time, Flaner," said Dara.

"How do I figure into this?" asked Henry on Dara's arm. They were sitting that close. "The ID?"

"Thematically. You're an impersonator. That's what this all hinges on. That and timing."

I didn't want him to talk about the IDs. That was for another day.

"Thursday night, two days ago, someone broke into my house and tried to kill me and Allison."

"That's when I got clobbered," she said.

"With great personal and olfactory sacrifice, I fought off the culprit. Next morning the blue Honda was there again. Timing."

"I didn't attack you," said Traard.

"Thursday afternoon, Allie and I ran into Stert at Albertsons, buying groceries. Melecio, don't you usually do the shopping for the household?"

The Cuban glanced at Kyi and Stert, at the cops and then back at me. "May I speak?"

"Why stop now?"

"Always," he said. "Unless there's some emergency."

"There was an emergency," I said. "Why were you following me, Traard?"

"I was hired to."

"Did you tell your employer where I lived?"

"First day's report."

"So your employer knew where I lived?"

"I just said that."

"Yes. Yes, you did." I nodded solemnly. "Is that employer here today in this room?"

"Yes, they are."

"Can you point them out to us?"

"Yes."

"Please do so."

Traard stood up, raised his finger and pointed straight at Critter on Garrett's arm.

"What the fuck?" said Dara.

"Hold on. I have an alibi," said Critter. "Ask Garrett."

"I don't know," said Garrett. "Thursday night, you say?"

"Traard, what the hell are you doing?" I asked.

"I thought it would be funny," he said. "Be more like you."

"I'm flattered. Point to the right one now. You're giving the puppet an aneurysm."

He pointed at Stert.

"There it is," I said.

Everyone stared and shook their heads.

"You'll need to do better than that, Tony," said Rogers.

"Really?"

"Fuck yeah, dipshit," said Dara.

"Thiha is a good boy," I said. "I think he has a good heart. He doesn't like what's going on, and he needs to be happy."

"Don't make me tell it," he said.

"I had no intention," I said, basking in the limelight.

"Timings," I said. "Sandi appeared at this doorstep two Fridays ago. Is she revealed as a fake then? Maybe, maybe not. I tend to think not. Instead she is nabbed. Kidnapped. Waylaid because she knows too much. Snatched because, I'm guessing here, hoping a bit, that Thiha actually put his foot down and kept her alive."

"What?" said San.

"Oh, you are paying attention. Good. Because this is your bit."

"I have been paying attention."

"You're right," said Thiha. "I stepped in."

"The party Saturday night set it all in motion," I said. "That night all the connections were made. Enzo and Traard, and me on the scent of Sandi as the main catalyst."

"I was hired the next day," said Traard. "I was just coming out of my...situation."

"Drugs."

"What kind of drugs?" said Deputy Rogers.

"He doesn't know."

"Where'd they come from?"

"The earlier bit about the drugged drink going to the wrong detective. Pay attention."

"Could you—"

"No."

"But—"

"He was hired by Kyi and Stert—Stewart?" asked Jay, the Ridez guy.

"Yes," said Osterlot. "Lotta moves. Gotta keep up."

The Spells player was right with me. I could tell he had the picture even though he'd just been introduced to the mystery that morning.

"Thiha unhappily writes letters to sponsors begging for money to keep Kyi in the lifestyle of the rich and exiled."

"Against your will?" asked Rogers.

Thiha shrugged.

"Grounding kids is not kidnapping," said Kyi. "So put that one away, Deputy."

"How does Enzo fit in?" asked Allie.

"Enzo represented an actress of dubious character who was adroit at playing Asian characters. Through him, the actress was hired to appear at the Drop Inn Comfy Quarters Inn in Sandy for a one-night performance as Sandi Wong—complete, I might add, with an authentic passport and borrowed credit card. Kelly confirmed to me that she made her up, and Enzo will confess later under torture that he drove her there and picked her up."

"Torture?"

"Kidding," I said. "Would American authorities torture anyone?"

Silence.

"Also of note, Sandi traveled with at least five bags. Drop Inn Sandi had only one."

Mittens spoke up. "True that. We saw it on the video."

"Bad timing now," I went on. "Stert killed her the night I told Bryan about her con game."

"What are you saying?" said Kyi. "That's a lie."

"My guess is that she tried to blackmail you too, Kyi. Can't have that. It's hard to get on eBay from C-Block."

"That's exactly what she was doing," said Enzo. "I tried to talk her out of it, but she thought she could milk him for more."

"But why all this to begin with? What was the threat?" said Osterlot.

"A double whammy," I said. "First, Kyi was using Thiha to impersonate —there you are again, Henry—a coup plot to return Myanmar, formerly Burma, to a monarchy. Thiha's letters were requests for money to finance a coup, but the money was really going to fund Kyi's lifestyle. He had people sending him stolen artifacts for the cause, some of it related to the last queen of Burma to give the movement authenticity. He sells the stuff on Southwick of Hollywood's poorly protected private server. Part of the notorious Dark Web, but without drugs. Sorry, Rogers."

"The stolen piece is a forgery, by the way," said San. "To help with your theme."

"I knew that."

"How?"

"Uhm, a hunch?"

"Sure," said Dara.

"The key is that Kyi didn't call the consulate to check on Sandi until Sunday morning, the day after the party, a week after she'd supposedly come and gone. Worse, he included a photocopy of her passport, meaning he had it then, hours before she supposedly took a very nice but economical room in her namesake city of Sandy, Utah."

"We take AAA," said Heather.

"How did Maddy pass as Sandi so easily?" I said. "Granted, Kelly does good makeup, but not that good. I think it was because we Americans have a surprisingly hard time differentiating Asian faces. It's a cultural thing. Asians do not have this problem. To them, maybe, we all look alike, but for us Americans, they too often do. It's something we need to work on. We don't see others like we should."

Everyone looked at San and Kyi and Thiha in sequence and then back at me.

"I think the coup idea was started by General Tayza when he was alive," I said. "Lots of money to start a coup, and when the general died in a tragic, and suspicious, car crash with Kyi's own son, named Phyo, a few years back, Kyi kept it going on the promise that Thiha, the General's son, would return and be king. Go monarchy!"

The crowd scanned all the Asians' faces again. A smile on San's face.

"Do you see it now?" I asked. "If I had a picture of the General, you'd see it clearer. Family relationship. Thiha here looks like Kyi, not the General. Thiha there is Phyo, Kyi's son. The real Thiha died in the car crash, and Kyi has had his son impersonating him ever since so he can buy ratty overcoats and shoelaces."

Thiha nodded. Kyi was fingering the pocket where he'd put the gun.

"Are you saying Kyi killed the general?" asked Jay.

"One could wonder."

A shadow crossed Kyi's face.

I was standing in his light.

"And now, let us meet Sandi Wong," said I. "I probably should have asked for her first. Do you guys have time to stay around while I explain it all to her?"

"What? She's here?"

"She's alive? Why not just kill her?"

"They promised me no killing," said Phyo, formerly Thiha.

Kyi looked at the boy with heartbreak and fear.

I went on. "Kyi told me four dudes live here, and yet two days ago, there was Stert in Albertsons, buying women's products. The emergency, remember? I challenged Stert's frail masculinity with an inane joke about it. Good times."

"Choke on it," Stert said.

"Good one," I said. "Really, that one works."

He scowled and gingerly shifted his weight.

"What now?" asked Allie.

"Melecio," I said. "If you could fetch Sandi? It might look good when you go in front of a judge."

The butler turned and disappeared down a hallway.

"Basement?" I asked Phyo/Thiha.

"Basement."

In a few moments he returned with a bedraggled but still stunningly beautiful Asian woman.

"Sandi Wong," I said. "I am Tony Flaner. Fah's friend."

Looking around the room, seeing no one she knew or liked, she rushed to me and threw her arms around me.

"That's about all of it," I said, peeling her off and giving her to Allie who took her to the couch and held her. "There should be a dozen cops outside by now and an ambulance for Sandi. Pretend you don't have that gun, Kyi. It'll be better for you. See you all in court later."

"That isn't all of it," said Sergeant San, standing up. He reached into his pocket and produced a long, folded official-looking document. "I have here an international arrest warrant and extradition order. My superiors would like to...talk to you, Adviser Kyi Tun."

44

ALLIE and I held hands as we walked down the hall, the squeak of my sneakers and the click of her pumps echoing off the industrial tile. We didn't have a lot of time. The maintenance man who'd let us in at seven-thirty said that we had to be out by eight. "Don't make me come looking for you."

"Like you could find us," I said. "We are the wind. We can hide in drafts, fold ourselves through locker slits, flow under doors, linger for decades in the cafeteria or woodworking shop." I made a swooshing sound and waved my hand in a circle eight to demonstrate.

"We'll be quick," said Allie, pulling me past the confused man. "What was that?"

"I'm not sure," I said.

"You're on a tear today," she said.

The cops had been about what I expected. They wanted to keep everyone for the duration but then settled on quick witness statements with contact information while they worked on jurisdiction, local levels and international concerns, department considerations. What kind of case was this? Smuggling? Kidnapping? Murder? Fraud?

I was only a little disappointed they let us go as early as they did. It meant I had to make the decision about going to the reunion or not. I could tell Frank Tomas wanted to ask me about it, but he didn't have the courage. If I decided to go, I didn't think I'd see him there. Then again, maybe I would.

Frank had spent months building a false front of success just for the reunion. He was a failure by his own measure and probably, tragically, by many others too. That made everything so much worse. He'd done nothing illegal. He hadn't stolen anything, conned anyone out of anything greater than a favorable impression among actors and movie movers. Who were they to call anyone a fraud? Frank might have raised the bidding on the *Boys in the Bush* script, but I suspect those filmmakers would be looking for different backing anyway.

I admired him a little, Frank. Unwilling to accept his own faults, he faked success. I can get behind that to a degree. "Fake it 'til you make it" is a valid life strategy. But Frank was working only for the short term, for the false impression he could never keep up. He ran up credit card bills for new teeth and photo ops for Facebook, renting a Jaguar to park it in the snow. It meant everything for him to be thought well of for a few days in his old home state.

In a way, it's the opposite of what I was facing. I feared that I'd tricked myself into an overblown portrait, and people thought too much of me. Success can do that. It's as bad as failure. It gets in your head. It makes you think you're an impostor in your own body. Frank lusted for that. I feared it. We were both wrong.

We all have those moments of doubt. Such is the cost of excellence. That's what Allie said. "If you get stuck, the trick is to keep good people around who can talk you off the ledge."

Allie is amazing. She says she has the same fears as I do. Impostor syndrome gets her too, she says, but I'll have to take her word for it. Of all the people I've ever known, she is the most comfortable in her own skin. She knows who she is and accepts it and goes on. That kind of confidence is breathtaking. I can best describe her as authentic.

She insisted on coming with me, to do this now, and maybe after—I still hadn't decided yet about reunion with me. She'd go with me, black eyes and bandages and all. "Anyone who asks about how I got them," she told me, "will hear the heroic story of your exploits and my part in them."

"Can't we just say you walked into a doorknob?"

The smell of sweet ink and raw paper met us like exotic perfume as we peeked in the door. The soft, smooth technological rhythm of a modern printer—*whoosh, chugga-chugga slide-slick-pop*, repeat—made a soothing song you could dance to.

"Mr. Smith," I called out. "Hunter."

The arts teacher looked up from his computer and smiled.

"Tony. Allison. What are you doing here?"

"We gotta talk."

"What happened to you?" he asked, seeing Allie's eyes.

"I beat her up when she wouldn't give me her hooking money. We're all made up now, aren't we, sweetie?"

"Sure thing, honey bear."

He blinked.

I squeezed her hand.

"Hunter," I said. "I know what's going on. You're not who you say you are."

"I am too." He said it in a way that made me look for deeper meaning.

"Okay. But you used to be Orion Peter Babb, graphic artist from San Francisco who now lives under an assumed, or rather new, identity as part of a plea deal."

He didn't say anything.

"You were, and are, a first-class counterfeiter who sells ironic pictures of the Eiffel Tower to stick it to the man. You are as political as you are talented."

"How'd you figure this out?"

Allie spoke. "He observed and deduced," she said. "Using his skills and knowledge and whatever opportunities presented themselves, he fit clues together until he saw the pattern. That's what a detective does, and my boy here, Tony Flaner, is a damn good one."

"We were in San Francisco. I ran into an old woman who knew you."

He nodded. "That could happen."

"Barion on the picture." I pointed to the Eiffel Tower on the wall. "Ba— Bagg. Rion, from Orion. Orion is the Hunter. Smith, well, that was just lazy."

"I thought it would fit in Utah."

"Oh. Yeah, Actually, it does. I take that back."

"Thanks."

"The ego signature is a bit trickier," I said. "The public domain sign. Another strike at the man?"

He shrugged.

Allie nodded. "Damn, you're good." She leaned in close and whispered in my ear. "Are we in danger here? You usually unmask villains with more witnesses."

"I'm not turning you in, Hunter. I'm actually here to warn you."

He looked shocked.

"You have handlers, I assume. People that cover for you here? The fact that you're still teaching with your overt views shows that the administration more than tolerates you."

"Yeah. The school actually gets paid to keep me here. Twice my salary."

"Your heart's in the right place," I said. "You made the cards to help out Oliver." It wasn't a question. "You knew where he lived, how he lived, and you fed him counterfeit cards to help his family."

"I never intended to hurt anyone," he said. "Thieving corporations, sure, but not real people. After I heard what happened at the tournament, I gathered them all up as best I could. I even went to Little Wars and bought all of them out. Curt, for all his stress, doesn't need more of that. And Randy was the last person I wanted to get in trouble."

"Do you ever buy drugs in that parking lot?" I asked.

"All the time," he said. "Have you tried the beige powder?"

"How do you get clients?"

"Dark web."

Allie pointed to her watch.

"I'm warning you also because Randy likes you. I like Randy. He's trying to figure out who he is. Trying out new identities like sale price shoes. He respects you. He needs people like you now. He's smart. He figured out your game before I did."

"He did?"

"He asked me to stay out of it. I meant to, but I figured it out anyway. He was trying to protect you and Jelissa, his crush, and Oliver."

"They're a cute couple."

"The police raided a house in Park City today. They'll find the false letter of authenticity you made for a Burmese vase. It's linked to the death of an actress in Provo and a kidnapping of a tourist. They'll search the actress's house and find at least four fake IDs you made for her."

"Oh."

"It'll be in the *Tribune* tomorrow."

"That soon?"

"So, you probably want to lie low for a while," I said.

"Okay."

"Is that the new ZX-2280?"

"Yeah. I got it overnighted. Testing it out now."

"Is that what you do with all the money you make on the IDs?"

"Exactly," he said. "All the Eiffel Tower money goes to the Public Domain Foundation."

"What are you making now?"

"Passports. You need one?"

"Nah, we're good."

"We gotta go," said Allie. "If we're going."

I wasn't so sure I wanted to, but I felt this was a good exit line, so I left with Allie on my arm.

"What about Randy's car, by the way?" Hunter said as we left.

"We're getting rid of it," I said.

Out in the parking lot, Allie asked, "When did you decide to get rid of the car?"

"The day I met Jelissa," I said. "The car puts out a strong signal, but it's the wrong one for who Randy is, or wants to be. He might not know what that all is yet, but he knows he wants it to be real. That dumb car isn't that."

"You've been thinking about Frank," she said.

"Among other things."

We got in the car.

"Are we going to the reunion or not?" she said.

"What do you think?"

"I think you're a big deal. You are a success, Tony Flaner. You can honestly and deservedly crow. In work and love and family, you're doing great. You have nothing to fear from your peers, old or new. And you know all this yourself. You proved that when you were confident enough to invite a reporter to the reveal today."

"I kinda did that to snub my nose at Traard."

"What about publicity?"

"Okay. I wanted to show off. You caught me."

"You played on hard mode today. If you'd have screwed it up, you'd have been toast. Maximum pressure and you nailed it."

"I did, didn't I?"

The inversion had not returned to pollute the valley. The sky was clear from the passing storm. The snow was white and pale on the ground, unmuddied for now. Above us, I could see stars and the first slip of moon creeping up from behind the eastern mountains.

"You know I'm going to use that hooker joke about your eyes again tonight, right?"

"Are you sure that's a good idea? It's funny, but they won't know what to think of you."

"That's their problem," I said.

Yeah, the air was clear.

A LOOK AT BOOK FIVE:
THE HERMIT OF BIG HORN COUNTY

In a world where everyone has something to hide, even the most unexpected places hold dark truths.

When a daring challenge leads Tony Flaner and his companions to the secluded corners of northern Wyoming, they find themselves disconnected from the digital realm and immersed in a reality they never imagined. Gone are the comforts of technology, replaced by the rugged landscape, no flushing toilets–*wait, what?*–and a sense of isolation that seems to permeate the very air they breathe.

But beneath the serene facade, danger lurks, and secrets take root.

Tony uncovers a world of old-fashioned motives and a chilling murder that shatters the tranquility of their retreat. As the layers of deception crumble, Tony must navigate through treacherous terrain, both physical and emotional, where manure piles high and the true nature of humanity is laid bare.

Unearth the hidden secrets of a remote wilderness in this gripping Tony Flaner mystery.

AVAILABLE OCTOBER 2023

ACKNOWLEDGMENTS

This book would not have been possible without all the fans who said nice things about my work, completely shattering my worldview and requiring me to wrestle with my own impostor syndrome.

ABOUT THE AUTHOR

Johnny Worthen is an award-winning and best-selling author of books and stories. Trained in stand-up comedy, modern literary criticism and cultural studies, he writes upmarket multi-genre fiction, symbolized by his love of tie-dye and good words.

"I wear tie-dye for my friends, but I write what I like to read," he says. "This guarantees me at least one fan and easy dressing in the morning."

Johnny teaches writing at the University of Utah and lives in a house with his wife, sons and assorted cats. There's also a lawn.

www.ingramcontent.com/pod-product-compliance
Lightning Source LLC
Chambersburg PA
CBHW010817250626
47156CB00011B/3103